LOVE'S DANGEROUS ENCHANTMENT . . .

The orchestra struck up a waltz and Caleb drew Lily easily into his arms. His eyes were alight with laughter as he looked down at her glowing face, but there was no mockery in his expression, and Lily felt a strange tug in the region of her heart. In that moment, something had been irrevocably altered within her.

Through dance after dance, Lily whirled in Caleb's arms, and it was only when he led her outside the mess hall that she realized she was breathless and much too warm.

"I'll never forget this night," Caleb said quietly.

"Neither will I," Lily confessed. "I wish it never had to end."

Caleb moved a step nearer and curved a finger under Lily's chin. "As naïve as you are, Lily-flower," he said gruffly, "you must know that something is happening between us."

She trembled at his touch, and the shivers that went through her were warm and sharp. "Yes," she admitted, as his mouth drew nearer to her own.

The kiss was inevitable and it was powerful. It left Lily sagging against Caleb's chest, her hands gripping the front of his uniform coat.

"Come with me," he said quietly, and Lily could no more have defied him than she could have reached out and snatched a star from the sky.

D0181047

Books by Linda Lael Miller

Angelfire
Banner O'Brien
Corbin's Fancy
Desire and Destiny
Fletcher's Woman
Lauralee
Lily and the Major
Memory's Embrace
Moonfire
My Darling Melissa
Wanton Angel
Willow

Published by POCKET BOOKS

Most Pocket Books are available at special quantity discounts for bulk purchases for sales promotions, premiums or fund raising. Special books or book excerpts can also be created to fit specific needs.

For details write the office of the Vice President of Special Markets, Pocket Books, 1230 Avenue of the Americas, New York, New York 10020.

LINDA LAEL MILLER

LILY AND THE MAJOR

POCKET BOOKS

New York   London   Toronto   Sydney   Tokyo   Singapore

For Harriet Vick,
who has the very special gift
of enjoying the little things in life

This book is a work of fiction. Names, characters, places and
incidents are either the product of the author's imagination or are
used fictitiously. Any resemblance to actual events or locales or
persons, living or dead, is entirely coincidental.

An *Original* Publication of POCKET BOOKS

POCKET BOOKS, a division of Simon & Schuster Inc.
1230 Avenue of the Americas, New York, NY 10020

Copyright © 1990 by Linda Lael Miller

All rights reserved, including the right to reproduce
this book or portions thereof in any form whatsoever.
For information address Pocket Books, 1230 Avenue
of the Americas, New York, NY 10020

ISBN: 0-671-67636-9

First Pocket Books printing December 1990

10 9 8 7 6 5 4 3 2 1

POCKET and colophon are registered trademarks of
Simon & Schuster Inc.

Printed in the U.S.A.

Prologue

Lincoln, Nebraska
December 9, 1865

*I*t was snowing, and the cold twilight wind swept up under six-year-old Lily's skirts to sting her bare knees, but she did not bend down to pull up her stockings. She was intent on the small crowd of people gathered in front of the railroad platform to stare at her and the other children traveling west on the orphan train.

There was a paper pinned to her shabby coat, with a two and a seven written on it. Lily knew that the two digits together made another number, but she couldn't reckon what it was because she'd never been to school. Her sisters had probably told her, but Lily's mind was amuddle with all the other things she was expected to remember.

Her name, no matter what anyone might say to the contrary, was Lily Chalmers, they'd said. Her sisters were Emma and Caroline. Her birthday was May 14, 1859, and she'd been born in Chicago, Illinois.

Lily felt Caroline's fingers tighten over her shoulders and

1

stood a little straighter. Her heart beat faster as a huge, bearlike man wearing a woolly coat stepped forward, assessing the small band of orphans with his narrowed eyes. She had not given up the hope that someone might want a family of three girls, even though Emma and Caroline had been preparing her for separation from the moment the train had rolled out of Chicago.

The bear-man chose two boys, and Lily gave a sigh of mingled relief and resignation. She looked at Emma out of the corner of her eye and saw a tear slide down her sister's cheek. Emma was seven and, by Lily's calculations, much too old to cry. She reached out, slipped her hand inside Emma's, and held on tight.

That was when the heavy woman stepped forward, stomped up the snow-dusted plank-board steps onto the platform, and marched over to the three girls huddling together.

"I'll take you," she announced imperiously, and for a moment Lily was full of joy, thinking she had been right in expecting someone to want all of them. Then she realized that the woman was speaking only to eight-year-old Caroline.

Caroline made a curtsy. "Ma'am, if you please," she ventured, in a breathless rush, "these are my sisters, Emma and Lily, and they're both good, strong girls, big enough to clean and cook—"

The woman shook her head. "Just you, miss," she said.

Caroline lingered long enough to embrace both her younger sisters. Her brown eyes were shimmering with tears, and the snow crested her dark hair like a circlet of flowers. Lily knew that, as the eldest and most responsible, Caroline had hoped to be chosen last, for she was the most likely to recall where to look for the other two.

"Remember all that I told you," she said softly, crouching in front of Lily and taking both Lily's hands in hers. "And when you get lonesome, just sing the songs we learned from Grandma, and that'll bring us close." She kissed Lily's cheek. "I'll find you both again somehow," she added. "I promise."

Caroline rose, turning to Emma. "Be strong," she said. "And remember. *Please* remember."

Emma nodded, tears slipping down her cheeks. She was the prettiest of the three sisters, by Lily's reckoning, with her copper-blond hair and indigo eyes, and she had the truest singing voice.

When it became apparent that no more would be chosen, the conductor herded the remaining children, Lily and Emma among them, back aboard the train. Lily didn't cry as Emma did, but there was a hard, cold lump in her throat, and her heart ached fit to shatter.

"We'll sing," Emma said, with inspiration and a sniffle, when the usual supper of dry bread and milk had been passed out to the children.

But the familiar songs sounded peculiar without Caroline to sing her part, and the words only made Emma cry again. In the end the little girls clung together in silent misery and tried to sleep.

Lily closed her eyes and remembered her mother talking with the soldier in the dusty blue suit.

"But they're my babies," Mama had cried, slurring her words the way she did whenever she had too much brandy. "What do you expect me to do with them?"

"Send them west, Kathleen," the soldier had answered, holding back the curtain that hid Mama's bed from the rest of the small flat and gesturing grandly.

"West?" Mama had echoed with a hiccup, preceding him around the curtain. She always did what men told her to do, but she got a swat on the bottom for her trouble all the same.

That was when Lily had first heard of the orphan trains. The soldier had told Mama what good homes those poor kids were finding out west, his clothes and hers dropping to the floor as he spoke. Their shadows were sleek against the curtain when Lily had gone outside to sit on the stoop and think, her chin propped in her hands.

3

She brought herself back to the present and snuggled closer to Emma, who was staring forlornly out at the night. Lily voiced the words no one had said before then. "Mama sent us away because of the soldier."

Emma's dark blue eyes were filled with gentle anguish as she nodded. "He wouldn't marry her if she kept us," she answered.

"I hate soldiers," said Lily, and she meant it.

Emma put an arm around her sister and held her close. "There's no point in hating anybody," she said. "Besides, we'll all be together again someday, just like Caroline promised."

Lily sighed. "I have to go," she told her sister.

Emma looked annoyed. "Oh, Lily, why didn't you take care of that when the train stopped? Now you'll have to use that awful slop pail in the back of the car!"

Lily's eyes, brown like Caroline's, grew wide. *"I have to go,"* she repeated insistently.

Properly disgruntled, Emma led her sister to the rear of the car and waited while she used the pot hidden behind the back of the last sooty seat. Some of the boys tried to look, but Emma gave them a piece of her mind and shielded Lily with her skirt.

The girls were back in their seats when it occurred to Lily that Emma might be among the orphans chosen next. Suppose Emma found a family and she didn't? If that happened, she wouldn't be able to go when she had to, for there would be no one to take her past those nasty boys and make a curtain for her when she pulled down her drawers.

Lily was afraid she'd wet, and the others would laugh and call her a baby.

Other worries soon gathered around, nipping at Lily like the dogs that frightened her in the streets at home. Maybe the people who took her in wouldn't like her, or they'd be mean-spirited. Or worse yet, maybe no one would want her at all, and she'd have to ride in that cold, smelly train forever and ever.

LILY AND THE MAJOR

After a very long time Lily drifted off into a fitful sleep and dreamed that Mama had changed her mind and wanted her children back. She called them her precious darlings and promised that they were all going to live in a lovely cottage close by the sea, just like the one Lily had seen in one of her grandmother's picture books.

The lurching of the train brought Lily awake with a cruel start. It was dawn, and she and Emma trooped out onto the platform once more with the others to be looked at by strangers.

A tiny, thin woman wanted to adopt Emma, who stood rooted to the platform, stiff and silent, while Lily clung to her skirts.

"Take my sister, too," Emma choked out after a few moments. "Please, ma'am—don't make me leave Lily."

The woman made a grunting sound of contempt. "I'm lucky to get one girl to help out around the place," she said. "If I brung home two, Mr. Carver would black my eyes."

At this the conductor interceded. He swept Lily up into his arms and hauled her back inside the train, fairly hurling her down into her seat. She was too stunned to cry out, too full of grief at so rude a parting from Emma to speak, but she got even all the same.

She leaned over and threw up in the aisle.

The conductor swore out loud, and that made the boys laugh, but Lily only turned her head and gazed numbly out the window.

Just as the train was pulling away from the little cluster of buildings gathered bravely together on the snowy plains Lily saw Emma waving at her. She was in the company of a fancy lady in a green dress and a feathered hat, and the other woman who had worried about getting her eyes blacked was nowhere to be seen.

Lily didn't eat breakfast that day, nor would she take the midday meal of wrinkly apples, cider, and bread.

In the late afternoon, with a new snowfall wafting down over the countryside, the train sounded its whistle and stopped again. Lily wouldn't have moved from her seat if the conductor hadn't grabbed her by the collar of her coat and thrust her out onto the platform with the others.

A plump fellow wearing a black suit pointed to her as he spoke to the woman at his side. There was a young man, too, but Lily paid him hardly any notice, for by this time she'd seen the little girl.

The child was a storybook vision, with fat yellow sausage curls falling past cheeks as perfect as Sunday china, and she wore a coat of crisp blue trimmed in shiny ribbon. She smiled at Lily and pointed.

"I want that one, Papa," she said clearly.

Lily stepped forward, as though drawn by an invisible string. She wasn't thinking or feeling much of anything, but she knew she didn't want to get back on that dreadful train.

The little girl climbed delicately up the platform steps and came to stand facing Lily. They were the same height, and both were fair, but there the similarities ended. Lily was wiry and thin, her pale hair astraggle, while the other child was plump and perfectly groomed.

"I am Isadora," the girl said importantly, smiling at Lily, "and Papa says I may have you for a playmate if I want you."

Lily shifted her weight from one foot to the other, unsure what to say. Now that Caroline and Emma were gone, maybe forever, it didn't much matter who took her home. She would just have to make the best of whatever happened.

Isadora frowned, her cornflower-blue eyes narrowing between thick, dark lashes. "You *can* talk, can't you? I want a friend that can talk!"

"I'm Lily," came the shy but firm response. "I'm six, and I can talk as good as anybody."

Isadora took Lily's hand and led her toward her beaming parents and the young man, probably her brother, who did not seem to share his family's delight at choosing an orphan. He was a great strapping boy with curly brown hair, and although he clearly disapproved of the proceedings, the expression in his blue eyes was a kindly one.

6

LILY AND THE MAJOR

"This is the one I want," Isadora announced. "I'm going to call her Aurora—no, that's too pretty." She turned and studied Lily somberly for a few moments. "I've got it. You shall be Alva. Alva Sommers."

Lily was taken to a waiting wagon and hoisted inside by Isadora's brother, who winked at her and smiled.

From that day forward everyone in the Sommers family addressed Lily as Alva, except for young Rupert. He called her by her rightful name, and when she told him about Caroline and Emma he wrote everything down so that she would always remember.

Chapter
❧ 1 ❧

Tylerville, Washington Territory
April 10, 1878

*T*he *rinka-tink-tink* of a tinny piano flowed out onto the street from the Blue Chicken Saloon, and greasy gray cigar smoke roiled out the open doors of the hotel dining room. Lily Chalmers consulted the cheap timepiece pinned to the bodice of her blue calico dress and nodded to herself, satisfied that she wouldn't be late for work.

Lifting her skirts with one dainty hand, Lily picked her way carefully through the mud and horse dung that littered the street. A little smile curved her lips when she reached the other side and stepped onto the wooden sidewalk. The land office was open for business.

The clerk, a young man with spectacles and pockmarked skin, stood behind the counter. He touched the brim of his visor when Lily entered. His gaze moved from her pale blond hair, done up in a chignon at the back of her neck, to her wide brown eyes and small, slender figure. "Mornin'," he said, with what Lily suspected was unusual enthusiasm.

Although she had never liked being assessed in that

particular way, she'd long since gotten used to it. Besides, nothing could take the glow off this perfect blue-and-gold day—not even the fact that she had to be at the Harrison Hotel in half an hour to serve another meal to a lot of noisy soldiers.

"I'd like to stake a claim on a piece of land, please," Lily said proudly. She took a folded map from her ancient beaded bag and held it out.

The clerk's eyes shifted to a place just beyond Lily's left shoulder, then back to her face. "Your husband isn't with you?" he asked. He looked disappointed now, rather than fervent.

Lily sighed and straightened her shoulders. "I don't have a husband," she said clearly.

There was a twitch in the clerk's left cheek, and his small eyes widened behind their spectacles. "You don't have a husband?" he echoed. "But you can't—you don't just—"

Lily had prepared for his argument, incoherently presented though it was. "Under the law, any able-bodied person of legal age may stake a claim to one-half section of land," she said, praying no one would demand proof that she had reached her majority. In truth, she was not quite nineteen. "One has only to prove up on their three hundred and twenty acres within five years, by building a house and planting crops."

The clerk was now thrumming the fingers of both hands on the countertop. He was clearly agitated. He started to speak, but his words came out in such a garble that they were unintelligible. Lily reached out to pat one of his hands.

"Be calm, now," she said in a gentle but firm voice. "Just tell me your name, and we'll work this all out amicably."

"Monroe," he replied. "My name is Monroe Samuels."

She nodded, pleased, and extended one gloved hand. "And I'm Miss Lily Chalmers," she responded sweetly. "Now, if we could just get down to business—I have another appointment very shortly."

Monroe took up the map Lily had laid on the countertop

and unfolded it. His Adam's apple jogged up his throat, then down again as he scanned the rough drawing of the land Lily had selected. He looked at her helplessly for a moment, then went to a shelf and took down an enormous book, which he opened with a flourish.

Lily stood on tiptoe, trying to make out the words marching neatly across the pages in a slanted black scrawl, but she was too far away.

"There is a five-dollar filing fee," Monroe said after clearing his throat. He seemed to expect Lily to be daunted by this announcement.

Again she opened her drawstring bag, this time taking out a five-dollar note. "I have it right here," she answered.

Monroe came and snatched up the map again, carrying it back to compare it with whatever was written in the book. "It might already be taken, you know."

Lily held her breath. Her land couldn't be taken—it just couldn't. Right from the very beginning she'd known God meant it to be hers and hers alone. She closed her eyes for a moment, summoning up images of the silvery creek shining in the sun, of the deep green grass and gently flowing bottomland where she meant to plant her crops. She could almost smell the stand of pine and fir trees that lined the southern border of her claim.

Monroe cleared his throat again, glanced at Lily's money as if to make sure it hadn't vanished, and dipped a pen to make a grudging notation in the book. "You need a husband to homestead," he fussed. "You're going to be dealing with Indians, and rattlesnakes, and outlaws—"

"We had all those things in Nebraska," Lily broke in politely, consulting her watch again. "And I survived. Now, if you'd just hurry . . ."

Scowling, Monroe wrote up a receipt and a temporary deed. "The half-section next to yours is already claimed," he warned. "Just make sure you've got your property line straight."

Lily scowled back. "I paced it off myself," she said.

Monroe did not look reassured. He snatched up the five dollars and shoved the deed and receipt at Lily. "Good luck, Miss Chalmers. You'll need it."

If the ink had been dry, Lily would have pressed the temporary deed to her bosom in triumph. She smiled at the petulant clerk to let him know he hadn't managed to discourage her, and she hurried out.

A stiff breeze made the certificate crackle between her fingers as she stood on the sidewalk inspecting it. For the first time in her life Lily owned something solid and real. Once she'd built her house and put in her crops she would be completely independent; never again would she be the interloper, the unwelcome burden.

She pursed her lips and blew on the deed like a child bending over a birthday cake and, when she was sure the ink was dry, rolled it neatly and tied it with a piece of string from her purse.

Her step was brisk as she hurried toward the hotel, where a long day's work awaited her.

She entered through the back way, recoiling as a blast of heat from the kitchen stove struck her. Carefully, she put her handbag and the precious deed away on a pantry shelf.

"There's a lot of 'em today," barked Charlie Mayfield, the cook, as he shouldered his way through the swinging door that led to the dining room, "and they're fractious."

Lily reached for her checkered apron, tied the strings at the back of her neck and at her waist, and nodded. "They're always troublesome," she said with resignation. "They're soldiers."

For Lily, those last two words said it all. She had no use whatsoever for men in uniform. They were invariably obnoxious, with no consideration for other people's rights.

Lily smoothed her hair once and set to work.

Later, as she passed between the crowded tables, gripping an overloaded tray in both hands, one of the soldiers reached out and wrenched hard at her apron strings. Pulled off balance, she stumbled, and the tray clattered to the floor.

Infuriated, the joy of her temporary deed forgotten for the moment, Lily whirled on her tormenter, a young infantry-man with a broad grin, picked up the mug of foaming beer in front of him, and flung the contents into his face. The other troopers whooped and cheered with delight.

A surge of heat moved up Lily's neck to throb in her cheeks and along the rims of her ears. Soldiers never seemed to care what trouble they caused, just as long as they had their good times.

She knelt and began gathering up the dirty cups, plates, and silverware she'd dropped with the tray.

The movements of her hands were quick and jerky, but she went still when she saw a pair of scuffed black boots come to a stop directly in front of her, and her temper swelled anew. These rascals had been harassing her with their exuberant mischief all morning, and she was through turning the other cheek.

She rose slowly to her feet and sighed as she felt the pins in her once-tidy hair give way, sending the silver-gold tresses tumbling down over her shoulders. Crows of amusement rose all around her as she set her hands on her hips and raised her chin.

The eyes that gazed down at her were just the color of maple sugar and shadowed by the brim of a dusty blue field hat banded in gold braid. A gloved hand reached up to remove the hat, revealing a thatch of golden-brown hair.

"On behalf of the United States Army, ma'am," a deep voice said with barely contained amusement, "I'd like to apologize for these men."

Lily reminded herself that the soldiers from nearby Fort Deveraux kept the hotel dining room in business, and that without them she wouldn't have a job. Nevertheless, she was near the end of her patience. "They would seem to be boys," she answered pointedly, "rather than men."

The barb brought a chorus of howls, whistles, and cries of mock despair.

The man looking down at Lily—a major, judging by his insignia—grinned rather insolently, showing teeth as white as the keys on a new piano. "They've been on patrol for two weeks, ma'am," he explained with elaborate cordiality, apparently choosing to ignore her comment on their collective bad manners.

Something about the curve of his lips made Lily feel as though the room had done a half spin. She reached out to steady herself by gripping the back of a chair. "I fail to see how that gives them the right to behave like circus gorillas."

The major's grin intensified, half blinding Lily. "Of course, you're right," he said. Every word that came out of his mouth was congenial. So why did she feel that he was making fun of her?

Lily found herself looking at the button-down panel on the front of his shirt and wondering about the chest beneath it. Was it as broad and muscled as it appeared, covered in a downy mass of maple hair?

With a toss of her head she shook off the unwelcome thought and knelt to finish gathering the crockery. She was surprised when the major squatted down to help, but she wouldn't meet his eyes.

"What's your name?" he asked.

Lily flung the last of the silverware onto the tray with a clatter. "It'll be mud if I don't get back to the kitchen and pick up my orders," she snapped.

The major took the heavy tray and stood with a sort of rolling grace while Lily scrambled inelegantly back to her feet. Just as she reached out to take the tray back someone pinched her hard on the bottom, and everything cascaded back to the floor again.

Lily cried out, spinning around in search of the culprit. "Who did that?" she demanded.

The unshaven, unwashed faces around her fairly glowed with innocence. It was obvious that no one was going to admit to the crime.

The major cleared his throat, and the troops, so rowdy only an instant before, immediately fell silent.

"That'll be enough," he said with quiet authority. "The next man who bedevils this woman will spend his leave time in the stockade. Is that understood?"

"Yes, sir," the men answered in rousing unison. One picked up Lily's tray and handed it to her, brimming with shattered plates and cups and dirty silverware.

She turned in a whirl of calico and stormed away, remembering the man who'd come into her mother's life years before and persuaded Kathleen to send Lily and her sisters west on the orphan train.

Soldiers. They were all alike.

In the cramped, sweltering kitchen she found Charlie in the expected state of annoyance. "These dinners are getting cold!" he complained, gesturing toward platefuls of fried chicken, mashed potatoes and gravy, and creamed corn.

Hastily Lily smoothed back her hair and pinned it into a chignon for the second time that day. "I know," she said, "and I'm sorry."

Charlie softened. He was an older man with thinning white hair and a crotchety manner, but he was basically kind. "I suppose the lads were pestering you a little. Serve them right if they had to eat their dinners cold," he said, but all the while he was filling clean plates from the pots and kettles on the stove.

Lily smiled at him and hurried out with the tray, keeping to the edge of the dining room in hopes of avoiding more trouble with the soldiers. But they were behaving themselves.

Reaching the table beside the corner window, Lily was taken aback to find the major there, along with an older man wearing the uniform of a colonel. An elegantly dressed woman with iron-gray hair and a sweet expression sat beside the ranking officer, and she smiled as Lily set a plate before her.

"You're new in Tylerville, aren't you?" the lady asked.

Lily bit her lower lip and nodded. She had no time to chat, but she didn't want to offend a customer. "Yes, ma'am," she answered. "I've been here a month."

The woman extended a gloved hand. "Welcome," she said. "My name is Gertrude Tibbet."

Lily glanced at the major, who was watching her with a look of humorous interest in his eyes, and swallowed. "I'm Lily," she replied. "Lily Chalmers."

"This is Major Caleb Halliday, an old friend of ours," Mrs. Tibbet went on cheerfully, indicating the man with the bold smile, "and beside me is my husband, Colonel John Tibbet."

Lily nodded politely at the colonel, a stout man with snow-white hair and a mustache to match. She ignored the major. Neither man stood, as they might have done under other circumstances.

"Let the poor girl get on with her work, Gertrude," Colonel Tibbet protested, chewing.

At that Mrs. Tibbet fell silent, and Lily turned and hurried away. She spent the rest of the day scurrying breathlessly from one table to another, filling coffee cups, carrying food, taking away dirty plates and silverware.

By the time the dining room closed hours later Lily's feet were throbbing, and she was so tired she could barely see. She spent another hour washing and drying dishes, then stumbled back to the storeroom beside the kitchen to fetch her bonnet and cloak. When she stepped out into the cool spring evening Major Halliday was waiting for her.

He tilted his hat. "Evening, Miss Chalmers," he said.

Lily glowered at him. "What do you want?"

The major smiled that insolent, melting smile of his. He had bathed, Lily noticed, and his uniform was fresh. He hesitated for a moment, then said, "I'd like to walk you home. It's dark, after all, and a town full of soldiers is no place for a woman alone."

Lily squared her slender shoulders. "My rooming house is nearby," she said in dismissal. "So I don't need an escort, thank you."

It was as though she hadn't spoken. Major Halliday fell into step beside her, settling his hat on his head with a practiced motion of one hand. "Where did you live before you came here?" he asked.

Lily sighed. The man was over six feet tall, and he probably weighed twice what she did. There would be no getting rid of him if he didn't want to go. "Nebraska," she replied, quickening her pace.

The major frowned. "That's a long way off. Do you have family in Tylerville?"

An old grief sounded inside Lily like a far-off bell as she thought of her lost sisters. Maybe, despite all her prayers and her letter-writing and her traveling from place to place, she'd never find them. She shook her head. "No family."

"Anywhere?" the major pressed.

Lily glanced at him. "I have an adopted brother living in Spokane," she answered. She wouldn't tell him about Emma and Caroline; that would be like baring a freshly bandaged wound. "Why are you so curious about me, Major?"

He smiled. "My name is Caleb," he corrected, ignoring her question.

"That's more than I care to know," Lily replied haughtily, and he laughed at that.

"I suppose it is. May I call you Lily?"

"No, you may not. I'm to be 'Miss Chalmers,' if you must address me at all."

He laughed again, and the sound was warm and richly masculine. "You've got all the warm congeniality of a porcupine, *Miss Chalmers.*"

"Thank you." Oddly, Lily found her thoughts straying back to his chest, of all things. He was a strong, well-built man, the kind who could put in a good day's work behind a plow without falling asleep over his supper, but there was no

16

reason to hope he'd ever become a farmer. Obviously, given his rank, Caleb Halliday had been a soldier for a long time, and he meant to remain one.

They had reached the rooming house, and Lily was both relieved and sorry. Stepping up onto the rough-board porch, she forced a smile. "Good night, Major," she said.

Just when she would have turned and run inside he caught hold of her hand. "Tell me why your brother let you come all this way by yourself." The words had the tone of an order, however politely they were framed, and Lily tried, without success, to withdraw her fingers from his grip.

"I am almost nineteen years old," she responded briskly. "I didn't ask Rupert's permission." Guiltily, she thought of how she'd left Spokane, where Rupert lived now, without telling her adopted brother good-bye or thanking him for his many kindnesses.

Another slow, smoldering grin spread across the major's face. "So you ran away," he guessed with distressing accuracy.

"No," Lily lied. "In any case, this is none of your business."

"Isn't it?" Major Halliday turned her hand in his and began stroking the tender flesh on the inside of her wrist with the pad of his thumb. The motion produced a series of disturbing sensations within Lily, not the least of which was a warm heaviness in her breasts and a soft ache in the depths of her femininity.

The door of the rooming house opened, and Mrs. McAllister, bless her nosy soul, peered out. "Time to come in, Lily. Say good-night to your young man."

Lily glared at Caleb. "He's *not* my young man," she said firmly. The day she took up with a soldier would be the day irises bloomed in hell.

Caleb's expression was as cocky as ever. "Not yet," he replied, in a voice so low that even the landlady's sharp ears could not have caught it. "I'll see you tomorrow, Lily."

Lily whirled in frustration and stomped into the house. It

17

had been a perfectly horrible day, and she was glad it was over.

After brewing a cup of tea in the kitchen she made her way up the back stairs to her room and sat down on the edge of her narrow, lumpy bed to remove her shoes. When they were off she stretched out with a sigh, pillows propped behind her back, and wriggled her cramped toes.

In order to keep from thinking about Major Caleb Halliday she turned her mind to Rupert. She knew she should write to her brother and tell him she was all right, but if she let him know where she was, he would surely come and drag her back to Spokane.

As much as Lily loved her brother, she couldn't live the kind of life he'd mapped out for her. She didn't want to teach school or sell coffee beans and yard goods at the general store. Or be forced to marry the first suitable man who asked her.

She smiled up at the darkened ceiling, her hands behind her head. Her temporary deed was safely tucked away.

Lily was going to be a farmer, once she'd saved the money to prove up on her homestead. This time next year she'd be planting fruit trees in her own sunny valley, with its fringe of timber. She'd set out a vegetable garden and start herself a flock of chickens, too.

Lily's smile faded. Before she could do any of that she had to have a cabin to live in. As determined as she was, she knew it would be impossible for her to cut down any of the huge Ponderosas that bordered her property, let alone drag them to the site she'd chosen and shape them into a house.

She sighed, getting off the bed to put on her nightgown. She'd find a way to get that cabin built. Somehow, she'd find a way.

Church bells awakened her with a persistent *bong-bong-bong,* and Lily tumbled out of bed muttering. She peeled off her nightgown and scrambled into drawers, a camisole, and a petticoat, then dragged her Sunday dress on over her head. She was going to be late again.

Lily fumbled with the cloth-covered buttons of her blue muslin gown and hastily brushed her hair. She was pinning it into place when Elmira McAllister rapped at the door of her room and called out, "Lily? Have you overslept again?"

It was one of Mrs. McAllister's rules that all lady boarders attend church faithfully. If Lily had had another place to live, she would have questioned the fact that male lodgers were allowed to sit in the front parlor and smoke of a Sunday morning, never giving the state of their souls a serious thought.

Clutching her Bible, Lily wrenched open the door and greeted her landlady with a slightly frantic smile and a breathless "Here I am!"

The plump, middle-aged woman replied with a "harumph." Her brown hair, streaked with gray, was pulled into its usual severe knot at the crown of her head, and her dark eyes moved over Lily with a look of suspicion. "I daresay the choir will be through the first hymn before we even reach our pews," she said. Then, with a sniff, she turned and led the way down the narrow staircase to the kitchen.

Although she knew it was anything but polite, Lily fell to watching Mrs. McAllister's wide hips brush the walls as she descended. It wouldn't be long, she reflected, before her landlady had to use the front stairs exclusively.

The sun was shining, and Lily noted with pleasure that the sky was the same deep blue as Mrs. McAllister's sugar bowl. The lilac bushes beside the back gate were just beginning to bud, and a spring rain had come during the night to nourish the awakening grass.

Lily drew a deep breath and wished devoutly that she might spend this morning on the half section of land that lay midway between Tylerville and Fort Deveraux. She'd have been closer to God there than in any clapboard church.

The musical "Amen" of the choir swelled out onto the spring air to meet Lily and Mrs. McAllister as they approached the front steps.

Inside, crowded onto the benches that held schoolchildren during the week, the townspeople closed their hymnals with a series of claps. Lily and her landlady took seats near the door, one on either side of the aisle.

Having registered this indication of Mrs. McAllister's disapproval, Lily squared her shoulders, lifted her chin, and focused her attention on the pastor, who was taking his place behind a makeshift pulpit. She started slightly when someone settled into the pew beside her, forcing her to move over.

Lily's brown eyes narrowed when she recognized Caleb Halliday. The major was dressed in a crisp blue uniform, his boots were polished, and he held his campaign hat respectfully in his lap.

He glowered down at her for a moment, as though she'd taken his seat, then turned his gaze toward the front of the church.

Once or twice during the next hour Caleb's muscled thigh actually brushed against Lily's skirts, and she felt as though she'd just dipped a ladle into a thunderstorm and taken a drink.

Because of the crowd, Lily wasn't able to escape quickly enough to evade Major Halliday. He was right behind her in the crush of people, and she was painfully conscious of his proximity.

Once outside under a maple tree she gulped fresh air and fanned herself with her Bible.

"Fine sermon, wouldn't you say?" the major drawled, his eyes dancing as he took in her flushed face and frazzled manner.

If Reverend Westbrook's sermon had been devoid of a single redeeming feature, Lily wouldn't have known it. She hadn't heard a word for worrying about Major Halliday and the odd feelings he produced in her. "It was fine indeed," she agreed grudgingly.

"I've always thought the Book of Proverbs to be particularly uplifting," he went on.

Lily longed to flee, and yet she seemed rooted to the spot like the tree she leaned against. "Y-yes," she said uncertainly. "Proverbs has much to inspire us all. Reverend Westbrook was wise to choose it as a topic."

Caleb's grin was slow and slightly obnoxious, and it caused a strange melting sensation in Lily's knees. "Perhaps he will someday," he said. "Today, of course, he talked about Jonah and the whale."

Lily felt color throbbing in her cheeks. "You delight in making a fool of me," she accused in a furious whisper.

"Not true," Caleb replied smoothly. "But I do like watching the sparks catch in your eyes when you realize you've just been had. May I walk you home, Miss Chalmers?"

"Certainly not. In fact, I would deem it a great favor if you would simply stop bothering me, Major." With that Lily thrust herself away from the tree and started toward the road.

Caleb reached out and caught hold of her arm, and she was forced to choose between turning to face him and making a scene. Since she knew Mrs. McAllister would be keeping a weather eye out for unseemly doings, she pretended that meeting Caleb's gaze had been her own idea.

"Come on a picnic with me," he said. It wasn't an invitation, but an order.

Color pulsed in Lily's cheeks, and she blinked, astounded at the man's arrogance. "I don't think that would be proper," she replied when she'd recovered a little. "After all, we hardly know each other."

Caleb sighed and replaced his hat. "And you obviously mean to see that we never do."

He sounded resigned and slightly wounded, and in spite

of herself Lily was sorry about that. She did find the major attractive, if entirely too tenacious. "I'll go if you can get Mrs. McAllister's permission," she said, feeling proud of her resourcefulness.

The twinkle in Caleb's eyes said he knew she expected her landlady to refuse the request without mincing words, but he turned and sought out that good woman in the crowd, where she stood chatting with two members of the choir.

Lily watched in mingled amazement and ire as Caleb made his way toward Mrs. McAllister, carrying his hat. He spoke politely to the woman, who rested one hand against her breast in delighted surprise and beamed up at him.

Presently Caleb returned, looking damnably pleased with himself. "She says I'm to have you back before sundown," he announced.

If Lily had been holding anything other than a Bible, she would have flung it down in pure exasperation. At the same moment, inexplicably, she wanted to kiss Mrs. McAllister for giving the picnic her blessing.

"Just how did you manage that?" she demanded as Caleb put his hat back on with a cocky flourish.

"I'm a very persuasive man," he replied, offering his arm.

Grudgingly, Lily took it. "And a very arrogant one."

Caleb chuckled. "So I've been told."

They'd reached a smart-looking buggy drawn by a coal-black gelding, and Caleb graciously handed Lily inside. She settled herself on the seat, making a great business of smoothing her skirts so that she wouldn't have to look at the major.

"Where would you like to go?" he asked.

Lily was caught off-guard by the question, since people rarely inquired about her preferences. A little shyly, she gave him directions to the plot of land she considered her own.

Caleb set off in that direction without hesitation, and Lily liked him for that. To keep him from finding out that he'd pleased her, she turned on the hard, narrow seat to glance behind her. Sure enough, a picnic basket was wedged into the narrow space. Tentatively she lifted the lid, and the scent of fried chicken tantalized her.

She couldn't help an appreciative little "ummmm," even though she was annoyed that Major Halliday had been so confident of her response to his invitation.

Caleb grinned. "So you like chicken, do you? You'd better watch out, Lily Chalmers—before you know it, I'll know all your deepest secrets."

Lily turned again and looked straight ahead at the rutted trail that led off into the countryside. The major's remark had given her the most unnerving feeling of intimacy. "You are too sure of yourself, sir," she replied stiffly.

"We'll see about that," he answered.

Lily squirmed on the seat. It appeared that nothing would do but the most straightforward approach. "If you're courting me, Major Halliday," she said, "it is only fair to tell you that I have no intention of marrying. Ever."

He unsettled Lily completely with a chuckle. "I'm not courting you," he answered, with such assurance that Lily was stung. "But you'll never make a spinster," he added.

"I will," Lily insisted through her teeth.

Caleb stopped the buggy and, with the black leather bonnet hiding them from the prying eyes of Tylerville, cupped Lily's chin in his hand and lifted it. His grasp was not painful, but it wasn't gentle, either. "You'll marry," he replied, "and here's the reason why."

Before Lily could make a move to twist away he kissed her. Those lips she'd found so appealing shaped hers effortlessly to suit them. Her breasts were pressed to his chest, and she could feel her nipples budding against him like spring flowers.

She gave a soft whimper as his tongue touched hers in a caressing flick, and the kiss went on. Endlessly.

When Caleb finally broke away Lily found her hands clutching his shoulders. Shamed, she let go of him and made to smooth her hair.

He took up the reins without a word and set the horse and rig in motion again.

They'd gone some distance before Lily could bring herself to speak. "You really should take me back to Mrs. McAllister's."

Caleb's eyes glowed like amber coals. "Not a chance, Miss Chalmers. We haven't finished our argument."

They *had* finished, as far as Lily was concerned, and he'd won. Never in her wildest dreams had she guessed that being kissed would feel like that. She could hardly wait to do it again. "What argument was that, Major?" she retorted.

"You said you'd never marry."

Lily sighed in spite of herself. "You were very forward just now."

"Yes."

"Would you care to be forward again, please?"

Caleb laughed. "That's one thing you won't have to worry about," he answered.

Lily waited, but he made no move to stop the buggy and kiss her a second time. She remembered how brazenly she'd behaved and flushed. If Mrs. McAllister ever found out, Lily would be out of the rooming house on her ear. "Do you like the army?" she asked when some considerable time had passed.

Caleb removed his hat and set it behind him, on top of the picnic basket, then ran splayed fingers through his hair.

"I've been a soldier since I was sixteen," he said, and there was a serious expression on his face now. "It's not a matter of liking it. I don't know any other kind of life."

Lily couldn't believe her own boldness. "Have you ever considered being a farmer?"

He turned his head to look at her, and Lily was startled by the amused rancor she saw in his face. "I'd sooner lead a raid on hell itself," he told her.

"Farming is good, honest work," Lily protested, incensed —and strangely wounded—that he didn't share her dream.

"If you've got no imagination," Caleb replied.

24

Lily bridled, folding her arms. "But soldiering is an *art*, I suppose. Well, you just try eating a sword for your Sunday supper—"

"Calm down," the major said, and though the words were spoken softly, they had the crispness of an order. In fact, Lily was as intimidated as the rowdy infantrymen had been the day before in the hotel dining room.

"Farmers are necessary to all of us," Lily pointed out. "Without them, we wouldn't eat. Soldiers, on the other hand . . ."

"Yes?" Caleb prompted when her voice fell away.

Lily cleared her throat. "I'm not claiming we don't need soldiers," she said diplomatically. "It's just that they do seem rather a luxury in a time of peace."

"You wouldn't say that if you'd ever been through an Indian attack."

Lily shivered at the images that came to mind. Unwittingly, the major had touched upon one of her deepest fears. "I thought the tribes around here were friendly," she said, her eyes widening as she looked up at Caleb.

His broad shoulders moved in a shrug. "If there's one thing I've learned about the red man, it's that he's unpredictable."

Lily bit her lower lip, thinking of all the nights ahead, when she would be alone on her little farm with no one to protect her.

Caleb favored her with an indulgent smile. "You don't need to worry, Lily. You're safe as long as you don't go wandering off into the countryside by yourself."

The reassurance didn't help. How on earth could she run a homestead single-handedly and not be alone? "I'll just have to buy a rifle and practice my shooting," she reflected aloud.

Even though they hadn't quite reached the valley, Caleb stopped the rig again. "What did you say?" he asked.

Lily sighed. "I want to practice shooting. I used to hunt grouse with Rupert, and—"

25

Caleb was staring at her as though she'd just said she planned to ride to the stars on a moonbeam. "A lady's got no business fooling with a weapon," he interrupted.

Lily sat up very straight. "You're certainly entitled to your opinion, Major Halliday," she said primly, "however antiquated and stupid it might be."

Caleb started the rig rolling again with a lurch, slapping the reins down on the horse's back. "What would you want with a gun?" he asked after a few moments had passed.

Although Lily knew her answer would start more trouble, she could no longer hold it back. "I'll need it for hunting, of course—and to protect myself, should the need arise. I mean to farm for a living, you see."

"By yourself?" There was a note of marvel in Caleb's voice.

"By myself," Lily confirmed as the horse and buggy topped a grassy knoll. Below lay the valley—her valley—dappled with purple and pink and yellow wildflowers, resplendent with spring.

For a few moments Lily had had doubts. But now, seeing her land, and her creek sparkling in the sunshine, she knew she would build her house and plant her fruit trees and crops. She could make it all come true if she just kept on working and planning, and she wouldn't need a man to help.

Especially not a soldier.

Chapter
❧ 2 ❧

*T*here," Lily said happily, drawing a deep breath and pointing. "Let's have our picnic right there, by the creek."

Caleb was silent as he guided the rig down the hill to the stream, and there was a look of surprise on his face. The horse drank thirstily of the pure water flowing from some distant spring while his master unloaded the picnic basket and a worn woolen blanket.

"Don't you like it?" Lily asked, climbing down from the buggy on her own and approaching Caleb. "Don't you think it's beautiful?"

Caleb gazed around him at the land, ran the fingers of his left hand through his hair, and took the basket from behind the seat. He flipped the blanket open to spread on the ground, then he looked at Lily in an odd, distracted sort of way. "Very beautiful," he answered gruffly.

Lily was pleased. Obviously Caleb was moved by the sheer grandeur of the landscape, just as she was. "I'm going to put my house right here," she announced, gleeful as a child as she extended both arms and turned in a circle. "The clothesline will be there, and the garden over here—"

Caleb was shaking his head, a look of sad amusement in his eyes. This was quickly displaced by a certain wariness. "You're not saying you mean to *live* here?"

Lily's good spirits deflated. "Of course I am. This is my property—or at least half of it is. I couldn't get a whole section because I'm not married."

Caleb folded his arms. The air between them seemed to hum. "You've filed a homestead claim on this place?"

Lily nodded. "I have the deed and everything," she answered proudly. "And I'm saving all my money. In another six months I'll have enough to stake myself to a good start."

Caleb sighed. His tone was indulgent; he might have been speaking to a child who wanted to play on the edge of a cliff. "It'll be October then," he pointed out. "The snow will only be a couple of weeks away."

Lily hadn't thought of that, for all her planning and scheming, but she didn't want Caleb to know. "I'll manage."

Caleb sat down on the blanket, and Lily joined him there, carefully smoothing her skirts. When he brought out the chicken Lily immediately helped herself to a drumstick.

Then she proceeded to make conversation. "Where did you grow up, Major?"

He smiled at the question, though Lily saw some old sadness move in his eyes. "Fox Chapel, Pennsylvania," he answered. "What about you?"

Lily looked away for a moment. "A little town outside of Lincoln, Nebraska," she said softly. "But I was born in Chicago."

"I know you have a brother in Spokane. Any sisters?"

For a moment the sorrow was nearly unbearable, coming upon her so suddenly the way it did. It was like a storm inside her spirit. "Two—Emma and Caroline. We were separated as children."

Caleb stopped eating to reach out and touch the back of Lily's hand. "I'm sorry," he said quietly. "What happened, if you don't mind my asking?"

Lily bit her lower lip, recovering. Finally she replied, "There was a new man in Mama's life—a soldier—and he didn't want any children around, so she put us on an orphan train headed west."

Caleb listened in silence, and if he felt pity for Lily, he didn't show it. She was grateful.

"Caroline was the oldest," she went on sadly, "then Emma, then me." She stopped to swallow. "When the train stopped they trooped us all out on the platform, and people could choose a child and take it home, no questions asked. I—I was young and naïve. I thought we'd all be chosen together, but it didn't happen that way, of course. Caroline got adopted somewhere in Nebraska, and Emma went the next day. I—I was all alone."

Caleb's hand closed over Lily's, the thumb making a soothing yet sensuous circle on her palm. "How old were you?" he asked, his voice gruff.

"Six," Lily answered, with a smile that soon faltered and fell away.

The major's grip tightened on her hand, but he didn't speak again. He just waited for Lily to go on.

Lily struggled against hopeless tears. She'd trained herself not to cry years before, but for some reason her resolve was weakening. "It was the soldier's fault," she said in a low, bitter voice. "Mama would never have sent us away if it weren't for him."

Caleb made no comment; he only looked at Lily as though he wanted to take her into his arms and hold her.

She drew a deep breath, let it out again. "I was adopted by a Presbyterian minister and his family as a—a playmate for their little girl." The grim lovelessness of life with the Sommers family came back to her, as crushingly dismal as ever. If it hadn't been for Rupert, she'd never have been able

29

to endure those years, and how had she repaid him? By running off without leaving so much as a farewell note.

"Were they cruel to you?" Caleb asked. "The minister's family, I mean."

Lily thought of the beatings she'd taken, the sparse meals allotted to her, the thundering reprimands, and the tattered clothes from the donation box on the church porch. She'd never been allowed to forget that she was a burden, taking up too much room. "Their son was good to me. He taught me to read and write and helped me with my work."

Caleb lifted her chafed, callused hand to his lips and kissed it lightly. "What do you want most in the whole world?"

She searched his handsome face, wondering if Caleb would understand, or if he would think her silly and frivolous. "I want to find my sisters. And I want a home of my own where nobody can tell me what to do."

Caleb nodded, and if he'd made any judgments of Lily's dreams, they didn't show in his eyes.

"I've been sending letters ever since I learned to write, trying to find them," Lily finished quietly.

"The west is a big place," Caleb reminded her in gentle tones. "They've probably married and taken other names—"

Lily glared at him. Maybe she'd just imagined that he empathized with her. "No matter what it takes, I'm going to find my sisters."

"How can you search for them and work a homestead, too?"

Lily folded her hands in her lap and looked at the china-blue sky for a long, long time. "When I was little and we were still in Chicago, my mother used to send me out for bread or a tin of tea, and I'd get lost on the way home. Caroline taught me to stay in one place until she came looking. She always found me."

Caleb released Lily's hand. "And you figure she'll find you this time, if you just stay put?"

Lily swallowed and nodded. Her eyes were stinging with tears. "She promised," she said.

Caleb didn't comment. They finished their meal of fried chicken, potato salad, and apple pie, and then he took Lily's hand and they got up from the blanket to walk around.

Lily showed Caleb the stakes that indicated her property line, and even though it ran square through the middle, she considered the whole valley hers. After all, nobody had built on the adjoining half section, even though a claim had been filed on it.

"What kind of crops do you plan to raise?" Caleb asked.

Lily folded her arms and gave a self-satisfied sigh. "I'm going to raise apples and pears—and grain."

Caleb looked out over the fertile land. Already it was carpeted with spring grass, even though patches of March snow lingered in places. "How do you plan to get the plowing done?" The question was a reasonable one.

"I've tilled fields before," Lily assured him. "Rupert's parents had a small farm in Nebraska. The reverend preached on Sundays and raised corn the rest of the week, and we had to help him. Except for Isadora, of course."

"Isadora?" They had returned to their picnic site, and Caleb was helping Lily fold the blanket. "Who's that?"

"She was Rupert's sister," Lily said, remembering the beautiful child with a certain bitter fondness.

A simple pull on the blanket brought Lily improperly close to Caleb, but she couldn't have let go to save her soul.

"You looked sad just then," Caleb said.

Lily nodded. "Isadora died of diphtheria the year we were ten."

Caleb let his end of the blanket fall to the ground and placed his hands on either side of Lily's head. His thumbs moved gently over her cheeks, and she was scandalized to find herself hoping that he meant to kiss her again. "You've had more grief in nineteen years than most people get in a lifetime," he said softly. "What you need is someone to take care of you. Very good care."

The last three words were spoken as a whisper against Lily's lips, and a shudder of need went through her as his mouth claimed hers. She would have sworn she felt his heart beating against her breast, but perhaps it was her own. She couldn't tell anymore.

Lily swayed slightly when Caleb withdrew, and he steadied her with strong hands. "If Mrs. McAllister ever found out about this," she muttered, dazed, "she'd throw me straight into the street."

Caleb chuckled. "What would you do then, Lily-flower?"

"I d-don't know," she answered.

He bent his head to touch his lips, just lightly, to the side of her neck. Lily shivered as a strange heat kindled there and danced along her flesh to pulse in the tips of her breasts. "You have other choices, Lily," he muttered, "besides grubbing in the dirt for a living."

Lily stepped back, knowing she would drown in sensation if she didn't get some perspective on things. She was entirely innocent when it came to the things men and women did together, but she sensed that Caleb was hinting at something scandalous. "Is this an indecent proposal?" she countered.

He smiled down at her. "I guess that's a matter of opinion," he answered. "I'd like you to be my mistress. You could have a fine house—"

Lily trembled with the effort to keep from flinging herself at Caleb Halliday in a hissing, spitting rage. Her words were evenly modulated and breathed, rather than spoken. "How dare you presume to suggest such a thing?"

The handsome face hardened. "I didn't 'presume' the way you reacted to that kiss," he replied.

Lily's cheeks flared with hurtful color. Just because she was alone in the world, forced to earn her living putting up with brazen flirtations and crude suggestions from soldiers and traveling peddlers, Caleb thought she was a strumpet. She wanted to sob at the injury, but she spoke calmly. "I think we'd better be getting back to town," she said. Not only had Caleb insulted her, but the sky was darkening and there were angry clouds gathering on the horizon.

Caleb set the picnic basket under the buggy seat and then hoisted Lily into the rig. He jerked his hat on, then climbed up beside her to take the reins.

A fanciful part of Lily's nature took over, one that had flourished during the lonely, difficult time she'd spent with the Sommers family. She pretended things were different.

In her mind, Caleb thought of her as a lady, and she didn't have to leave her land. She imagined living there, and bringing cold creek water to Caleb in the fields. He'd be wearing plain clothes instead of a uniform, and his shirt, open midway down his chest because of the heat, would cling wetly to his flesh. . . .

She brought herself sharply back to reality. Caleb was no gentleman, and he'd already made it clear that he was no farmer, either. Besides, she didn't know him well enough to indulge in such fancies.

Mrs. McAllister was waiting on the front porch, her hands clasped together over her apron, when Lily and Caleb arrived at the boarding house. She smiled happily and hurried down the walk. "Would you care to come back at seven for supper, Major?" she asked, without sparing Lily so much as a glance.

If she had, Lily would have discouraged her from tendering the invitation. The prospect of sitting across the table from Caleb Halliday, knowing he thought she was a trollop, was patently unappealing.

Besides, one had to take a personality as strong as Caleb's in small, measured doses. Like castor oil.

"I'd like that very much," Caleb said, hat in hand. He got down from the buggy and came around to help Lily. "Thank you, Mrs. McAllister."

Lily blushed and tightened her lips at the sensations stirred by the touch of his hands on either side of her waist. Avoiding both her landlady's eyes and Caleb's, she thanked the major stiffly, excused herself, and hurried into the house.

She was brewing tea in the kitchen when Elmira McAllister joined her there.

"Such a nice young man," she said, going straight to the stove to check the ham. "You could do worse than a major in the United States Army, Lily Chalmers."

Lily sighed and sat down to wait for her tea to steep. She was too proud to say that Caleb was looking for a mistress, not a wife. "I'm not in the market for a husband, Mrs. McAllister—especially not a bossy one like Caleb Halliday."

"Humph," said Mrs. McAllister. "If ever a young lady needed the strong guiding hand of a good man, you do."

Lily smoothed her hair. She didn't understand what she'd done to warrant such an opinion. She supported herself, and she was a dependable tenant, always paying her rent on time, never venturing into the kitchen after eight o'clock or leaving soggy towels about after her bath the way the male boarders did.

Mrs. McAllister seemed disappointed that Lily had let her remark pass. She touched the crust of a pie cooling on the windowsill with an experienced finger, then brought it to the counter. "Every girl's got to use whatever blessings the good Lord's given her, be they brains or beauty."

Lily waited resentfully.

"You've a comely face and figure," the older woman went on, slicing the pie into eight generous pieces. Normally there would have been twelve, but Mrs. McAllister obviously wanted to impress Caleb Halliday. "If you're smart, you'll encourage the major."

"Why?" Lily was willing to grant that Caleb was handsome, and he was a fine, sturdy man in the bargain, but neither of those qualities explained why Mrs. McAllister was so adamant. She certainly hadn't displayed these sentiments when other men had come to call on Lily.

"You haven't been in Tylerville long enough to know, I guess," sighed the landlady. "He's from a very prominent family back east, Lily. Whoever marries him will have money, position, respectability."

Lily ached with fury. Caleb was reserving *those* assets for the woman he considered suitable to bear his name and his children. Well, maybe she didn't have money and position, but she was respectable. She'd never done anything truly wrong, except perhaps for letting Caleb kiss her twice and enjoying it both times. And nobody knew about that. "What about love?" she asked. "Does it mean anything that I don't love the man?"

"It's too early to be deciding that," Mrs. McAllister retorted. "Many's the marriage that began in friendship and blossomed into love as the years went by. It was like that with my own Mr. McAllister." She paused to sigh. "I married him because my papa told me to—he had a farm that adjoined ours, you know—but I came to care very deeply for my husband, Lily. Very deeply indeed."

Lily was amazed. She had never seen this sentimental side of Elmira McAllister. "You must miss him very much," she said gently.

Mrs. McAllister nodded, looking wistful, but then she was her normal, stern self again. "There's no point in pining," she said briskly, and she swept out of the kitchen, leaving Lily alone with her tea and her thoughts.

Lily refilled her cup, added milk and sugar, and went up the back stairs to her room. There she sat at the rickety little desk in front of the window, took out paper, pen, and ink, and began yet another letter, addressed to the marshal of yet another western town.

She asked the same questions as always, signed the letter, and tucked it forlornly into an envelope. She'd probably mailed out a thousand such inquiries over the years to marshals and newspapers in Nebraska and points west, and she'd never received even one answer.

No one, it seemed, knew the whereabouts of either Emma or Caroline Chalmers.

Lily wondered sometimes if both her sisters were dead. Maybe they'd been struck down by cholera, or diphtheria, like Isadora. Maybe they'd been killed by Indians, or washed away in a flooded river. . . .

"Stop," Lily instructed herself. Caroline and Emma were alive and well, she knew that in her heart. If she just stayed in or near Tylerville, just as she'd stayed by a lamppost or a street sign when she was lost as a child, one of them would find her.

Only it seemed less and less likely with every passing year. Not for the first time, Lily considered the possibility that her siblings didn't *want* to find her. In all likelihood they had husbands and children and no room in their busy lives for a lost sister.

Maybe they'd forgotten she even existed, or given her up for dead.

Lily's mind drifted back into the past.

"If you died, nobody would cry," Isadora said, pouring real tea from a china pot into a doll-sized cup and shoving it across the toy table. She was an exquisite child, as beautiful as any of her dolls, with her glistening golden curls and cornflower-blue eyes.

Nine-year-old Lily's stomach grumbled, and she made a slurping sound as she drank the tea.

Frowning with disapproval, Isadora reached out and slapped at Lily's hand. "Don't do that, Alva," she said, using the made-up name Lily hated. "You sound like a terrible pig. Act like one, too. I don't think anybody will come to your funeral."

"Rupert will," Lily dared to say, her chin quivering.

Isadora shook her head. "Rupert's going away to be a teacher," she said. "He won't ever think about you again, once he's gone. Everybody's going to forget you, except for me, of course."

LILY AND THE MAJOR

Suddenly Lily was filled with unreasoning, aching rage. Isadora had spoken the truth, and Lily hated her for it. She leapt out of her chair, rounded the table, and slapped Isadora's rosy cheek with all her might.

Isadora emitted a startled shriek, which brought her mother trundling across the farmhouse's big kitchen. Bethesda Sommers entangled a strong, work-hardened hand in Lily's hair, wrenching her away from her daughter.

"Willful child!" she screamed. "It was the devil's doing, your coming here!"

Tears of pain and fear burned in Lily's eyes, but she wouldn't let them fall. She didn't cry out once, not even when Mrs. Sommers dragged her across the kitchen and beat her with a wooden spoon.

Lily was lying on her bed in the attic hours later, her body bruised and covered with welts, when Isadora arrived with her supper, which consisted of a glass of milk and a slice of bread.

"Rupert went to town with Papa," the child said smugly. "He doesn't even know you have to stay here until Mama's through being mad with you." She paused to smile. "Like I said, nobody thinks about you but me."

Tears blurred Lily's vision when she wrenched herself back to the present and reached for another sheet of paper. Resolutely, she dipped her pen and selected a town from the list she'd copied from one of Rupert's geography books. Then she began a new letter.

Wearing only his trousers, Caleb lay stretched out full length on the lumpy bed in his hotel room, his hands cupped behind his head. He recalled with pleasure how Lily had looked, standing beside the stream that day, telling him about her dreams of happy independence.

He smiled. She honestly expected to work a piece of land all by herself—what an innocent she was.

Caleb's amusement faded as he considered how quickly

the rigors of homesteading would turn Lily hard and cynical, her great expectations notwithstanding. In another year she'd be work-worn and gaunt, with lye-reddened hands and empty eyes. Some man would come along and marry her, and for a time maybe things would be better. Maybe, at last, she'd feel she belonged.

But then there'd be babies, one after another, until there were too many. Lily would die, taking her dreams with her. The man who had used her up would bring another bride to her cherished land, and the cycle would start all over again.

The bedsprings complained as Caleb sat up, thoroughly depressed. He didn't usually take such a dark view of things, but meeting Lily the day before in the hotel dining room had turned his thought processes upside down. He was obsessed with the woman, wanting to shelter her, to dress her in beautiful gowns and show her off, to make up for the hard years.

To bed her.

He'd even begun to have thoughts about going home and facing his family.

With the bed railings pressing cold against his bare back, Caleb closed his eyes and returned, in his thoughts, to the sprawling Pennsylvania farm where he'd grown up. . . .

He was eleven years old, and he was hiding in the hayloft, fighting against the sobs that hammered at the back of his throat. His father had died six months before, and now his mother was dead, too—the doctor had just told Caleb so.

And it was all because of that stupid baby. Caleb wished it had been the one to die, instead of his mother.

"Caleb?" The voice belonged to his older brother. At twenty-one, Joss was already a man, and he'd been running the farm since the accident that had killed Aaron Halliday, their father. "Come on, boy—I know you're in here somewhere, so speak up."

Caleb swallowed. He was afraid to answer, afraid he'd start bawling and never be able to stop.

Joss repeated his name, and Caleb squeezed his eyes shut,

38

sending a silent prayer toward heaven. Let him tell me it was all a mistake. Let him say Mama isn't really dead.

The rickety rungs of the wooden ladder creaked, and when Caleb opened his eyes Joss was climbing into the hayloft. His handsome face was streaked with field dirt and sweat or, perhaps, tears, and he wore the simple shirt and trousers of a farmer. Like Caleb, he had amber eyes and dark blond hair, though his was curly instead of thick and straight.

"You sure don't make things easy," he said with a sigh, coming to sit beside Caleb in the hay, his broad back to the weathered wood of the barn wall.

Caleb's misery was pure and exquisitely painful. "It's that damn baby's fault," he managed to get out. "She killed Mama."

Joss caught Caleb's face in one huge, callused hand and gazed straight into his eyes. His expression was stern, and so were his words, though they were spoken gently. "Don't you ever let me hear you say anything like that again, boy. If you do, so help me God, I'll take you to the woodshed and whip you proper. That little girl in there is our sister, and we're going to look after her. She's a Halliday."

Caleb's composure was shattered. It was real, then— because Joss wouldn't deny it, it was real. Mama was truly dead, and the three of them, Joss, Caleb, and that squalling, red-faced baby girl, were all that was left of the family.

A hoarse sob ripped itself from Caleb's throat, and he felt Joss's powerful arm slip around his shoulders.

"You do all the crying you've got to do," Joss said quietly, his chin resting against the top of Caleb's head. "In time the hurting will stop. And I'm going to take care of you, boy—you and little Abigail. Don't you worry, because I'm always going to be right here."

I'm always going to be right here. The words echoed in Caleb's mind years later as he sat in the hotel room, remembering. Joss was still on the farm, but things had gone terribly wrong one hot day during the war, and as far as Joss was concerned, Caleb was as dead as their mother and father.

Abigail had written that there was even a stone in the family plot with Caleb's name carved in it.

A crushing sense of loss descended on Caleb. He flung himself off the bed and away from thoughts of his bull-headed brother.

He went to the window and looked out on the dried mud of the town's main street. Tomorrow he'd have to return to Fort Deveraux and his work there. He'd be forced to leave Lily.

A wagon jolted past, loaded with supplies for the fort, and Caleb turned away, rubbing his jaw thoughtfully. There had to be some way to bring Lily back with him.

He toyed with the idea of hiring her as his housekeeper instead of installing her in a house in Tylerville, but he knew what would happen if he did that. The resultant gossip would take the rigid pride out of Lily's backbone and the insolent snap from her brown eyes. And she wouldn't agree to such a plan anyway.

Caleb paced. Mrs. Tibbet, the colonel's wife, was always looking for a housekeeper. Every time she hired one the lady would marry a soldier departing for home and leave the Tibbets' employ.

A slow grin spread across Caleb's face. If Lily accepted the position, she would be close at hand, and he'd have an opportunity to win her over to his way of thinking. He'd court her, after a fashion, though he had no intention of marrying her or any other woman, and he'd teach her the pleasures of a good man's bed.

A pang of guilt struck his middle as he remembered Bianca and the way she'd looked when he'd told her he wouldn't be calling on her again because he'd met someone else. She'd turned away, her shoulders very straight, and said she didn't care much for being a soldier's mistress anyway.

Caleb exiled Bianca from his mind, just as he had Joss.

He opened his watch for the thousandth time and saw that it was finally time to go to supper at Mrs. McAllister's. He went to the mirror, brushed his hair, and put on his shirt and then his uniform coat—the one with the gold epaulets.

There were no flowers to be had in all of Tylerville, except for wild blossoms blooming in colorful profusion at the edge of town, and Caleb wasn't about to let his men see him picking daisies and hollyhocks. He persuaded the storekeeper to open his door, even though it was Sunday, and bought a box of fine French chocolates.

When he reached the boarding house where Lily lived she answered the door herself. Her attitude was one of resignation rather than welcome, and Caleb suppressed a smile. The time would come when she would greet him by flinging both arms around his neck and pressing that delectable little body to his.

Her eyes, brown as coffee, dropped to the fancy box in Caleb's hands. "Good evening," she said coolly.

Caleb's mind filled with an unbidden image of her in the parlor of the grand house in Fox Chapel, wearing silks and satins and graciously greeting his guests of an evening. He'd be the envy of every man north of the Mason-Dixon line.

He shook off the idea. He was looking for another mistress, not a wife.

"Hello," he replied somewhat belatedly.

Lily stepped back to admit him, her gaze catching on the chocolates again. It was Caleb's aim to make her look at him just the way she was looking at that red satin box.

He extended the candy and knew by the pleasure in her eyes that she'd received few gifts in her life. And for one insensible, fevered moment Caleb wanted to give her everything. He wanted to drag the world to her feet and make it bow.

"Thank you," Lily said, accepting the chocolates with both hands.

41

Caleb felt relief surge through him. All he had to do was show Lily how gracious life could be, and she would forget her silly ideas about homesteading a hardscrabble farm.

"Won't you sit down?" Lily asked, indicating a horsehair settee facing Mrs. McAllister's parlor fireplace.

"After you," Caleb said, and when Lily took a seat on the settee he joined her.

Lily lifted one corner of the chocolate box and peeked inside. "Do you suppose Mrs. McAllister would notice if I ate just one piece before supper?" she whispered.

"Eat the whole box if you want," Caleb replied, oddly touched.

Lily cautiously chose a chocolate from the box and popped it into her mouth. Caleb watched as she rolled it around on her tongue, savoring it, and his blood turned hot as kerosene in his veins.

"Would you like one?" she asked, holding the box out to him.

Caleb drew a deep breath and let it out slowly. Time. He had to give things time. "No, thanks," he said hoarsely.

Lily looked delighted that she didn't have to share, the greedy little scamp, and Caleb wanted to laugh. He also wanted to carry her off to his bed and make her completely and inexorably his own.

He drew another deep breath.

Elmira McAllister swept into the room just then, all smiles. She was a handsome woman, Caleb thought wryly. In fact, she rather resembled his first sergeant.

He rose immediately to his feet, took the lady's offered hand, and kissed it. In a sidelong glance at Lily he saw her slide the candy box under the cushion of the settee.

"Major Halliday," the landlady trilled, "I can't tell you how honored we are to have you come calling."

Caleb didn't know exactly how to respond to that remark, so he brushed it off by seating Mrs. McAllister in a nearby chair.

When dinner was served the other tenants were conspicuously absent. Caleb wondered if his hostess had ordered them to eat in their rooms.

"You've got chocolate on your chin," he whispered to Lily when the landlady went to the kitchen for the first course.

It was wonderful watching her reaction. She dipped the tip of her table napkin into her water glass and dabbed hastily at the spot Caleb indicated with the touch of an index finger. Sometime in the future, when she was warm and contented from their lovemaking, he'd confess to Lily that there had never been a speck of chocolate on her face at all.

Mrs. McAllister hurried in with a tureen of soup just then, or Caleb would have kissed Lily soundly on the mouth. When her hand accidentally brushed his thigh he felt himself harden fiercely and was grateful for the concealing tablecloth.

He shifted uncomfortably in his chair when Mrs. McAllister went out for the main course.

"Is something wrong?" Lily asked, her dark eyes wide as she studied his face.

"No," he lied. "What happened to the other boarders?"

Lily leaned close to him; he felt her breast against his upper arm and groaned inwardly as his condition worsened. "Mrs. McAllister enticed them to stay away," she confided. "She wants me to marry you, so I'll have money and position."

Caleb knew Lily had hoped to shock him. "Would you do that?" he asked smoothly. "Marry a man for money and position, I mean?"

"I'm not going to marry anyone," Lily insisted.

"So you've said," he replied, and he slipped his hand under Lily's arm. He hoped she'd stick by her decision, since a married woman wouldn't do as a mistress.

She started slightly as he brushed his fingers over the sensitive flesh on the underside of her forearm, and a delightful apricot blush pulsed in her cheeks, but she made no move to rebuff him. "She'll be back at any moment!" she hissed.

"Wrong," Caleb replied with a slight shake of his head. "She wants us to be alone together as much as possible."

He saw in Lily's eyes that she knew he was right. "This is most improper," she said.

Caleb moved his fingers in a slow, feather-light circle, watching with satisfaction as her breasts rose on a quick breath and a pulse tapped its beat at the base of her neck. She tilted her head back for a moment and closed her eyes as he touched her, and he knew a soaring triumph. He'd been right. For all her innocence, Lily's blood ran warm as mulled wine in her veins.

Much as Caleb would have loved giving Lily a lesson in pleasure, he knew he mustn't move too fast. He withdrew his hand just as Mrs. McAllister came in with the roast chicken.

Lily flashed him a look, her color still high, and turned her attention to the meal.

When dinner was over—and the hour seemed interminable to Caleb—he asked permission to take Lily out for a walk in the moonlight.

It was Mrs. McAllister who readily agreed; Lily was looking at him with stormy eyes.

He led her into the relative privacy of the McAllister apple orchard.

Lily leaned against a tree, her hands behind her, her pose unconsciously thrusting her beautiful breasts forward and sharpening the sweet anguish Caleb was feeling. "I'm not a loose woman," she said firmly, without preamble, "and I won't be your mistress, no matter how many boxes of chocolates you give me."

Caleb rested one hand on the gnarled trunk of the tree she leaned against and bent toward her. "That's the last thing I think, Miss Chalmers," he informed her. "That you're a loose woman, I mean."

"Is it?" She blushed again. Fetchingly, he thought. "You've kissed me twice today, Major Halliday. And tonight at the table, you—you—"

"I touched you," Caleb said softly. "And you let me."

Lily sighed. "I don't know what possessed me."

"I do," came the easy reply. "You're supposed to feel like that when the right man touches you, Lily. It's natural."

She stared up at him. "It is?"

Caleb nodded. "Not only that, but it gets better."

Lily swallowed. "It couldn't."

"But it does," Caleb argued gently. "One day soon, when you're ready, I'll show you."

"It seems to me that you expect rather a lot for a pound of chocolates," Lily protested.

Caleb laughed. "Rebel while you can," he said. "Very soon things will be different."

She looked as though she didn't believe her ears. "Of all the audacious, low-minded—"

He ran his thumb along her jawline, delighting in her fury and her fire. Taming her was going to be pure joy. "Yes?"

It took a mere brush of his lips to make her tilt her head back for his kiss. Caleb wondered if she was sophisticated enough to know how much he wanted her.

He'd kissed her thoroughly when she finally placed both hands against his chest and pushed.

"It's hopeless," she gasped out defiantly. "So stop trying to convince me!"

Caleb smiled and allowed one of his hands to stray, ever so lightly, across her breast. He felt her nipple grow instantly taut against his knuckles. "I mean to have you, Lily Chalmers," he warned, his voice barely more than a breath. "The time will come when you'll stand at your window watching for me."

She gaped at him.

"I see we understand each other," he said, putting his hat back on and stepping back to see Lily better. She was like some delicate, exotic flower blooming in the moonlight.

"Suppose I tell you that I never want to see you again?" she managed after a long time, her voice a breathless whisper.

Caleb knew he looked a lot more confident than he felt. "You won't," he answered.

"What makes you so sure?"

"The kiss we just shared."

"You say and do the most outrageous things, Major Halliday."

He touched her chin with the tip of one index finger. "I'm leaving tomorrow, Lily."

Maybe he was imagining it, but he thought he felt her quiver. "Leaving?" she asked in a small voice.

"I'm going back to Fort Deveraux."

He could see she was mentally gauging the distance between Tylerville and the fort, and that eased some of his anxiety about leaving her. "You'll probably forget all about me," she said.

Caleb chuckled ruefully. "I couldn't do that if I tried," he answered. "And I don't intend to try. Lily, there's an officers' ball at the fort next Saturday night. Will you go with me?"

Her alabaster throat moved as she swallowed, and it was obvious that she was searching her mind for reasons to refuse. "I don't have a proper dress—"

"That won't be a problem. I have a friend who'll be able to come up with something for you to wear."

Lily's eyes narrowed. "What friend?" she demanded.

Caleb wanted to shout for joy. She was jealous! "You met her in the dining room yesterday—Mrs. Tibbet."

"Her clothes would never fit me," Lily protested.

"No," Caleb agreed, "but her niece's would."

He knew then that she wanted to go to the ball, and the knowledge made him exuberant.

"Where would I stay? The fort must be ten miles from here—I could never get back to Mrs. McAllister's in time to go to bed."

"You could spend the night with Colonel and Mrs. Tibbett. There probably aren't two more acceptable chaperons in the whole territory."

Lily smiled uncertainly, and the eagerness in her face twisted Caleb's heart. "I've never been to a ball," she said in a speculative tone of voice. "Would I get another box of chocolates?"

"Only if you promise not to eat them in front of me," Caleb replied, remembering the agonies he'd suffered watching her roll the sweet around on her tongue. Then, after planting a light kiss on Lily's mouth, he escorted her back to the house and took his leave.

Chapter

⤜ 3 ⤛

The next morning, while Lily was lingering over a late breakfast and doing her best to steel herself for another shift at the hotel dining room, Gertrude Tibbet came to call. She rapped lightly on the glass pane in Mrs. McAllister's kitchen door and smiled when Lily leapt to her feet.

After smoothing her hair and straightening her skirts Lily admitted the unexpected guest with a quiet "Good morning."

Mrs. Tibbet nodded graciously. "Hello, Lily."

"Won't you sit down?" Lily asked, suddenly remembering her manners.

"Thank you," the older woman said, "but I can't stay long. Caleb tells me he's invited you to the officers' ball at Fort Deveraux on Saturday evening."

Lily swallowed. She should have refused him, she knew, but she'd never been to a ball, and she knew this might be her only chance. "Yes, ma'am. He did."

Gertrude Tibbet smiled again. "He also said that you

were quite properly concerned with your reputation and refused to attend unless suitable arrangements could be made."

Color pulsed in Lily's cheeks. She wondered what else the major might have told Mrs. Tibbet—had he admitted kissing her, for instance? Or confessed he wanted Lily to be his mistress? "That's true," she said belatedly, beginning to clear away the breakfast dishes because she was nervous and needed something to do with her hands.

Mrs. Tibbet's small shoulders seemed to swell beneath her black sateen cloak as she took a deep breath. "Well, then, I've come to solve the problem. The colonel and I would be delighted if you'd consent to stay with us on Saturday evening. Major Halliday could see you back to Tylerville on Sunday afternoon."

Lily's eyes were wide. "That's very kind of you, Mrs. Tibbet, but you see, I don't—"

"You don't have a dress," the older woman finished for her. "Don't worry. I'm sure something of Sandra's would fit you."

Lily wavered. Heaven only knew when she'd be invited to a ball again, with a gown provided and everything, and besides, nothing more would come of it. She'd never take up with a soldier, after all. "I—I just have to ask my landlady."

Mrs. Tibbet arched stone-gray eyebrows. "Your landlady?"

Lily sighed and dropped her voice to a whisper. "She's pretty much of a fussbudget, Mrs. McAllister is," she confided. "If I do anything she disapproves of, I won't have a place to live."

"I see," said Mrs. Tibbet, but she didn't look as though she saw at all. Lily thought she seemed puzzled.

"If you'll just wait here," Lily said hopefully, "I'll come back straightaway with an answer."

Mrs. Tibbet nodded, and Lily dashed out of the room. She found Mrs. McAllister changing the sheets on Mr. Arguson's bed.

Hastily Lily explained Caleb's invitation to the officer's ball and Mrs. Tibbet's offer to put her up while she was at Fort Deveraux.

Mrs. McAllister beamed at the idea. "Before you know it, Lily Chalmers," she said buoyantly, "you'll be carrying the major's dinner to the table of a night, instead of waiting on strangers at the hotel."

Lily felt a stab of shame, knowing Caleb had quite another purpose in mind. He was a scoundrel, and he deserved whatever happened to him. But for just one shining, magical night Lily would pretend he was a prince. "You don't object to my going, then?"

The landlady favored her with a stern look. "See that you mind your manners, that's all. No gentleman will buy the cow when he knows he can get the milk for nothing."

Lily managed not to roll her eyes until she'd turned her back on Mrs. McAllister and stepped into the hall again. Caleb had come right out and admitted that he had no intention of "buying the cow"—he only wanted to rent it.

Lily smiled sadly. He wasn't going to succeed, of course. She meant to wear a ball gown and glass slippers for a night, then forget she'd ever heard Caleb Halliday's name.

She found Mrs. Tibbet waiting patiently in the kitchen.

The colonel's wife chuckled at Lily's shining face. "You don't need to tell me, dear," she said. "Your expression has done that." She embraced Lily lightly, then stepped back. "There is a stage to Fort Deveraux on Saturday morning," she added, pressing a coin into Lily's hand. "Here is your fare."

Lily felt almost as though she'd been visited by a fairy godmother. "Thank you," she said, a moment before Mrs. Tibbet opened the back door and walked out.

In her room Lily got down on her knees, dug one of her Sunday shoes out from under the bed, and hid the coin in its toe. While in that opportune position she offered up a quick prayer that she might hear from Caroline and Emma soon and thanked God for her invitation to the officers' ball.

Mounted soldiers, row after row of them, filled the street outside the hotel when Lily arrived for work. Although she saw a few of the young men look at her in a sidelong fashion, there were no catcalls or teasing remarks.

A glance toward the front told her why they were so well-behaved. Caleb, riding the same blue-black gelding that had drawn the buggy the day before, when they'd gone on their picnic, had called them to attention.

Lily paused at the door of the dining room, fascinated by the man's air of strength and command. She wanted him to look at her so that she could snub him, but he didn't spare her so much as a glance.

"Sergeant Haywood," he said in a crisp tone. Before he spoke the street had seemed utterly silent, except for the nickering and fidgeting of some of the horses.

A man in the front row saluted briskly. "Yes, sir."

Caleb returned the salute. "Take over my command. I'll catch up to you in a few minutes."

"Yes, *sir*," answered Sergeant Haywood, a heavyset man with a red beard and mustache. He rode up beside Caleb, lifted one arm into the air to reveal a crescent of sweat, then shouted, "Forward!"

As the troops spurred their horses Caleb rode over to where Lily stood, dismounted, and wrapped the reins around a hitching post. Then, with his hat in one hand, he stepped up onto the wooden sidewalk to face her.

It seemed a long time passed before the clatter of hooves began to recede into the distance. The air was full of dust, and Lily used one hand to fan some of it away.

Caleb grinned at the gesture. "Sorry," he said.

Even though Lily had been on a picnic with this man, even though she'd been *kissed* by him, she still felt shy and awkward in his presence. "That's quite all right," she replied.

He took one of her hands into fingers gloved in soft leather and stroked the chafed flesh lightly. "I'll be looking forward to meeting the stage next Saturday," he told her.

Gazing up at him, Lily swallowed hard. She'd never known anyone who could affect her with ordinary words in quite the way Caleb did, and she suspected he had the power to make her exchange her old dreams for new ones. That was a frightening thing.

"Lily?"

She realized she hadn't answered him. "I'll be looking forward to Saturday, too," she said. That was only half true, she thought, because a part of her dreaded the week's end the way a sworn sinner would dread Judgment Day. Caleb had a frightening sort of power over her.

For a moment it really seemed as though the major meant to kiss her good-bye right there on the sidewalk. In the end, though, he only smiled again, put his hat back on, and turned to stride back to his horse. Once he was mounted he studied Lily for a long moment, then rode off after his men.

Lily was left feeling disgruntled and confused. She didn't *like* Caleb Halliday. He was rude, arrogant, and insufferable. His intentions toward her were not at all honorable.

So why had she agreed to have anything further to do with him?

Lily sighed. Because she was starved for a little magic, that was why. Because one wonderful night was not too much to ask out of a lifetime of hard work. She opened the door of the dining hall and went inside, nearly colliding with a customer in the process.

She smiled her apologies and hurried into the kitchen. Although the small restaurant was practically empty, the stagecoach from Spokane was due in only fifteen minutes. Before long the place would be brimming with hungry travelers and workers from the saw mill. After greeting Charlie Lily snatched a clean apron from the peg beside the pantry door and put it on.

"These pies is burned!" Charlie bellowed once he'd opened the oven door.

Sure enough, the kitchen was soon filled with black

smoke. Coughing, Lily opened the back door to let in some fresh air.

Charlie went right on swearing, just as though it were Lily's fault he'd forgotten to take the pies out of the oven. She filled a tray with clean silverware and fled into the dining room to begin setting tables.

She was just finishing up when the stage rolled to a stop outside and emitted only two passengers. One was a beautiful dark-haired woman wearing an amethyst-colored traveling suit. The other was Lily's adopted brother, Rupert.

Lily stood perfectly still as Rupert opened the door for the woman in his usual courtly way and then stepped inside himself. His dark blue eyes blazed as he looked at Lily.

"So this is where you've been," he accused.

In her mind's eye Lily saw herself slipping out of the small house she and Rupert had shared, all her belongings stuffed into a single worn valise.

Rupert had been unreasonable, but she regretted the worry she'd surely caused him. She noticed how tired he looked, and his shabby schoolmaster's clothes were dusty from hours on the road. His dark, curly hair, normally so springy, was limp, and there were ridges where he'd run his fingers through it.

The woman passenger glanced at Lily, smiled distractedly, and found herself a place to sit. "I'll have coffee, if you don't mind," she called out in a voice that reminded Lily of the delicate chimes of a music box.

"I have to work," Lily informed Rupert, turning to hurry away to the kitchen.

Rupert grasped her arm and wrenched her around to face him. "You might have written and told me you were all right," he whispered furiously.

Lily lifted her chin a notch but made no attempt to pull away. Rupert might be a schoolmaster, but he was strong. "You would only have come to fetch me and drag me home."

"That I have," he ground out.

"Lily!" roared Charlie from the kitchen.

"Sit down, Rupert," Lily hissed, "before I lose my job!"

Surprisingly, Rupert obeyed. He looked a little stuporous as he took a table and gazed out the window.

Lily fled into the kitchen. "There are only two of them," she told Charlie.

"I don't give a damn if there's two or twenty," Charlie answered impatiently, dragging a few coins from the pocket of his trousers and handing them to Lily. "We have to have pie. You go over to Mrs. Halligan's and see if she's got any."

With a sigh Lily dropped the money into her apron pocket and slipped out the back door, closing the screen door carefully behind her so no flies would get inside.

She should have known Rupert would come looking for her, she thought with a sigh, lifting her skirt so the hem wouldn't be soiled as she crossed the alley behind the hotel. Now what was she going to do? She couldn't run away again; this time she'd be leaving too much behind—her valley, for example.

And Caleb.

Not that it made any difference to her if she ever saw *him* again.

The widow Halligan, who baked to supplement the small stipend her husband had left her, happened to have two sweet potato pies on hand, and Lily bought them both. She was crossing the alley, one pie balanced in each palm, when Rupert rounded the corner of the hotel.

Lily smiled. "Thought I'd run away again, didn't you?"

Rupert blocked her way into the kitchen, folding his arms across his brawny farmer's chest. "When it comes to you, most times I don't rightly know what to think," he replied. "Get your things, Lily, because you're coming back to Spokane with me."

"Oh, no, I'm not," Lily answered. Her arms were getting tired, and Charlie was probably growing more crotchety by the minute. "I have a job here, and I have land of my own. Furthermore, next Saturday evening I'm going to Fort Deveraux and dance at the officers' ball."

Rupert's eyes were bulging a little. That meant his patience was seriously strained, and Lily retreated one step. "Land of your own?" he echoed, sounding horrified. "What the devil do you mean by that?"

"I've filed a claim on a homestead," Lily hissed, glancing toward the kitchen window. If she lost this job because of Rupert's interference, she was never going to forgive him. "Now will you please let me pass?"

When she tried to step around Rupert he moved in front of her again. His jaw was set at an obstinate angle, and it was clear there would be no reasoning with him.

Lily had no choice but to lob the pie in her right hand into his face.

While he was still sputtering in shock and wiping away globs of sweet potato Lily marched into the kitchen and set the other pie down on the counter.

"That's all she had?" Charlie demanded.

Lily drew a deep breath, held it for a moment, and let it out slowly. "Actually, there were two," she answered truthfully. "My brother is wearing the other one."

Rupert burst through the back door at that very moment, living proof that she'd spoken the truth.

Charlie gave a hoarse snort of laughter, then shook a floury finger at Lily, "Brother or no brother, young lady, I won't have you treatin' my customers with disrespect. It ain't like I don't have anybody else that wants your job, you know."

Lily bit her lower lip, thinking of all the seed and lumber and tools she meant to buy with her earnings. "I'm sorry, Rupert," she said after a long moment.

Rupert was using his handkerchief to wipe the last of the sweet potato pie from his face. "My good man," he said to Charlie in a serious tone of voice, "this young woman is a fugitive."

Charlie looked horrified. "You mean she done broke the law?"

Rupert favored Lily with a brief, triumphant glance, and she tensed. Whatever Rupert said, Charlie would believe him. That was how it was with men.

"Not exactly."

Lily let out her breath at Rupert's answer.

"What do you mean, 'not exactly'?" Charlie demanded.

Rupert squared his shoulders like a man bearing up under crushing tragedy. "The truth is, this woman is my wife. She abandoned me and our two sick children just a month ago."

"That's a lie!" Lily raged, knowing exactly what Charlie's reaction would be. "Rupert is my brother!"

"Shame on you," Charlie scolded, shaking his finger at Lily again. "Sittin' in church like a decent woman, ridin' out into the country with the major—for shame!"

Rupert gave Lily a discerning look. "What major?" he asked.

Lily picked up the remaining pie and flung it into his face. Then she turned on her heel and left because she didn't need Charlie to tell her that she was fired.

She was halfway to Mrs. McAllister's house when Rupert caught up with her again.

"If I were any man but myself," he said, "I would turn you over my knee and blister your backside!"

Tossing the second sweet potato pie had not been revenge enough for Lily. She threw back her head and screamed, "Help! Somebody *help!*"

Old Marshal Lillow hobbled out of the Blue Chicken Saloon. He peered at Rupert's sweet potato-strewn countenance through thick spectacles and said, "What's this? What's this?"

Lily didn't quite have the heart to follow through and have Rupert arrested for a rascal. After all, he'd been her only real friend while she was growing up. He'd taught her to read and write, defended her against his own parents, provided for her after the Sommerses died. He had only her best interests at heart. "Everything's all right, Marshal," she said evenly, avoiding Rupert's gaze.

"Who was that screamin' for help, then?" the lawman asked reasonably.

Lily bit her lower lip.

"We didn't hear anyone screaming," Rupert put in. Taking Lily's elbow firmly in hand, he ushered her away.

Looking back over one shoulder, Lily saw the marshal scratch his chin and wander back into the Blue Chicken. She stopped cold, refusing to go another inch.

"I'm nineteen years old, Rupert Sommers," she said, "and I will not be dragged home like an errant schoolgirl. I'm making a life for myself, and you have no right to interfere!"

Rupert scowled at her, but she could tell he was beginning to see reason. "What did you mean back there when you talked about having land of your own?"

"I've filed a homestead claim, and I intend to prove up on it," Lily answered, meeting her brother's angry gaze.

"Unmarried women cannot homestead!"

"You're wrong, Rupert," Lily replied. "They can, and I did."

"Of all the—"

"If you take me home, I'll only run away again."

Rupert sighed and shoved a hand through his hair. He was a mess of road dust and pie filling, and the flics were starting to gather around. "Drat it all, Lily Chalmers!"

She stood on tiptoe to kiss his cleft chin. "You've made me lose my job," she sighed, "and I don't know where I'll get another."

"You'll just have to come home with me," Rupert insisted. "Besides, I didn't get you fired. You did that yourself."

There didn't seem to be any point in arguing. "Come along," Lily said with a sigh, linking her arm through her brother's. "I'll take you to Mrs. McAllister's and see if she won't let you take a bath."

Rupert balked at that. "I'll have a bath at the hotel, thank you. After all, that's where my baggage is."

"Very well. We'll go there, then. While you're having your bath I'll try to talk Charlie into taking me back."

Rupert rolled his eyes, and they walked toward the hotel again.

The dining room was full of mill hands wanting coffee and pie, and Charlie was at his wits' end trying to fill their mugs and explain that there wasn't any pie to be had.

Lily walked up and took the heavy blue enamel coffee pot from his hand. "I'll do that," she said crisply. "You just go in and do your baking so we don't have this problem at suppertime."

Charlie glared at Lily for a moment, but he let her stay. Rupert collected his valise and rented himself a room, and when Lily saw him again an hour later he was his usual tidy, if somewhat frayed, self.

"You'll let me stay in Tylerville, won't you?" she asked when her shift was over and she was washing a mountain of dishes.

Out of habit, Rupert took up a dish towel and began to help with the task. "I shouldn't."

"But you will?"

"I don't see that I have any choice. Knowing where you are will be something of a comfort, at least. I was very worried about you, Lily."

Lily averted her eyes for a moment. "I know," she said softly. "And I'm sorry."

"About this major you went out riding with—"

"It was all perfectly respectable, Rupert. I had Mrs. McAllister's blessing."

Rupert narrowed his eyes. "Any chance you'll marry this fellow?"

Lily hated to disappoint him. It would have settled his mind to know his sister planned to wed someone like Caleb Halliday. "None at all," she said with a shake of her head. "He's a soldier. Besides, he's not cut out to be a farmer."

"We've got farmers aplenty around Spokane, if that's what you want."

"I don't want a farmer, and you know it," Lily reminded her brother patiently. "I want to *be* a farmer."

"I'll leave you here to learn your lesson on one account, Lily Chalmers. You've got to promise that you'll come home to Spokane when you fail."

Lily smiled and patted his cheek with a sudsy hand. "Very well, Rupert—I promise. If I fail at being a farmer, I'll come home."

Rupert nodded, though he still looked a little uncertain. When they'd finished the dishes he waited while Lily locked up the dining room and then walked her to Mrs. McAllister's house.

That good lady appeared on the porch when they arrived. She was carrying a lantern and holding Lily's carpetbag in one hand.

"So," she hissed, at the sight of her tenant. "There you are! And I thought you were so sweet and innocent—"

Lily's mouth dropped open.

"Now see here—" Rupert began lamely.

"I wouldn't think you, of all people, would defend her," clucked Mrs. McAllister, inching her way down the front steps to hold Lily's bag over the front fence. "Poor, deserted husband. And those little babes at home, crying for their mama—"

"I don't have a husband!" Lily cried, catching hold of her bag before Mrs. McAllister dropped it.

"There's been a terrible misunderstanding," protested Rupert.

"I should say there has," huffed Mrs. McAllister. "Just wait until Major Halliday hears that he's been courting a strumpet!"

Lily stomped one foot in frustration. "Now look what you've done, Rupert Sommers," she cried, near tears. "You've ruined everything!"

"Madam," Rupert reasoned sturdily, "this young woman

is not my wife, she is my sister. It should go without saying that there are no babies."

Mrs. McAllister looked deflated. "Then there's no husband?"

Rupert shook his head solemnly.

"I see," said the landlady, opening the gate.

Lily stepped through it with her head held high. "I trust that I still have a room."

Mrs. McAllister sighed. "I reckon you do—for the time being, anyhow. But I still want to know how that story got started."

Lily gave Rupert a look fit to strip the fur from a bear's hide. "My brother will be happy to explain," she said. And then she marched into the house, climbed the stairs, and locked herself in her room.

When she came down to breakfast the next morning Rupert was sitting at the kitchen table, sipping coffee.

"What are you doing here?" Lily asked inhospitably.

"I've come to say good-bye."

Lily was chagrined. "You mean you're leaving? Just like that?"

Rupert nodded. "I've got a school to run, remember?" He paused to waggle a finger. "Don't forget your promise— you'll come home immediately when things go wrong."

Lily was stung by his certainty that she would fail, but she wasn't about to argue. He was letting her stay and try to achieve her dream, that was the important thing. "I promise," she said softly. "And I'll write often."

Rupert reached out to squeeze her hand. "That would be nice."

Lily had been wondering about something most of the night. "How did you find me?"

"The postmaster told me you were here."

Lily nodded. Of course. Some of the letters she'd written to the marshals of various towns in Washington Territory must have passed through Spokane. "You've really been very understanding, considering," she ventured to say.

Rupert smiled. "I only want you to be happy, Lily. Happy and safe."

Lily thought of the lonely winter nights she would spend on her farm, with the wolves and the wind howling in the darkness, and she shivered.

"What is it?" Rupert asked, alarmed.

Lily reassured him with a soft chuckle. "It's nothing."

That morning when the stagecoach set out for Spokane, Rupert was on it. Lily was left with a lonely feeling that would have been all-encompassing if she hadn't had the officers' ball to look forward to. That was going to be the adventure of a lifetime.

Charlie hadn't completely forgiven Lily for upsetting his routine the way she had, and he was cranky and demanding all through her first shift.

When she arrived at the rooming house that night, however, there was a parcel lying in the middle of the bed. The return address said simply, *Tibbet. Fort Deveraux, W.T.*

Overcome with curiosity, Lily tore away the twine and ripped open the package.

Inside the box was a lovely gown of lavendar lawn. The sleeves were puffy, trimmed with the most delicate lace imaginable, and the neckline, while certainly within the bounds of propriety, was anything but demure.

Lily scrambled to the cracked mirror over her bureau, holding the glorious dress to her bosom. The pale amethyst color was becoming, at least in the dim light of her room.

She pulled off the calico dress she'd worn to work and carefully put on the dancing gown. Except for being a fraction too large at the waist and several inches too long, it fit her perfectly.

She whirled, imagining herself in Major Halliday's arms, looking up into those wonderful, impudent, whiskey-colored eyes of his. . . .

Lily stopped. She was going to have to be careful not to forget that Caleb's intentions were not honorable. To him she was just an amusement, something to play with. His interest in her was as selfish and thoughtless as Isadora's had been.

With a sigh, still holding the dress, Lily sat down on the edge of her bed. For all of that, Caleb was haunting her waking moments as well as her sleep. For instance, this afternoon, when she'd been helping Charlie bake dried apple pies, she'd gone right ahead and imagined what it would be like to lie in bed with Major Halliday.

Lily's cheeks burned at the memory. Mortified, she stood up quickly and went downstairs to borrow Mrs. McAllister's sewing basket. She concentrated hard on altering the lavender gown until she couldn't see clearly anymore, then tumbled into bed and dreamed that she was hoeing corn in her own garden.

She backed along the row, hoeing and hoeing, until she collided with the scarecrow. When she looked, Caleb was standing there in the scarecrow's clothes, smiling down at her. He swept her into his arms and kissed her, and Lily didn't resist.

In fact, she awakened with a start, breathing hard and feeling an embarrassing ache deep in her middle. It was a pain she didn't understand, except for the surety that Caleb would know how to ease it.

Lily sat up in bed, wrapping her arms around her legs and resting her chin on her knees. The room was bathed in moonlight, and the lavender gown, carefully hung beside the door, seemed enchanted. She could almost believe it would leap down from the peg all on its own and dance around the room.

With a sigh Lily crawled to the foot of her bed and looked out the window. She could see the neighboring houses clear as day, and the sky seemed to be bursting with stars, all competing to see which could shine brightest.

She got up, found the box of French chocolates where she'd hidden it in her bureau drawer, and lifted the lid. After helping herself to a bonbon she crawled back into bed, taking the candy with her.

The chocolate melted on her tongue, and Lily sighed with contentment. She wondered why Caleb had been so uncomfortable when she'd eaten that first piece of candy. Wasn't that why he'd given it to her, to eat?

With a shrug Lily took another chocolate from the box and popped it into her mouth, where she rolled it slowly from one cheek to the other. Then she let it rest in the center of her mouth, sucking gently so the flavor would last. Men were such strange, incomprehensible creatures, giving a lady a present and then tugging at their collars and squirming in their seats just because she enjoyed it.

When she saw Caleb again on Saturday she'd ask him to explain. Smiling, Lily put the candy box away and stretched out to sleep.

Chapter
❧ 4 ❧

The stockade stood on a high, grassy butte, rising like a castle of pine logs against the cloudless blue expanse of the sky. Daisies grew around its base, resembling a fluffy white moat. Between the hard-packed ruts that made a road of sorts, yellow and scarlet monkey flowers nodded in the spring breeze.

Lily drew her head back inside the stagecoach and sat up a little straighter on the hard seat. In another few minutes she was going to see Caleb again.

Not that she was excited.

She loosened the strings of her new yellow bonnet, which matched her dress. "We're almost there," she said to the soldier who sat facing her.

The man's expression revealed a distinct lack of enthusiasm. "I surely did miss that place," he drawled, pushing back his billed hat to an impudent angle.

In the distance a bugle sounded, and Lily looked out again

to see men in blue coats moving along the parapets. The great doors of the stockade opened inward as the stagecoach approached.

"You here to do laundry for the men, ma'am?" the soldier asked, taking in Lily's trim dandelion-yellow dress. All during the trip he hadn't said two words, but now, apparently, he wanted to make conversation.

Lily shook her head. "I've been invited to the officers' ball."

The thin, wiry corporal leaned forward on his seat. He was not a comely man, with his unfortunate complexion and discolored teeth, and the smell of his clothes made Lily wish she hadn't spoken to him. "Whose lady are you? You look to be the sort Lieutenant Costner might pick. Or maybe Cap'n Phillips."

Lily tugged at her gloves—part of the getup she'd spent some of her precious savings to buy—and squared her shoulders. "I am the guest of Major Caleb Halliday, if that is any concern of yours."

The soldier sat back abruptly, bumping his hat askew. "I'm really sorry if I aggravated you, ma'am," he said quickly. "I surely didn't mean to."

The stage was rolling through the open gates of the fort, and Lily had better things to think about than some soldier's poor manners. Pleased that she had been able to put the man in his place with so little effort, she tied her bonnet strings again and neatened the skirts of her dress.

Looking out the window, she saw that Fort Deveraux was a small city unto itself; there was a store and a post office, and a few well-dressed women wheeled wicker baby carriages along the wooden sidewalks.

The stage driver stopped the coach in front of a small building with flags on either side of its door and almost immediately came back to assist Lily. He was a good-looking dark-haired man with a manly mustache and laughing brown eyes, and he doffed his battered, dusty hat as she alighted.

"I'll be looking forward to having you ride with us again, miss," he said easily.

Lily smiled at him, allowing him to help her onto the sidewalk.

Gertrude Tibbet was waiting for her, accompanied by a strikingly attractive woman with dark hair who looked vaguely familiar. There was no sign of Caleb, though. Lily was careful to hide her disappointment.

"Hello, Lily," Mrs. Tibbet said fondly. "I'd like to introduce you to my niece, Sandra Halliday."

"Hello," Lily said, suddenly feeling so awkward that she wished she could get on the stage again and head straight back to Tylerville. It might be coincidence that Sandra's last name was the same as Caleb's, but a sinking feeling in the pit of her stomach said it wasn't.

"You were expecting Caleb, I know," Sandra said soothingly, and in that moment Lily remembered her. She was the woman who had come into Tylerville on the same stage as Rupert nearly a week before. "I'm afraid only the army can depend on him. The rest of us have to take our chances."

"Sandra," Mrs. Tibbet scolded good-naturedly.

Sandra pointed an elegantly gloved finger toward the parade grounds, which were across the road from where they stood. "There he is. He does make a dashing figure, doesn't he?"

Lily's legs were cramped from the long ride in the stagecoach, but she forgot such annoyances as she watched the troops moving in skillful, ever-changing patterns, like bits of blue glass in a kaleidoscope. Caleb was their commander; he rode the familiar black gelding, and it danced beneath him as he shouted orders.

Forgetting Mrs. Tibbet and Sandra, at least for the moment, Lily crossed the road to stand at the edge of the parade grounds. She took off her bonnet to let the breeze cool her scalp and the back of her neck.

A column of soldiers had been riding toward her in

perfect order, but in the instant when Lily removed her bonnet everything went awry. The fellow in the lead seemed to forget all about the drill.

Every semblance of order was thrown to the winds as the young man, whooping and hollering, galloped toward Lily. His blue cap flew off his head and was trampled by the mounts of the other men of his humble rank, who approached her just as eagerly.

Lily retreated a step, fearing she'd be run down, and it was then that her eyes pivoted to the imperious man with yellow stripes down the sides of his trousers.

Caleb gave another order, and the half-dozen deserters reined their horses around and returned to rank. They remained in formation, their backs rigid, their gazes fixed straight ahead, while their commanding officer rode toward Lily.

He touched the brim of his campaign hat with a gloved hand and spoke to her in an abrupt voice. "God knows I'm glad to see you, Lily," he said, though his expression belied his words, "but you shouldn't be here. You're distracting the men."

Color blossomed in Lily's cheeks. "I expected you to meet my stagecoach, since you said you would."

Caleb sighed and resettled his hat, even though it had looked perfectly all right in the first place. "I thought it would be better if Mrs. Tibbet did that."

Lily nodded stiffly. Perhaps she'd presumed too much. After all, the major had never pretended that his feelings were noble. For that matter, neither were hers; she was using Caleb, just as he had planned to use her. "I'm sure you're right," she said, starting to turn away.

He stopped her with a low murmur. "You look like spring sunshine in that dress."

She wet her lips nervously with the end of her tongue. No answer came to her beyond a muttered, grudging "Thank you."

"I'll see you later, at the Tibbets'." With that, Caleb touched the brim of his hat briefly and then turned and rode back to his men.

Mrs. Tibbet and her niece had crossed the road, Lily discovered, and were standing only a few feet away. Sandra held the handle of Lily's ancient carpetbag in both hands.

"That was quite a show the men just put on," said Sandra. "I wouldn't be in their shoes right now for anything."

Feeling vaguely alarmed, Lily turned her head and saw Caleb riding alongside the column of transgressors. Although his voice didn't carry, she knew the men were being reprimanded, and she felt partially responsible for their severe circumstances. "What will he do to them?" she asked, worried.

Gertrude Tibbet touched her arm. "Turn them into some of the finest soldiers in the United States Army," she said reassuringly. "Come, Lily. Let's go and get you settled. No doubt you're ready for some tea and a good long chat."

Lily glanced back at Caleb once more before walking away with Mrs. Tibbet and Sandra.

"Auntie tells me that Caleb has taken quite a shine to you, Lily," Sandra remarked as the three women strolled beneath trees that were just sprouting spring leaves.

"Now, Sandra, Miss Chalmers is our guest." Mrs. Tibbet linked her arm with Lily's. "Don't be baiting her."

Sandra laughed, and the sound was musical. "Stop fussing, Auntie," she said. "I'm not going to say anything scandalous."

Lily felt as though she were standing on the edge of a high precipice. She could no longer bear the suspense. "You have the same last name as Caleb," she said.

Sandra was quiet for a moment, then she put a friendly arm around Lily. "I'll probably get three days in the stockade for this," she said, "but somebody should have told you, and it's obvious no one has. Caleb and I used to be married."

Lily was speechless, even though she'd suspected the truth from the moment she'd been introduced to Sandra.

Mrs. Tibbet stopped in front of a two-story shuttered house with awakening rosebushes in the yard. She opened the gate for them to step through. "No one will ever accuse you of being subtle, my dear," she said to her niece.

Lily was wondering if it was too late to get back on the stagecoach and go home. What kind of situation was this?

Sandra gave her a little push through the gateway. "Don't worry, Lily—much as I'd like to, I'm probably not going to offer any competition for Caleb's affections. I'm out of his good graces, you see."

"Sandra!" Mrs. Tibbet protested, and this time she sounded as though she meant it.

Sandra said no more, but she was still smiling.

"Perhaps I should just go back to Tylerville," Lily said uneasily.

Mrs. Tibbet was advancing up the porch steps, holding her billowing skirts in her hands. She used just one word to dispense with Lily's idea. "Nonsense."

"But . . ."

The front door was opened, and Lily followed Mrs. Tibbet inside.

"You'd think it would concern Caleb that you and I are here together, wouldn't you?" Sandra chimed as they entered a cluttered parlor. There were framed photographs on every surface, and potted palms stood in the corners.

"Why should it?" Lily asked crisply.

Mrs. Tibbet waved at her niece in a dismissive fashion. "Give me that satchel, Sandra," she said, her tone impatient. "I'll show Lily to her room, and you can make tea. While you're at it, my dear, you might meditate on the wisdom of interfering where you don't belong."

Sandra sighed dramatically and swept off in a rush of fashionable skirts toward the back of the house.

"Caleb should have told me," Lily said forlornly when she

and Mrs. Tibbet were alone in the room that had apparently been selected for the major's guest.

Mrs. Tibet set the carpetbag on a little chest at the foot of an attractive brass and ivory bed. The colorful quilt cheered Lily; it was just the kind of thing she planned to have when she moved into a house of her own. "Yes, he should have," she agreed with a little sigh. "Knowing Caleb, I would guess that it never occurred to him. He doesn't quite think of Sandra in the way a man usually does of a former wife."

Mystified, Lily sat down on the edge of the bed. Divorce was almost unheard of. How could Caleb have such a casual attitude toward Sandra that he wouldn't even take the trouble to mention her? "Wh-what happened between them?"

"I'm afraid you'll have to ask Caleb and Sandra about that. Just keep in mind that they have very different versions."

Lily wanted more than ever to go back to Tylerville and forget she'd ever met Major Halliday. One night at a ball wasn't worth such humiliation. "Which of them should I believe?"

Mrs. Tibbet paused at the door of Lily's room and smiled. "Why, both of them, my dear. They're equally truthful—it's just that things of this nature are so much a matter of perspective."

Lily was more baffled than ever, but asking more questions obviously wasn't going to get her anywhere. After Mrs. Tibbet had gone she opened her valise, carefully removed the precious lavender dress, and hung it inside the oak wardrobe.

She sat down in a rocking chair beside the window, looking out at the bustling fort and wondering if Rupert's parents had been right about her. They'd always said she didn't have the sense God gave a doorpost.

And now here she was, in a stranger's guest room, looking forward to an evening with a man brazen enough to say outright that he wanted her for a mistress, a man who hadn't troubled to tell her that he just happened to have a spare wife who'd be staying in the same house.

"Caroline," Lily said in a whisper, "what should I do?"

Her sister wasn't there to answer, of course, but Lily longed for her. Caroline had always known what to do about everything. Wherever her eldest sister was, Lily felt sure she'd grown into a woman of firm opinions.

There was a soft knock at the door, and then Sandra stepped in. She was truly a vision in her white cotton dress trimmed in eyelet, with her luscious dark hair and spirited eyes. She'd probably broken Caleb's heart, and he didn't talk about her because he couldn't.

"Good heavens," Sandra demanded, "what are you thinking about? You look like an abandoned child."

Lily drew up her dignity around her and managed a smile. "I was thinking about you and Caleb," she said honestly.

Sandra sat down on the chest at the foot of Lily's bed, and Lily turned her chair to face her. "You're in love with him," Sandra said in a delighted whisper.

Lily thought of her half-section of land, of the corn crops and fruit trees that would one day grow there. She forced herself to remember that Caleb wanted to keep her, not marry her. And, of course, there was the fact that he was a soldier. "No!" she protested, guarding her dreams.

Sandra folded her hands in her lap. Her amethyst eyes sparkled with mischief. "I don't believe you."

"I don't care," Lily snapped, out of patience.

Sandra laughed. "You needn't be so testy about it. Caleb never loved me, Lily—I'm no worry to you."

"If he didn't love you, why did the two of you get married?" Lily asked reasonably.

Sandra's slender shoulders moved in a pretty shrug. "My aunt and uncle are among Caleb's oldest friends. I suppose we were sort of thrown together."

Lily found the courage to ask, "Did you love him?"

71

Sandra thought carefully. "I don't think I knew what love was until it was too late and I'd lost him."

A terrible sadness swept through Lily. "But you love him now?"

"Yes," Sandra said with a small, resigned sigh. "For all the good it does me. I had hoped Caleb might see things differently if I came back, but I was too late. You're here."

Lily was sitting on the very edge of her chair. Not since her years with the Sommers family had she felt like such an intruder. "I'll go back to Tylerville," she promised. "If only the stage hasn't left."

Sandra reached out and closed her hand over Lily's. "You mustn't go—you belong here, with Caleb."

"You seem to think this is much more serious than it is," Lily hastened to explain. "I hardly know Caleb. We sat together in church, and he came to supper one night, but—"

"His eyes glowed when he told me about the picnic," Sandra interrupted.

Lily wondered if he'd mentioned kissing her. "He—he told you?"

"We talk about everything," Sandra said. "Caleb regards me as a friend."

These people were simply too sophisticated for her, Lily decided. She might have known she wouldn't fit in, wouldn't even understand their thinking. "You must tell him how you feel!"

Sandra's smile was a sad one. "I tried. He patted me on the shoulder and said, 'We get along fine this way, Sandy. Let's not botch it up by talking about love.'"

Lily had to laugh, even though she was on the verge of tears. Sandra's imitation of Caleb's manner had been hilariously accurate. A moment later, though, Lily's face was serious again. "I'm so sorry, Sandra. Maybe if you wait for a while, he'll come around."

Sandra shook her head. "Once the major makes up his mind, a blast of dynamite wouldn't change it." With that she stood and smoothed her skirts, avoiding Lily's eyes. "Auntie sent me to tell you that the tea's ready," she said, and then she went out.

After freshening up a little Lily reluctantly descended the stairs.

Mrs. Tibbet was waiting in the parlor, a silver tea service gleaming on the wheeled cart beside her chair. There was no sign of Sandra.

"My niece has a headache," Mrs. Tibbet explained, gesturing for Lily to take a chair.

Privately, Lily suspected that Sandra was weeping, and that made her feel even worse. Nonetheless, she accepted the cup of tea Mrs. Tibbet held out to her.

There was milk on the tea cart, along with sugar, but Lily added neither to her cup. "Is there a stagecoach tomorrow?" she asked.

Mrs. Tibbet shook her head. "No, dear. Caleb plans to drive you back to Tylerville himself."

Lily fidgeted uncomfortably at the thought. The trip would take at least two hours, and she wasn't prepared to spend such a long time alone in his company. "You speak of him so kindly," she remarked, "when he broke your niece's heart."

Gertrude Tibbet touched the chignon of glowing silver hair at her nape in a gesture Lily suspected was habitual. "As I told you, my dear, there are two sides to this story. Before you condemn Caleb for a rounder, perhaps you'd better listen to his account."

Lily swallowed a sip of her tea. "Sandra's still in love with him," she heard herself say.

Gertrude actually chuckled. "Is that what she told you?"

Before Lily could reply, there was a rap at the front door. Gertrude made no move to get out of her chair, and Lily was about to answer the summons, thinking her hostess hadn't heard, when Caleb strode into the house. He was carrying the ever-present campaign hat in one hand.

"Hello, Gertrude," he said, bending to kiss the older woman's crinkled cheek. Even as he did so, however, his eyes were fixed on Lily.

Gertrude patted his gloved hand. "Sit down, dear. Lily was just telling me that Sandra is madly in love with you."

Caleb laughed, to Lily's amazement, and tossed his hat onto a settee. After peeling off his gloves he made his way through the forest of bric-a-brac to the liquor decanter waiting on the sideboard. He poured himself a drink with all the aplomb of a person who has spent a great deal of time in a house and feels welcome there.

Lily watched with rounded eyes as he tossed back the drink, set his glass down with a clunk, and came to sit at the end of the settee. He was so close that she could catch the sunshine-and-bruised-grass scent of him. "Well?" she demanded.

Caleb rubbed his chin with one hand, as though stroking a beard he didn't have. "Gertrude," he began, "could you excuse us for a few minutes, please?"

Lily's hostess nodded, rose from her chair, and left the room.

Lily hated to see her go. "You brought me here under false pretenses," she accused in an angry whisper, her eyes snapping as she glared at Caleb.

"That's not true," he replied, his tone damnably sensible. "I'm not married to Sandra or anyone else. I have every right to take you to a dance."

"You might have mentioned her!"

"I would have, of course. She wasn't here when I met you, Lily—she arrived the day I got back to the fort."

Lily bit her lower lip for a moment. His reply sounded so logical. "But she loves you."

Caleb gave a ragged sigh. "So she says. Talk is cheap with Sandra. What matters is that I don't love her in return."

Lily imagined having this man's love and then losing it, and the emotion that ensued was almost indiscernible from grief. "How can you be so cold and calm about this? That woman was your wife!"

The warmth left Caleb's eyes. "That really depends on how you define the word 'wife,'" he retorted. "Now, are you still going to the dance with me tonight, or has Sandra convinced you I'm a scoundrel?"

Despite everything, Lily's heart still leapt a little at the thought of spending an entire evening in this man's arms. She lowered her eyes for a moment, then forced them back to Caleb's face. "I'm still going," she said softly.

Caleb's grin was bright enough to push back the shadows in the corners of the Tibbets' parlor. "Good," he whispered, and then he bent forward far enough to kiss Lily lightly on the mouth.

She tasted on her own lips the brandy he'd just drunk, and the experience brought that strange, hurting warmth to her loins again.

"I'm back," Mrs. Tibbet chimed in friendly warning, stepping into the room with a steaming cup of coffee and a plateful of cookies. She handed the coffee to Caleb and set the cookies on the tea cart. "Have you seen the colonel this morning, Caleb?"

The major shook his head. "No. He's barricaded behind his office door, working on the budget."

Mrs. Tibbet laughed. "That always puts him in a fine state of mind."

Caleb chuckled. "Right. And it probably explains why Costner and Phillips took their troops on patrol today."

The light banter made Lily feel better. She'd been starting to see herself as one of those shameless homewreckers she'd read about in the penny dreadfuls. "They'll be back in time for the officers' ball, of course," she remarked, mostly to join in the conversation.

Caleb gave her a look of good-natured warning. "It won't matter whether they are or not. You're saving every dance for me, Miss Chalmers."

Lily's cheeks warmed at the intimacy of his tone. One would have thought that Mrs. Tibbet wasn't even there, the way he talked. "I imagine I can dance with whomever I like," she said, to put Caleb in his place.

He wouldn't be put. "As long as that whomever is me," he responded.

In that moment it seemed to Lily that lightning had crept out of the sunny spring sky to crackle in the room. She didn't speak, because she knew Caleb would have an answer for anything she said. He could be so dreadfully bossy.

Just then Sandra came down the stairs. Although there was a hint of redness around her eyes, she was utterly composed. She smiled and crossed the room to greet Caleb, and, like a gentleman, he stood.

Sandra's hands closed over his, and she rose on tiptoe to kiss his cheek. "Hello, darling," she said.

He gave her an annoyed look. "Hello, Sandra."

"Everyone will be very glad, I'm sure, to know that I'm feeling better," she announced to the room in general, turning away from Caleb to assess the contents of the cookie plate. After due consideration she selected a macaroon.

When she sat down it was on the settee where Caleb had been, and she held his hat fondly in her lap, toying with the tassels on the gold braid. "I suppose you and Lily have been planning your night at the officers' ball," she said wistfully.

Caleb reached out to reclaim his hat. "I believe you're going with Lieutenant Costner," he remarked.

"I believe I am," Sandra answered, smiling her beautiful smile.

"Have a wonderful time," Caleb replied shortly. Then he surprised everyone in the room by taking Lily's hand and hauling her to her feet. "Come with me," he commanded.

Lily was too startled to protest, and too eager to escape that room, which suddenly seemed more crowded than ever.

Caleb led her outside, along the porch and into a shadowy, screened-off room that overlooked the beginnings of a garden. "No matter what Sandra says," he told her, "I want you to remember this."

Lily stared up at him. "What?" she asked as he pulled her close. She could feel the brass buttons on his paneled shirt pressing against her bosom.

Instead of answering, Caleb bent his head and kissed her, his mouth gentle at first, then fierce. She struggled for a moment before giving herself up to the hurricane of sensation his lips and tongue created within her.

She couldn't breathe when he let her go; it was as though he had been her air supply.

He smiled at her disgruntled expression and kissed her forehead lightly. "I'll see you at dinner, Lily-flower," he said. And then he was putting on his hat and walking away.

Lily stood alone on the sun porch for a long time, breathing deeply and waiting for her blush to fade. She knew Mrs. Tibbet and Sandra would guess what she'd been up to if she returned to the parlor in her present state.

When she returned Sandra was placidly nibbling another cookie, and Mrs. Tibbet was out of the room.

"I see Caleb has brought you around to his way of thinking," Sandra remarked.

Lily was chagrined that the aftereffects of Caleb's kiss still showed, and after all her efforts at composure, too. "It might be a good idea if you and I didn't discuss Caleb," she said evenly.

Sandra got up, crossed the room to a cabinet, and returned with a sewing basket. "You may be right," she agreed. "Tell me about yourself, Lily. Where were you born?"

"Chicago," Lily answered, thinking back to those relatively happy days before the soldier had come along and convinced her mother to give up her children. "What about you?"

"I'm from Fox Chapel, Pennsylvania, like everyone else in this house," was Sandra's reply. She was frowning with concentration as she threaded a needle.

Fox Chapel. Lily remembered Caleb telling her that he came from that same town. "I see."

There was nothing malicious in Sandra's voice or manner when she spoke again. "I hear you plan to homestead. That's a very ambitious idea for a woman, isn't it?"

Lily let out a sigh. Sandra could only have learned of Lily's plans by talking with Caleb. Why was it that every subject seemed to lead back to the major? "I think I can manage it."

"We often think we can manage things—or people. And then it turns out that we can't."

Lily looked with longing at the door. "I believe I'll just go out for a short walk, if you don't mind."

Sandra smiled at her. "I could go with you," she suggested. "My headache is gone now."

Hastily, Lily shook her head. "I won't be long," she promised. And then she made her escape.

Since she knew what lay in the direction she and Sandra and Mrs. Tibbet had taken earlier, Lily headed off in the opposite one. She passed a dozen other houses like the Tibbets', and then there was an open field. Beyond that was the most depressing collection of shanties Lily had ever seen.

She ventured closer, driven by curiosity. Dirty, naked children played in front of the tumbledown shacks while raucous women shouted at them.

Lily glanced back over one shoulder to reassure herself that she hadn't imagined the elegant two-story houses with their neat picket fences and budding rose gardens. She took another step closer to the shacks.

"What do you want, lady?" a little girl asked with a revolting sniffle.

Lily looked at the urchin in despair, unable, for the moment, to speak.

The child tried again. "You lookin' for your man?"

As the meaning of the little one's words sunk in Lily took a step backwards. "No."

"Sometimes ladies come down here to Suds Row lookin' for their men. When that happens, there's usually an awful cat fight."

Lily tried to smile. "I suppose there is. D-do you live here?"

The scamp put out a grimy hand and smiled. "I'm Elsie."

"My name is Lily," she responded, after a lapse of a second or two, and shook the child's hand. "Elsie, do the soldiers come here very much?"

Elsie nodded. "Them what wants a woman or a clean shirt do," she answered.

Lily was sickened. "And the colonel allows that?"

The child shrugged. "We don't see him down here. He's got a wife. Besides, he's probably too old to want snugglin'."

The fire of wrath burned in Lily's soul. She understood hardship all too well, and the fact that it existed in the midst of plenty only made matters worse.

She whirled, skirts in hand, and stormed back toward the center of the fort. Maybe everyone else was afraid to confront Colonel Tibbet with the plight of these people, but she wasn't.

Chapter
❧ 5 ❧

Since Lily didn't know exactly where to look for Colonel Tibbet, she began her inquiry in the general store.

Glad of the shadowy interior, which cooled her temper a little, she assessed the merchandise available. There was tobacco and flour, calico and bullets, boot blacking and licorice. Lily spotted a dime novel with the intriguing title *Typhoon Sally, Queen of the Rodeo*, but she didn't consider purchasing it. She'd spent enough on her dress, gloves, and bonnet.

Behind the counter stood a rotund man wearing a sergeant's stripes on the sleeve of his shirt. He was only a little taller than Lily, his head was bald, and his eyes were a twinkling, kindly blue. "Hello, there, miss. How can I help you?"

Lily drew herself up to her full height of five feet, two and a half inches. "I'm looking for Colonel Tibbet. Could you please direct me to his office?"

The sergeant's friendly smile revealed a shadow of bewilderment. "Thinking of enlisting, ma'am?" he teased.

Some of Lily's normal good humor was restored, and she returned his smile. "I don't believe I'd make a very good soldier. Now, if you'll just advise me as to where I might find the colonel—"

"Right next door," answered the sergeant, cocking a thumb in the direction of the log building with flags on either side of its door. "But I wouldn't bother him for anything less than a full-scale Comanche attack if I was you."

Lily frowned. "There aren't any Comanches around here."

"Exactly," replied the sergeant with a waggle of his index finger. "Colonel Tibbet is a fine man, miss. But when he's got to deal with those fellers back in the capital, well, some of his good Christian nature just up and deserts him."

Lily recalled the conversation between Mrs. Tibbet and Caleb concerning the colonel's antipathy for going over some budget, but she couldn't allow herself to be daunted. She thanked the sergeant kindly for his assistance and set out for the building next door.

There Lily found a handsome young corporal seated behind a desk. He smiled and got to his feet. "Corporal Pierce at your service, ma'am," he said quickly.

"I'm here to see Colonel Tibbet," Lily announced, lifting her chin.

"I'm afraid he's very busy—"

"I'll only take a moment of his time."

Corporal Pierce's dancing blue eyes swept over Lily's yellow dress. "I don't suppose you're going to be at the dance tonight," he ventured, lifting one hand to smooth his light brown hair.

Before Lily could make a response the door of the inner office opened, and Colonel Tibbet was standing in the chasm. "Corporal, go and fetch me some coffee from the mess hall right away."

"Yes, sir." The young soldier looked at Lily and shrugged, as if to say, *here's your chance.* Then he hurried out to obey the colonel's order.

Lily cleared her throat loudly just as the older man would have closed his door again. "Excuse me, sir, but I'd like a word with you."

Colonel Tibbet looked startled; obviously he hadn't noticed Lily before. And he didn't remember her from their brief meeting in the hotel dining room. He narrowed his eyes and scratched one florid cheek. "Who are you?"

"My name is Lily Chalmers, Colonel, and I'm here to report a disgrace."

"Lily Chalmers." The colonel seemed to be sorting through mental files for the name. "Ah, yes—you're the little waitress who caught Caleb's eye back there in Tylerville."

"Yes." Lily felt diminished by the colonel's words, but she didn't know how to correct him. In fact, she had only enough courage to confront him about that awful place where the soldiers took their laundry and their scurrilous attentions.

"Looking for the major, are you?" Colonel Tibbet asked with a jovial chuckle.

Lily shook her head quickly, her cheeks heating at the suggestion that she would be so audacious as to pursue Caleb at his colonel's office. "I'm here about Suds Row," she said bravely.

The colonel came out of his office and shut the door behind him, frowning. "Suds Row?" He seemed to encircle the phrase, pondering. "What earthly connection could you have with such a place, young lady?"

Lily took a step forward, mainly because she felt like going into retreat. "I happened to pass by on my walk. How can you allow that kind of ignominy to exist?"

The colonel looked surprised, but not affronted. His manner was more one of indulgence than offense. "Now, Daisy—"

"Lily." She said her name firmly.

"Lily, then. Suds Row is not the kind of place a young woman of your delicacy should ever be exposed to. If you would just stay away from that part of the fort while you're here—"

Lily was stunned. "You mean you're just going to *ignore* it? Colonel Tibbet, we're talking about a place where women sell themselves to men!"

He chuckled and smoothed his mustache. "Yes. Well, Caleb's done it this time, I'll say that for him."

Lily stiffened. "I beg your pardon?"

The colonel cleared his throat loudly. "You must excuse me. I have work to do—dratted budget. Congress expects us to operate on nothing more than their good wishes, you see." With that he turned, went back into his office, and closed the door behind him.

The smells and images of Suds Row filled Lily's mind, and she was just about to storm into the colonel's private office when Corporal Pierce returned, carrying a coffeepot in one hand and a mug in the other. He looked at Lily's flushed face and smiled.

"I see you had your chat with the colonel."

"For all the good it did me," Lily conceded. Then she brightened. "Why don't you let me carry that in?" she asked, indicating the coffeepot.

The corporal shook his head immediately. "No, ma'am," he said, looking worried. "I've got thirty days' leave coming up next month, and I don't want to spend it in the stockade."

With that the young man disappeared into Colonel Tibbet's office, and Lily was left to face the fact that her impromptu crusade had gotten her exactly nowhere. There was nothing to do but give up in temporary defeat; she would confront the commander of Fort Deveraux again, over his own supper table.

As Lily was going out the door, deep in thought, she all but collided with Caleb. In fact, she would have if he hadn't caught her upper arms in his hands and stopped her.

"What are you doing here?" he asked. Although his tone was not unkind, he obviously wasn't pleased to see her.

Lily couldn't have him think for even a second that she'd been chasing after him. "I wanted to talk to the colonel about Suds Row."

Caleb looked out-and-out shocked. When Corporal Pierce returned to his desk at that same moment he pushed Lily outside onto the sidewalk and demanded, "What the hell do you know about the Row?"

Lily folded her arms and looked stubbornly up into Caleb's eyes. "You're not the man I thought you were, if you can look the other way when something like that is going on. Caleb, there are *children* in that place."

He gave a heavy sigh. "Lily, there are certain realities in this world—"

"Yes," Lily interrupted. "Like disease, and corruption."

Caleb rolled his eyes. "All right," he sighed. "I'll admit Suds Row is a disgrace. But it's also a necessary evil."

"Only a man would say that."

A muscle tightened in Caleb's jawline, then relaxed a little. "Is that so? Then you just march down there and ask those women if they want to be sent packing. Tell them you're personally going to see that they never have to sleep with a man for money or wash a soldier's shirts again. Do you know what they'll do, Lily?"

Lily swallowed, no longer so certain of herself. "What?"

"They'll run you off like they would a coyote in a chicken pen!"

"I don't believe you." Lily's eyes widened. "You're only defending Suds Row because you like to visit there yourself."

Caleb closed his eyes for a moment in an obvious struggle for patience. "I don't go near the place, except to have my shirts washed," he declared in a furious whisper.

Lily felt wildly relieved, though of course she wouldn't

have revealed that. She could barely admit it to herself. "What this place needs is a good, honest laundress," she announced.

"A laundr—" Caleb's anger subsided suddenly, replaced by a disconcerting light in his eyes. "Right here?"

Lily envisioned herself waxing wealthy. "Yes." She laid a thoughtful finger to her chin. "I'd need a place to live, though."

Caleb started propelling her down the sidewalk. "Of course, you could always forget the laundry business and take a position as a housekeeper."

Lily looked up at him suspiciously. "For whom?"

He hesitated. "For me," he ventured in an uncertain tone of voice.

"Never," Lily replied. "My reputation would be in shreds in a matter of minutes."

He treated her to a blinding grin. "Probably with good reason," he boasted. When Lily gave him a withering look he came up with another suggestion. "Gertrude is always looking for a housekeeper."

"Housekeeping pays no more than waiting tables," Lily reasoned as they came to a stop in front of the Tibbets' front gate.

"True," Caleb conceded, "but a housekeeper doesn't have to pay for her room and board."

The idea had its merits, although Lily favored the plan to wash clothes for a living. It would be hard work, but there'd be plenty of money in it. She'd have her plow and building supplies in no time.

"I couldn't live in the same house with Sandra," Lily said, laying a hand on the neatly painted gatepost.

Caleb looked genuinely exasperated. "We'll talk about this later," he snapped, and then he turned and strode away, resettling his hat as he went, leaving Lily to stare after him in baffled annoyance.

Sandra was still engrossed in her needlework when Lily entered the house.

"How was your walk?" she asked.

Lily sank into a chair. "Depressing. I've just had my first look at Suds Row."

Sandra wrinkled her pretty nose. "If you're smart, you'll forget you've ever seen the place. The nice women on the post pretend it doesn't even exist."

To Lily it seemed a stupid approach. "That's like ignoring a sickness—it just gets worse and worse."

Sandra shrugged but did not look up from her sampler. "Those nasty women deserve whatever they get."

"Do they?" Lily demanded. "What about the soldiers who trade with them—what do they deserve?"

Sandra's pretty lips curved into a mischievous little smile. "Cooties," she answered, "and I'm sure they get them. Among other things."

Agitated, Lily tried to smooth the loose tendrils of hair at the nape of her neck back into their earlier arrangement. "At least it's only the unmarried men—"

"Naïve girl," Sandra put in.

"You don't mean—?"

"A lot of women would just as soon their husbands didn't trouble them in bed, Lily. So they pretend to be stupid when the men start telling them they shouldn't have to ruin their soft hands doing wash."

Sandra wasn't much older than Lily, but she'd been married, and she obviously had a broader view of the world.

"Not Caleb?" Lily whispered, horrified.

Sandra laughed. "My, no. No snaggletoothed washerwoman would appeal to him. He kept a mistress in Tylerville—she's there still, I think."

Lily's eyes went so wide they hurt. So *that* was why Caleb and Sandra had been divorced. He'd been unfaithful. To think she'd let a rascal like that kiss her, and give her chocolates! Excusing herself in rather a tremulous voice, Lily got out of her chair and made for the stairway.

Ten minutes later she came down to the parlor carrying

her valise. Mrs. Tibbet had returned, and she looked upset. "Lily—you're not going, are you?"

"Yes," Lily answered.

Sandra set aside her needlework at last. "Well, whatever for?" she wanted to know. "And how do you intend to get back to Tylerville without a stagecoach, may I ask?"

Lily's face was warm. "I'll walk if I have to," she vowed.

"What did you say to her?" Mrs. Tibbet demanded, her hands resting on her hips as she glared at Sandra.

"I merely told her that Caleb kept a mistress in Tylerville. It's perfectly true, and I'll bet he still visits her!"

"Sandra, you are my own dear sister's child, and I love you for that reason, but I will tolerate no more of your interference! Do you hear me?"

Lily was chagrined at having started such a row, especially between family members. "Good-bye, Mrs. Tibbet. And thank you." She nodded at Caleb's former wife. "Sandra."

Mrs. Tibbet reached out for Lily's forearm, clasping her gently. "Please don't go, dear. You don't understand—"

"I'm afraid I do," Lily said.

Mrs. Tibbet's gaze had shifted to her niece. "Caleb will turn you over his knee when he finds out about this, Sandra, and I won't do a thing to stop him, I promise you."

Sandra bit down on her lower lip. "Caleb *did* have a mistress," she insisted after a moment.

"Tell her why," Mrs. Tibbet pressed.

There was a fetching ruddiness to Sandra's cheeks. "Because he and I didn't—we didn't have normal marital relations."

Lily was baffled, and she didn't try to hide the fact.

"Caleb never came to my bed once the whole time we were married," Sandra said miserably.

Lily had never heard of such a thing. "He preferred that woman in Tylerville to his own wife?"

Sandra lowered her eyes and shook her head. "No. Caleb became my husband as a favor to my aunt and uncle. He never had any intention of making me a real wife, and he annulled the marriage as soon as decency allowed."

Lily looked at Mrs. Tibbet, mystified, and the older woman nodded confirmation. "Sandra was expecting a child," she said quietly. "The man in question deserted her, and Caleb stepped in. There was a miscarriage, and he asked for his freedom."

Lily set down her valise and sank into a chair. She had never felt sorrier for anyone than she did for Sandra in that moment. She said nothing; her emotions were in upheaval.

Sandra hurled her needlework aside and ran up the stairs.

"Will she be all right?" Lily asked.

Mrs. Tibbet smiled at her. "Oh, yes," she said gently. "Sandra will be just fine. Did I hear you say you'd been to Suds Row today?"

Lily nodded. "It's a terrible place."

"I know," Mrs. Tibbet agreed. "I've been trying to get John to do something about it for the longest time. He says he'll be retiring soon, and then it will be Caleb's problem. The major is second in command, you know, and when John gives up his commission Caleb will be made a colonel."

The last of Lily's hopes that Caleb might choose to become a farmer—hopes she hadn't been aware she harbored—died then. She excused herself and went upstairs to lie on the guest room bed, thinking, and soon she fell asleep.

All of a sudden she was small again, and she was back in her mother's flat in Chicago. The soldier was there, too, lying with Mama on the other side of the canvas curtain, and Lily could hear them fighting.

She was scared, watching their shadows move violently against the curtain, and she tried to get out of bed. She had to stop the soldier from hurting Mama.

But Caroline restrained her, gripping her arm hard and holding on. With her free hand she covered Lily's mouth.

"He isn't hurting her," Caroline whispered.

Lily was still afraid. She watched her mother's shadow reach up and grip the railings of the headboard, and she was moaning just the way she'd done a few months before, when a baby was supposed to come.

There hadn't been any baby, just a lot of blood and, like now, a lot of carrying on.

Lily's eyes blurred with tears; they slipped down her cheeks to shimmer against Caroline's hand. She hated that soldier with his dusty blue coat and his brass buttons. She hated him enough to kill him.

Caroline and Emma began to sing, very softly, to comfort her. Their grandmother had made up the words and the tune, just for them.

> *Three flowers bloomed in the meadow,*
> *Heads bent in sweet repose,*
> *The daisy, the lily, and the rose. . . .*

Lily opened her eyes. Shadows were creeping into the room, and the echo of the old song lingered in her ears. She sat up with a start, still half in the dream, thinking her sisters must be close by. But Lily soon realized the voice belonged to Sandra, and the song was not the one she remembered.

She rose from the bed, automatically reaching up to smooth her hair, and fought back the tears that were always near when she dreamed of a reunion with her sisters and then awakened to find that she was still alone. There was fresh water in the crockery pitcher on the washstand, and Lily poured some into the basin and splashed her face.

Soon she was feeling better, though there was still a hollow little ache in one corner of her heart. Perhaps if she stayed at Fort Deveraux and found a way to start her laundry business, she could afford to hire a Pinkerton man. Surely a detective would be able to find her sisters.

There was a rap at the door, and Sandra came in without waiting for an invitation. "I hope you're not angry with me," she said softly. She had exchanged her white eyelet-trimmed dress for a dancing gown of gossamer pink silk trimmed in pearls, and she looked like one of Isadora's dolls come to life.

Lily shook her head. "I'm not angry."

"You won't tell Caleb that I said he had a mistress, will you?"

Lily wasn't about to promise any such thing, and she said nothing. Caleb was obviously one of those men who felt that keeping a mistress was his right, whether he was married or not, the rounder. And she might very well want to throw the fact in his face.

"He'll *kill* me!" Sandra wailed, crossing the room to Lily's rocking chair and collapsing into it.

Lily thought it a good time to change the subject. "You look very lovely tonight."

Sandra immediately brightened. "I think Lieutenant Costner has serious intentions toward me," she confided.

Lily sighed. Only hours before Sandra had claimed to love Caleb. Now she was beaming because another man liked her.

"Of course," Sandra went on, "it won't matter, because I'm going back to Fox Chapel and marry someone else."

Since Lily's back was turned, Sandra couldn't possibly have seen her roll her eyes. "I wouldn't do anything hasty if I were you," Lily counseled, trying to undo the buttons of her dress.

Sandra immediately came to her aid. "You're a fine one to talk about impulses, Lily Chalmers. Uncle John is downstairs right now telling Auntie and Caleb how you gave him the dickens in his own office."

Lily thought perhaps she had been a little rash, confronting the colonel that way. After all, social changes never came quickly. "Is he angry?"

"Uncle John?" Sandra finished with Lily's buttons and started lifting the dress off over her head. "That lamb? He's much too sweet to hold a grudge."

Lily didn't ask about Caleb's reaction because she didn't want to know. "I was hoping I could take a bath before I dressed for the ball," she said.

"There's a tub just down the hall," Sandra volunteered. "And I suppose there's water in the tank, too." She disappeared, returning only moments later with a pink satin wrapper. "Here, put this on," she said, tossing the pretty garment to Lily.

Lily pulled the wrapper on over her camisole and petticoat and followed Sandra out of the room. She led her to a bathroom, complete with a commode, and struck a match to light the wick under a giant black tank.

"The water won't be very hot," Sandra warned, "but the kerosene flame will take the chill off, anyway." With that she began turning a recalcitrant spigot. Soon water was tumbling into the claw-footed bathtub.

Lily looked at the modern wonder in amazement and was startled into motion when Sandra shoved a fluffy white towel and a bar of soap at her.

"Here, silly," she said good-naturedly. "And be quick about it. Auntie will hold dinner until everyone is present, and I'm starving."

After closing and bolting the door Lily peeled off the borrowed wrapper and tested the bathwater with a cautious toe. It was tepid, but that was no hardship. She turned off the spigot a few minutes later, climbed into the tub and bathed hastily.

Soon she was back in the guest room, feeling fresh and eager for the ball to begin. She pulled the lavender dress on over fresh underthings and stood back to admire herself in the mirror.

The lace edges of her camisole showed. Although she pushed them down inside her dress, they only popped out again.

Lily quickly removed the offending undergarment and pulled the dress bodice up again. She felt daring and strangely free, knowing she was bare beneath the gown.

She was just putting the finishing touches on her hair when Sandra came to collect her.

"Oh, Lily," the other woman said happily, "you look *wonderful!*"

Lily hoped that was truly the case. Although she knew there was no future for her and Caleb, she would remember this night all her life, and for some reason she couldn't explain, she wanted him to do the same. "Thank you," she said shyly.

Sandra took her hand and tugged her out into the hallway. "Come on, hurry. There's roast chicken for supper!"

Lily was suddenly hungry, and Sandra didn't need to urge her anymore. The two went downstairs together, chattering like the best of friends, and burst into the dining room.

Caleb was there, standing beside the window with the colonel. Both men were sipping brandy, and when his gaze fell on Lily, Caleb looked as though he might drop his snifter.

In the end he set the glass aside and came toward her, taking one of her hands in his and raising it to his lips. She had no words, Lily decided, to describe how handsome he looked in his impeccably tailored dress uniform.

He was so magnificent, in fact, and his mouth was so warm against the back of her hand that Lily thought for a moment she might have to sit down.

His golden eyes laughed at her, but gently, and with affection. He kissed her hand once more before releasing it and took obvious delight in the little shiver she gave.

Lily turned away so quickly that she almost caught her foot in the hem of her gown and went sliding across the dining room floor. In fact, it was Caleb's quick grip on the sides of her waist that kept her upright.

Like a bird resettling its ruffled feathers, she squared herself and proceeded toward Mrs. Tibbet, who was watching her with affectionate amusement.

"You look very lovely," the woman said to Lily.

"Thank you," Lily replied. "Not only for the compliment, but for sending the dress to me in Tylerville."

"Sending it?" Mrs. Tibbet looked bewildered, but then her eyes connected with someone standing behind Lily, and she said quickly, "Oh, yes. You're quite welcome, my dear."

Lily turned her head and saw Caleb just behind her. His gaze shifted from Mrs. Tibbet to Lily, but before he could speak there was a mild ruckus at the front of the house. Sandra soon entered the dining room on the arm of a nice-looking man wearing a lieutenant's uniform.

He glanced uncomfortably at the colonel and then at Caleb, but for Lily he spared a broad smile.

"This is Lieutenant Costner," Sandra told Lily, giving her beau's arm an eloquent little shake. "Robert, I'd like to introduce you to Miss Lily Chalmers."

The lieutenant's brown eyes shifted to Caleb's face and then back to Lily's. The smile vanished. "Hello, Miss Chalmers," he said hoarsely.

"Lieutenant," Lily responded with a slight nod of her head.

"Enough of this nonsense!" boomed the colonel, startling everyone. "It's time we had something to eat. Everybody sit down."

Caleb was careful to seat Lily beside him. The colonel sat to her right, at the head of the table.

"Don't you think Lily looks splendid in that dress, Caleb?" Sandra chimed as her aunt reached out to take the lid off the tureen and began ladling soup into delicate china bowls.

Although Caleb's glance across the table at Sandra was

civil enough, Lily found it had its lethal elements. "Yes," he answered evenly.

"Did you make it yourself, Lily?"

Lily was surprised at Sandra's question. Since Mrs. Tibbet had sent the dress, she'd assumed it was a gown Sandra herself had grown tired of. "No," she answered. "It was given to me."

Sandra flinched as though someone had kicked her under the table. She glared at Caleb but said nothing else. She accepted the soup that had been handed to her and passed it on.

When everyone had been served and the colonel had taken some of his soup, he turned to Lily and said, "Well, how is our lovely houseguest tonight?"

Before said guest could open her mouth to answer, Mrs. Tibbet broke in. "Lily's been telling me about her visit to Suds Row," she said pointedly. "The place is an absolute shame, dear, and it shouldn't be tolerated."

The colonel fixed his wife with a quelling look. "The Row is hardly a suitable dinner topic," he pointed out.

Mrs. Tibbet immediately subsided, and Lily was surprised. She hadn't seen her hostess as the type to be intimidated by a husband, even one as compelling as the white-haired colonel.

"All the same—" Lily began, but she felt Caleb's thigh bump against hers and fell silent. Now she was sure he'd either nudged Sandra with the toe of his boot or stepped on her foot when she'd begun talking about Lily's dress.

"Lily's thinking of starting up a laundry business," Caleb announced, his spoon poised in one hand.

Mrs. Tibbet choked on her soup and had to press a napkin to her face.

"A strictly legitimate one, of course," the major went on, and he gave Lily a sidelong look that said, *See how crazy your idea is?*

Her expression conveyed the message that he was mistaken if he thought he'd dissuaded her. Now that she had come up with the plan of hiring a Pinkerton man, as well as earning the money for the things she'd need for her homestead, she was more determined to succeed than ever. "There must be a little house I could rent somewhere on the post," she reasoned.

Mrs. Tibbet was fluttering her napkin in front of her face.

"There's no such thing," grumbled the colonel.

"There is that little place the teacher lived in before they built on to the schoolhouse," ventured Lieutenant Costner, and everyone in the room glared at him except for Lily and Sandra.

He lowered his eyes to his soup.

"Thank you, Lieutenant," Caleb said with a note of dangerous cordiality in his voice. "I'll remember this."

Chapter

❧ 6 ❧

For that one night Lily suspended all her doubts and reservations about the major. As far as she was concerned, the buggy waiting in front of the Tibbet house was a glass coach, and Caleb was a prince. She felt truly regal as he helped her up into the seat.

Behind them Sandra and her lieutenant were getting into another rig, and their laughter added to the festive feeling of that warm April night.

It was a moment before Lily realized that Caleb lingered on the sidewalk, looking up at her with the light of silver stars shimmering in his eyes. Her name sounded hoarse, coming from deep in his chest.

"Yes?"

But Caleb only shook his head, rounded the buggy, and climbed up to settle himself beside Lily. The seat of the rig was narrow, and it put them in scandalously close proximity. Through the skirts of her dancing gown Lily could feel the hard length of Caleb's thigh pressing against her leg.

She squirmed slightly and was rewarded with one of Caleb's obnoxious grins.

"Uncomfortable?" he asked.

Lily swallowed. She'd *never* been so uncomfortable, and she hoped the feeling would last a lifetime. "I'm fine."

He chuckled and brought the reins down lightly on the horse's back, at the same time releasing the brake with a motion of one foot.

The ball was to be held in the mess hall, which stood in the middle of the post, near the parade grounds. As they drew nearer, Lily saw golden light spilling into the darkness from doors and windows and heard laughter and music. She was drawn to the merriment, but at the same time she wanted to go on being alone with Caleb under the shadowy covering of the buggy's bonnet.

At last they reached the large log building, and Caleb brought the rig to a stop. He came around to lift Lily down from the seat, his hands encircling her waist.

Her heart beat faster at the intimacy of his touch, and when her breasts brushed against his chest as he lowered her to the ground a tremor of elemental need went through her. "Will you dance with me?" she asked in a whisper, gazing up at him. "Will you be the first?"

He touched her cheek with an index finger, and for once his smile did not mock her. Indeed, it was like a caress, very private and special. "I want to be the first," he said gruffly. "Believe me."

Before Lily could think of a suitable response they were surrounded by eager young soldiers wanting to make her acquaintance. Clearly, enlisted men were allowed to attend the ball as well as officers.

Lily saw a muscle tighten in Caleb's neck, then slacken again. He cleared his throat, and the flock of privates and corporals receded as though he'd thrown hot water on them.

But they didn't go far.

Lily was bewitched and would have been content to stand there facing Caleb for eternity, but he finally took her arm and ushered her toward the open door of the mess hall. Several of Lily's new admirers followed close behind.

The inside of the building was crowded. The vast majority of the revelers wore uniforms, but there were several women, too.

Caleb didn't seem to see anything or anyone but Lily, and when the small military orchestra struck up a waltz he drew her easily into his arms.

Only then did Lily suffer a misgiving. She'd done very little dancing in her life, and she was certain she would bumble everything. "Caleb, I—"

The light of his smile burned away her qualms as the sun would sear dew from the grass. "You're the most beautiful woman here," he assured her. Then the music swept them both away into a swirling river of blue uniform coats and brightly colored dresses.

After a few missteps the art of dancing came back to Lily, and she could feel her face glowing with the joy of it.

Caleb's eyes were alight with laughter as he looked down at her, but there was no mockery in his expression, and Lily felt a strange tug in the region of her heart. In that moment something had been irrevocably altered within her, but she had no way of knowing what was different.

Through dance after dance Lily whirled in Caleb's arms, and it was only when he led her outside that she realized she was breathless and much too warm.

He handed her the glass of punch he'd appropriated from the refreshment table on the way out. "I'll never forget this night," he said quietly.

Lily held the cup in both hands and took an unladylike gulp before remembering her manners. She dropped one hand and sipped. "Neither will I," she confessed when her thirst had been satisfied. A certain sadness possessed her. "I wish it never had to end."

Caleb tilted his head back to look at the starry sky for a moment before meeting her gaze directly. "It doesn't have to end, Lily. We could be together."

She nearly dropped the small glass cup. Lily knew what he meant, and, for her, the magical mood of the evening had been spoiled. "We hardly know each other," she said in a chilly voice.

He moved a step nearer—they were almost as close as they had been when they were dancing—and took the cup from her hand. After setting it on the porch railing he curved a finger under Lily's chin and lifted. "As naïve as you are, Lily-flower," he said gruffly, "you must know that something is happening between us."

She trembled at his touch. "Yes," she admitted as his mouth drew nearer to her own.

The kiss was inevitable, and it was powerful. It left Lily sagging against Caleb's chest, her hands gripping the front of his uniform coat.

"Come with me," he said quietly, and Lily could no more have defied him than she could have reached out and snatched a star from the sky.

He took her across the road, to the building where Colonel Tibbet's office was. It was dark there, but Lily wasn't afraid because a strange feeling of enchantment possessed her.

They entered a room, and, after closing the door, Caleb left Lily to light a lamp. In the flickering glow Lily saw a desk, bookshelves, and a long leather couch.

Caleb stood by the sofa, and when he held out a hand to Lily she went to him.

"They'll know we're gone," she protested, using the last vestiges of her willpower. She knew Caleb had bewitched her, either while they were dancing or while they were standing close beneath the stars, but she couldn't break the spell.

He shook his head. "We'll be back before anyone misses us."

"Caleb—"

He kissed her forehead lightly. "Shhh." His hands came to rest on her bare shoulders, the thumbs making soft motions against her collarbone.

Lily could feel the hard wall of his torso and his thighs against her, and she sensed the steely strength of him. "You're—you're going to compromise me," she fretted, but she couldn't bring herself to step out of his embrace.

"Umm-hmmm." Caleb bent his head to nibble at the sensitive flesh beneath Lily's right ear, and she moaned softly.

"I'll be r-ruined for any other man—"

"You don't want any other man," Caleb reasoned as he continued his tender torment, "so what does it matter?"

Lily shivered, but she didn't speak.

Caleb reached around behind her and began unfastening the back of her dress. "I have to look at you, Lily. If I don't, I'll go crazy."

Lily would not have permitted any other man on earth the brazen liberty Caleb took then, but she had no power to stop him, and somehow he knew that. He drew down the bodice of her gown so that her breasts were proudly bared.

Until that moment Lily had believed that women had breasts only so they could nurture babies. Now her horizons were broadening significantly.

Caleb touched her very lightly, circling one nipple with the tip of his finger, causing the rosebud to tighten, and Lily stiffened as a new pleasure knifed through her.

She drew in a sharp breath as Caleb trailed his fingers across her chest to the other breast. She could not believe she was allowing such an impropriety, let alone enjoying it.

"Caleb," she whispered, closing her eyes for a moment.

She felt him withdraw and opened her eyes again to see that he was unbuttoning his uniform coat. He shrugged out of the garment and tossed it aside.

Some of Lily's lost reason was restored, and she lifted her arms to cover herself self-consciously, but Caleb immediately reached out, clasped her wrists in gentle hands, and lowered them again. Then he wrapped his arms around Lily's waist and bent to taste one of her nipples with a flick of his tongue.

Lily gasped and put her hand to the back of his head, instinctively pressing him closer.

He chuckled and rewarded her with a suckling motion that made her groan, then reached out to turn down the wick in the lamp. Although he was a man made of shadows, Lily knew the whiteness of her skin made her clearly visible.

"You're too short for this," Caleb muttered, and he gripped Lily by the waist and easily lifted her high off the floor. Her dress fell away in the process, but she was only half aware of that.

She gripped Caleb's shoulders with her fingers as he clasped his arms together beneath her bottom and drew her nipple back into his mouth. She felt herself growing moist in quite another place, and that mysterious ache was back, fiercer than ever.

Presently he carried her to the couch—she felt the cool grip of the leather as he laid her there—and she sought his face with her hands while he took away her petticoat and her drawers and the dainty slippers Sandra had lent her.

"Why, Caleb?" she whispered.

He found the nest of curls at the junction of her thighs and began to stroke her lightly. Skillfully. "There's no other way to convince you that you belong with me," he answered, his voice low and hoarse. "Part your legs for me, Lily."

Her knees separated of their own accord, and Caleb's fingers continued their circular caresses, setting Lily's insides afire even as she grew moister.

"It's not fair that you can touch me and—ooooooh—I can't touch you," Lily fretted as her hips began the dance Caleb was teaching them.

He laughed softly. "That would scare you, I think," he said, and then he couldn't talk anymore because his mouth was occupied with her breast again.

Lily began to thrash on the couch; the pleasure was too great, she couldn't bear it. It was building and building inside her, threatening to erupt like Vesuvius. "Oh—Caleb —something is happening to me—I—"

He let her nipple go briefly. "Something is happening, all right. But it's perfectly natural, Lily. Stop worrying and let me show you what it means to be a woman."

Her back arched in wild concert with his hand. "Caleb," she gasped in delicious desperation. *"Caleb."*

"It's all right, Lily. Your body knows what to do."

"Oh—my—God—"

Suddenly he left her breast, and his fingers stopped stroking Lily to part her. She gave a primitive cry when his tongue touched the little nubbin of flesh where her womanhood had been hiding.

Her body seemed to go wild, thrashing and flailing to escape Caleb even as it fought to encompass him. Caleb caught his hands under her bottom and held her to his mouth like a vessel, and his grasp was firm enough to still her rebellious hips. She gave a long, lusty groan, low in her throat, as her body and soul convulsed in unison.

When the fierce spasms had subsided to a steady quiver Caleb lowered her gently to the couch and stroked her thighs with his hands.

"Let me touch you," she said again, and this time Caleb put her hands to the front of his shirt. She groped to unbutton it and spread her hands over his bare chest.

He drew in his breath when Lily touched his nipples, and the realization that she had power over him, just as he had over her, was intoxicating. Emboldened, she lifted her hands to the back of his neck and pressed him into another kiss.

After a long time he broke away. "Oh, Lily," he said with a raspy chuckle, and his tone made the words a complete sentence in themselves.

"Caleb," she pleaded, rising up far enough to find one of his nipples with the tip of her tongue.

Caleb trembled, and his hands fell to his sides. He allowed her to taste him at her leisure, then shifted so that he was sitting beside her on the couch. He pulled off his boots.

"Once this happens," he said, "things will be different for you, Lily."

She lay still, watching him move in the shadows. He was a magnificent man. "But not for you?"

He turned and looked at her, and she could feel the heat of his amber eyes in the darkness. He shook his head in a movement so slight that it was almost imperceptible. "I won't be giving up anything. But you will."

Lily knew he was right, knew she should put on her clothes and leave before any damage was done, but she was possessed of a strange, sweet inertia. She bit down on her lower lip and waited for him to put out the mysterious fire within her.

He poised himself over her, lean and agile as a prowling jungle beast. His long frame trembled with his effort at restraint. "Lily, are you sure—?"

She nodded her head slowly and ran her hands along the sides of his rib cage. "You'll be the first, Caleb," she told him. However unnecessary the words might have been, they were important to Lily.

He sighed. "It hurts the first time," he warned.

Lily laid her hands to his taut buttocks and pressed him toward her. "I don't care, Caleb. You said you'd show me how to be a woman—now you have to keep your word."

Caleb reached down to prepare her with his fingers, caressing and then claiming her with a sudden thrust of his hand. Her back arched as the heat began thrumming through her again, and Caleb withdrew his fingers only to replace them with the tip of his shaft.

Lily's hands were moving up and down his back now, gently urging him. "Take me, Caleb."

He pressed just a little further into her, and Lily began to whimper, needing something she couldn't begin to define. He dropped his mouth to hers and whispered against her lips, "Only once. It will only hurt once, Lily."

She trusted him utterly and drew him into her kiss. He

caught her cry of mingled pain and pleasure when his manhood was driven home in a single powerful stroke.

There was a stinging sensation, a feeling of being too full, but this was soon replaced by something more elemental. Lily's body craved friction, and her hips began rising and falling by instinct.

Caleb went rigid upon her and moaned, "Lily, stop—please stop—"

His pleading only heightened her pleasure, and she had to have the sweet conflict he would have denied her. She flung herself at him, a she-cat claiming her mate, and his control was shattered. He rode her with a smooth, rhythmic ferocity that made the flesh of his back slick beneath Lily's hands.

Lily felt wonder, as well as an explosion of delight, when his powerful body buckled upon hers. After a long moment he collapsed, nearly crushing her beneath his weight. Gasping for breath, he shifted her so that she lay on top of him.

"I didn't plan that," he managed, just as the full measure of what she'd done was beginning to dawn on Lily.

She flung herself away, eyes burning with tears, and groped in the darkness for her drawers and petticoat. "You knew exactly what you were doing!"

Caleb rose from the sofa and began putting on his clothes. "Lily, I only meant to show you what I could make you feel. I wanted to stop when you were satisfied, but you wouldn't let me."

The fact that what he said was true only shamed Lily further. What had possessed her to do such a stupid, brazen thing, she wondered frantically as she yanked on her drawers and tied the strings firmly. One minute she'd been dancing, the next she'd been thrashing beneath Caleb Halliday like a wanton.

She gave a strangled cry of frustrated rage and struggled when she felt Caleb's hands close on her shoulders. She'd never meant for this to happen; it was as though someone else had taken over her body.

"It's all right, Lily," he said gently, and she sank against him, sobbing.

He held her until she'd stopped crying, and he brought her her petticoat and dress. He waited while she dressed, then lit the lamp again.

"I'm sorry," he said, buttoning his paneled shirt.

Lily made a largely useless effort to right her hair and glared at him. "Take me home!"

Caleb sighed, gestured toward the door with a sweeping motion of one hand, and turned down the wick in the lamp again.

Lily was through the door and outside in the crisp evening air before he caught up to her.

"I said I was sorry," he hissed, grasping her by the elbow when she would have kept walking.

Lily sniffled furiously. "Wonderful!" she whispered. "You ruin a girl's whole life, then you tell her you're sorry! Damn you and your arrogant assumptions, Caleb Halliday!"

He hauled her against his chest, and his eyes glittered in the light of the moon. Music sailed out into the night from the mess hall.

"Stop acting like this was all my idea," Caleb ordered furiously. "The truth is, most of it was *yours,* and you damned well know it!"

"Mine?!" Lily cried. *"I* wasn't the one who took my clothes off!"

Caleb's nose was not more than half an inch from Lily's. "Maybe not," he countered, "but you sure as hell helped take *mine* off!"

Lily was mortified, and she glanced wildly around her to see if anyone had overheard Caleb's accusation. "I got carried away!" she whispered.

Caleb sighed. "We both did," he admitted. "Come on, I'll take you back to the Tibbets'."

Lily was a little calmer, but she bridled all the same. "I can take myself back, thank you."

Caleb cursed under his breath and propelled her toward one of the buggies that lined the street in front of the mess hall. Before she could escape him he'd thrust her up into the seat.

She folded her arms across her chest and looked straight ahead. "Just suppose I do get married someday. What am I going to tell my husband on our wedding night?"

Caleb's shoulders moved in an insolent shrug. "I guess you'll just have to pretend, won't you?"

The darkness hid the blush that flooded her face—at least, Lily hoped it did. "After tonight, Caleb Halliday, I never want to have anything to do with you. I don't want to see your face or hear your name!"

Caleb released the brake lever and brought the reins down on the horse's back with a snap, but he didn't speak until they'd pulled up in front of the Tibbets' house. "I'll be here to get you at eight tomorrow morning," he said. "Be ready."

Lily wanted to slap him, but she didn't quite have the nerve. "If it's all the same to you, *Major,* I'll just wait until Monday and take the stagecoach back to Tylerville. Even with renegade Indians and outlaws around, it's bound to be safer!"

Caleb glowered at her for a moment, but then he started to laugh.

Lily elbowed him hard in the ribs, furious that he could find anything funny about the situation. "Stop it!" she cried, starting to clamber down from the buggy.

The horse drawing the rig began to nicker and prance nervously at the disturbance, and Caleb made things worse by reaching out and clasping Lily by the arm. Her bottom landed on the buggy seat with a humiliating thump.

"You know," Caleb said evenly, "it's likely to take me a good month to train you."

Lily struggled against a volcanic burst of temper. *"Train me?"* she echoed in outraged disbelief.

Caleb nodded. "You've got a lot to learn, Lily-flower.

We'll start with the respect a woman has for her man and progress to public deportment."

By then Lily was so angry that she couldn't speak, only sputter. But when Caleb came around to lift her down from the buggy seat she lost her composure completely and began to pound at his impervious shoulders with her fists.

Caleb set her away from him easily, and she clenched her hands at her sides.

"I hate you, Caleb Halliday," she vowed.

He kissed her lightly, and she caught the spicy female scent of her own body. "Of course you do, darling," he said, propelling her toward the Tibbets' front gate.

"And what happened tonight is never going to happen again!"

"Wrong," Caleb said confidently. "It's going to happen thousands of times, in thousands of different places."

Before Lily could come up with a suitably scathing answer the door opened, and Mrs. Tibbet came out on the porch. "Caleb? Lily? Is the dance over already?"

Caleb was solicitous as he ushered Lily up the stone walk. "Lily has a slight headache," he said sympathetically, "but I'm sure she'll be fully recovered by eight o'clock tomorrow morning when I stop by to pick her up."

Lily couldn't bring herself to make a scene in front of Mrs. Tibbet, not when the woman had gone to so much trouble to make her stay at Fort Deveraux pleasant and comfortable. She managed a hateful smile for Caleb and said, "Good night and thank you for a truly remarkable evening."

His lips curved into a secretive grin. "Until tomorrow," he said, with a little bow.

Lily wanted to clout him over the head, but she overcame that desire and followed Mrs. Tibbet into the house.

"I'll get you some powders for that headache," the older woman fretted. Lily finally noticed that her hostess was wearing a wrapper, slippers, and a nightcap.

She shook her head. "Please don't trouble yourself. I'm sure a little sleep is all I need."

Mrs. Tibbet looked at her in an assessing fashion. "Well, if you're sure. How was the dance, dear?"

Lily was too fond of Mrs. Tibbet, and too ashamed of her own actions, to tell the entire truth. "I had a marvelous time," she said, for the dancing had indeed been wonderful. Then I gave myself to Caleb, added a voice in her mind.

Later, alone in her room, Lily allowed herself to remember how it had been with Caleb. Despite the initial pain, loving and being loved by that man had been the most glorious experience of her life. Her cheeks warmed at the memory, and she busied herself with her ablutions. There was a faint soreness in her thighs and her most private place that reminded her of those incredible minutes when Caleb's body had been joined to hers, and although she knew she'd made a serious mistake, she was no longer ashamed.

There had been something indescribably right about what they'd done together. She just couldn't let it happen again, that was all.

Lily stripped off the beautiful lavender dress and laid tentative hands to her breasts. They'd been nothing more than a bother to her until Caleb had touched them, brought them a life they'd never had before.

Quickly Lily drew her hands away and put on her nightgown. It was wrong to touch herself; Mrs. Sommers, Rupert's mother, had claimed a person could go to hell for it. Being a preacher's wife, Bethesda Sommers had been in a position to know those things.

After polishing her teeth and brushing her hair Lily tossed back the pretty quilt and crawled between smooth linen sheets. Emma, she thought, as she did every night, Caroline, I'm doing my best to stand still so you can find me.

Imagining what her sisters would look like after all these years was a bittersweet game that Lily played. It made her feel closer to them, but it also invariably caused her to wonder if they'd changed so much she wouldn't recognize them even if she passed them on the street.

Lily felt tears gathering and blinked them back, hearing

Caroline's childlike voice as clear as a bell in her mind: "Don't be a crybaby, Lily-dilly. Nobody likes a crybaby."

She ran her hands down over her nightgown, over her hips and her thighs. Her body was sore, but so was her pride. Dear heaven, when she thought of the way she'd responded to Caleb . . .

The bed seemed broad and lonely, and she pretended that Caleb was lying beside her, naked and strong. He'd told her that the loving would never hurt after the first time.

A bleak feeling filled her. There was never going to be a second time, so it didn't really matter.

Lily knotted one hand into a fist and bunched the heel of her palm against her mouth. Caleb would come for her in the morning, to drive her back to Tylerville in his buggy. How in the name of heaven was she going to face him?

She turned onto her side and closed her eyes, determined to sleep. Soon, because she was exhausted, both emotionally and physically, she drifted off.

She dreamed about the soldier.

He'd struck Mama—beautiful Mama, with her dark hair and bright brown eyes—with the back of his hand.

Suddenly, in that strange way of dreams, Lily was grown up, and she had Rupert's hunting rifle in her hands. She pulled the trigger, and there was a loud report; then Mama's soldier clutched his belly, blood bubbling past his fingers, and toppled to the floor.

"Lily," he said, and he had golden eyes now, and maple-sugar hair. He was Caleb, and he was dying.

Lily awakened sitting bolt upright in bed, her cry of terror still echoing in the room.

Chapter

❧ 7 ❧

Caleb sat at the writing table in his room off the main barracks, rubbing one thumb idly over the frame of an old photograph. He felt the pull of the past and resisted it by remembering Lily's ire after the episode in his office.

He grinned. He'd boasted that taming her would take a month, but he suspected the job might require a lifetime instead.

His gaze shifted to the serious, beloved faces in the photograph. His mother stood behind his father's chair, one hand resting on her husband's shoulder, and Joss, a handsome five-year-old, stood staunchly at her side.

Memories pulled Caleb inexorably backward in time.

Caleb would be thirty-three years old on his next birthday. At sixteen he'd run away to join the Federal Army, and he'd been a cavalryman ever since. He remembered himself as a skinny private, all eyes and Adam's apple, hardly knowing one end of a rifle from the other, yet confident of his ability to single-handedly save the Union.

He'd learned fast that war was no schoolyard game, and

many a night he'd lain shivering in his bedroll, wishing to God he could go home. He'd wondered, too, whether Joss, his older brother, was lying on another patch of ground somewhere, wanting the same thing.

Finally Caleb's mind settled on the day his relationship with his elder brother had changed forever. . . .

"You can't do this!" Susannah, Joss's pretty new bride, sobbed, clutching at the front of her husband's shirt. "We need you, Caleb and Abbie and I! I won't let you go!"

Caleb had watched in disbelief as his brother gently removed Susannah's hands and bent to kiss the part in her thick auburn hair. "I can't just stand by and watch this happen," he said gruffly.

"It isn't your fight," Susannah pressed frantically. "This is Pennsylvania—we're a part of the North—"

Joss's eyes moved to Caleb's rigid face. They had cousins down in Virginia, and Joss was siding with them and with the South. "Right is right," he said. "A man should be able to choose how he wants to live without interference from the government."

At last Caleb spoke, and his words echoed through the spacious study, even though he said them quietly. Later the unwitting precognition of those simple sentences would haunt him. "If you fight, Joss, it'll be against your friends and family. It'll be against me."

Joss released his hold on the shoulders of his weeping wife, his face taut with emotion. "You're sixteen years old," he said, his voice gruff. "You've got no business fighting a war—not on either side."

"I'll be fighting this one," Caleb maintained quietly. "I'm signing on with the Federal Army."

Joss gripped Caleb by the lapels of his shirt, nearly wrenching him off his feet. *"You will stay right here,"* he said through his teeth.

Caleb swallowed hard. Joss was bigger and stronger, and he'd been running the Halliday family for five years. But he wasn't the only one with principles and political beliefs. "I'm going to fight," Caleb said.

Joss raised his hand as if to backhand Caleb, but in the end a look of pure sadness filled his eyes. He thrust Caleb away and stormed out of the house without looking back.

Late that night Caleb packed his saddle bags with food— he was perennially hungry—and rode out.

Months passed before he and Joss met again.

Grieved to the depths of his spirit, Caleb avoided thinking about the tragic reunion and turned his mind to another part of the war.

He'd been wounded at Gettysburg, not in the body, but in the soul. Every rebel he'd shot or bayoneted had had Joss's face, and those first three days of July, 1863, had left Caleb numb inside. Later he'd witnessed Lee's gallant surrender at Appomattox.

Soldiering was a lonely life, often a frustrating one. There were times when Caleb thought he'd go insane if he had to put another platoon of privates through their paces on the parade grounds.

But now there was Lily, and she'd changed everything.

As soon as he'd brought her around to his way of thinking and she was safely ensconced in a proper house, Caleb decided, he would go back to Pennsylvania and make an attempt at setting things right.

Maybe he would even leave the army and take his proper place in the world.

Lily was up and dressed long before eight o'clock the next morning. In fact, by the time breakfast was served she had already located the schoolhouse and peered through the windows of the tiny cottage across the street.

"I'd like to rent that small house Lieutenant Costner mentioned at supper last night," she announced as she speared a sausage and passed the platter on to Colonel Tibbet.

Her host exchanged a level look with his wife. "To start your laundry business, I presume."

Lily nodded.

"My dear," Mrs. Tibbet said quickly, "if it's work you want, I can provide it. I'm desperate for a housekeeper—"

Lily interrupted her hostess with a smile. "You are so kind," she said sincerely, "and I've come to depend upon you as a friend. It wouldn't be fair for me to accept the position when I intend to quit the moment I have money enough to move onto my homestead."

Mrs. Tibbet sighed. "I do understand, dear," she said gently, and her gaze shifted to the colonel. "John, that house is a waste, sitting empty like that."

The colonel's face grew even more ruddy than usual. "Don't tell me you're in favor of this young woman's preposterous plan, Gertrude!"

"I *am* in favor," Mrs. Tibbet insisted.

"Lily, you'll ruin your hands," Sandra put in with a concerned frown. "All that lye soap." She paused to shudder. "And of course everyone will think you're selling yourself as well as your services."

"Poppycock," said Mrs. Tibbet.

"Gertrude," warned the colonel, "I will thank you not to use strong language."

"If you don't let Lily have that house," pressed his wife, "I will invite her to live here and conduct business from our kitchen!"

Both Sandra and Lily sat tensely in their chairs while invisible darts flew back and forth between the Tibbets.

Finally the colonel pushed back his chair and grumbled, "Very well, Lily may have the house. But I'm warning you, Gertrude—there will be trouble, and you'll have yourself to thank for it."

Lily wanted to shout for joy. She was in business! Soon she'd have all the money she needed. When the Pinkerton man she meant to hire located Emma and Caroline they would find her to be a woman of property, with her own pigs and chickens.

Life was glorious.

Sandra was gazing at Lily in amazement. "What will Caleb say?"

Lily was about to respond that she didn't care what Caleb would say when he came strolling into the dining room and demanded good-naturedly, "What will Caleb say about what?"

"Dratted women," the colonel muttered, tossing down his napkin and bolting out of his chair. "They don't know how to listen. They don't know how to obey. If the army were made up of them, we'd all be British subjects."

Caleb grinned at his superior officer's disgruntled remarks and helped himself to a cup of coffee from the silver pot standing on the sideboard. The colonel sank back into his chair with an exaggerated sigh.

"Sit down and have some breakfast, Caleb," Mrs. Tibbet said, but his eyes were on Lily now, curious and wary.

He drew back a chair beside Lily and sat. "Thank you," he said to the mistress of the house, "but I ate at the mess hall. What's going on here?"

"Lily's starting up a business," Sandra piped, her eyes dancing at the prospect of an uproar in her aunt and uncle's dining room. "Uncle John is going to let her live in the schoolmaster's cottage."

Lily braced herself, but when she managed to meet Caleb's gaze she was surprised to see that he was smiling.

"You're not going to like the laundry trade, Lily," he said evenly. "But I'd be a liar if I said I wasn't glad you were staying."

Lily had to avert her eyes because she was remembering the night before and the way she'd behaved with this man. It all seemed so brazen in the bright light of day. "Of course, I will have to go back to Tylerville to get my things and resign my job," she said. "I don't know what Mrs. McAllister will say about my coming to live on an army post, however."

"If we're going to make the trip and get back within the day," Caleb remarked, finishing off his coffee, "we'd better be leaving."

Lily squirmed slightly in her chair. Caleb already thought he had the right to tell her what to do about everything. If she didn't take a firm approach with him, he was going to have her dancing at the end of a string like a puppet. "I'll just remain here and take the stagecoach tomorrow," she said sweetly. "But thank you all the same."

In the distance church bells began to chime.

"Oh, my goodness," Mrs. Tibbet fretted, squinting at the watch pinned to the bodice of her brown sateen dress. "If we don't hurry, we'll miss the opening prayer."

"Heaven forbid," said Sandra, who was watching Lily and Caleb avidly.

"Come along, Sandra," the colonel said gruffly.

"I'll clear the table while you're gone," Lily offered, hoping that Caleb would leave the house with the Tibbets and Sandra and give her a little time to plan. She hadn't really expected the colonel to give in on the issue of the schoolmaster's cottage so easily; his capitulation had left her with a great many things to think about.

As luck would have it, Caleb remained behind.

Lily's hands were unsteady as she cleared the table, despite all her practice at such tasks. She could feel Caleb's eyes on her, and she knew he was remembering the night before, just as she was.

"You needn't think I'm staying at Fort Deveraux because of you," she said without looking at him. "In fact, I believe it would be better if you just tended to your own business and left me completely alone."

"Do you?" he asked, and, catching hold of the back of her yellow dress, he hauled her easily onto his lap.

Lily spread her hands on his chest, her brown eyes widening, but she didn't push herself away. She couldn't quite work up the impetus to do that. "Y-yes," she answered belatedly.

He touched her breast with the tip of one index finger, causing her nipple to harden beneath her clothes. "Perhaps you need some convincing," he said, his voice at once soft and ragged.

"Wh-what sort of convincing?" Lily asked, because she was by nature adventurous and just a bit on the impulsive side. She had to know what he'd say.

Caleb pretended deep thought. "Well, since there's nobody here but us—and there won't be for at least two hours, because the chaplain is a long-winded man—I could spread you out on this table and have you for breakfast."

Lily was shocked, but she was also intrigued. It was her abrupt understanding of this latter fact that gave her the power to bound out of Caleb's lap and cross to the other side of the room. "You would force me?"

"I wouldn't have to force you," Caleb said easily, "and we both know it. In five minutes I could have you volunteering for duty."

Lily knew he was right, and that infuriated her. She turned away and began slamming lids onto the various dishes on the sideboard. "Don't you know when to give up?" she snapped.

Caleb came up behind her, turned her into his arms, and held her close. "When was the last time you gave up on something you wanted, Lily?"

"I never give up. It's cowardly."

He smiled, his hands resting lightly on the sides of her waist. "Persistence is an admirable quality. Perhaps you've noticed that I have it, too."

Lily was desperate for a barrier to throw between them; she was beginning to have thoughts of lying on Mrs. Tibbet's tablecloth in total surrender. "I couldn't love a man who keeps a mistress," she threw out.

He withdrew slightly. "What?"

"Sandra told me. She said the woman lives in Tylerville."

Caleb looked taken aback, but only for a moment. "She does," he answered. "But when we parted company, she was talking about going back to San Francisco. She has a prospective husband there."

Lily's eyes widened. "You parted company?"

"Of course," Caleb replied. "Did you think I was going to go on visiting Bianca while I was seeing you?"

"You weren't faithful to Sandra," Lily pointed out.

"I also wasn't sleeping with her."

Lily lowered her eyes. "I don't understand."

Caleb lifted her chin. "Sandra is my little sister's best friend," he said gently. "She's family to the Tibbets. I married her because she was in trouble. Is it getting any clearer?"

"You're really a very honorable man," Lily allowed with a sigh.

Caleb arched an eyebrow. "That's bad?"

"It makes it much harder to resist you."

"Resisting me will prove impossible, Lily."

"You are the most presumptuous—"

He turned his head to glance back at the table. "You'd just fit between the biscuits and the butter dish," he commented idly.

Lily resisted an urge to smash his instep with her foot. He'd gotten his way. She was going to agree to let him drive her back to Tylerville. And the reason was simple: If they stayed here, she might end up doing something scandalous. If they were in a moving buggy, there would be less chance of that.

"Just let me finish clearing the table," she said, pretending the decision had been hers alone, "and then I'll get my valise and write a note for Mrs. Tibbet."

Caleb's hands cupped her bottom very lightly and very briefly. "I'll clear the table," he said. "Go ahead and get ready to leave."

Lily was flabbergasted. She'd never known a man to voluntarily undertake a household chore before. Why, even Rupert, as kind as he was, had always expected the female members of the family to take care of such things.

"Go on," Caleb said gently.

Lily hurried upstairs and packed her things. Then, after finding paper and pencil on top of Mrs. Tibbet's writing desk in the parlor, she composed a note thanking her hostess and explaining that she had gone with Caleb.

She doubted that her friend would be surprised.

The dining room was spotless when Lily returned, and Caleb was standing at the window with his back to her, looking out on a temperamental spring day.

"I hope it won't rain," Lily said, feeling very shy all of a sudden.

Caleb turned and smiled at her. "Whatever happens, Lily," he said, "I'll take care of you."

Soon they were in Caleb's buggy again, heading through the fort toward the great gates. Since most everyone was in church, there were only a few Suds Row urchins to stare at them as they passed.

Caleb sensed Lily's pain at seeing them and reached out to lay one hand over hers. "What are you thinking?"

Lily was silent until the gates had been opened and Caleb had been saluted and waved through. "I know how they feel, Caleb—always on the outside of things."

He squeezed her hand and brought it to rest on his knee. "Is that how you felt, growing up?"

Lily had told Caleb a little about her separation from her sisters and her adoption by the Sommers family the day of their picnic, but she'd never admitted what it had really been like living with them. In fact, she'd never discussed that with anyone—not even Rupert.

"The Sommerses wanted me as a playmate for their daughter, Isadora. She was the light of their lives—beautiful as a fairy princess."

"Was she unkind to you?"

Lily shrugged. "Sometimes, but Isadora was too shallow to be really cruel." She paused to reflect. "But I was a doll to her, not a person."

Caleb's silence was an encouraging one.

"When we were ten, and Isadora died of diphtheria, Charles and Bethesda—Reverend and Mrs. Sommers— were furious with God. They couldn't believe, after all their dedication, that He'd taken their cherished daughter to heaven and left them burdened with me. They treated me accordingly."

Caleb's hand tightened on Lily's.

"If it hadn't been for Rupert, life would have been intolerable. When he left home I went with him and served as his housekeeper—until I ran away to Tylerville and filed my homestead claim."

"You never saw the Sommerses again?"

Lily shook her head. "They're dead."

"How long have you been trying to find your sisters?"

"Ever since I learned to write," Lily sighed. "Not one of my letters was ever answered. Besides, Caroline and Emma wouldn't look the way I remember them, so my descriptions probably aren't very helpful."

Caleb lifted her hand to his mouth, kissed the knuckles lightly, and let her go. "Have you ever thought about hiring a detective?"

Lily nodded. "I mean to engage a Pinkerton man," she said, "even if I have to wait another year to build my house."

"I'll pay for the investigation, Lily."

She looked at him in amazement. "I couldn't be obligated."

"You wouldn't be."

Lily shook her head. "Thank you for offering, Caleb, but it really wouldn't be proper."

"What about last night? Was that proper?"

Lily blushed. "Are you suggesting that you should *pay* me for that?"

Caleb's grin was slow and arrogant. "Of course not. That would make you a—laundress."

Another gibe about her business plans. Determined not to allow him to bait her, Lily turned her attention to the cloudy sky. A chilly wind blew over the prairie land that surrounded them, and Caleb produced his uniform coat from behind the seat. With one hand he draped it over Lily's shoulders.

"Thank you," she said grudgingly.

Caleb laughed. "It will take a lifetime," he said.

Lily looked at him curiously. "What will?"

"Never mind," he replied.

Fifteen minutes later the rain began. Although it was only a drizzle, Lily knew that the road would soon be wet and muddy and the traveling difficult. She half expected Caleb to turn the horse and buggy around and head back to Fort Deveraux, but he didn't.

When, after an hour, the weather grew really bad, he pulled the rig into a copse of pine trees to wait out the storm.

"We could go back to the fort," Lily suggested uneasily. She wondered what the chances were of their being set upon by hostile Indians.

"It's just a cloudburst," Caleb said in a dismissive tone, getting down from the buggy to stretch his long legs.

The horse nickered and began nibbling contentedly on the moist spring grass.

Lily, wearing Caleb's coat over her dress, folded her arms impatiently. She wanted to be *moving,* whether it was toward the fort or toward Tylerville. Stopping under a bunch of trees was nothing but a waste of time. And suppose there was lightning?

At that moment a blast of thunder rent the sky, and Lily fairly flung herself out of the buggy and into Caleb's arms.

He lowered her slowly to the ground, making her feel every inch of his torso as she passed. With one finger he traced her jawline, his mouth drawing closer to hers with every passing second.

Lily whirled away from him, nearly slipping in the grass. Although the air was moist, the rain did not reach them.

"Are you afraid of me, Lily?"

She hugged herself and shook her head, aware that she must look very silly in that oversized coat. "No. I don't believe you'd ever hurt me or force me to do anything I didn't want to."

He spread his hands. "Well, then?"

"But I am afraid of your power over me," Lily went on. "Sometimes I think you could make me do anything."

"Has it ever occurred to you that you might have the same kind of power over me?"

Lily shook her head. "I know I don't." Suddenly she started to cry. "Any woman could do what I did last night."

Caleb came to her and drew her close. "Lily, that isn't true."

She let her forehead rest against his shoulder and wept. "It is!" she wailed.

Caleb held her face, hooking his thumbs beneath her chin, and made her look at him. She closed her eyes, only to have him gently kiss her lids. "Lily, listen to me. I've got feelings for you that I've never had for anyone else. Ever."

Her hands were drawn to his shoulders, where they rested lightly. "But why? Why me, Caleb?"

He kissed her lips lightly. "Because you're beautiful— because you're strong—because somewhere, sometime, an angel wrote our names in a book. I don't know why, Lily. And the why of it doesn't matter."

Lily liked the idea of an angel writing her name in a book, but she still wasn't convinced that Caleb wasn't using her. Maybe she had been an innocent until just the night before, but she'd known for a long time that a man would say anything to get a woman to lie down with him. The smart ones, like Caleb, could come up with some very pretty words. "You're right. It doesn't matter, because you're going to stay in the army, and I'm going to homestead my land."

Caleb's expression was one of pure exasperation. "You little idiot. How the hell do you propose to plow fields, fend off Indians and outlaws, and build a house all by yourself?"

Lily was wounded. "Maybe I won't be by myself," she said, wanting to hurt him in the same way he'd hurt her. "Maybe I'll meet a soldier at Fort Deveraux—one who wants to be a farmer. We could get married, and I wouldn't be alone." She started to turn away from him, intending to go back to the buggy, but he grasped her arm and wrenched her back.

"You're mine," he breathed through his perfect white teeth. "And I'll kill the man who lays a hand on you."

"I'm not yours!"

"You are," Caleb argued. "I saw to that last night."

Lily was outraged. He was treating her like a piece of land, one he'd homesteaded and laid a permanent claim to. "I told you, last night was a mistake."

Deftly, he turned her so that her back was pressed to his chest. Lily was angry, but she wasn't afraid. Even in anger she knew she had nothing to fear from Caleb.

"What are you doing?" she spat.

Although Caleb's arms held her like a giant manacle his hands were gentle on her breasts. Her nipples responded instantly, traitorously, to his touch. "I'm convincing you," he said, his lips moving along her neck.

Lily struggled, but it was useless. "Caleb Halliday, you let me go!"

"All right," he said huskily, and he relaxed the pressure of his arms, though his hands remained on Lily's breasts, caressing her. "Go ahead, Lily. Step away."

It was humiliating, but Lily found she couldn't move. What he was doing felt too good; it was meeting some deep and mysterious need. A need as old as womankind.

"Go on," he said, and Lily felt the front of her skirt rising as one of his hands clasped it. "Walk away, Lily."

"Damn you," she gasped. She felt the cold, drizzly breeze through her drawers as her skirt was lifted.

"Hold this," Caleb ordered softly, and she did. She actually clasped her skirt in one hand and held it for him, and her defiant obedience brought a low chuckle from his throat.

He untied her drawers, and, because they were too big in

the first place, they fell unceremoniously to her ankles. She kicked them away.

Caleb put one foot between Lily's feet and made her broaden her stance, and she quivered as his hand massaged her bare abdomen. "Caleb," she pleaded.

"Yes?" His voice was a raw whisper muffled by the tingling flesh of her neck. He found her secret place and plundered it gently, using her own dampness to heighten her sensitivity to his touch.

"I—despise you."

"I can see that," he answered as she thrust her head back against his shoulder and groaned with helpless pleasure. The practiced motions of his hand were faster now, and a burning tremor was beginning deep inside Lily.

She pressed herself shamelessly to his hand, still holding her skirt for him, and her head moved from side to side in delirium. "Oh, dear God, Caleb—*Caleb*—"

Knowing somehow that her untutored body was about to erupt with passion, Caleb increased his efforts and sent Lily spinning into the sky to become a part of the thunder and the lightning.

When it was over she turned to him, feeling a strange, determined peace. But she did not drop her skirts. "Take me, Caleb," she said. "Make love to me like you did last night."

He shook his head, but she could see his manhood swelling against the front of his trousers. "You'll be sore. Another time, Lily."

"Now," she said, reaching out to caress him as boldly as he'd caressed her.

Caleb groaned. "Lily—"

She spread his coat on the damp ground and lay down on it, holding up her arms. Her skirt lay crumpled around her waist, leaving the lower half of her body naked.

In the coming moments Lily could believe Caleb's earlier assertion that she had the same power he wielded. He could not fight her. He sank to his knees on the ground and opened his trousers while Lily unbuttoned his shirt.

He brought down the front of her dress and bent to suckle her breast through the flimsy fabric of her camisole, and Lily groaned at his teasing.

He entered her slowly, cautiously, but Lily saw a conqueror looking out of his eyes, a primitive warrior claiming his woman, defying her to resist him.

The pleasure was so keen that Lily was soon in a fever, clinging to Caleb, begging him for the relief only he could provide. He gave her more and more of himself until Lily's body convulsed in a series of violent spasms and she shouted her triumph to the sky.

Caleb's release came moments later, and Lily caressed his chest and face and shoulders in a gentle frenzy while he threw his head back and, with a hoarse cry, spilled his seed deep within her. Lily comforted him in the aftermath while his body still trembled with the ferocity of his satisfaction.

After a time he sat up. He raised Lily's dampened camisole so that he could admire her bare breasts. In the moist, cool air their tips tightened like roses closing back into buds. With his handkerchief he began to cleanse her.

Although the motion was infinitely tender, it set Lily afire again. Caleb continued the gentle ministrations until she cried out, arching her back in soft surrender.

"Can you live without that, Lily?" he asked minutes later when she was dressing, her face averted in embarrassment. "Can you lie alone in your bed every night for the rest of your life and remember how it was?"

She ignored him, climbing back into the buggy seat, his coat settled around her shoulders again. The scent of Caleb rose from the cloth, a treacherous comfort. "Let's go on," she said. "The rain is letting up."

Caleb swore quietly and joined her in the buggy, taking the reins in his hands. An hour later they arrived at Mrs. McAllister's rooming house in Tylerville.

The opinionated widow greeted Lily's news with an

approving smile. It was obvious that she expected her departing tenant to give up the crazy idea of starting a laundry business after a week or so and throw all her energies into reining in Caleb Halliday.

Lily and Caleb had Sunday dinner with Mrs. McAllister after calling on Charlie Mayfield so that Lily could quit her job, and then they drove back to the fort. Although the roads were muddy and the horse was tired, they didn't stop. They didn't talk much, either.

"Where are you staying tonight?" Caleb asked reasonably.

Lily had no idea; her mind had been so full of Caleb that she hadn't thought about that. Nor had she collected her savings from the bank in Tylerville or bought the equipment she would need to wash clothes. Although the schoolmaster's cottage was a cozy little place, it would require some preparation before she could move in.

"You could spend the night with me," he suggested when Lily didn't answer his question. "I've been staying in the barracks, but I have a house."

She glared at him.

"Forget I said anything," Caleb sighed. And he turned the buggy toward the Tibbet place.

Chapter
❧ 8 ❧

With help from Sandra and the loan of some basic household items from Gertrude Tibbet Lily was able to move into the schoolmaster's cottage three days after her return to Fort Deveraux. She put up placards around the post, said a prayer, and waited for her clients to arrive.

She was stringing up clothesline that bright Wednesday morning when her first customer rounded the tiny house to find her in the backyard.

It was the soldier who had ridden with her on the stagecoach the previous Saturday morning, and Lily had to force herself to smile as she greeted him.

His eyes moved over her in an unsettling sweep, then he held out an armful of dirty shirts. "I need these washed and pressed," he said. "The name's Judd. Judd Ingram."

Lily lowered her arms from the post where she'd been tying one end of a clothesline, suddenly aware that Private Ingram was looking at her breasts. "If you'll just leave your things there, on the back step . . ."

He laid the clothes down where Lily had asked. "I thought maybe we could go inside and talk a while."

Lily swallowed. She'd been warned that men would expect other services besides the washing of their clothes, but she hadn't truly believed it. Not until now. "I'll be busy with this for some time," she hedged, indicating the clothesline.

The slender, wiry man grinned and swaggered over to her. "Here. Let me do it." With that, he elbowed Lily aside and reached up to make a firm knot in the line.

The smell of him made Lily's eyes water. "Thank you," she said in a hesitant voice.

Ingram turned to beam down at her, having finished his task. "There. Now let's go inside."

Lily's bewilderment was replaced by indignation. She placed her hands on her hips and met Judd Ingram's eager, icy gaze. "I don't think you understand, Mr. Ingram," she said. "I'm here to wash clothes, and that's all I do. If you'll come back tomorrow afternoon, I'll have your things ready by then."

The soldier looked disappointed, then annoyed. "What's the matter? Ain't my money as good as the major's?"

Lily flushed with fury, but financial prudence kept her from slapping her first client across the face. Beneath her rage was the painful fear that Caleb had boasted about conquering her. "I'll thank you to explain that remark."

"Major Halliday's been whistlin' under his breath ever since the dance Saturday night, when you two went off together," Judd replied insolently. "Major Halliday lectures, and he hollers, but he don't whistle."

"Your laundry will be ready tomorrow," Lily said coldly, and then she took Judd Ingram's dirty shirts from where he'd left them on the step and went inside her tiny house. She bolted the door the moment she'd closed it, and through its glass window she watched as Ingram slapped his cap against one leg and then stormed away.

She was building a fire under the big wash kettle she'd bought at the general store when a second visitor arrived.

The woman was taller than Lily and sturdy as a man, and her complexion was pockmarked. Her hair, pulled back from her face in a fashion so severe as to look painful, was a nondescript brown. Her broad hands were red, the skin cracked open in places, and she ran them down the skirts of her plain calico dress in a gesture of frustration.

"You the one that hung up them signs around the fort?"

Lily looked at the caller for a moment before nodding and going on with getting her fire started. She said nothing, waiting for the woman to state her business.

"I'm Velvet Hughes," she finally said, rubbing her right hand against her skirt once more before offering it in a stiff and patently unfriendly greeting.

Lily spared no time to consider the disparities between the woman and her name. It was obvious that this call wasn't social. "My name is Lily Chalmers," she answered, taking the offered hand. It felt swollen and callused.

"I reckon you're new around these parts and don't know the rules," Velvet allowed. "You can't take up in the laundry business if you don't live on Suds Row."

Lily folded her arms. "I hadn't heard that rule."

"You've heard it now."

Lily ran the tip of her tongue over her lips and stood up a little straighter. "Who made this rule?"

"We did," Velvet replied calmly. "We what live down on the Row, I mean. We don't allow nobody to break it, neither."

Lily stood her ground. "I'm afraid it's impossible for me to come and live on Suds Row, since I paid out a good part of my savings to rent this house." She paused and smiled warmly. "But thank you for inviting me."

Velvet's unfortunate complexion reddened. "You don't understand. There ain't no shacks left down there no way. We want you to stop takin' in wash."

Lily made herself take a step closer. It was her policy to do that when she felt like turning tail and running. "Are you threatening me, Velvet Hughes?"

Velvet sighed. "I reckon there will be trouble if you don't take heed," she admitted, and there was a sorrowful expression in her eyes. "Pretty thing like you could have any man you set your cap for. Why would you want any part of what we do?"

Lily knew Velvet wasn't talking about washing trousers and shirts, underwear and stockings. Mingled with the battle-ready challenge she felt was a sense of abject pity. "I've got plans for the money."

The visitor gave an unladylike snort of contempt. She looked Lily over in a way that was patently derisive and said bluntly, "You think you're real smart, don't you, miss? Just a mite better than them what live on the Row. Well, you'd better just watch yourself, 'cause my friends and me, we might see to it that you ain't so pretty no more."

Fear braided itself around Lily's spine, but she kept her back straight and her chin high. She'd dealt with a good many bullies in her life, and she hadn't let one get the better of her yet. She walked past Velvet to the rusty pump and began drawing water for the first batch of wash. "I'm disappointed that you don't want to be friends," she remarked.

Velvet shook her head in amazement as she watched Lily carry the first bucketful of water over to the kettle and pour it in. Lily suspected that, for all her rough talk, Velvet had never really gotten the knack of browbeating people.

She was staring at Lily now. "You're just going to go right on takin' in wash, ain't you?" she marveled. "Here you got a man like the major to look after you, and you want to do this!" She waved her arm in a wild gesture that took in the clotheslines and the big cast-iron wash kettle.

Lily stopped on her way back to the pump for another bucketful of water. For the second time in a day someone had thrown her relationship with Caleb in her face. "What do you mean, I've got the major to look after me?"

A delicate blush pooled beneath the coarse surface of Velvet's skin. Clearly, a trace of modesty lingered in her spirit from earlier, more innocent days. "I think you know," she said, and her light green eyes held a nervous challenge.

Lily fought to hold onto her temper. That was another thing she'd discovered: A person who couldn't control her emotions was at a disadvantage. "I'm not a prostitute," she said evenly, and with dignity. "Furthermore, I refuse to believe that all the women on Suds Row ply such a scurrilous trade. Do you?"

Velvet's eyes widened in shock, as though Lily had flung cold water into her face. Her mouth and throat moved, but no sound came out.

"You'd better go now," Lily said, beginning to work the pump handle again. "I have work to do."

Velvet started to say something, then closed her mouth and stomped angrily out of the yard. Lily finished filling the laundry kettle, added wood to the fire at its base, and tossed Judd Ingram's filthy shirts in to soak.

All day soldiers arrived with dirty clothes to be washed and hopeful glances at Lily's compact, womanly shape. She met them all in the front yard and tactfully set them straight on the nature of her business.

By nightfall, when Sandra came to call carrying a plate covered with a blue and white checkered napkin, Lily was exhausted but filled with the pride of accomplishment. If every day was like this one, she would have the money she needed in no time at all.

Sandra looked around the cottage and shook her head. Lily had to admit it wasn't a prepossessing place, since there was only one room. Except for her bed, which was kitty-corner from the kitchen stove, there was only a table, two chairs, and a bookcase for furniture. The light of twin kerosene lanterns dispelled the dense darkness at the windows.

She smiled and poured coffee into two mugs. It was nice to have company, even if she was too tired to think straight.

Sandra shoved the plate at her when she sat down. "Auntie says you're to eat every bite of this."

Lily removed the checkered napkin gratefully, finding a hearty dinner of fried chicken, corn kernels, and a boiled potato beneath. She got up to fetch a fork, then smoothed the napkin in her lap and began to consume the first real meal she'd had all day. "Thank you."

Sandra was tapping one foot as she sat across the table from Lily, still looking around. "I see you've had a great many customers," she remarked, gesturing toward the pile of clean clothes waiting to be pressed.

Lily nodded, swallowing a bite of chicken. "I'm not sure I can keep up with them all," she confided.

Sandra glanced uncomfortably at the bed. "You don't let them come inside, do you? They're sure to get the wrong idea if you do."

Lily shook her head quickly and felt her cheeks pinken. In truth, she was not thinking about the ideas her customers might get. She was wondering what it would be like to share that narrow bed with Caleb.

"I did have a visit from a Suds Row woman today," she said. "Her name was Velvet, though I must say Burlap would have suited her better."

Sandra leaned forward and waggled one finger. Her lovely pink cotton dress made Lily's old calico look like a washed-out rag. "You be careful of those women, Lily Chalmers. They're tough as men, some of them."

Lily shrugged. "I sensed a certain gentleness in Velvet, despite her appearance and her manner. I don't think she wants the life she has."

"If she didn't want it, why would she do the things she does?" Sandra reasoned in a somewhat testy tone. "You're naïve, Lily."

Lily lowered her fork. "Not everyone is privileged like you are, Sandra. It takes money to live."

Sandra sighed. "So you're still on your bandwagon. You won't be able to change Suds Row, Lily—or those women.

If there's one thing I've learned in my short life, it's that people only change when they want to."

"I can talk to them—try to be their friend."

"Their friend!" Sandra hooted as though Lily had made a joke. "Their *friend?* Lily, you'll be lucky if they don't tar-and-feather you and throw you off one of the parapets. You're a threat to them—you're taking away the two things they value most: their money and their men!"

Lily felt guilty at the thought of taking the money, but she had no designs on the men. "I won't be here long."

Sandra waved one hand at her. "I know, I know. You're only going to wash clothes until you can hire a Pinkerton agent and build your silly cabin. Sometimes I think you're addlepated."

Lily pushed her plate away, though it was still half full, but said nothing.

Sandra was examining her fingernails, her lower lip curved in a practiced pout. "I'm leaving Washington Territory. And when I go, Lily Chalmers, you'll miss me, because whether you believe it or not, I'm your friend."

"You're going away?"

Sandra nodded. "Yes," she said, with a dramatic little sniffle. "It's breaking my heart to see Caleb besotted with another woman." She looked pointedly at Lily. "I can't bear it, so I'm going home to Fox Chapel."

Lily felt duly chagrined, though she couldn't rightly imagine Caleb "besotted" with anyone. He was much too practical-minded for that. "I will miss you," Lily allowed.

Sandra sniffled again, as if to say that was as it should be. "I'll write," she offered.

"I'd like that," Lily answered, hiding a smile behind her coffee cup. She suspected that Sandra wanted to be kept up on Fort Deveraux gossip rather than to nurture a new friendship.

With an earnest sigh Sandra leaned forward in her chair. "Caleb has promised to see me safely back to Tylerville, since he has business there," she blurted out.

Lily wondered how long she'd been waiting to impart that bit of information. Although it aroused a painful jealousy within her, she didn't let on. "That's nice," she said, getting up to test one of the flatirons heating on the stove.

"Well, I'd better be going," Sandra told her, covering the plate with the checked napkin again and starting for the door with it. "I do hope there aren't any privates or corporals lurking outside in the darkness."

Lily rolled her eyes. "If you're scared, Sandra, I'll be happy to walk you back to the Tibbets' house."

Sandra gave her an injured look. "Thank you very much for your concern, but I'll see myself home," she announced. And then she was gone, taking Mrs. Tibbet's plate and napkin with her.

Although Lily longed to fall into bed and sleep, she still had at least two more hours of work to do. Resolutely she spread the first shirt on the table and began to iron it.

The next morning she awakened before dawn. Soldiers came for their laundry, paid Lily generously, and brought more dirty clothes.

At midday, when Lily was scrubbing long underwear, her hair drooping around her face in damp loops, her dress wet with perspiration and wash water, Caleb arrived. He looked crisp and cool in his flawlessly laundered uniform, and he grinned at Lily's dishevelment as he swept off his hat. Under one arm he carried an intriguing blue satin box.

"Hello, Major," Lily said, and she went right on scrubbing.

Caleb approached. "Put down those long johns and look at me, Lily. I've got something to give you."

She glared resentfully at his perfectly pressed coat, thinking of his plans to escort Sandra back to Tylerville. "Who washed your clothes?" she demanded.

"Your competition," he answered easily. "After all, if I brought my laundry to you, it would be like paying you, wouldn't it? And I know how you feel about that."

Lily stiffened at having her own logic thrown back in her

face, then went on scrubbing. The washboard was rubbing her knuckles raw. "Sandra tells me you're going to Tylerville with her," she said, careful not to look at him.

"Lily, if you don't stop that washing and look at me, I swear I'll throw you over my shoulder and carry you inside like a sack of grain."

Because she knew Caleb wouldn't be afraid to carry out his threat she stopped working and glared up at him impatiently.

He laughed. "You're a bad-tempered little creature. Maybe it will take me two months to get you in line rather than one."

Lily's eyes were drawn to the satin box despite valiant efforts to avoid looking at it. "Is that for me?"

"Yes."

She reached for the box, knowing it contained her favorite indulgence: chocolate.

Caleb withheld the temptation. "Not only bad-tempered," he teased, "but greedy, too."

Defiantly, Lily went back to her washing, and Caleb immediately hoisted her off her feet. The breath went out of her when her stomach struck his shoulder, but she managed to kick.

Caleb gave her a hard swat on the bottom and strode through the maze of clotheslines to the back door, where he stood her summarily on the stoop. The expression snapping in his eyes was not one of mischief when he jammed the box of chocolates into her hands.

"I've had enough of this nonsense," he announced. "You're moving in with me. From now on, you're going to be my housekeeper."

Lily's backside was stinging as badly as her cheeks. "I'm staying right here!" she said fiercely.

Caleb remained on the ground, his eyes level with Lily's. "My house is two doors down from the Tibbets'. I'll expect you to be there waiting when I get home. Preferably with dinner on the table."

Lily would have clouted him over the head with the candy box if not for the distinct possibility that her chocolates would be squashed. She whirled, stormed into her little house, slammed the door closed, and drove the bolt home.

"Saturday," Caleb called to her, and she watched through the window as he put his hat back on and strode out of the yard.

Thirty precious minutes passed before Lily had the nerve to go outside again. She comforted herself with a chocolate cream bonbon and the sure conviction that God would strike Caleb Halliday down with a lightning bolt somewhere between Fort Deveraux and Tylerville for his arrogance.

"I tell you, Caleb," Colonel Tibbet expounded with energetic sincerity, "you're going about this all wrong. You've let the woman see that you want her, and that was a tactical error. Puts me in mind of Custer over at the Little Bighorn. Damn it, he let those Indians catch him with his pants down!"

Seated behind his desk, his jacket draped over a nearby chair, Caleb sighed. The colonel was right; he'd tipped his hand. Maybe in the frenzy of lovemaking he'd even told Lily straight out that he loved her—he couldn't be sure. "I wish I could take back that ultimatum I gave her," he said wearily. "Even if Lily wanted to move in with me, her pride wouldn't allow it."

The colonel was leaning against the framework of the window, his arms folded across his chest. He smoothed his white mustache with a thumb and forefinger before replying thoughtfully, "I'd say you're making the wrong offer. A woman like Lily—well, she won't live under your roof unless she has a wedding band on her finger. She wants to be your wife—she just doesn't know it yet."

Caleb chuckled ruefully at that. "I'm not looking for a wife. I want her for a mistress."

Colonel Tibbet spread his hands. Well past sixty, he was still a fine figure of a man. "In that case, you're probably wasting your time. Best thing to do is go on seeing Bianca in Tylerville and forget about Lily."

"I can't forget Lily," Caleb confessed, gazing out the window. "I'm obsessed."

The colonel shook his head. "Then stop paying so much attention to her, at least. Let her wonder just a little about your affections. Women can be perverse creatures, Caleb— give them an advantage and they'll beat you into submission with it."

Caleb couldn't help grinning. "Is that what Gertrude did to you?"

The colonel's smile was fond. "She tried, God bless her, but I woke up to the situation in time to save myself. I put my foot down, let her know who was boss." He paused to take a pipe from his pocket and clamp it between his teeth. "That's what you've got to do with Lily."

Caleb let out a heavy sigh and leaned forward in his chair to riffle through the paperwork on his desk. Always an organized man, he was now hopelessly behind on his reports and evaluations. Because John Tibbet was the best friend he'd ever had, the difference in their ages and ranks notwithstanding, Caleb let his doubts show. "You don't know Lily. She's determined to get along without me. And what if she falls in love with someone else?"

"Can't happen," the colonel answered with certainty. "Lily's already in love with you. She needs to have the fact made plain to her, that's all."

Splaying the fingers of his right hand, Caleb shoved them through his hair. Maybe John knew what he was talking about. And it wasn't as if his own efforts were working. "So you think I ought to ignore her for a while?"

The colonel chuckled and rubbed his hands together with good-natured glee, Father Christmas in a blue uniform. With a nod he said, "You'll have her proposing marriage within the month."

Caleb didn't bother to repeat that he had no intention of

marrying Lily or anyone else. It was getting to the point where he didn't know *what* he wanted.

At the general store Lily couldn't help splurging on the book she'd noticed before: *Typhoon Sally, Queen of the Rodeo.* Business was good, and she was feeling rich.

On her way home with her shopping basket over one arm Lily noticed Caleb walking toward her. She was prepared to snub him and already had her nose in the air when he crossed the road without so much as a smile or a touch to the brim of his hat.

Lily felt uneasy. Hardly more than an hour before the man had ordered her to be waiting in his house when he got home from Tylerville. She quickened her pace as though by walking faster she could distance herself from the disturbing feelings she had for Caleb.

She wouldn't exactly call them love, she reflected. But she surely felt passion—scandalous passion—and she didn't like the idea of Caleb traveling with a woman who frankly admitted she cared for him.

Something prickled at the back of Lily's neck as she approached her small house, which was directly across the street from the schoolhouse. The children were outside playing noisy games in the April sunshine, and Lily smiled at their joy, but her uneasiness deepened as she turned her attention back to the cottage.

Something was very wrong.

She took her purchases in through the front door, glancing around the one-room place and even peeking under the bed before she closed the door. It was when she set the shopping basket on the table and went to the back window that she saw what had happened.

The clotheslines were down; shirts and trousers had been ground into the mud. Her entire morning's work was ruined.

Fury kept Lily from weeping. She opened the cottage's

rear door and stepped out onto the sagging little stoop. Her wash kettle had been overturned, and her soap flakes, carelessly left outside, had been dumped over the wreckage like lumpy snow.

Lily's eyes burned like fire, but she blinked back her tears and bit down hard on her lower lip. Velvet and her bunch had gone a long way toward putting her out of business, but they weren't going to make her cry.

Clutching her skirts in her hands, she waded through the destruction, setting the wash kettle up again—it would take forever to refill it and heat new water—and rescuing the clothes from the dirt. When everything was picked up and the kettle was filled and just beginning to bubble over a new fire, Lily began rehanging her clotheslines. She'd taken time and care to wipe the mud from the lines.

At last the tasks were completed. Lily went inside and heated water then carefully washed her face and hands. She took down her hair, brushed it with a thoroughness born of pure outrage, and pinned it up again.

And then she put a clean apron over her calico dress and set out for Suds Row.

Lily was too angry to be intimidated when she reached the place and was greeted by cold stares from the ragged children and their hard-eyed mothers.

She stopped at one rickety fence and demanded, "Where does Velvet Hughes live, please?"

The woman was leaning over a scrub board and washtub, but she stopped her work to glare at Lily. Her eyes moved over Lily's tidy hair and calico dress with a sort of desolate contempt. "Right there," she answered, gesturing toward the tumbledown shack next door.

"Thank you," Lily said, sweeping up both her chin and her skirts as she approached Velvet's gate.

The latch came off in her hand, and she was still making her way up the dirt path when Velvet herself came out onto the stoop. Her hands were resting on her generous hips, and her eyes were narrowed. "What do you want?" she asked, running the words together as though they were all one.

Lily looked around her and saw that half a dozen other Suds Row women were watching from their dooryards. Then she focused all her attention on Velvet. "You tore my laundry down and stomped it into the dirt," she accused evenly. "I just came here to tell you that it'll take a lot more than a silly prank like that to drive me off."

Velvet started slowly down the steps, her manner calculated to frighten Lily. "I didn't go near your place after we talked," the woman vowed.

Even though Lily knew Velvet would probably best her in an out-and-out fight, since she was nearly twice her size, she was too angry to be afraid. She took another step nearer, just to let Velvet know she wouldn't be browbeaten. "You're a liar."

The laundress made to lunge at Lily, but someone called out, "Velvet, she's the major's woman!"

At that, Velvet stopped where she was.

It was Lily who was stung to fury. "That's not true!" she said, sweeping all those downtrodden, destitute women up in one glance. "I don't belong to any man, and you don't have to, either."

There was a sudden silence, except for the creaking of the sagging screen door on Velvet's shack. Private Ingram appeared in the opening, shirtless and barefoot, his thin brown hair rumpled. "You get in here, woman," he said to Velvet. "Right now."

Velvet cast a defiant glance back at him, but Lily could see that she was weakening. "I never touched your damn laundry," she spat, then she turned and obeyed Private Ingram's summons.

Lily felt vaguely sick to her stomach as she walked away.

Back at home she rewashed and rehung all the laundry, and by the time the clothes were dry enough to press or fold it was stone dark outside.

Lily opened the pretty blue satin box Caleb had given her and took out a chocolate—she and Sandra had consumed the remains of the first box while looking at Mrs. Tibbet's stereoptic pictures. The candy gave her a certain guilty pleasure, and she fixed herself a modest supper and went back to work.

Pressing the shirts and trousers took hours, and it was late when Lily finally set her work aside, got ready for bed, and read a chapter of *Typhoon Sally* to relax her mind.

She was in bed, exhausted and in a state resembling despair, when she finally allowed herself to think of Caleb. She remembered how it was when he'd kissed her, and held her, and taken the tips of her breasts into his mouth. She recalled the weight of him, the way he fit between her legs, the feel of his bare back under her hands.

And even though the stove had gone out, Lily felt warm.

Chapter

❧ 9 ❧

Velvet felt Judd Ingram's eyes following her as she got out of bed that rainy April morning and put on her flannel wrapper. Standing in front of the streaky mirror affixed to the wall, she studied herself, turning first in one direction and then in the other. She wished she was dainty and fair-haired, like the major's Lily, but there was no sense in wanting something that could never be.

She saw Judd's reflection in the mirror, watched as he raised himself to sit with his back against the iron headboard. He took a cheroot and a match from the rickety little table beside the bed and began to smoke.

The smirk on his face made Velvet turn to face him directly. "What are you grinnin' at?" she wanted to know.

He rested one hand on his narrow, almost concave chest and drew deeply on the smoke of the cheroot before answering. "You," he replied. "And all them big ideas spinnin' in your head right now. You're wastin' your time thinkin' you don't need me and the money I give you."

Velvet supposed she wouldn't have been so angry if she hadn't been coming to the same conclusion. She went to the wall and laid a hand to her one good dress, a black and white checkered percale, feeling pride in its starchy freshness. Maybe she was wasting her time, just like Judd said, but she knew she had to do something to make her life better. If there was a way off of Suds Row, a way out from under Judd Ingram's thumb, she wanted to find it.

He threw back the covers, annoyed at her silence. "You listening to me, woman?"

"Yes, Judd, I'm listenin'," Velvet replied. She was afraid of him when he got that look in his eye.

Judd strode across the room and took a painful grip on her arm, whirling her around to face him. "You ain't sweet, pretty little Lily," he reminded her, shaking a finger in front of her nose, "and folks ain't gonna fall all over themselves to look after you like they do for her. You listen to her, you let her get your hopes up that things is gonna be better, and you're in for a bad fall."

Velvet bit down on her lower lip, too scared to fight Judd, willing him to let her go.

His eyes narrowed as he bent closer to her, and he spoke through his teeth, his breath foul from last night's whiskey. "I ain't through with you yet," he rasped out, and then he dragged Velvet back to the bed and flung her onto the lumpy mattress.

He opened her wrapper, revealing her heavy breasts and her belly and private place.

Velvet closed her eyes and prayed it would be over fast. Judd was never a tender lover, but when he got in a mood like he was in now, he liked to be rough.

Sometimes it helped, Velvet had learned, if she just stared up at the ceiling and thought of something else. She remembered coming west on the wagon train with her pa and her brother Eldon. Except for the awful way she'd missed Hank, those had been good times, though surely not easy ones.

Then the cholera had taken Eldon, and Pa had drowned crossing the Snake River. . . .

Judd was nearly through; she could tell by his rapid breathing and the quick, fevered movements of his hips. He was thin, but his lean muscles were sinewy, like little corded bands of steel, and Velvet ran her hands up and down his back, urging him on.

When he stiffened in release he flung his head back and cried, "Lily—oh, God—Lily—"

Velvet wasn't surprised that he was pretending she was someone else, but a cold shiver rolled just beneath the surface of her skin. In the next few moments she had to carry on like she was pleasured, because Judd would slap her if she didn't.

She arched her back and, taking a page from Judd's book, made him into Hank in her mind. To her surprise, her body suddenly tensed in involuntary elation, and the hoarse cries coming from her throat were real.

Judd laughed breathlessly, moving down just far enough to roll one of Velvet's nipples between his teeth. "See there?" he gasped out. "You do need me."

Yes, Hank, Velvet answered from the place within her where her spirit hid. Yes, I need you.

He circled the nipple with the tip of his tongue, and Velvet moaned, her hips already seeking new contact with his.

"Say it," Judd ordered.

"I need you," Velvet whispered as the rain battered at the thin, leaky roof above. Minutes later the sound was drowned out by her moans of release.

The rain was merely a dull drizzle as Lily hurried through the streets toward the Tibbet house, where there was to be a going-away party for Sandra. She devoutly hoped Caleb wouldn't attend and, at the same time, prayed that he would.

Lily pulled her tattered corduroy cloak more tightly

around her as a gust of wind blew a chilling mist toward her. She recalled that she had only a little wood left for the stove and wondered where she would get more, since the nearest trees were several miles from the fort. Even if she managed to chop one down, she couldn't imagine how she'd ever get it back home.

Lamplight glowed in the windows of the Tibbet house, since it was a gloomy day, and Lily put her worries out of her mind as she opened the gate and hurried up the walk.

She knocked at the door and was admitted by Corporal Pierce, the good-looking, dark-haired young man who worked in Colonel Tibbet's office and had leave time coming up soon.

He smiled broadly and ran one hand over his slicked-back hair. "Hello, Miss Lily," he said, and he made a great business out of helping Lily off with her cloak, as if she hadn't removed it on her own a thousand times. "Would you like some punch and cake?"

Lily cast a surreptitious glance around the crowded parlor and saw Caleb standing on the far side of the room, a cup of punch in his hand, speaking with Sandra's friend, Lieutenant Costner. He met Lily's look, as quick as it was, but there was time enough for her to see the lack of interest in his eyes.

"Yes, please," she said brightly to Corporal Pierce, who was still standing attentively at her side. "Punch and cake would be very nice, thank you."

While the corporal hurried off to the refreshment table Lily scanned the room again, this time slowly, her gaze deliberately skirting Caleb. Despite her cool demeanor, however, she felt bruised.

Just a day before he'd brought her candy and demanded that she come and live with him. Now he didn't seem aware of her existence.

"My first name is Wilbur, ma'am," the corporal confided, returning with a plate of cake and a cup brimming with pink punch. Lily spotted a nearby chair and wended her way

144

toward it. Reaching her destination, she sat down, balancing her cake plate on her knees, and gazed up at her new friend with her most devastating smile.

"Wilbur," she echoed, saying the name as though it were somehow Olympian and anyone bearing it would surely have wings upon his feet.

Wilbur crouched beside her. "I know those rumors aren't true," he said earnestly. "About your washing business, I mean."

Lily might have choked on her first bite of cake if she hadn't seen out of the corner of her eye that Caleb was watching her. She set her punch on the figurine-cluttered table beside her chair and patted Wilbur's cheek affectionately. "Thank you, Wilbur," she said softly.

The young man fairly beamed. "I'll bring my wash over tomorrow, if that's all right with you."

Lily risked a glance at Caleb and found that he was concentrating on a conversation with a plump blond woman wearing a blue sateen dress. "That'll be fine," she answered distractedly. "Of course, if it's raining again, everything will take longer."

Before Wilbur could make a response Gertrude Tibbet appeared. Lily thought she looked very nice in a gray silk frock with a matching jacket, and her blue eyes were bright with laughter. "Well, hello, Lily. I'm so glad you could spare a few hours from your laundry enterprise to come to our party."

Seeing Mrs. Tibbet, Lily recalled an idea that had been brewing in the back of her mind since her first encounter with the Suds Row woman. She returned her hostess's smile. "It was kind of you to invite me."

Mrs. Tibbet put one hand to her forehead. "I don't begin to know how I'll get everything back to normal, though. It will take hours just to wash the dishes."

The older woman already looked tired; she'd probably spent much of the day preparing for the party. Sandra had been around to assist, of course, but there was no telling how much help *she* would be. "I'll be happy to stay and lend a hand," Lily offered. "There is something—or I should say someone—I'd like to talk to you about, however."

Mrs. Tibbet looked pleased. "Caleb?" she asked, causing Lily to wince and Corporal Pierce to frown.

Lily was quick to dispel that notion. "No. I have a—a friend who might want a housekeeping position," she announced. Considering that she hadn't raised the subject to Velvet Hughes, it was a rash statement, but Lily didn't care.

The older woman's face shone with interest and relief. "Oh, Lily—you must send her to see me at once."

"I will," Lily promised, wondering what she was going to do if Velvet had no interest in the position.

Mrs. Tibbet said a few more words and then moved on. A sidelong glimpse of Caleb showed that he was talking to Sandra now, and his eyes were full of that special laughter. Lily felt her throat go tight and sore.

"Are you all right?" Wilbur asked, sounding really concerned.

Lily recovered herself and smiled at her companion. "I wonder if you'd see fit to walk me down to Suds Row, Wilbur," she said quietly. "There's someone I want to see."

Wilbur's eyebrows knitted together for a moment. "Suds Row?" he echoed.

Lily nodded, swallowing another bite of cake.

"I reckon you mean to go there even if I don't escort you," Wilbur said.

Again Lily nodded. "Yes, I do, but I'd rather have your company, Wilbur." She lowered her eyes for a moment. "I'd feel safer that way."

Wilbur rolled gracefully to his feet. "You just say the word when you're ready to leave, Miss Lily, and I'll take care of everything after that."

Lily reached out and squeezed his hand. She genuinely liked Wilbur, and she knew she'd have to be careful not to give him the wrong impression. Leading him on was the furthest thing from her mind, but she did want Caleb to see her leaving the party on the arm of another gentleman.

The more scandalous the major's thoughts on that subject, she reasoned, the better.

There was another knock at the door, and Wilbur hurried off to answer. While he was engaged Lily finished her cake and punch and carried the dishes into the kitchen.

Sandra was there, dressed in peacock blue, her face buried in a dish towel as she sobbed at the top of her lungs.

"What is it, Sandra?" Lily asked, setting her dishes in the heaping sink so she could put an arm around Sandra's shoulders.

"I don't want to go!" Sandra wailed.

Lily's voice was gentle, reasonable. "Then don't."

Sandra lowered the dish towel with shaking hands. "I've fallen in love," she confided tragically. Her beautiful violet eyes were red-rimmed and puffy, and the end of her nose was a glowing pink. She indulged in an inelegant sniffle.

"Caleb?" Lily asked with a sinking heart.

But Sandra shook her head. "Not at all. It's Lieutenant Costner I love, and he's asked me to marry him."

"Then what is the problem?" Lily asked, annoyed to feel so relieved.

"Uncle John won't give us his blessing. He says I'm impulsive, that I haven't thought this through."

Lily believed the colonel was probably right, but she still felt sorry for Sandra. "You'll just stay, then. In time your uncle will know your feelings for the lieutenant are real."

Sandra dabbed at her eyes with the dish towel. "There may not be any time, Lily," she said miserably. "I think I'm expecting."

Lily was shocked, but she did a good job of hiding the fact. She said nothing, waiting for Sandra to go on.

"The night of the ball Robert and I got carried away. We slipped away to his room in the barracks, and—and—" Sandra began to cry again, the sound muffled by the dish towel as she pressed it to her face once more.

"Sandra, that was only a few days ago," Lily reasoned. "How could you possibly know—"

"I was supposed to get the curse," Sandra broke in in a desolate whisper, "and I didn't. It's always just as regular as can be!"

Lily sighed. "Perhaps you'd better tell your aunt," she said, but Sandra shook her head wildly at the idea.

"I can't—not after what happened before."

"I don't think you have any choice."

"You do it—you tell them for me!" Sandra cried. "They both like you. They'd understand if you explained it."

But Lily shook her head. "It's your place to tell them, Sandra, not mine. But I will send Mrs. Tibbet in to see you if you'd like."

Sandra drew a deep, quivering breath, then nodded in reckless decision. "All right," she snuffled.

Lily went out, found her hostess, and sent her back to the kitchen. She was just rejoining the party when Wilbur appeared again.

"The rain's let up a little, Miss Lily. Maybe we'd better head for Suds Row right now, if we're going."

Lily nodded her agreement, and before she could even make her excuses Wilbur was back with her cloak. He draped it over her shoulders in a solicitous way.

The weather was still cool, and Lily lifted the hood of her cloak as she and Wilbur moved down the walk to the gate.

"Where are you from originally?" she asked, to make polite conversation.

Wilbur smiled, revealing teeth as fine and white as Caleb's. "Kansas," he replied. "My folks have a farm there."

"Do you miss Kansas?"

He considered, then nodded. "Yes, ma'am, I do. But a man's got to make his own way in the world, and I'm no farmer."

Lily felt a twinge of disappointment at that, even though she hadn't consciously considered Wilbur as a life partner.

"That's what I want to be more than anything," she said. "A farmer."

It was plain that Wilbur was disappointed, too. "A farmer? You, Miss Lily?"

She nodded. "I came west on an orphan train," she explained. "Ever since then I've wanted a place all my own. I plan to raise my own crops and sleep under my own roof and not be accountable to anybody."

Wilbur's stride was easy, his arms swinging at his sides, but his expression was troubled. "I don't reckon you're the type of woman that changes her mind very often, are you?"

Lily shook her head. "No, Wilbur. I'm not."

He turned a bright smile on her. "Well, I was planning on courting you. But I guess we can be friends. That's probably easier than courting anyway, and it won't make my palms sweat."

Lily laughed and linked her arm through Wilbur's. "We can be the best of friends," she said.

Caleb stood on the Tibbet porch, gazing after Lily through the thin veil of rain sliding down from the porch roof. He'd been employing the tactics the colonel had recommended, and he'd liked the results—until he'd noticed Lily leaving the house with Corporal Pierce.

When he'd seen her take that green kid's arm and look up at him as though he'd just cured all the ills of humanity in a single sentence, Caleb had wanted to vault over the porch railing and run after them, shouting protests like a fool. He ached, knowing Lily wouldn't have made such a familiar gesture with him, even after all they'd been to each other.

Saddened, Caleb turned and opened the door to go inside. He almost collided with Gertrude Tibbet.

"There you are," she said somewhat breathlessly, fanning herself. "Mercy, but it's warm in there, with all those people crowded in like pickles in a crock."

Caleb smiled and stepped back, knowing from long experience that Gertrude wanted to talk.

"Where's Lily?" she asked, still fanning herself with one hand as she sat down on the porch swing.

Caleb leaned against a pillar, his arms folded across his chest, his back to the disappearing figures of Lily and her friend. He moved his shoulders in a shrug. "How would I know?"

"I'd guess you know *exactly,* Caleb Halliday."

He chuckled ruefully. "Guilty," he said. "I just saw her leave with Corporal Pierce."

Gertrude frowned for a moment, but then the disturbing thought, whatever it was, moved on, and her face was all mischief and amusement. "She was watching you, you know. Stealing glances whenever she thought you weren't looking."

The knowledge made Caleb feel better. "What was it you wanted to talk to me about?" he prodded.

Gertrude sighed. "It seems Sandra isn't going back to Fox Chapel after all. She and Robert Costner are in love."

"I see," Caleb said noncommittally. He wished Sandra every happiness, but he had little confidence in her judgment; the woman didn't know her own mind.

"She believes she may be pregnant."

Caleb refrained from commenting.

"Considering what happened last time, I have to take into account the distressing possibility that she's right. She wants to stay, Caleb, and marry Robert."

Had they been discussing anyone else, Caleb might have suggested that marriage could settle a woman down. Since they were talking about Sandra, he said nothing of the kind. "Is Costner the father?"

Gertrude smoothed her skirts, modestly lowering her eyes at the delicacy of the subject. "Yes, according to Sandra, he is."

Caleb felt sorry for the young lieutenant because he knew how flighty and irresponsible Sandra could be. "I wish them all the best," he said with resignation.

"That's kind of you, keeping in mind all that's gone before. I'm afraid I still need a favor, though."

"What?" Caleb asked, and his voice sounded wary even though there were few things he would refuse this woman.

"Sandra decided, during our discussion, to go home to Fox Chapel for the wedding. Lieutenant Costner will join her there in a few weeks, when he has completed his tour of duty. I'd like you to see my niece safely to the train in Spokane."

Even though Caleb dreaded the prospect, he agreed readily. And he had other reasons for cooperating besides his fondness for Gertrude Tibbet. For one thing, in Spokane he could make arrangements to hire the Pinkerton agency to find Lily's sisters.

"Lily's brother lives in Spokane, you know," Gertrude said in an offhand tone.

Lily had mentioned her adopted brother to Caleb, but he couldn't remember the man's name. "Any idea what he's called?"

Gertrude smiled as though some cherished secret suspicion had been confirmed. "No, but if you asked Lily, I'm sure she'd tell you."

Caleb had his doubts that Lily would even speak to him, but he nodded an acknowledgment anyway, his gaze straying down the street in the hope of seeing her return.

Gertrude chuckled. "It's wonderful to see you falling in love at last, Caleb. I was beginning to think I'd never dance at your wedding."

Caleb went to the porch swing and sat down beside her, taking her hand in his and giving her knuckles a brief kiss. He didn't know if he was in love, but he wasn't about to spoil Gertrude's delight. "If I can't have you," he teased, "I'll have to settle."

"She'll still be giving you trouble when you're ninety, you know. Lily's exactly what you need, Caleb. She'll try your patience many a time, but she'll also bring out the best that's in you. And she'll give you fine, handsome children."

Caleb allowed himself to imagine Lily bearing him a child and felt his groin tighten. "Are you suggesting that I court her?" he asked in a light voice, to cover the sweet despair he felt.

"I know what John told you," Gertrude answered, "and to a great degree I think he's right. Lily's the kind of person that's got to be challenged; she doesn't believe that anything worthwhile comes easily."

Caleb got up and walked to the porch railing again, bracing his hands on the whitewashed wood, searching the distance for Lily, but there was no sign of her. "I think she may drive me crazy before too long," he said.

Gertrude laughed, and the swing hinges creaked. She came and patted him gently on the back. "That's a sure sign she's the right one," she said. And then she went back inside to the party.

Caleb remained outside. He had an idea that, for him, the party was over.

When Lily and Wilbur reached Velvet's ramshackle house on Suds Row Judd Ingram wasn't in evidence.

Lily was mightily relieved about that. "May we come in?" she asked as Velvet gazed at her callers in bewilderment through the rusted, torn screen door.

Velvet sighed and stepped back. She was wearing a wrapper, and there was a high flush to her face. "Lord knows why you'd want to," she muttered.

"I've come to talk to you about another kind of work," Lily ventured bravely, looking around the one-room cottage. Although it was shabby, and in such poor repair that it looked as if it might fall over, the place was spotlessly clean.

"What kind of work?" Velvet asked, tightening the belt of her worn wrapper and eyeing Lily with suspicious hope.

"Housekeeping. Mrs. Tibbet is badly in need of someone to clean for her, and cook meals—"

Velvet let out a guffaw of rude laughter. "Mrs. Tibbet, is it? The wife of the colonel himself? She wouldn't let nobody like me come to her back door, let alone dust the gewgaws in her fancy parlor!"

"You won't know that until you talk with her, will you?" Lily challenged, folding her arms and jutting out her chin. Wilbur stood uneasily at her side, and it occurred to Lily that he was probably no stranger to this place.

"Can you get me a in-tro-duction, Miss Snooty Shoes?" Velvet countered.

"Yes, I can, as a matter of fact. That's why I'm here—to ask you to come back with me right now. Mrs. Tibbet's having a party, and there's going to be a mess to clean up afterwards. This is your chance to show her what you can do."

At last a hopeful look came over Velvet's face. She narrowed her eyes at Lily. "Is this a trick?"

Lily began to tap one foot in impatience. "It would serve you right if it was, after what you did to my wash, but the fact of the matter is that Mrs. Tibbet has need of a housekeeper. Someone she can count on."

"Wait outside, the both of you, while I put on some clothes," Velvet grumbled, waving Lily and Wilbur toward the porch.

They went to stand on the steps. The rain was coming down hard again, and Lily looked forward to going home to her little place. She'd have a light supper, then heat water for a nice hot bath. And after the bath she'd read more about Typhoon Sally.

"I'm ready," Velvet announced gruffly, appearing on the porch in a neatly pressed black and white dress and carrying an umbrella with one bent spoke. "This better not be no joke, little Miss Lily, because if it is, I'll sell you to the first Indian that comes down the road."

Lily stifled a smile at that and squeezed Wilbur's arm, since he was glowering at Velvet. "It's all right," she said softly. "She doesn't mean any harm."

"We'll see about that," put in Velvet, who evidently had very good hearing.

They reached the Tibbet house just as the drizzle became a downpour and they dashed in through the back door.

Mrs. Tibbet was there, frantically trying to wash up a few dishes so that newly arrived guests could be served.

Velvet edged the older woman away from the sink with a motion of her broad hips. "I'll take care of that, missus," she said.

Mrs. Tibbet stared at Velvet, and then at Lily. "Who is this?" she demanded. She sounded stern, but there was a note of hope in her voice.

"May I present Miss Velvet Hughes," Lily answered, tying an apron around her waist and reaching for a dish towel even as Velvet brought the hot water kettle from the stove. "She'd like to be your new housekeeper."

"I can speak for myself," Velvet said, blushing and avoiding Mrs. Tibbet's gaze. "It's true I want a job, ma'am."

"You may work for me today," Mrs. Tibbet said. "We'll discuss the future after all these people have gone and I've had a chance to put up my feet and take a sip of tea."

"Here, soldier," Velvet said gruffly, thrusting a bucket into Wilbur's hands. "Go get us some water."

Wilbur started to shove the bucket back at Velvet, but after a glance at Lily he went to the pump in the backyard and began working the lever.

"Here, now," Mrs. Tibbet protested as Lily started drying and putting away the dishes her hostess had managed to wash. "You're a guest in this house."

Lily smiled and continued to work. "You wouldn't take away the first real chance I've had to repay you for all your kindness, would you?"

Mrs. Tibbet was about to protest, but then she saw that it was no good. She left the kitchen to entertain her guests, Wilbur went back outside for another bucket of well water, and Lily set to work. Beside her Velvet hummed a little tune as she scrubbed dainty crystal dessert plates.

Chapter
❧ 10 ❧

Good luck," Lily said to Velvet when the last dish was washed and they were alone in the kitchen. Wilbur had gone to the barracks, and they could hear the final guests saying their farewells to the Tibbets.

Velvet looked panic-stricken, standing there in her best dress, her hands dripping soapy water. "You're not going to leave me to talk to her all alone, are you?"

"Yes," Lily replied firmly, raising both hands to smooth back her steam-dampened hair. "You're perfectly capable of winning the position on your own." With that, she took her cloak from the peg beside the back door, draped it over her shoulders, lifted the hood, and tied the strings under her chin.

She was opening the door when Velvet stopped her with a hoarse "Lily?"

Lily stopped and looked back over one shoulder. "Yes?"

"Thank you."

Lily smiled. "You're welcome, Velvet."

It was very dark, except for pools of light from the street lamps, and Lily hurried along the sidewalk, anxious to get home. When she arrived at her tiny house smoke was curling from the chimney and the windows glowed golden.

Lily went up and stood in the empty flower bed to peer in through the glass, and she was incensed to see Caleb sitting at the table, smoking a pipe as if he owned the place.

She shoved open the door and stormed inside to demand, "What are you doing here, Caleb Halliday?"

He gave her a distant, noncommittal glance. "You were almost out of firewood," he said, "so I brought you some from my place. I'll have more delivered in a few days."

"Couldn't you have told me that without walking into my house and making yourself at home?"

The insolent grin she expected did not curve Caleb's lips. He only sighed and drew once on his pipe before saying, "April evenings can be cold. I wanted to make sure you were warm, that's all."

Lily felt foolish, and she was strangely disappointed in Caleb's reaction. "Well, I don't like smoking in my house," she snapped.

"When you get a house that belongs to you, and not the army, I guess you'll be able to dictate things like that," Caleb responded evenly. He sounded abjectly bored. "Sit down, Lily. We have some things to talk about."

Too weary to argue, Lily took off her cloak and sat, her chin propped in her hands.

"Have you had your supper?"

"I'm not a child, Caleb. I'll eat when I'm hungry."

His powerful shoulders rose in a shrug, and he got up to help himself to coffee from the pot on Lily's stove with not so much as a by-your-leave. "Fine. Tell me about your brother."

Lily narrowed her eyes as Caleb sat down again, coffee mug in hand. Not only was the man presumptuous, he was thoughtless, too. It wouldn't have hurt him to pour a cup for his hostess. "His name is Rupert Sommers, and he's a schoolteacher," she said wearily.

"And your sisters?"

Lily got up and went to the stove for coffee of her own, mostly in order to hide her reaction to the question. On nights like this, when she was tired and a little discouraged, it seemed she'd never find them. "I've told you about them. What more do you want to know?"

"I'm just generally curious," Caleb replied. "Indulge me."

"Their names are Caroline and Emma. Caroline is the eldest—she'd be twenty-one by now. She has dark hair and brown eyes. Emma is twenty, and her hair is the color of copper and gold mixed together. Her eyes are blue."

"Is that all you know about them?"

"I haven't seen them in thirteen years, Caleb." Lily came back to the table holding her coffee mug in both hands. "We used to sing together," she recalled wistfully as she sat down again. The words of the special song trailed through her mind.

Three flowers bloomed in the meadow . . . heads bent in sweet repose . . . the daisy, the lily, and the rose . . .

"Emma had the truest voice," she said aloud. "And Caroline liked to boss everybody around—especially me."

For the first time Caleb spared a slight grin. "That's natural, since you're the youngest."

Lily heard Caroline's voice in her mind, husky and brisk. *Hurry up and button your shoes, Lily-dilly . . . don't cry, everything will be all right, I promise . . . when I get big I'm going to be rich and buy you the prettiest dresses in the world . . . .* "Do you have brothers and sisters?"

The expression in Caleb's eyes was one of profound sorrow, though he quickly disguised it. "I have an older brother, Joss, and a younger sister, Abigail."

"Do they live in Pennsylvania—in Fox Chapel?"

Caleb nodded remotely, then countered with a question

of his own. "You and Emma and Caroline all had the same father?"

That seemed rather personal, but Lily was too weary to spar with Caleb. She just wanted her supper and a bath. "I don't know," she said honestly, because the shame had worn off a long time ago. "But we all went by the same last name."

Caleb shoved back his chair and stood. "Sandra and I have to get an early start tomorrow," he said lightly. There was still that strange distance about him, as though he'd never held Lily in his arms, never moved inside her in unrestrained passion.

She was relieved, but she was also hurt. A woman's virtue was a precious thing, and she'd given it to him. Now he seemed to have no more than the most superficial interest in her. "Good night, Caleb," she said as he went to the door.

He didn't even meet her eyes directly, much less kiss her. "Good night," he answered, and Lily knew from his tone that his mind had gone on without her, like a train she'd just missed.

Lily told herself it was just as well that Caleb's ardor had cooled, since she had no intention of marrying him anyway. She got the bucket from behind the stove. The water for her bath might as well be heating while she made herself supper.

After she'd had her potato and two thick slices of bacon Lily fetched the largest wash kettle from its peg by the back stoop and set it in the middle of the floor. Soon steam was rolling up as she poured pot after pot of hot water into it.

Because she had only thin calico curtains to cover the windows, Lily blew out all the lanterns but one before taking off her clothes and stepping into the tub. She was standing there, naked as a Greek statue, when the door suddenly opened and a gust of cool night air raised goosebumps all over her body.

"I forgot my hat," Caleb announced flatly, but his amber eyes burned as they moved over Lily's naked form.

She covered both breasts with her arms and lifted one thigh in an attempt to hide herself. She was so angry that for a long moment she just stood there, staring and shivering. Then she snapped, "Get out."

"You should lock the doors at night, Lily," Caleb reasoned, collecting his hat from the peg beside the door. "I could have been a client."

Lily was seething. "Believe me," she ground out, "I'll lock it the moment you step outside."

Caleb chuckled and walked around behind Lily for another perspective. She turned, of course, but she wasn't quick enough.

She watched in helpless fury as he tossed his hat onto the table and raised his hands to his hips. "You know, Lily," he remarked easily, "if you don't get on with that bath of yours, the water's going to get cold."

"I'd be happy to finish my bath," Lily hissed, "if only you'd leave!"

He laughed, then caught her suddenly around the waist with his hands. He raised her out of the water, and she was trapped against his chest. "I want a good-bye kiss first," he said.

"You'll be lucky if I don't bite off your nose!" Lily spat. She prayed no one was passing by the window and seeing her naked body silhouetted against Caleb's frame.

"Will I?" He carried her across the room and tossed her onto the bed.

Before Lily could get up he was stretched out beside her, his hand making a tantalizing circle on her bare stomach. She whimpered and turned her head to one side, searching inside herself for the power to resist him and finding nothing there but yearnings of the most primitive kind. He took advantage of her motion to trail his lips along the length of her neck.

"Tell me to go away, Lily," he challenged in a velvet whisper. "Tell me you don't want me, and I'll leave."

Lily moaned and dragged in a gasping breath when he left her neck suddenly and closed his lips over a distended nipple. Sweet fire raged through her as Caleb reached down to part her legs with his hand.

"What's the matter, Lily?" he asked between greedy forays at her breast. "Could it be that you have even more passion than pride? Remarkable." His hand caressed her until she was warm and wet and twisting.

He stopped her by thrusting his fingers deep inside, and she arched her back and uttered his name in a low, lusty cry.

"Take me," she whispered, writhing as he ministered to her with a gentle ferocity that singed her very soul. "Oh, Caleb, please . . ."

He reached out to turn down the wick on the last lamp, then quickly removed his clothes. When he stretched out over Lily he raised her hands above her head and closed her fingers over the iron bars of the bedstead.

She held on tighter and tighter as he slid down her body, pausing here and there to kiss, to suckle, to caress. She was thrashing from side to side like a wild creature, entrapped, by the time he caught her hips between his commanding hands and forced her to lie still for his entrance.

Her palms perspired, making her grip on the bedstead tenuous, and she tilted back her head in ecstasy as he slowly filled her with himself. Instinct caused her to bend her knees so that she could take more of him.

Lily could tell by the quivering in Caleb's long, muscular body that he was barely able to control himself, and she wanted to push him over the edge. Still holding onto the bars above her head, Lily raised her hips in a quick upward thrust, and the motion dragged a fevered groan from him.

The bedsprings creaked as he drove into her once, twice, a third time, and Lily bit down on her lower lip to keep from shouting her desires and needs for everyone in the fort to hear.

With each joyous collision of their bodies Lily became more and more excited. When the friction became too sweet and too fiery to be borne any longer, Caleb caught her cries in his mouth and sent his own back to her.

In one ferocious moment his forceful body tensed, and his groan echoed through Lily to curl her toes.

For a long time they lay still together, naked, gilded by the strained moonlight pouring in through the curtains. Then Caleb got up without a word and put his clothes back on.

Lily pulled the quilt over her and rolled to one side so that her back was to him. Now that her passion had been appeased, her pride was back in force, and it was painfully bruised.

She heard the clank of metal against metal, then felt a cold rush of air as Caleb opened the back door and went out. She knew he'd gone to the pump for more water.

Lily didn't move until much later, when he crossed the room to swat her lightly on her quilt-covered bottom. "Your bath water is hot again," he said quietly. "Lock the door when I go."

Lily turned to look up at him. "Caleb—"

He laid an index finger to her lips to silence her. "There's been enough nonsense," he told her matter-of-factly. "I'll be away for a day or so. When I get back I want to find you living in my house, where you belong."

Before Lily could recover enough to respond, he was gone.

She immediately dashed across the room and drove the bolt home, though it struck her, even then, that it was a little like locking the barn door after the horse had gotten away.

Without bothering to light any lamps Lily found the steaming tub in the darkness and sank into it. She could wash away the scent of Caleb, she knew, and the traces of his passion. But the need of him was a pounding ache deep inside her, where she couldn't reach.

She took a long, thorough bath, then dried herself off and put on a prim flannel nightgown. If it hadn't been for the soft glow of satisfaction within her she might have been able to pretend that Caleb Halliday had never existed.

161

In bed Lily pulled the covers up to her chin and cried, damning Caleb with everything that was in her and, at the same time, hurting because he'd left her to sleep alone.

First thing the next morning Velvet arrived at Lily's door wearing her good percale dress again and carrying a single tattered suitcase. "I'm movin' in with the Tibbets this mornin'," she told Lily, with as much exuberance as if they'd been friends forever. "And I've got you to thank for it!"

Lily, who couldn't do wash because the weather was even worse than it had been the day before, was writing another letter asking for information about her sisters. "Nonsense," she replied. "You're a good worker, and Mrs. Tibbet needed a housekeeper, so you got the job. It wasn't anybody's doing but your own."

Velvet set her suitcase down and smoothed her skirts. "Do I look all right?"

Lily nodded. "I've got some coffee made, if you'd like a cup."

But Velvet shook her head. "No time. I don't want to be late."

Lily felt disappointed, since company was especially nice on a rainy day. "I imagine you'll have a room of your own at the Tibbets'," she said.

Velvet nodded proudly. "It's got the prettiest lace curtains, and those folks have a bathtub and a commode right inside the house."

Lily smiled. "Impressive, all right." Her expression sobered. "What about Judd?"

"I don't want no more truck with the likes of him," Velvet vowed with an angry motion of one hand. "And I figure he'll leave me alone, since he's scared of the colonel."

Lily had a feeling Judd might not be that easily intimidated, but she didn't want to spoil Velvet's good cheer, so she just nodded.

Velvet took up her suitcase and opened the door to go. "You watch out for Judd," she warned earnestly. "He can't be trusted nohow."

Lily promised to be careful, and for good measure she left the table and locked the door as soon as Velvet had gone. Standing at the window watching her new friend hurry down the walk, Lily was possessed of a strange loneliness, a yearning for things she didn't have, people she didn't know, and places she'd never seen.

Turning back to the table, she finished the first letter. After consulting her geography book she sighed and began another.

"I know what I'm doing, Caleb Halliday," Sandra insisted, clutching the edges of the buggy seat as the rig jostled over rain-rutted roads.

Caleb favored her with a sidelong look. "I hope so," he answered. "You've been able to get by with one failed marriage, but two would put you on all the wrong lists."

Sandra let go of the buggy seat and tugged at one of her gloves. Caleb knew the gesture was born of habit, not necessity. "I don't need any lectures from you," she said. "You aren't my husband anymore."

"I never was," Caleb pointed out with a shrug.

Sandra settled herself again and made an obvious search of her mind for something to talk about. Then she brightened. "I'll be seeing Joss and Abigail soon. Is there anything you want me to tell them?"

Caleb stiffened on the seat and quickened the horse's pace, even though he knew it was moving fast enough. He didn't look at Sandra. "No."

He felt a small hand come to rest on his arm. "Caleb . . ."

He forced himself to relax. "All right. Tell Abigail I miss her—and I liked the socks she knitted for me last Christmas."

Sandra's sigh was on the dramatic side. "Honestly, Caleb, you can be such a curmudgeon. What will it take to make you go home—a family funeral?"

Caleb glared at Sandra, purposely trying to intimidate her. He didn't like talking about home, or even thinking about it. But there was no ignoring the fact that the war had split the Halliday family like a piece of dry firewood, and there would be no mending it.

"The war's over," Sandra pressed softly, "and your side won. Why can't you go back and shake your brother's hand and put the whole thing behind you?"

"You don't understand," Caleb bit out, and this time he succeeded in forcing Sandra to subside a little.

"I should think you'd want them all to meet Lily," she muttered, gazing out at the land with its rolling prairies and distant fringes of pine trees.

The mention of Lily reminded him of the night before, when he'd interrupted her bath, and Caleb smiled. "Lily's got no desire to meet my family," he said. "In fact, she doesn't want anything to do with me or mine."

Sandra looked up at him from beneath dark, dense lashes. "Watch out for her, Caleb. If the men of Fort Deveraux have the wrong idea about Lily, so do the women—and they'll tear her apart if they get the chance."

Caleb frowned. "What are you saying?"

"It isn't just those bawds down on Suds Row that Lily has to look out for. Did it escape your notice that the 'good' women at my party snubbed her in that ever-so-gracious way they have? They don't like her, Caleb, and they won't miss an opportunity to let her know it."

"Gertrude likes Lily," Caleb maintained.

"That will take her only so far. She's prettier by half than any girl on the post, and now she's got that infernal laundry business going. Lily's proud, Caleb, and that's her weakness. They'll relegate her to Suds Row if they can."

Caleb resisted an urge to go back to Fort Deveraux, snatch Lily up, and take her with him to Spokane. If she was at his side, no one would hurt her—he'd see to that. "Women," he muttered furiously.

Sandra patted his arm in silent sympathy.

When Lily reached the general store with her letters in hand to mail, she got a surprise. There was an envelope waiting for her, forwarded many times. It bore a Chicago return address, and the handwriting was vaguely familiar to Lily.

Her heart lurched. The letter was from Caroline . . . or Emma . . . it *had* to be. Fingers trembling, she tore open the envelope.

A piece of paper wafted to the ground, and Sergeant Killoran, the storekeeper-postmaster, recovered it for her. "You look a little peaky," he said, ushering her to a chair and pressing her into it. "You'd best sit for a spell."

Lily's throat closed as she read the letter enclosed, and her eyes burned with unshed tears. The message had been written not by either of her sisters, but by Kathleen Chalmers Harrington—her mother.

Shock made it impossible to concentrate on the contents of the letter, and Lily finally let it rest in her lap while she struggled to regain her composure.

"You'd better have a sip of this," Sergeant Killoran said kindly, handing her a cup.

She took one sip of brandy, then another.

"Bad news?" the sergeant asked.

Lily shook her head, then nodded, then tried again to read the letter through. The years had been good to her, Kathleen wrote, but there hadn't been a day when she hadn't regretted sending her children away. She had spent years searching for them after being divinely delivered from her penchant for the demon rum, but until she'd hired a good detective agency she'd had no luck.

Now Kathleen sincerely hoped that "her beautiful girls" would forgive her and come home to her bosom, since she didn't expect to live much longer.

Lily put down the letter and looked at the bit of paper Sergeant Killoran had recovered from the floor for her. It was a bank draft for seven hundred and fifty dollars, and it bore Kathleen's own signature.

Seven hundred and fifty dollars! It was a fortune.

Lily swallowed hard as she gazed disbelievingly at the money. With this she could make all her dreams come true—or, at least, most of them. There was, of course, a conflicting urge to fling the money back in her mother's face.

She took another sip of the brandy and read the letter through again. She remembered life in Chicago, how often she'd been hungry and frightened there. She remembered the soldier swatting Kathleen on the bottom, and the way their two shadows had intertwined behind the canvas curtain. She crumpled her mother's letter into a ball, walked across the room to the stove, and tossed it in with the envelope.

She left the general store in something of a daze, absently fanning herself with the bank draft that would buy lumber and seed and pay the Pinkerton man . . . if she didn't decide to return it.

Lily was nearly home when she realized that if her mother had managed to track *her* down, she might have found Emma and Caroline, too. Kathleen Harrington could be the only person on earth who knew where her sisters were.

Her heart pounding in her throat, Lily whirled and ran back to the store. Without a word to any of the clucking ladies looking at the new display of yard goods she yanked open the stove door. To her relief, the handle was cold. There was no fire within.

She retrieved the letter and envelope.

"I saw her myself," one of the women was saying. "She was sitting right there in that chair, drinking brandy like a man."

Lily didn't even try to identify her critic. She refolded the letter neatly and tucked it back inside the envelope along with the bank draft. Then, with her chin held high, she walked out of the general store and hurried home.

Sitting at her table, she read the letter again and again, for her mind was in such a state of confusion that it was difficult to understand the simple, straightforward words.

Finally she got out her paper and pen and ink again and started a letter of her own.

"Dear Mama," it began.

Lily tore the paper to shreds before the ink was dry. Kathleen Chalmers Harrington might think she could win her youngest daughter back with a few airy lines, but she was wrong.

"My dear Mrs. Harrington," Lily wrote. Finding that she could live with that salutation, she went on writing. She informed her mother that, although she regretted the fact, she couldn't get away from her "interests" in the west. She lifted her head again as she thought about the bank draft. Then, her hand shaking with excitement even though she knew it might be weeks or even months before she received an answer, Lily inquired as to the whereabouts of her sisters.

She recomposed the letter four times before she was satisfied. Then, after hiding the bank draft under the flyleaf of *Typhoon Sally,* she set out for the general store again. Where money was concerned, Lily was torn between pride and practicality.

Sergeant Killoran looked at her with friendly concern before weighing her letter and taking the postage money she held out. "Is everything all right now, Miss Lily?"

For the first time in thirteen years Lily had real hope of finding Emma and Caroline. "Yes," she answered. "Everything is wonderful." She thought of the seven hundred and fifty dollars at home in her book and smiled. Practicality had come out the winner. "Everything is perfect."

On Saturday morning, when the stagecoach arrived, Lily was waiting for it, her ticket in hand, her valise sitting beside her on the wooden sidewalk.

The handsome driver greeted her with a grin and a tip of his dusty hat. "My name is Sam Hargrave, in case I've neglected to offer it," he said.

Lily smiled at his boldness. She was a woman of means now, and that meant she could be generous. "Will we be leaving soon?" she asked.

Sam nodded and settled his hat on his head again. "Yes, ma'am. Soon as I've given these horses some food and water and let them rest for half an hour or so, we'll be on the road."

"Thank you," Lily said. She was turning to go back inside the store to wait when a familiar female voice hailed her. She lifted her yellow bonnet back onto her head so that her eyes were shaded from the bright sunshine, and she saw Gertrude Tibbet approaching.

"You're not leaving us, are you?" Mrs. Tibbet asked, taking both Lily's hands in hers. The worried expression in the woman's eyes warmed Lily's heart.

She shook her head. "I'll be back on next Saturday's stage," she said. "I've got some business to attend to in Spokane, that's all."

Mrs. Tibbet did not look reassured. "Is there anything wrong, my dear? If there is, John and I could surely be of assistance—"

"Everything is fine," Lily broke in gently. "I've come into a small . . . inheritance, and I want to deposit it in a bank and order implements for my farm."

The older woman shook her head from side to side in gentle amusement and squeezed Lily's hands. "Just as long as you're coming back. By the way, my dear, your friend Velvet is working out very well. She's the best housekeeper I've ever had—so eager to please."

Lily was delighted.

"I'm even thinking of taking her home to Fox Chapel with us when John retires. Provided she hasn't married a soldier and deserted us by then, of course."

The mention of Fox Chapel reminded Lily of Caleb, and

the smile faded from her face. She wondered whether he even remembered telling her to wait at his house for his arrival home. It wasn't likely that he did. Anyway, Lily knew she was going to be much better off once she'd forgotten him.

Mrs. Tibbet gave her a farewell kiss on the cheek, said something Lily didn't catch because her mind had been wandering, and then disappeared into the general store. Two ladies Lily recognized from church walked by, and she smiled at them.

They glared at her and swept their skirts aside, and Lily felt as though she'd been slapped. She climbed inside the stagecoach to wait, her cheeks flaming. Her first thought was that they knew about her interludes with Major Halliday, but she dismissed that idea soon enough. It was her laundry business and the presumption that she was a woman of loose principles that had caused them to snub her.

Lily wanted to run after the women and tell them that she'd never taken money from a man for anything but washing his clothes, but her pride wouldn't allow that. She sat very still inside the coach, her handbag in her lap, and waited for Mr. Hargrave to announce that they were leaving.

A heavy woman accompanied by an adolescent girl climbed into the coach and settled across from Lily with such energy that the whole vehicle shook.

"Hello," said the girl, smiling at Lily.

Before Lily could return the greeting the young lady's mother reached out and slapped her daughter soundly on the hand. "Don't you speak to *that woman* again, Alvinia Baker!"

Lily's mouth tightened. It promised to be a long trip.

Chapter
❧ 11 ❧

*E*ven though Caleb had known in the core of his being that Lily would not be waiting in his house when he returned from Spokane, he was disappointed not to find her there. As he walked through the dusty rooms where the furniture looked misshapen under coverings of cloth he imagined the changes Lily's presence would have wrought in the place.

It was cold and dank in that house, but Lily would have had fires burning on both the hearths and in the kitchen stove. The rooms were dark and smelled musty, but if Lily had been there, the good scents of bread baking and of woman would have been in the air, and the windows would have glowed with light.

Caleb sighed. He was getting pretty fanciful these days, he thought to himself. The plain, unvarnished reality was that while Lily might surrender her body to him—her own needs drove her to do that—she had no intention of surrendering her dreams.

After a few more minutes of solitude Caleb left the house he'd moved out of after his parting from Sandra and returned to his buggy. His horse was tired, so he drove slowly toward Lily's cottage.

He knew the moment he rounded the corner that something was different—and wrong. When he reached the gate he realized that the place was as empty as the house he'd just left.

Caleb strode up the walk and knocked at the front door all the same. When there was no answer he went around back. No laundry hung on the clotheslines, and there was no fire burning under the wash kettle. He tried the door only to find it soundly locked.

Exasperated—and more than a little worried—Caleb left his horse and buggy at the gate and walked down to the Tibbet house. A plain woman wearing a mobcap and a blue percale dress answered his knock.

"Yes, sir?"

Caleb asked for Gertrude and was admitted. He found his friend seated in her parlor, happily stitching a sampler.

"Where's Lily?" he asked without preamble.

Gertrude smiled. "Sit down, Caleb, and calm yourself. She hasn't gone to the ends of the earth. I presume Sandra boarded her train without incident?"

Hat in hand, Caleb took a seat on the settee and nodded impatiently. "She'll be in Pennsylvania by the end of the week."

"I envy her in some ways," Gertrude said with a sigh.

Caleb could barely sit still. "About Lily," he prompted.

Gertrude didn't look up from her embroidery. "She's gone to Spokane to buy nails and seed and such as that. Came into some kind of windfall. She got on this morning's stage and left."

Caleb was on the edge of the settee. "For Tylerville?"

"For Spokane," Gertrude repeated.

"What kind of windfall?" Caleb pressed.

Mrs. Tibbet shrugged. "I wouldn't know, dear. She only told me that she'd come into some money and meant to buy things for her farm."

Caleb swore under his breath and got to his feet. He had so much to say to Lily, and presents to give her, and here she'd taken off on some wild goose chase. She really meant to move to that damned farm, the stubborn little chit.

"Lily will be home next Saturday, Caleb," Gertrude said in a tone that was probably meant to be both stern and soothing. "And all your fretting and swearing won't bring her back a moment sooner."

Caleb wasn't sure of many things at that moment, but he did know he couldn't wait a full week to see Lily again. He took out his pocket watch, the one Joss had given him on his twelfth birthday, and flipped open the case. He'd passed the stage on his way out from Tylerville, and he knew he could catch it if he rode a fast horse.

After a rather abrupt good-bye to Mrs. Tibbet he strode out of the house and back down the street to where he'd left his horse and buggy. His own gelding was too weary for him to ride, so he drove to the stables.

Twenty minutes later he was in pursuit of the stagecoach. Fifteen minutes after that he was walking back toward Fort Deveraux. His borrowed horse had thrown a shoe.

The stop in Tylerville was a brief one, but Lily had a piece of pie in the hotel dining room where she'd worked before going to Fort Deveraux and chatted with Charlie for a while. To her relief, the unfriendly woman and her daughter were nowhere around when she returned to the stage. In fact, it looked as though she would have the vehicle entirely to herself until, at almost the last moment, a lovely auburn-haired lady arrived. She had a great deal of baggage, and she ordered Sam Hargrave around until it had all been secured in a fashion she approved of.

When she took a seat across from Lily she smiled wanly and said, "Hello."

This was certainly an improvement over her ill treatment at the hands of that Fort Deveraux woman. "Hello," Lily responded warmly. "My name is Lily Chalmers."

"Miss or Missus?"

"Miss, but please call me Lily."

"Of course I will. I'm Bianca Parrish, Lily, and I'm very glad to meet you. Tell me, what's your destination?"

Lily smiled, liking Bianca instantly for her dancing blue eyes and friendly face. "I'm traveling to Spokane. And you?"

Sadness flickered in Bianca's eyes for just the briefest moment. "San Francisco," she said after a short hesitation. "I'm afraid things didn't work out very well for me here."

"I'm sorry," Lily told her sincerely.

Bianca shrugged her elegant shoulders and intensified her smile. "Don't be. I'm going to be married when I get home, and I'm sure I'll be happy enough."

Privately, Lily thought Bianca shouldn't get married if she was no more excited about it than that, but she didn't say so. After all, the woman was a stranger to her. "Did you have a business here?" she asked, just to make conversation.

The stage jerked into motion, and Bianca put one hand on her feathered hat to keep it in place. She was wearing a dress of green silk and carrying a handbag that matched precisely. "You might say that. I was waiting for a man to marry me—I hope this doesn't shock you, Lily, but it's such a relief to speak frankly—and he came to me and said he'd found someone else."

Again Lily was filled with sympathy. "That's terrible."

"Luckily, there's a man in San Francisco who's been waiting for me for years. I wired him that I'd come home if he still wanted me, and he replied that he'd be waiting."

Lily thought it strange that an attractive, intelligent woman like Bianca should take such care that she had another man to go to, but again she kept her thoughts to herself. She was just glad to have company during the trip.

"San Francisco must be a wonderful city," she said. "I've always wanted to go there."

Bianca nodded and glanced out the window at the countryside. There were a great many pine trees towering on either side of the road. "I guess one place is about the same as another," she said with a little sigh. Her smile was determinedly brighter when she met Lily's eyes again. "Tell me, what are you planning to do in Spokane?"

Lily explained that she meant to buy equipment for her farm, but she said nothing about hiring the Pinkerton agent to search for her sisters. Bianca was still too much of a stranger for Lily to share so delicate a hope.

The miles between Tylerville and Spokane passed quickly, and the growing city was visible in the distance when suddenly there were shouts and the stagecoach came to a sudden stop.

Lily heard Sam Hargrave swear up in the box of the coach, and for one terrible moment she thought they'd been set upon by bandits. She was completely shocked when Caleb wrenched open the stage door.

"You've changed your mind," Bianca said softly.

Lily's gaze shifted from Caleb to Bianca and back again. Even with his face shrouded by the shadow of his hat brim Lily could see that Caleb had gone a little pale.

"No," he answered flatly.

"Damn it, Major," Sam complained from the box, "I got a schedule to keep!"

"Hold on," Caleb said distractedly. "Lily, I've got to talk to you."

An awful suspicion was forming in Lily's mind. Bianca had been talking about a man she'd hoped to marry, and when she saw Caleb, she'd said, "You've changed your mind."

Lily folded her arms. "I'll be at my brother Rupert's house on Division Street," she said, though a moment later she regretted sharing the information.

Bianca had taken a handkerchief from her bag, and she

was drying her eyes with it. Her shoulders trembled slightly as she wept.

"Rascal," Lily said to Caleb, wrenching the door closed. "Fiend!"

"Lily!" Caleb shouted.

Sam yelled to the horses, and the coach raced into motion. Lily moved to sit beside Bianca and lay one hand on her shoulder.

"Caleb was the man you wanted to marry," she said quietly, bracing herself for the reply even though she knew full well what it would be.

"Yes," Bianca sniffled. "And I have a feeling you're the woman he favored over me."

Lily's emotions were a welter of confusion. She didn't know whether to be furious with Caleb or to disregard the incident completely. After all, she had made no promises, and neither had Caleb. It wasn't as though he had betrayed her. And yet she hated to think of him loving any other woman in the same intimate ways he'd loved her.

"Well?" Bianca prompted when Lily didn't answer immediately. "Aren't you?"

"I don't know," Lily replied.

"What do you mean you don't know?"

Lily sighed. "I have no claim on Major Halliday's affections, Bianca. Nor do I want one." She spoke from her mind, overruling the distinctly separate dictates of her heart.

Bianca began to cry again. "You can't possibly know how wonderful it was, being held in his arms. . . ."

A stab of pain went through Lily, but she weathered it with no change in her expression. "If you truly love him, perhaps you shouldn't go."

Bianca shook her head. "Once the major's mind is set, there's no turning back. Caleb married without love once, but he'd never do it again. He was too unhappy."

Lily remembered Sandra saying that Caleb's mind couldn't be changed by a blast of dynamite once he'd made it up on a subject, and she had a hunch both women were right. Caleb was the most hardheaded man on earth.

"He must love you," Bianca went on brokenly, "if he'd follow you all this way."

Lily shook her head. She couldn't bear for Bianca's words to be true, or for them to be a lie. She wished she'd never met Caleb Halliday, never danced with him, never eaten his chocolates and appeased his needs. "He's just angry because I didn't obey his orders," she said finally. "My guess is that he'll ride back to Fort Deveraux and forget all about me."

Bianca shook her head. "Not Caleb. The gates of hell itself won't stop him if he wants you."

Lily didn't know what to say to that, so she just patted Bianca's hand and kept silent until the stagecoach had come to a stop in front of the Grand Hotel.

"I truly hope you'll be happy," she said when she and Bianca had both alighted. Caleb was standing at a distance, she saw at once, looking miserably uncomfortable. Sam Hargrave was hauling baggage down from the top of the coach.

Bianca nodded and kissed Lily's cheek. Then, with one unreadable look at Caleb, she hurried into the hotel.

Lily immediately stormed over to Caleb. She couldn't let on that, against her better judgment, she was glad to see him. "You've broken that poor woman's heart," she accused.

"I told you I kept a mistress before we met," Caleb answered, sounding a little defensive for all his recalcitrant stance. His uniform, usually so impeccable, was crumpled and covered with dust. "And I told *her* that we'd never be married."

"I don't think we have to discuss this on the street." Lily's voice and manner were prim as she turned away to claim her single valise. She smiled at Sam. "Thank you, Mr. Hargrave, for a very comfortable ride."

Sam grinned at Lily and lifted his battered hat. "Any time

you want to travel with us, Miss Lily, we'll be more than happy to have you."

Caleb was grumbling about something when Lily took her valise from Sam and started off down the street. It wasn't far to Rupert's house.

"Just a damn minute," Caleb barked, bringing her up short with a quick grasp on her elbow. "Where do you think you're going?"

"To my brother's home," Lily replied, her chin high. "Kindly unhand me, Major. If you don't, I'll scream."

Reluctantly Caleb let go of Lily's arm. He swept his hat off his head and then put it back on again in a single furious motion. "I want to know what you're doing here," he hissed, keeping up with Lily's short strides easily when she set out for Rupert's home.

Wagons and buggies rattled by on the brick street, and Lily indulged in a secret smile. "I've become a woman of means, Caleb," she said, still walking briskly. By that time he'd taken her valise, so she swung her arms at her sides. "I'm going to buy all the things I need to homestead my land."

"That's crazy. Who's going to protect you from Indians and outlaws?"

"I am," Lily answered without pause, though inside she didn't feel so confident. "I suppose I'll marry one day, though."

Caleb swore softly. "Fine. Marry anybody you want to," he snapped.

"Thank you," Lily replied in a dulcet tone. "I will." She turned onto a side street, and her spirits lifted because she could see Rupert's small house in the distance.

"Tell me where you got the money for this harebrained project!" Caleb demanded.

Lily looked up at him out of the corner of her eye. "I sold myself to every man on the post," she whispered. "I let them do everything you've ever done."

Caleb was practically apoplectic. "I'm warning you, Lily Chalmers—"

"Of what?"

Just as Lily would have entered Rupert's front gate Caleb caught hold of her again. He dropped the valise to the ground and gripped her by both shoulders. "Tell me."

Lily sighed. "I don't know exactly where the money came from, Caleb," she said moderately. "My mother sent it. Apparently her circumstances improved considerably after she got rid of us. Now, since I've answered your question— and may I say it was none of your business in the first place—will you stop carrying on in public?"

Caleb glowered at her and let go of her arm. "We have to talk."

Lily worked the gate latch. "Why?"

"Because when you go in there you're going to find out that I've been here asking questions, that's why."

Lily's hand froze in midair. "What?"

"I've hired a Pinkerton man to look for your sisters, Lily."

Lily was stunned. "I told you—"

"That you didn't want to be obligated. I know. But I wanted to do this for you, and I can afford it, so I went ahead."

Before Lily could think of an answer, Rupert appeared in the doorway of the little frame house and shouted gleefully, "Lily! What brings you here?" He gave Caleb a friendly smile. "Good to see you again, Major."

While Lily was embracing her brother she was looking at Caleb and wondering. The man was such a mystery, one minute making love to her as though there could never be another woman for him, the next crossing the street to avoid her. He expected to dictate Lily's comings and goings even though they were practically strangers, for all their intimacies, and he'd followed her all the way from Fort Deveraux to Spokane just to find out what she was doing.

He had to be loco.

Caleb touched the brim of his hat and nodded an acknowledgment to Rupert, then spoke to Lily in the clipped, authoritative tone she'd heard him use with his soldiers. "We'll leave for the fort tomorrow," he announced.

"*You* may do whatever you please, Major," Lily responded coldly, "but I'm staying here. I have business to attend to."

"Shall I explain to your brother why I have a claim on you?" Caleb asked, his tone a mockery of indulgence.

Lily felt her face go hot as a stove stoked for cooking.

Rupert looked pleasantly baffled. "Did I miss something here?"

Caleb relented just in time to save himself from a kick to the shins. "Tomorrow," he repeated. And then he excused himself and started to walk away.

"Come back for supper!" Rupert called after him, and this time it was her brother Lily wanted to kick. "So," he said, putting an arm around her shoulders and escorting her toward his small wooden house, "you've finally come to your senses and decided to settle down and make a real life for yourself. The major seems like a fine man to me."

Lily wondered if Rupert had overlooked the fact that she and Caleb hated each other. "He's a pompous, overbearing, bullying ass," she replied.

Rupert grinned. "Just what you need," he retorted.

As luck would have it, Caleb appeared at supper that night. His uniform had been shaken out and pressed, and his butterscotch hair gleamed with cleanliness. He brought Cuban cigars for Rupert and a delicate china figurine for Lily.

She looked at him in bewilderment, and he smiled at her as though there had been no disagreement at the front gate only a few hours earlier.

"I want to marry your sister," he announced after he and Rupert had consumed the better part of a chicken, along with mashed potatoes, gravy, and corn, at the simple table in Rupert's kitchen.

Lily had no illusions that Caleb meant what he said. It was just that even he wouldn't have the gall to stand there flat-footed and tell Rupert he wanted to keep his sister as a mistress.

He and Rupert each took a cigar and lit up.

"Don't I have anything to say about this?" Lily demanded, slamming the cast-iron skillet she'd been about to scour back onto the stove top.

Caleb leaned forward in the fog of blue smoke that curled between him and Rupert and said confidentially, "I've compromised her, you see. There's nothing to do but tie the knot before she's ruined."

Lily would have exploded if she hadn't been so surprised at Rupert's reaction. He should have been angry—outraged, even—but he only sat back in his chair and puffed on that damnable cigar. "I see," he said.

"I will not marry this—this *pony soldier!*" Lily raved. "He's only fooling, anyway! Do you hear me, Rupert? *There will be no wedding!*"

Rupert assessed her thoughtfully. "Is it true that he's compromised you?"

Lily's face was red as an ember. She couldn't have answered that question to save her life.

"There might be a child," he reasoned. "Did you ever think of that?"

"Yes," Caleb collaborated. "Did you ever think of that?"

Lily groped for a chair and sank into it. Pregnancy was a possibility she hadn't once considered. She'd been too wrapped up in her problems for that. "Shut up, both of you," she murmured, feeling ill.

"I think you'd better marry the major," said Rupert.

"I think I'd sooner marry the devil," countered Lily.

Caleb chuckled. "Isn't she beautiful?"

Rupert frowned. "Personally, I think she needs a spanking."

"I agree," said Caleb.

"Will you two please stop talking about me as if I weren't here? And it would take a bigger man than either of you to get the best of me."

Caleb leaned forward in his chair. "Is that a challenge?"

"No," Lily said, and the word took a great piece of her pride with it as it left her mouth.

"I thought not," said Caleb.

"Don't push your luck," said Lily.

Nothing was resolved that night.

On Sunday morning, after a sleepless night spent worrying that she might be pregnant, Lily went to church and prayed that God would make Caleb go away and leave her alone. Provided she wasn't expecting, that is—she hadn't bled since before she left Tylerville.

When she returned to Rupert's house there was no sign of either Caleb or her brother. She scavenged in the cupboards until she found the ingredients for a dried apple pie, and she was rolling out dough when there was a knock at the door.

"Come in," she called without thinking.

The door opened, and Caleb stepped inside. "I want to apologize for last night," he said, his hat in his hands, his expression as innocent as an altar boy's. "The truth is, I don't think we should get married."

Lily was beginning to get disturbing ideas about the rolling pin in her hands. His disclaimer came as no surprise to her, of course; she'd known he was an out-and-out scoundrel all along. "Oh?"

"We'd do nothing but fight. And make love, of course. I think we'd better just stay away from each other from now on."

Lily had prayed to hear these words that very morning. So why did they hurt so much? "What if I'm pregnant?"

Caleb shrugged as though they were talking about the possibility of a splinter or a stubbed toe. "I'd take care of you both, of course."

"Like you took care of Bianca, I suppose."

Caleb's grin was infuriating. "Yes."

Lily began tapping her palm with the rolling pin. "But you don't think we should be married."

"Absolutely not," Caleb replied firmly.

"What if *I* think we should be?"

He grinned. "If you propose to me, Lily-flower, I might reconsider. You'd have to be suitably humble, of course."

Lily made a strangled sound of rage and rounded the table, wielding the rolling pin like a battle ax.

Caleb easily wrested it from her hand and tossed it aside before pulling her into his arms. She squirmed, but there was no escaping, and when he caught her chin in one hand and forced her head back for his kiss she was lost.

When it was over, and Lily was breathless, Caleb set her away from him. "When you change your mind, you know where to find me."

Lily glared up at him. "I'll dance in hell before I'll come crawling to you, Caleb Halliday!"

He laughed, more in amazement than good humor. "If I didn't think you might be carrying my baby, I'd turn you over my knee right here and now and blister your behind!"

"I'm not carrying your baby!" Lily stormed out of the house toward the woodshed, bent on getting kindling for the cook stove.

Caleb followed, cornering Lily against a sawhorse, and laid a possessive hand on her abdomen. "We'll see about that in a few months," he vowed. His fingers moved downward to tease her most private place, and even through her skirts and petticoats Lily felt herself catch fire.

Her breath came hard and fast. "Caleb—*stop*—"

He withdrew his hand, only to press his hardness against her, and Lily groaned under her breath. In that moment she hated Caleb for his ability to get past her reason and play havoc with her very soul.

"Rupert will be home any minute," she fibbed, practically moaning the words.

"Liar," Caleb replied, his voice low and husky. "He's

having Sunday dinner with the pastor's daughter. She's sweet on him, you know. They'll probably get married soon." All the time he was talking Caleb was lifting Lily's skirts, and she was powerless to stop him.

She tried with the last of her will to turn away, and she would have fallen over the sawhorse if Caleb hadn't caught her.

He moved in closer, kissing the nape of her neck. The woodshed was shadowy and fragrant, and Lily ached as her pride and her resilient young body did battle.

Caleb raised her skirts to her waist and brought down her drawers, and still Lily didn't fight him. She only gripped the sawhorse with both hands as wave after wave of heat rolled over her. Instinct made her bend forward; pleasure made her cry out softly as he slid into the velvety depths of her femininity.

No longer concerned with her skirts, Caleb raised his hands to Lily's breasts, straining beneath her dress, and kneaded them gently as she met every thrust of his hips with a parry of her own. As his pace increased so did hers, and when a violent climax racked her Lily bit down hard on her lower lip to keep from letting him know how he'd pleasured her.

Caleb plunged deep and then, with a low moan, spilled his warm seed into her. He remained joined with her, his hands moving on her breasts, his breath coming in short gasps.

Lily was amazed when she felt him growing hard again, and she tried to wriggle free. He withdrew, but only long enough to sit down on the chopping block and turn Lily to face him. Then he brought her sleekly down onto his rod, and she felt it straining within her, as powerful as ever. She let her head fall back in surrender as Caleb began unbuttoning the front of her dress.

She whimpered when he bent forward to nip gently at a nipple still covered by her muslin camisole, and she tried to bare herself.

Caleb clasped her wrists in his hands, holding them away

from her body. He continued to enjoy Lily's breasts through the thin barrier of her camisole, and the pleasure—between that and the slight, tantalizing motions of his shaft within her—was an exquisite torment.

"Caleb," she pleaded, arching her back so that her breasts were thrust toward him.

He untied her camisole and laid it aside to suckle, and Lily's freed hands went immediately to his head. She tangled her fingers in Caleb's hair and held him to her, beginning to rock feverishly on his lap. Finally, in wild desperation, she sought his mouth with hers, and he kissed her, claiming her with his tongue even as he claimed her with his manhood. And she rode him shamelessly into an explosion of searing glory, her legs wrapped tightly around his hips as she drew his essence from his body into hers.

Chapter

❧ 12 ❧

*T*hat night, parted from Lily and sleeping fitfully in his hotel room, Caleb dreamed of his brother Joss, and of the battle that had changed both their lives.

The air was hot, filled with the smells of fear and blood. Screams and exploding shells seemed to echo against a placid blue sky. Young and desperately afraid, Caleb lay on his belly behind a little rise, his hands slick with sweat where he gripped his rifle.

A day before, an hour before, Caleb would have sworn that the devil was nothing more than a myth made up to scare women and children into behaving themselves. Now, with a sense of evil lying over him like a smothering shroud, he was a believer.

The lieutenant in charge of Caleb's squad shouted an order to advance. Praying that dying wouldn't hurt too much, Caleb bolted to his feet and charged with the others through a volley of gunfire.

Finally they gained a copse of trees. Caleb took a quick inventory of his body parts, amazed that he was not only alive, but whole.

The lieutenant gave an order to spread out, and Caleb watched as the other troops scattered to obey. He was to hold the ground where he stood. With his heart in his throat he looked around him.

That was when he spotted a tattered piece of gray cloth hidden in the brush. God, Caleb pleaded, whoever he is, let him already be dead so I won't have to kill him.

He moved closer and found a rebel lying facedown in the bushes, one arm blown away. Bits of flesh clung to the foliage.

With bile rising in his throat Caleb crouched beside the man, prodding him gently in the ribs with the tip of his bayonet.

"You alive, Johnny?" he asked in a throaty whisper. Sweat soaked his shirt, making it cling between his shoulder blades and along his chest.

Caleb's heart sank when the reb turned his head and looked up at him. The wan, filthy face was Joss's, and, remarkably, he smiled at Caleb, showing a set of perfect teeth. "Hello, little brother," he said.

Caleb closed his eyes tight, sick with horror. "Jesus," he whispered, but the word was a prayer, not a curse.

"They're going to find me in a few minutes, Caleb," Joss said, his voice as steady and calm as it had been years before when they'd both been boys and he'd taught Caleb to ride and shoot. "They'll put me in a prison camp, and I'll rot."

Caleb knew what Joss was going to ask of him, and he was already shaking his head. "No!" He sobbed the word.

Joss spoke quietly. "You've got to do it, boy. You've got to put me out of my misery right here and now—if you don't, I'll die a lot slower."

Tears were streaming down Caleb's face, mingling with the gritty dust that covered him. "You're my brother," he rasped.

Joss groaned, and Caleb had a profound sense of his brother's pain as well as his fear. "In the name of God, Caleb, help me. I've got nobody else but you."

Caleb's mind raced. He knew the prison camps were terrible places, and there was never enough food and medicine, but he couldn't put a bullet into his own brother unless he fired the next one into himself. And he wanted to live.

He looked back over his shoulder and spotted his sergeant approaching. He swallowed hard, starting when he felt Joss's one remaining hand grasp him by the wrist. "We've got a prisoner here," Caleb called out. He dragged one sleeve across his face, wiping away sweat and tears.

"Damn you, Caleb," Joss spat. "Damn you to hell for a traitor and a coward!"

The sergeant squatted by Joss and grimaced at the sight of his wound. "This one won't last long," he said. "Better take him behind the lines all the same."

By then Joss was only half-conscious. He kept muttering curses, but that wasn't unusual with a rebel prisoner. The sergeant had no way of knowing that the two men, one a friend and one a foe, were brothers. Nor would he have cared, Caleb decided, for this was war, and all the ordinary rules had been suspended.

Hauling Joss to his feet and draping his brother's one good arm over his shoulder, Caleb started back toward the line, passing corpses in blue and corpses in gray.

Joss came to and looked straight into Caleb's eyes just before they took him into the medical tent, where men from both sides screamed in pain. "Judas," he whispered, and he spat in Caleb's face.

Caleb bolted awake, but he could still feel his brother's spittle on his cheek, and even though he knew it was imaginary, he wiped it away.

Other elements of the dream lingered, too. His gut was twisted within him, and he was sweating despite the coolness of the evening. The despair was as real and as deep

187

as it had ever been. "Damn you, Joss," Caleb whispered, "leave me alone."

He sat up in bed, wishing Lily was there. He wouldn't even have needed to touch her; just watching her sleep would have soothed him.

Caleb shoved the splayed fingers of his right hand through his hair. He had to go home to Fox Chapel, face Joss, take his place in the family again. He wanted his share of the land and the horses.

And he wanted Lily at his side, now and forever.

Sweating, Caleb sank back against his pillows with a heavy sigh. Lily had about as much use for him as Joss would; he'd made every possible mistake with her.

His body ached as he remembered having Lily in the woodshed that day. Dear God, what was it about her that made him want her that way?

Caleb turned onto his belly, but that was worse—he kept imagining Lily beneath him. He rolled onto his back again and resolutely closed his eyes.

A long time passed before he slept, and when he did he had the same grisly dream over again from start to finish.

Lily woke up early the next morning and, out of habit, made Rupert's breakfast. He was standing in front of the cracked mirror next to the stove, full of buckwheat pancakes, straightening his collar when there was a summary knock at the door.

Lily braced herself, fully expecting Caleb, but when Rupert admitted the visitor she was confronted with a pretty blond woman with wide blue eyes and pouty lips.

"Who is this, Rupert?" the caller demanded, giving Lily a look that was decidedly unfriendly and not a little insulting.

Rupert chuckled and gestured toward Lily. "It's only my sister. Lily, may I present Winola Ferring?"

"Hello," Lily said with reserve.

Winola nodded curtly. "It's almost time for school to

begin," she said to Rupert in a whiny tone that set Lily's teeth on edge. "We'll be late."

Rupert turned to Lily, beaming. "Winola teaches first and second grades," he said.

Lily, who loved children but hadn't the patience to make a vocation of teaching them, managed a smile. "So you and Rupert work together."

"Yes," Winola allowed, a little friendlier than before.

"Isn't that nice," Lily remarked, and she meant it. Rupert had been alone too long; he needed a wife, and it was time he had children. If he married Winola, or anyone else, she would be happy for him.

Winola linked her arm possessively through Rupert's. "It was wonderful to meet you, Miss Sommers," she said, dragging him toward the door.

"Chalmers," Lily corrected. "It's Miss Chalmers."

Winola's blue eyes went very wide. "You told me she was your sister," she said to Rupert in an accusing voice.

"My parents adopted Lily when she was six," Rupert hastened to explain. The glance he gave his sister was a beleaguered one.

"You'll be leaving soon, I suppose," Winola said to Lily, and she looked hopeful.

Lily wanted to laugh. "Don't worry, Winola," she replied. "I won't be around long."

Winola made a sniffing sound and propelled Rupert out of the house.

Humming, Lily cleared away the remains of breakfast, stacking the dishes in the sink to be washed later, and she put on the bright yellow bonnet that matched her dress. She tugged her gloves into place as she left Rupert's little house, her handbag dangling from her wrist.

It was a lovely day out, bursting with all the sweet promises of spring, and Lily felt truly joyous as she hurried along the sidewalk toward the center of town, where all the shops and mercantiles waited, filled with fascinating wares.

Her first stop was the bank, where she deposited the draft her mother had sent and obtained a letter of credit to show the merchants. The second was the town's largest general store, known for its selection of farm implements and hardware.

Lily ordered a plow, a keg of nails, and a cook stove, asking that they be sent to Tylerville right away.

She was looking at seed and garden tools in another store when Caleb materialized at her side.

"Hello, Major," she said coolly, going right on with her business. She'd chosen a hoe, a spade, and a shovel, and she set them next to the counter.

His jawline was taut. "Lily," he replied with a stiff nod of his head.

"I'm surprised you're still here," she went on airily as she scooped up a handful of seed corn and watched the hard yellow kernels slip through her fingers. "Don't you have soldiers to boss around, or someone to blindfold and shoot?"

Standing next to Caleb was like being on the slopes of a volcano about to erupt. All the same, he spoke quietly. "Come next door and have a cup of coffee with me. Please."

The request was so uncharacteristically reasonable that Lily stopped what she was doing to gaze up at Caleb in surprise. "I suppose I could do that," she allowed.

After telling the clerk she'd be back in just a few minutes to complete her shopping Lily took Caleb's arm and let him usher her into the restaurant next door. They were seated at a table, cups of coffee steaming before them, before Caleb spoke to Lily again or even met her eyes.

"I'm leaving the army," he said.

Lily felt hope leap within her breast. Maybe Caleb had changed his mind; maybe he wanted to be a farmer after all. She held her breath, waiting for him to go on.

"I want to go back to Pennsylvania."

Lily's hopes plummeted. She could only stare at Caleb in misery. "I see," she said finally, with dignity.

190

Caleb reached into the pocket of his uniform coat and brought out a small box. "I want you to go with me, Lily," he told her, setting the box in front of her.

She opened it, hands trembling, to find an exquisite diamond ring inside. The larger center stone glittered and winked at her from amid the surrounding smaller gems. Her finger fairly burned, waiting to wear that ring.

"I can't," she said resolutely, snapping the box closed and shoving it back toward Caleb.

He leaned forward in his chair and lowered his voice. "Don't sit there and tell me you don't care for me, Lily, because I know you do. Yesterday you gave yourself to me in a woodshed, remember?"

Lily colored to recall the wanton way she'd behaved, and she lowered her eyes. "I do care," she answered, "but I don't want to leave my land, and I don't want a husband."

"You'd marry me if I agreed to stay and farm that damnable land with you?"

Again hope stirred in Lily's heart. "Yes."

"You just said you didn't want a husband."

Lily bit her lower lip. "If we were going to live in the same house, we'd have to be married, wouldn't we?"

Caleb pushed the ring box back across the table. "Has it ever occurred to you that I could promise to live on the farm, marry you, and then take you anywhere I damn well please, whether you want to go or not?"

"You're not making a very good case for marriage," Lily answered, ignoring the ring box and taking a steadying sip of her coffee. The truth was, she had never once considered the possibility Caleb had suggested; she knew he was honest to a fault.

"Damn it," he whispered, "I should have done it. I should have told you I'd homestead with you and then married you!"

"I would never have forgiven you, and you know it. It would have soured everything between us."

"Not everything," Caleb argued, making Lily blush again.

191

"Must every conversation we have come back to that?"

Caleb took the ring from the box, and then he lifted Lily's left hand and shoved the diamond unceremoniously onto her finger. "I think the fact that you would probably let me make love to you damn near anywhere has some bearing on what we're talking about, yes!"

Lily looked around furtively to see if anyone was listening. Fortunately, the restaurant was nearly empty, and the few other diners were sitting some distance away. "There is absolutely no need for you to be so arrogant," she fretted, trying to pull the ring off. It was just a tiny bit too small and wouldn't come over her knuckle.

Caleb's amber eyes were glittering with triumph when she looked up at him. "Perfect fit," he said.

Lily pushed back her chair. "I'll get it off if I have to have my finger amputated," she replied, preparing to leave.

"Get out of that chair and there will be a scene you'll remember until the day you die," Caleb promised.

Lily sat down again. "I don't want to marry you, and I don't want to go to Pennsylvania, so why can't you just leave me alone?"

"Because I love you," Caleb answered, and he looked as surprised to find himself saying the words as Lily was to hear them.

"I beg your pardon?"

"You heard me, Lily."

"You said you loved me. Did you mean it?"

Caleb drove one hand through his hair. "Yes."

Lily stared at him and stopped trying to get the ring off her finger. "You're just saying that. It's a trick of some kind."

Caleb laughed, but there was no humor in the sound. "Believe me, it's no trick—it's a fact I'm going to have to live with for the next fifty years."

In that moment Lily wanted to say yes to Caleb's proposal. She wanted the right to lie in this man's bed at night and revel in his touch; she wanted his children and his laughter and even his fury. But she was suddenly afraid. Sooner or later she might drive Caleb away, just as her mother had driven her father away. She might end up drinking, as Kathleen had, and even whoring. Wasn't she doing that already, after a fashion? Caleb boasted that he could take her anytime and anyplace, and he was right. Why, things might even progress to the point where she abandoned her own children.

Now, it crossed Lily's mind that she might be like her mother. Thinking back on the way she'd behaved with Caleb, she had to consider the possibility.

Lily blinked back tears of shame and horror. She pushed back her chair and bolted out of it.

Caleb called to her, but she didn't stop. Holding her head high, she went back to the mercantile, back to her ordering.

All the fun had gone out of it.

Lily had bought everything she needed by noon, including the lumber for her house. She gave directions for delivery, then walked slowly back to Rupert's place.

He wasn't there, of course, since school would be in session for several more hours, and there was no sign of Caleb either. Her head pounding, Lily lay down on the narrow bed in the kitchen that had been hers when she lived with Rupert.

She was certain there had never been a woman more confused than she was.

An hour's nap brought the headache under control, and Lily got up, went to the sink, and covered her left hand with slick soap. Caleb's ring still wouldn't come off her finger.

Frustrated, she turned to the wall calendar and did some calculations. They brought the headache back full force and drained the color from her face. She could be pregnant.

Common sense told Lily to go to Caleb, admit that she loved him, and marry him right away, but her fears were stronger. And they told her that history was repeating itself. She was becoming another Kathleen.

Lily was a strong woman, not given to tears, but the

prospect of living the life her mother had was more than she could bear. She sat down at Rupert's table, rested her head in her arms, and sobbed.

At suppertime Caleb still did not appear, and Lily was troubled by that, though she tried to tell herself she was relieved.

Rupert ate hungrily of the meal she'd prepared, but Lily had little appetite. She kept pushing her portion of meat loaf from one side of her plate to the other, and every time there was a noise from the street she started, barely able to resist leaping out of her chair and running to the window to look for Caleb.

"I guess Major Halliday's gone back to Fort Deveraux by now," Rupert ventured, scooping another slice of meat loaf onto his plate.

"He wouldn't leave without saying good-bye to me," Lily said, and the moment the words were out of her mouth she wished she could call them back.

Rupert arched one eyebrow. "I'm surprised at you, Lily. You allowed the man liberties, and yet you treat him like a typhoid carrier. Do you love him or not?"

Lily's cheeks throbbed with embarrassment. "It happens that *I'm* surprised at *you,*" she retorted. "I expected you to be angry about what I've done with Caleb—instead you act as though he was somehow entitled."

A long moment passed before Rupert replied. "I know you're not promiscuous, Lily—that would have shown up long before now. If you were intimate with the major—and it does seem that you have been—I'd guess it was because you love him."

"Or because I'm just like my mother," Lily said with real despair. Her eyes were brimming with tears when she looked imploringly at Rupert. "She let men take liberties, too. All sorts of men."

"You've been with other men besides Caleb?"

"Of course not!"

"Well, then, there you have it. Kathleen was Kathleen, and you're Lily, and never the twain shall meet."

Lily sighed. "I think maybe the twain *will* meet," she said, drying her eyes. "If Mama could find me, she might very well know where Emma and Caroline are, too."

Rupert had read the letter from Kathleen soon after Lily's arrival. He nodded. "It's possible. Are you thinking of visiting her in Chicago, Lily?"

Lily shook her head, then nodded. "Oh, I don't know!" she wailed in desperation. "Caleb has me so mixed up—"

"I see he gave you a ring," Rupert remarked, glancing at the twinkling diamond on Lily's finger.

"I'm only wearing it because it won't come off."

"Why did you put it on in the first place?"

Lily sighed. "I didn't—Caleb did."

"I see. We've come full circle, Lily—back to my original question, which you so neatly evaded. Do you love Caleb Halliday?"

Lily lowered her head. "Yes," she answered weakly. "I think about him all the time, and I get cold chills and hot flashes, just like when I had the flu. I even feel a little bit sick to my stomach."

"It's love, all right," Rupert said. He sounded very worldly wise for a schoolmaster who had only now gotten around to considering marriage. "And you don't want to marry him because you think you might be like your mother?"

Lily wanted to make her case by explaining how hot-blooded and wanton she was with Caleb, but it wouldn't be delicate to speak too specifically of such things with a man. "It's more than that," she said. "I've got my heart set on a place of my own, and on finding my sisters. Caleb wants to leave the army and go back to Pennsylvania to live. Marrying him would change the whole course of my life."

"Love often does that."

Lily was incensed. "Why do *I* have to be the one that does the giving up and the changing? Why not Caleb?"

"I see your problem," Rupert announced. "Neither one of you is the sort to back down from a decision once it has been made. I guess it would be better if you just stayed here and tilled your land while he went back east. He'll probably meet some pretty girl and forget all about you."

Just the thought made Lily's blood run hot as kerosene. "He won't either," she argued. "He'll see reason and stay here with me. I know he will!"

Rupert shrugged. "For your sake, Lily, I hope you're right. Now, tell me, what about this idea of traveling to Chicago? Are you going to do it?"

"I'm hoping I won't have to," Lily answered. "I wrote Mama and asked her if she knew where my sisters are. If she does, I'm sure she'll write back and tell me."

At that moment there was a knock at the front door. Lily bounded out of her chair, then caught herself and returned to the table. "You answer it," she whispered to Rupert, already assembling an appearance of indifference.

Rupert complied, but the caller was only Winola. She smiled coolly at Lily as she took off her bonnet.

"Rupert and I usually work on our lesson plans after supper," she announced, making the pursuit sound intimate.

Lily wondered if she was expected to vacate the premises. "Go right ahead," she said, standing up to begin clearing off the table. She was abysmally disappointed that Winola wasn't Caleb. "I'll try not to disturb you."

The glint of Lily's diamond must have caught Winola's eye, for she suddenly grabbed her hand. "You're engaged!" the schoolmistress crowed, obviously delighted.

Lily started to correct Winola's misconception, but Rupert leapt into the conversation before she could finish.

"Yes," he said quickly, and with great exuberance. "Lily's marrying a man named Caleb Halliday. He's a major in the army."

"Oh," Winola said, looking much friendlier. "Well, congratulations, Lily."

"Thank you," Lily answered, shooting one murderous look at Rupert before she went on with the task of setting the kitchen to rights.

Soon Rupert and Winola were comfortably seated at the table, their heads close together, working out their lesson plans for the next day. They seemed to have forgotten Lily entirely, and even when she deliberately dropped a cast-iron skillet to the floor they didn't look up.

With a sigh she put on her shawl and went out for a walk. Maybe if she had some fresh air and exercise she would fall asleep easily that night, instead of lying there having foolish thoughts about Caleb.

She headed directly for the Grand Hotel, where she assumed Caleb was staying. She strode up to the desk and asked after him.

"Major Halliday's checked out, ma'am," the young clerk explained. "But you might speak with Mrs. Parrish. She and the major were together earlier this evening."

Lily squared her shoulders automatically. She thanked the clerk and turned to go.

"Mrs. Parrish is in the dining room," the young man called after her in a helpful tone of voice.

Lily started toward the door, but in the end her curiosity overrode her considerable pride. She would go into the dining room and speak to Bianca.

She entered, glancing from side to side, only to see Caleb sitting with Bianca near the windows. There was a candle in the center of the table, and its light flickered like liquid gold over their features. They were laughing, their heads close together.

Lily might have turned and walked out without either of them seeing her, but she wanted Caleb to know that *she* knew he was a two-timing, back-stabbing bounder. So she summoned all her courage, squared her shoulders, and marched over to the table.

"Good evening, Bianca," she said cheerfully. "Caleb."

Caleb rose from his chair, but there was no guilt in his expression, only challenge.

"Lily!" Bianca cried, sounding genuinely pleased. "Do join us. We were just talking about—"

"I couldn't," Lily interrupted. "My brother is expecting me home at any moment." In truth, Rupert had either forgotten her or was hoping that she would stay away for a while so that he and Winola could spoon. "I just wanted to tell you good-bye, Bianca. I hope your journey will be a pleasant one."

"I may not be leaving," Bianca said, unaware she'd driven an invisible spike through Lily's heart with those innocent, brightly spoken words. "Caleb has convinced me that I shouldn't be too hasty."

"I can just imagine that he has," Lily said warmly, never looking at Caleb, although she was conscious of him in every fiber of her being. She glanced at the big regulator clock on the wall nearby. "It's getting late—I'd better hurry home," she said. "It was good seeing you again, Bianca."

With that, Lily turned and walked away at a brisk pace, her chin high, her eyes burning with tears she was too proud to shed. She hoped Caleb would follow her and offer some explanation, but he didn't.

When Lily arrived at Rupert's house she peeked into the front window and saw her brother kissing Winola with unrestrained passion.

With a little sob of frustration and heartbreak Lily sat down on the front step to wait, her chin propped in her hands. It seemed the whole world was romancing tonight—except for her, of course.

Chapter

❧ 13 ❦

*L*ily couldn't wait until the following Saturday to travel back to Fort Deveraux. It was too painful knowing Caleb was in Spokane, renewing his friendship with Bianca Parrish. So she bought a sturdy pinto gelding from the man at the livery stable, along with a saddle and bridle, and trousers and a shirt from the mercantile. Then she packed her valise.

After writing a short note of farewell to Rupert, which she left propped against the sugar bowl in the middle of the kitchen table, Lily mounted her horse and set her face toward Fort Deveraux. By nightfall she would be in her own little cottage across from the schoolhouse, making plans to move onto her homestead.

She wasn't more than five miles outside of town when she began to wish she'd bought a hat and some proper boots as well as denim trousers and a shirt. The sun was so bright that it made her squint, and her scalp was sweating, making her hairline damp and sticky. Worse, the horse she'd purchased was determined to show her he deserved his name:

Dancer. He liked to prance and do little sideways jigs, but he had a problem with straight ahead.

Lily had serious doubts that he'd do as a plow horse.

When twilight came Lily was still miles from Tylerville, let alone Fort Deveraux. Resigned, she found a little rock-walled canyon, gathered a few twigs, and tried to start a fire.

Sally of *Typhoon Sally, Queen of the Rodeo* had once set a pile of wood ablaze by rubbing two sticks together. Lily tried that and found out fast that the process was overrated. Whenever she'd needed a fire, she'd used matches.

Dancer, meanwhile, seemed perfectly content. There was a stream nearby where he could drink, and the ground was covered with sweet green grass.

For Lily the pickings were slimmer. She hadn't brought along any food, having expected to reach her destination well before nightfall, and now she'd go hungry. She didn't have a gun or a knife, and even if she had, she would have been hard put to kill some unsuspecting little creature and eat it. She sat down on a fallen log next to her nonexistent fire and propped her chin in her hands to consider her fate.

"What would Typhoon Sally do?" she asked herself, and Dancer, and the waving green grass that stretched for miles, practically unbroken by trees, in every direction. No answer came to her from within or without. She looked up at the sky and hoped it wouldn't be cold that night.

It was then that she felt the first tickle, about midway up her spinal column. That was followed by another tickle, and another, and suddenly they were all over her. Lily bounded off the fallen log and looked down to see that it was swarming with red ants.

With a startled scream she began tearing off her clothes. Her shirt went first, and then her trousers, and then her shoes and stockings. There were ants in her hair, between her toes, everywhere on her body. She danced and swatted wildly in a futile attempt to escape them.

Caleb rode up just as she was trying to submerge herself in

an ice-cold creek no more than six inches deep. Calmly he hung his hat on the horn of his saddle, then he put his hands on his hips, an infuriating grin spreading across his face.

"Ants?" he inquired cordially.

He was at once the first and last person Lily would have wanted to see. She sat up in the creek, her hair dripping, her arms covering her breasts, ants banished at last. Her legs and bottom were so numb from the cold that she couldn't even feel them. Teeth chattering, she made a strangled sound of rage and shouted, "G-give me my clothes!"

Caleb picked up the trousers and the shirt and the stockings, which were scattered about with abandon, and assessed them with mischief twinkling in his eyes. "These can't be your things, Lily—they look like they'd belong to a half-grown boy."

Lily struggled to her feet. She didn't want to show herself to Caleb, but if she stayed in the water any longer she wouldn't be able to walk. Furiously, shivering with cold, she struggled to the shore. "You know very well they belong to me!" she raged, tearing the clothes from Caleb's hand and starting to put them on.

It was a difficult task, since her skin was wet, but she managed. When she turned around again Caleb was squatting beside her fire, and a small blaze was just catching under the wood.

Lily glared at him. "How did you do that?" she demanded.

"I lit a match," Caleb responded. "Elementary stuff."

Giving a wide berth to the log where the ants kept residence, Lily found a smooth rock and, after a careful inspection, sat down upon it to pull on her shoes. When that was done she reached out for her valise and opened it.

She was brushing her sodden, badly tangled hair when Caleb spoke again.

"Hungry?" he asked.

Lily's stomach grumbled. "Yes," she admitted grudgingly.

Caleb fetched his saddle bags and tossed them to Lily. "There's some hard candy in there. Maybe that'll hold you until I can shoot a rabbit."

Lily fairly clawed open the leather flaps. After a few moments of ferreting through the bags she found the candy and popped several pieces into her mouth. "I suppose you think I don't know how to survive in the wilderness," she began, her words garbled by the candy. "But the fact is . . ."

Caleb turned away, pulling the pistol from his holster and spinning the chamber with a practiced thumb. As Lily watched he took bullets from his belt and loaded the gun. "We'll talk about your survival later," he said uncharitably. Then he turned and strode away into the gathering darkness.

A few minutes later the sound of a shot echoed through the evening air, and Lily winced. Still, she was glad to see Caleb stride back into the light of the campfire. Using a pocket knife and several small tree branches he made a spit and put the freshly skinned rabbit on to roast.

By that time Lily had consumed all the hard candy in Caleb's saddle bags, but she was still ravenous.

"Were you following me?" she asked, hugging her knees and watching her supper cook.

"Yes," Caleb answered in his direct way. He sat down across from Lily, and the firelight did a primitive dance over his features. "I wanted to see how you could get by on your own."

He didn't need to tell Lily that she'd failed the test miserably; she knew, and her pride had been stripped as bare as the supper rabbit. "I thought I could reach Tylerville, at least, before nightfall."

Somewhere in a nearby copse of pine trees an owl hooted, and in the distance coyotes howled at the rising moon. Caleb glanced toward Dancer, who was grazing a few yards away. "You might have made it if you hadn't bought such a fool horse."

Lily felt called upon to defend Dancer, even though she

privately agreed. "He's pretty," she said after taking several moments to search her mind for something favorable to say.

Caleb stood up to turn the rabbit on its spit. "Look how far that got you."

"I suppose *your* horse could make better time."

"Without a doubt," the major answered. "As it is, we're both stuck here for the night, so there isn't much sense in arguing."

Lily rested her chin on her updrawn knees and sighed. Now that Caleb was there the night didn't seem quite so dark, and she had to admit she would have been half-starved by morning if not for him. All the same, agreeing with him didn't come easily. "Did you persuade Bianca to stay on in Tylerville?"

Caleb favored Lily with an infuriating grin as he sat down again, this time a little closer to her. "Maybe," he replied.

Lily lowered her eyes. "That's certainly a vague answer."

"We can talk about Bianca another time. Right now I want to know why the hell you took off like that. You could have run into a lot of trouble out here by yourself."

She sniffed, hoping Caleb wouldn't guess how near tears she was. "I've told you before—I'm not afraid to be on my own."

Caleb stirred the fire, and a shower of crimson sparks rose up to mate with the silver stars scattered across the sky. "Only because you haven't got the good sense to be," he replied, but his tone wasn't inflammatory.

Tired and discouraged, Lily let her head rest against the rounding of his shoulder and sighed. "Are you and Bianca taking up again?"

Caleb laughed. "Hardly. But I'll admit I enjoyed letting you think that for a while."

"Surely you don't believe I cared," Lily bluffed with the last of her bravado. It was getting cold, even near the fire, and she hugged herself.

Caleb took off his coat and put it over Lily's shoulders.

The scent and weight of it brought back memories that made her cheeks grow warm. "You didn't care?"

Lily considered, recalling Reverend Sommers's thunderous declarations that all liars go straight to hell when they die. "Maybe I cared a little," she said in a small voice. "Just a very little."

He caught her left hand in his and lifted it so that the diamond sparkled in the firelight. "I see you haven't cut off your finger yet."

Lily smiled sleepily. "That would have hurt too much." She paused to sniff the air. "Is that rabbit ready? I'm starved."

Caleb prodded the meat with the tip of his knife. "Not quite," he answered, settling down beside Lily again. His arm slipped around her shoulders, and she was too tired, she told herself, to shrug it off.

She turned her head to look up at him. "Thank you," she said softly.

"For what?" Caleb asked, watching her face with an expression of tenderness that made her throat constrict.

"For fixing that rabbit," Lily replied, "and for not yelling at me or giving me a lecture on my foolhardy ways."

Caleb kissed her forehead lightly, the way one might kiss a grubby, disgruntled child. "Believe me, if I thought it would help, I'd yell."

Lily drew a deep breath and let it out slowly. Except for her ravenous hunger, she felt content. "I think I should have bought a rifle. It's time I learned to shoot better."

"Now there's a reassuring thought," Caleb remarked in a wry tone of voice. He speared the rabbit again, took it off the spit, and deftly cut it into pieces, which he laid carefully on a tin plate from his saddle bags.

Lily picked up a large chunk of the steaming, fragrant meat and bit into it. "This is good," she said with her mouth full.

Caleb kissed her greasy lips. "What an interesting addition you'd be to afternoon tea in Fox Chapel," he laughed.

Lily was hurt. "What an embarrassment, you mean."

"Never."

Assuaged, at least for the moment, Lily continued to eat, and when the meal had ended she and Caleb went down to the stream together to wash their faces and hands.

"You're really a very good cook," Lily remarked. They were so far from the fire that Caleb was little more than a moving shadow in the darkness.

"Thanks," he responded lightly. "If you have any business to take care of, you'd better do it now, because you're not going to want to leave the fire by yourself."

He was right, but Lily was mortified at the prospect of relieving herself with a man present. "Turn your back," she said, unbuttoning her trousers.

Caleb laughed. "I can't see you, Lily. It's too dark."

"I don't care."

Lily heard the rustle of small stones as he turned away. Naturally, the moon came out from behind its cloud the moment she crouched, bathing her and the rest of the landscape in silver light. A man of his word, Caleb was indeed facing in the other direction.

"I hope there aren't any Indians looking on," Lily said, fastening her trousers.

Caleb chuckled. "So do I, Lily-flower, but for entirely different reasons."

She walked confidently toward the snapping heat and comforting glow of the fire. "You're just trying to scare me."

Caleb had taken his bedroll from the back of his horse when he unsaddled it. Now he smoothed it out on the grassy ground. "You can keep the first watch," he said, sitting down on the bedroll and pulling off his boots.

Lily's eyes were wide. "What do I do if I see something?"

"Scream," Caleb replied, settling down into the makeshift bed and gazing up at the stars. His voice sounded as though he might nod off at any second.

"You can't just leave me out here," Lily reasoned. "If I'm not scalped, I'll freeze to death."

The firelight flickered in Caleb's whiskey-colored eyes as he looked at her and tossed back the blanket. "Be my guest," he said in a low voice.

Lily hesitated for only a moment, then she was sitting next to him, pulling off her shoes. "This is highly improper, of course," she said as she snuggled in beside Caleb.

"There's no denying that."

Lying spoon fashion with Caleb, Lily could feel his masculinity against her buttocks. She shifted, trying to avoid the contact, but he shifted with her. She turned to face him, knowing he would win because he always did. "You can kiss me if you want to," she offered.

He wrapped his arms around her and cradled her close. "Maybe in the morning," he yawned.

"You're not fooling me, Caleb," Lily told him bluntly. "You're hard."

"So is the ground. Go to sleep, Lily."

She couldn't close her eyes, even though she was exhausted. She was too aware of Caleb's scent and warmth and strength. Soon she'd be homesteading and he'd be back in Pennsylvania, courting someone like Sandra, but for tonight he belonged to Lily alone. She began unbuttoning the front panel of his shirt.

"Lily."

She kissed the hairy, muscled wall of his chest. "Ummm?"

"Stop it."

Lily found a masculine nipple, hidden in down, and teased it with her tongue, eliciting a low, rumbling groan from Caleb.

But he grasped her wrists and thrust her roughly onto her back. "Enough, Lily."

Her eyes were wide with confusion and hurt as she looked up at him. Not in her wildest imaginings would she have guessed that Caleb wouldn't want her.

"You're always so headstrong," he marveled in a furious whisper. "So impulsive. You just do whatever comes into that demented little brain of yours, whether you have any idea of what you're letting yourself in for or not."

Lily tried to free her hands, but he wouldn't let them go. In fact, he pulled them high above her head and held them easily with one hand. With the other he unbuttoned her flannel shirt.

"Caleb," she whispered, "stop it!"

"You started this," he answered, "I didn't." And he continued opening the buttons of her shirt until she was naked to the waist.

"I didn't mean—"

"The hell you didn't," Caleb interrupted, and he lowered his head to take the straining peak of Lily's bare breast into his mouth.

An involuntary groan escaped her, and she struggled again, without success, to free her hands. Caleb responded by spreading his fingers over the warmth of her belly and suckling all the more greedily.

Lily twisted from side to side, but he followed her with his mouth, and his hand deftly undid the buttons on her trousers. She felt them sliding downward over her hips. When they reached her knees Caleb positioned himself above her, letting her hands go at last.

She meant to push him away, but instead she found herself caressing the nape of his neck. "Caleb," she murmured just before his mouth covered hers in a savage kiss.

When he broke away his eyes glittered, catching fragments of moonlight and turning them to amber. "God help me, I know I should turn away from you," he breathed, "but I can't. I need you so much, Lily. So much."

With one powerful stroke he was inside her, and Lily arched her back in glorious surrender, gazing up at the millions of stars spattered across the sky and making a low, crooning sound in her throat.

Caleb moved slowly, involuntarily, upon her. "You little witch," he rasped.

She was kissing the base of his throat, where a pulse beat

furiously. Her hands moved beneath his shirt and down over his taut buttocks, pushing his trousers out of the way as they passed.

"I can't hold back," he groaned, and his hands slid beneath her bottom, lifting her to receive a ferocious, driving stroke. "I can't stop—oh, God, Lily—*Lily . . .*"

She waited for pain, for fear, for Caleb had never taken her with such primitive voracity; even in the moments of greatest intimacy there had been a restraint in him, however tenuous. Now there were no constraints; he was like a wild stallion, unpredictable, ruthless, driven by instinct.

Lily thrust her hips upward to receive him, and he lunged deep inside her, his head back, his teeth bared in the singular fury of passion. Even as her own body was racked with brutal tremors of satisfaction she soothed him, her hands caressing his face, his magnificent chest, his muscled back.

When he gave a warrior's shout of victory and went still upon her Lily was almost overwhelmed with tenderness. She held him as he lay gasping and spent in her arms.

"Damn you!" was the first thing he managed to say.

Lily laughed, even though there were tears in her eyes. "Such tender words."

"I could strangle you, you little vixen." The words were still labored, and the anger in them was all too real. "You refuse to marry me, and yet you feel free to crawl into my bed and drive me straight out of my mind."

She circled his nipple with the tip of one finger, delighting in the way his flesh grew taut in response. "Would you believe me if I said I was sorry?"

"No," he bit out, pushing her hand away. "And stop that!"

Lily kissed his chin. "Don't be so crabby, Caleb. How many times have you seduced me? I was only giving you some of your own medicine."

He chuckled and fell to her neck, kissing the night-cooled,

ivory flesh until it grew warm under his lips. This second time Caleb loved Lily with excruciating slowness, drawing response after response from her before taking her completely.

When it was over Caleb pulled her close and kissed the top of her head. "Good night, sodbuster," he murmured.

Lily slept deeply, dreamlessly, and when she awakened the sun was shining in her face and Caleb was nowhere about. For a terrible moment she believed he'd left her, and she raised herself on one elbow to look around.

The horses were both tethered nearby, but there was no sign of Caleb.

Lily buttoned her shirt and righted her trousers, which had worked their way down around her ankles. She was climbing out of the bedroll when Caleb returned, grinning.

"Morning," he said, running his eyes over Lily's rumpled clothes with amused appreciation.

Feeling strangely shy, Lily averted her eyes. "Good morning," she mumbled. Seeing her shoes a short distance away, she fetched them and sat down on Caleb's bedroll to tie the laces.

"We'll get some breakfast in Tylerville," he announced, starting to saddle Lily's horse. "While we're there you'd better put on a dress and do something with your hair. There's going to be talk enough when we come back to Fort Deveraux together."

Lily dreaded the prospect. Now that her return was imminent she remembered the unfriendly woman on the stagecoach, and the two ladies who had whisked their skirts aside when they passed her on the sidewalk. "There are times when I wish I'd never left Spokane in the first place," she confided despondently.

Caleb's smile was warm and reassuring. "As much trouble as you are, I'm still glad you did," he answered.

Lily looked at him and then glanced quickly away again. She'd been brazen the night before, and the memory shamed her, reminded her that she was no better than her mother had been. "People don't dare snub you," she pointed out brokenly. "Women don't pull their skirts aside or forbid their children to speak to you."

He came to her and pulled her to her feet. "What are you talking about?"

She explained haltingly, in a small voice. "They think I'm a tramp," she finished miserably, and then she covered her face with both hands. "And maybe they're right."

Caleb pulled her hands down and shook his head. "Lily, all you've got to do to shut them up is marry me. Do that and they'll be polishing your shoe buckles."

"I can't," Lily whispered. "Caleb, you know I can't, and you know why."

With a ragged sigh he released her. He kicked dirt over the last of the fire and went back to finish saddling the horses.

An hour later he and Lily rode into Tylerville. Even though they avoided the main street of town, they still drew plenty of notice.

Caleb rented a room for Lily at the hotel, ordered fresh, hot water sent up, and then disappeared into the saloon. Lily climbed the stairs to her room, valise in hand, hair falling around her shoulders in a series of tangles. Two elderly women stared openly at her trousers and shirt as she moved along the upper hallway.

She put her tongue out at them and unlocked her door.

She was sitting slumped on the bed when a maid arrived with a huge bathtub, which she set in the middle of the room. The woman was plump, with dark hair and severe features, and her eyes moved over Lily's clothes and hair with frank curiosity.

"Your man said to send up breakfast, along with the hot water."

"Major Halliday is not my man," Lily said tartly. She was too discouraged and too weary to defend herself properly.

"He gives the orders and you follow them," the maid pointed out. "That means he's your man."

Lily was stumped for an answer, but she glared until the woman wilted a little and crept out of the room.

Charlie Mayfield brought her breakfast in person, and he whistled in amazement when he saw her clothes. "Pants? The major's got you wearin' *pants?*"

"It was my idea," Lily said defensively, wrenching the tray out of his hands and stomping over to the table beside the window. "Furthermore, I'm getting tired of everyone going around assuming that I do a somersault every time Caleb Halliday snaps his fingers!"

Charlie cackled at that. "He's got his work cut out for him, the major has. But I figure he's man enough to handle the job."

Lily lifted the lid off a plate of sausage, eggs, and fried potatoes and began to eat. Her motions were quickened not only by temper, but by hunger. "If he's down there telling everyone that he's got some kind of hold over me," she said between bites, "he's lying!"

Charlie was as tickled as a gossipy old spinster. "He didn't have to say nothin'. Just bringin' you in here and orderin' up breakfast and a bath said it all."

Lily supposed it did, and her shoulders sagged in temporary defeat. "I'm ruined," she said.

"I reckon that's so, unless you marry him. People'll come around soon enough if you do that."

"I'm not going to sign away the next fifty years of my life just to keep the gossips happy," Lily said, waving a buttermilk biscuit for emphasis.

Charlie shook his head, marveling. Before he could offer a reply, however, there was another knock at the door, and Lily called out a grudging "Come in!"

The maid entered again, burdened down with two bucketfuls of steaming hot water. Charlie looked at the tub, then at Lily, shook his head again, and walked out muttering.

By the time Lily had finished her breakfast the maid had carried up enough water to fill the tub.

Lily locked the door after the woman was gone, then put a

chair under the knob for good measure. Caleb had walked in on one of her baths before; he wasn't going to get a second opportunity.

The water was cooling rapidly, so Lily took a fast and vigorous bath. When it was over she put on drawers and a camisole and petticoat, then took her good yellow dress from her valise and shook it out.

It was still wrinkled when she put it on, but there was no helping that. She took the chair out from under the doorknob, turned the key in the lock, and left the room with her head held high.

She found Elmira McAllister just starting up the stairs. "So it's true," Lily's former landlady gasped, laying a hand to her breast. A spot of color glowed on each cheek. "Folks saw you riding into town sneaky-like with Major Halliday. So I was sent to find out. Are you his wife or not?"

"It's none of your business whose wife I am, if I'm anybody's," Lily replied, but she was careful to let the ring Caleb had given her show. The diamond was practically as big as a bird's egg; let the town's busybodies talk about *that*.

"You'll regret being so uppity when no decent woman will have you to tea or sit next to you in church."

Lily's aplomb deserted her. "Mrs. McAllister, I—"

She was cut off. "You've had your warning, Lily Chalmers," the older woman said, shaking a finger in Lily's face. "Just remember the words of St. Paul—it's better to marry than to burn!"

With that she stormed off, leaving Lily to wonder whether she had a friend left in the world. By now even Gertrude Tibbet and Velvet Hughes had probably turned against her.

Chapter

❧ 14 ❧

When Caleb didn't return to the hotel immediately Lily went to look for him. She checked the saloons first, peeking in over the swinging doors, and was vastly relieved not to see him there among the midday revelers.

He wasn't in the general store or the land office or the blacksmith's shop, either. That left the livery stable.

Arriving there, Lily found Caleb hitching his horse to a buggy. Dancer was in a nearby stall, contentedly chewing grain.

Lily smoothed the hopelessly rumpled skirts of her best dress and approached. "I'm ruined," she confided miserably. "Everyone hates me."

"I don't," Caleb pointed out.

Lily was not consoled. "You're a man," she retorted, "and that doesn't count."

Caleb arched his eyebrows at that but said nothing.

"Your people back in Pennsylvania—what are they like?"

Caleb finished his work and turned to face Lily, his arms

213

folded. Because the barn was shadowy and he was wearing that blasted campaign hat of his she could barely see his face. "Decent, hardworking, ordinary enough."

"Rich?" Lily inquired.

"Yes, you could say that."

Lily sighed. Marrying the major might eliminate her current dilemma, but once the back-east Hallidays got a good look at her the snobbery would begin all over again. Caleb's family would wonder what had possessed their long-lost son to choose an orphan with a questionable reputation for his wife.

He curved a finger under her chin and lifted it. "They'd take to you immediately, sodbuster," he said. "It's me they've got no use for."

"And if they didn't?"

"They would. Now let's get back to the fort—that is, unless you want to stop at the church and get married first."

Lily thought for a moment, then shook her head.

Caleb sighed, walking away to bring Dancer out of his stall and tether him to the back of the buggy. Lily didn't wait for him to help her but stowed her valise under the seat and climbed up on her own. She averted her eyes when Caleb settled in beside her, released the brake lever, and took up the reins.

He whistled to the horse, and it bolted forward, drawing the rig out through the double doorway of the stable into the bright sunlight. "Our children are going to be remarkably stubborn," he commented as they started down the main street of town.

Lily tried to ignore the avid stares of passers-by. "We aren't going to have any children," she said. Some instinct caused her to lie. "My—my monthly arrived today."

Caleb fell silent, and in a sidelong glance Lily saw his disappointment. She laid a hand on his arm but could not bring herself to admit the truth. If the major believed there was no child—indeed, no possibility of a child—he might stop pursuing Lily. The sooner he gave up, the sooner she could get on with building up her homestead and finding her sisters.

She bit down on her lower lip. Of course, if there was a baby growing inside her, would it be fair to let Caleb go back to Fox Chapel without ever knowing he was about to become a father?

The quandary made Lily feel sick to her stomach, and she put it aside to enjoy the warm sunshine of the day. Wildflowers were blooming in profusion along both sides of the rutted country road, and the sky was that particular, pungent shade of blue that always made her throat go tight.

They traveled in relative silence until they reached Lily's land. There Caleb stopped to let the horses rest and drink from the creek.

Lily scanned the surrounding area with satisfaction, but her smile faded when she saw the Indians lining the top of the small rise to the south. There were six of them, and they were carrying rifles.

"Caleb," Lily whispered.

He turned from the horses to glance at her curiously. "What?"

"Indians," she managed to say. "Over there, on the rise!"

He turned in a leisurely fashion to look toward the hillside, making no move to take his pistol from its holster or dive for the rifle Lily had seen him put under the seat back in Tylerville. "Son of a gun," he remarked, sounding interested but not alarmed.

Impatient, Lily started to reach under the seat.

"No sudden moves, sodbuster," Caleb warned calmly without even glancing in her direction. "They don't take well to things like that."

Lily sat still as a stone, her fingers itching for the rifle even though she didn't have the faintest idea what to do with it. *Do something!* she wanted to scream as the Indians rode down the hill at a cautious pace. "They'll probably scalp me," she fretted through her teeth.

"If they don't, I will," Caleb replied.

At that, Lily fell silent. Her eyes grew wider and wider as the Indians rode nearer on their squat, stout ponies. Their dark hair hung down around their shoulders, but that was their only similarity to the illustrations in *Typhoon Sally* and the other books Lily read with such relish. Instead of being bare-chested, like literary savages, they wore oddly cut calico shirts. Rather than loincloths they sported ordinary trousers, and their moccasins weren't moccasins at all—they were plain black boots of the type available in any mercantile.

The man wearing the brightest shirt rode forward, holding his rifle at the angle at which he might have held a spear. "This Blue Coat's woman?" he demanded, gesturing toward Lily.

Caleb shook his head. "She's her own woman. Just ask her."

Lily's heart was jammed into her throat. She had an urge to go for the rifle again, but this time it was Caleb she wanted to shoot. "He lies," she said quickly, trying to make sign language. "I am too his woman!"

The Indian looked back at his followers, and they all laughed. Lily thought she saw a hint of a grin curve Caleb's lips as well but decided she must have imagined it.

"You trade woman for two horses?"

Caleb lifted one hand to his chin, considering. "Maybe. I've got to be honest with you. She's a lot of trouble, this woman."

Lily's terror was exceeded only by her wrath. "Caleb!"

The Indian squinted at Lily and then made an abrupt, peevish gesture with the fingers of one hand.

"He wants you to get down from the buggy so he can have a good look at you," Caleb said quietly.

"I don't care what he wants," Lily replied, folding her trembling hands in her lap and squaring her shoulders.

The Indian shouted something.

"He's losing his patience," Caleb warned, quite unnecessarily.

Lily scrambled down from the buggy and stood a few feet from it while the Indian rode around her several times on his pony, making thoughtful grunting noises. Annoyance was beginning to overrule Lily's better judgment. "This is my land," she blurted out all of a sudden, "and I'm inviting you and your friends to get off it! Right now!"

The Indian reined in his pony, staring at Lily in amazement.

"You heard me!" she said, advancing on him, her hands poised on her hips.

At that, Caleb came up behind her, and his arms closed around her like the sides of a giant manacle. His breath rushed past her ear. "Shut up!"

Lily subsided, watching rage gather in the Indians' faces like clouds in a stormy sky. "Caleb," she said, "you've got to save me."

"Save you? If they raise their offer to three horses, you'll be braiding your hair and wearing buckskin by nightfall."

The Indians were consulting with one another, casting occasional measuring glances in Lily's direction. She was feeling desperate again. "All right, then, but remember, if I go, your child goes with me."

"You said you were bleeding."

Lily's face colored. "You needn't be so explicit. And I lied."

"Two horses," Caleb bid in a cheerful, ringing voice.

The Indians looked interested.

"I'll marry you!" Lily added breathlessly.

"Promise?"

"I promise."

"When?"

"At Christmas."

"Not good enough."

"Next month, then."

"Today."

Lily assessed the Indians again, imagined herself carrying firewood for miles, doing wash in a stream, battling fleas in a tepee, being dragged to a pallet by a brave. "Today," Lily conceded.

The man in the best calico shirt rode forward again. "No trade," he said angrily. "Blue Coat right—woman much trouble!"

Caleb laughed. "Much, much trouble," he agreed.

"This *Indian* land," the savage further insisted. With that, he gave a blood-curdling shriek, and he and his friends bolted off toward the hillside again.

Lily turned to face Caleb. "I lied," she said bluntly. "I have no intention of marrying you."

He brought his nose within an inch of hers. "You're going back on your word?"

"Yes," Lily answered, turning away to climb back into the buggy. "I was trying to save myself. I would have said anything."

Caleb caught her by the arm and wrenched her around to face him. "And there's no baby?"

Lily lowered her eyes. "There's no baby."

"I should have taken the two horses when they were offered to me," Caleb grumbled, practically hurling her into the buggy.

Lily said nothing, and she was glad when she saw Fort Deveraux rising in the distance. After that band of Indians the ladies of the post didn't seem so intimidating.

Caleb let Lily off at her cottage without so much as a word of farewell. Given his mood, she didn't envy the soldiers under his command.

Carrying her valise in one hand, Lily went through the gate and up the walk without looking back. When she was inside she locked the door, stumbled over to the bed, and lay down on it, trembling. Soon she was going to be living on that land all by herself. The Indians could return at any time, and she might not win a second argument with them.

A determined knock at Lily's door made her sit bolt upright. After drawing a deep breath to compose herself she crossed the cabin and peeked out the front window.

Velvet was standing on the step.

Lily opened the door anxiously. "Velvet, come in!"

Velvet gave Lily an odd look and stepped inside. "Mrs. Tibbet sent me over. She and the colonel want you to come to supper tonight."

"How did they know I was back?"

"The whole fort knows that," Velvet scoffed. "There's lots of talk about you and the major goin' off together and all."

"We didn't 'go off together'!"

Velvet assessed Lily's travel-rumpled dress as she took a seat at the table. "I don't figure the facts matter much. As far as the people on this post is concerned, you're the major's mistress."

Lily grabbed the coffeepot off the stove, dumped the stale grounds into the trash, and started toward the back door. She went outside and pumped water into the pot while Velvet came to stand in the doorway, watching. "I suppose you think I should marry Caleb, like everyone else."

"If he'll have you," Velvet replied.

Before Lily could frame a reply to that Judd Ingram rounded the house and vaulted over the back fence. He glared at Velvet, who shrank back a step or two.

"I suppose you think you're real smart and real fancy," Judd growled, pushing his cap to the back of his head.

"Get out of here, Judd," Velvet said, but the order sounded lame.

He drew a sleeve across his forehead. "When the Tibbets send you packing back to Suds Row I'll be waiting. But it ain't gonna be easy getting on my good side again, Velvet."

Lily was tired of arrogant, pushy males. She'd already dealt with Caleb and six Indians that day, and she was finished with diplomacy. After taking careful aim she drenched Private Ingram with a coffeepot full of cold water.

"Get off my property," Lily warned. "And you'll leave Velvet alone from now on if you know what's good for you!"

Judd started toward Lily, but he stopped himself in midstride, swore, and stormed away.

Lily felt a hand close over her arm and looked up to see Velvet standing at her side. "You watch out for Judd," Lily's friend whispered. "He don't have no use for nobody what spites him."

Lily lifted her chin, even though she felt an elemental, lingering fear. When and if there was trouble, she'd face it straight on. For now, there was no sense in worrying.

The photographer had stopped his wagon beside the parade grounds, and he was setting up his cumbersome camera. Although he had a pronounced limp, there was a familiar deftness about him that made Velvet stop for a moment as she headed back to the Tibbets'. Her heart beat a little faster when the sunlight caught in his coppery-brown hair.

He looked so much like her own Hank.

Velvet wanted to call out that dear name, to see if the man would turn his head at the sound, but her throat was closed up tight. Her legs were no more nimble; although she knew Mrs. Tibbet was waiting for news of Lily, she couldn't move.

Hank, she thought.

As though she'd shouted, he turned to look at her. "Velvet?" he said, and suddenly he was moving awkwardly toward her.

God in heaven, after all those years, after all those men, somehow Hank had found her.

Shame stung Velvet; she knew she could not face him. Even though Hank had been the betrayer, leaving her standing at the altar, she wasn't about to let him see what she'd become. She lifted her skirts and ran wildly down the dusty street.

"Velvet!" Hank shouted after her. "Wait!"

She ran on and on, past the Tibbets' place, stopping only when she reached Lily's cottage across the street from the schoolhouse.

Lily was pumping water to fill the big wash kettle in her backyard, since several of her customers had already been by to drop off their dirty shirts. Suddenly Velvet returned, looking pale as porcelain and gnawing on her lower lip.

"He's here!" she sobbed. "Oh, Lily, he's *right here* at Fort Deveraux!"

Lily took her friend's arm and pulled her inside the house.

"He's here!" Velvet cried again.

"Hush!" Lily ordered, and then she dragged Velvet to a chair at the table and went to the stove to pour hot coffee for them both. "Who's here, for heaven's sake?" she asked when she was sitting and Velvet had regained some of her self-control.

"Hank," moaned Velvet, her face full of despair and yearning.

Lily was still completely puzzled.

"He was the man I was going to marry," Velvet managed to get out, drying her face with the corner of her apron. "He's a photographer now, looks like, but he was a farmer when I knew him. Courted me right and proper. I had a new dress and everything, but when the weddin' day came, Hank didn't show up at the church."

Lily reached out to close her hand over Velvet's in an effort to console her. "Your father should have shot him," she said with conviction.

Velvet gave a wail of despondency, then lapsed into a prolonged bout of snuffling. Lily fetched a yellow bandanna from the wash and handed it to her, and she blew loudly before going on. "Pa said I was better off without the rascal and made me come west with him and Eldon—that was my brother."

"Maybe Hank had a reason for not showing up at the wedding. Did you ask him?"

Velvet sniffled and shook her head. "A woman's got to have some pride," she said.

Lily thought of some of the things she'd done with Caleb and reflected that she'd once believed the same thing. "What are you going to do?"

"I don't know," Velvet said, her broad shoulders trembling beneath the shoulders of her starched calico dress. "I can't stand for Hank to know about Suds Row, Lily, and about Judd."

Lily sighed. "Did he see you? Hank, I mean?"

Velvet nodded. "I turned around and ran like the devil was after me."

"You'll have to face Hank sooner or later. In a community this small, you're not going to be able to avoid him."

Velvet's face fell while timid hope flared in her eyes. "He'll never understand."

Lily was angry. "He's in no position to go around *understanding* anyway. Didn't he ask you to be his wife and then leave you high and dry?"

Slowly Velvet nodded. "I can't talk to him. I'd be too scared."

Lily sighed. "Velvet Hughes, I have work to do. I can't sit around here all day trying to persuade you to do what you know is right."

"I know what's right?" Velvet looked patently unconvinced.

"You certainly do," said Lily with resolution.

"You won't talk to him for me?"

Lily stood up. "Absolutely not. I'm your friend, Velvet, not your nursemaid."

For all Lily's strength of purpose, Velvet looked so crestfallen that in the end she gave in and set off for the parade grounds.

The photographer was engrossed in taking pictures of serious-faced young soldiers. Lily waited—barely flinching when the flash powder exploded with a fiery *poof*—for him to notice her.

"Velvet sent you," he guessed. He was quite a handsome man, with dark auburn hair and quick brown eyes.

Lily nodded and introduced herself.

"Why did she run away?" Hank wanted to know.

Thinking of Velvet standing at the altar, waiting in vain for this man to marry her, filled Lily with ire. "People run away for all sorts of reasons," she said. "You ought to know that."

Hank looked honestly baffled. "I'm afraid I don't understand," he said.

Lily drew a deep breath and let it out again. She had work to do, and the day was practically gone. "She waited for you at the church, and you didn't come."

"I had a reason for that."

"Maybe you'd best share it with Miss Hughes, then," Lily responded. "A good day to you, sir." With that, she turned and walked away.

"Miss Chalmers?"

She stopped and looked back inquiringly over one shoulder.

Hank smiled broadly. "Where would I find Velvet, provided I wanted to explain myself and all?"

Lily felt her lips curve slightly. "She works for Colonel and Mrs. Tibbet," she answered, and then she continued on her way.

When Lily arrived home she threw herself into her work, but by sunset she knew it was hopeless. She'd have to stay up all night to keep up with her orders, and after the events of the past few days she was simply too tired for that.

After carefully closing the curtains, she washed her face and hands and repinned her hair. She'd exchanged her soiled yellow dress for a crisp calico earlier.

Lily's steps were slow as she approached the Tibbet house. She did hope Caleb hadn't been invited to supper, too, but she knew it was almost inevitable that he had been.

Velvet greeted her at the door with a worried look. "Did you see him? Did you talk to Hank? What's he doing here?"

"How can I answer your questions if you fire them at me like bullets from a Gatling gun?"

Velvet narrowed her eyes in an intimidating fashion even as she admitted Lily to the house.

"He's going to come and see you," Lily said, sticking her chin out to show she wasn't going to cower just because someone made a face at her. Hadn't she sent six Indians packing that very day, with almost no help from Caleb?

As if the thought had conjured him, Caleb appeared in the parlor doorway. He had obviously bathed and shaved and was wearing a fresh uniform and polished boots. His whiskey-colored eyes moved over Lily's calico dress with something that resembled amusement flashing in their depths. "Hello, Lily."

Lily's greeting was cool. "Major."

"Come in," he urged, "and face the music."

Something in his tone made Lily want to flee, but she wasn't about to give him the satisfaction of running away. She lifted her chin and advanced into the parlor.

Mrs. Tibbet was there, speaking with the chaplain, Captain Horatio. Once again Lily wanted to run; once again she stood her ground.

"Good evening, Mrs. Tibbet. Captain Horatio."

The captain only nodded, but Gertrude rushed over, linked her arm with Lily's, and half dragged her into the colonel's study, which was at the rear of the house.

It smelled of cigar smoke and beeswax, and there were paintings of famous Union generals on the walls. Lily was too much on her guard to notice anything more.

"My dear," Mrs. Tibbet began with stern affection, "I really must speak to you about your conduct."

Lily had to stand very straight and bite down hard on her lower lip to keep from crying. Mrs. Tibbet was her only friend, aside from Velvet, and her disapproval hurt terribly.

"Why won't you give up this silly idea of homesteading?" Gertrude went on. Her tone of voice was moderate, but her blue eyes were snapping. "I can't help thinking you're just being stubborn, Lily. Caleb is well able to provide for you, I assure you. He comes from one of the finest families in Pennsylvania—I've known the Hallidays a long time."

Lily looked down at the floor for a moment, gathering her courage. "You wouldn't understand," she said softly.

Gertrude sighed. "Do sit down," she told Lily kindly,

taking a chair herself. "Now what is it that I would find so difficult to understand?"

"I love Caleb very much," Lily began in a shaky voice, "but I'm not the woman for him."

Mrs. Tibbet raised her eyebrows. "Oh? And why not?"

Lily leaned forward in her chair and lowered her voice to a whisper. "I think I may be like my mother."

"How so?" Mrs. Tibbet asked, smoothing her skirts.

"She was—she drank. And there were men. Lots of men."

"Oh, dear," said Mrs. Tibbet seriously. "And you drink?"

Lily swallowed. "Well—no."

"Then there are men."

"Only Caleb," Lily said quietly. "But he can make me do and say the most shameful things. I'm so afraid it's because I'm—er—hot-blooded."

Mrs. Tibbet looked as though she might be trying to suppress a smile. "You wouldn't be the first girl who'd given herself to a man before marriage, Lily. It isn't a wise course of action, but it happens often enough."

Lily drew in a deep breath. "I suppose the drinking would come later," she said, discounting Mrs. Tibbet's remarks as mere kindness. "And then the men. No, I'm sure I'm better off going on with my life just as I've planned."

There was a rap at the door, and then Velvet put her head inside. "Pardon, missus, but dinner's ready, and the men say they're going to eat without you if you don't hurry."

"We'll be there in a moment," Mrs. Tibbet answered. "And tell the men that if they don't wait, they'll have me to deal with."

"Yes, ma'am," Velvet replied with a hint of laughter in her voice. The door closed with a click.

Mrs. Tibbet turned back to her guest. "If you were my own daughter, Lily, I would tell you the same thing. You couldn't do better than Caleb Halliday if you searched the world over for a man. Don't throw away a chance at real happiness—it might be the only one you get."

Lily pushed herself out of her chair and went to stand at

the window. From there she could see the moon rising above the roof of the house next door; it looked as though it had just squeezed out of the chimney. "Sometimes I think I know what I want. I'll decide that I want to marry Caleb and forget all about having a homestead. But then I remember what Mama was like."

"Lily, you're not your mother."

"No," Lily agreed sadly, turning to face Mrs. Tibbet, her hands clasped in front of her. "But Mama was young and happy once, and she must have thought she was in love with my father. She married him, she had his children. And then something changed, and she began to drink. Papa went away—I don't even remember him—and the men started coming around, one after the other . . ."

Gertrude came to take Lily's hands in her own. "Things will be different for you," she said quietly. "You're strong, and so is Caleb. Oh, Lily, don't be afraid to take a chance."

At that moment the colonel thundered from the hallway that he was going to have his supper right then whether the women cared to come to the table or not, and Lily smiled. "I promise I'll think things through very carefully, Mrs. Tibbet."

"Don't take too long," Gertrude answered, ushering her toward the door of the study. "Fate can take the strangest twists and turns, sealing us off from someone when we least expect it."

At supper Caleb and the colonel discussed military tactics while Lily and Mrs. Tibbet talked of dress patterns and the need to reform Suds Row. For all Lily could tell, Caleb wasn't even aware of her presence; but when dinner was over and she excused herself to leave, he immediately volunteered to walk her home.

Chapter
❧ 15 ❧

The moon seemed to ride on Caleb's right shoulder as he stood facing Lily at the door of her cottage. The walk there from the Tibbet house had been accomplished mostly in silence, but now he swept his hat from his head and cleared his throat.

Lily braced herself.

"There's something I've got to tell you—about your homestead," he began.

"If you're planning to give me another lecture, Caleb, kindly keep it to yourself."

A muscle bunched in his jaw, then relaxed again. "All right, have it your way. Good night, Lily."

She waited for Caleb to kiss her, but he only put his hat back on, turned, and went down the steps. Lily watched him for a few moments, then opened her door and entered.

The interior of the cottage was dark, and Lily felt a tremor of fear as she groped for the lamp she'd left on the sideboard, along with a box of matches. She heard a movement in the blackness and dived for the door, a scream gathering in her throat.

A strong hand clamped over her mouth before the sound could escape, and though Lily struggled, she was dragged back inside the cottage. Her attacker was wiry and strong, and he smelled of liquor and stale sweat. She knew who he was even before he pulled her over to the table and struck a match to light the lamp, even before he gagged her with a bandanna and tied her hands behind her and came around to face her.

"Go ahead and try to get away," said Judd Ingram. "That'll make it all the sweeter."

Lily was terrified, but she wouldn't allow Judd the satisfaction of knowing that. She let the expression in her eyes tell him what she thought of his kind.

He rounded the table and cupped her chin in one hand. "What a pretty little thing you are. I bet you just carry on something fierce when the major's loving you. Well, tonight I'll be the one who gives you what you need."

If Lily hadn't been gagged, she would have spit in his face. She lifted her chin to a defiant angle and glared.

Judd strode over to the bed and flung back the blankets and the top sheet. While he was doing that, Lily looked wildly around the room for some way of escape. Her only chance, she realized, lay in creating a diversion.

She bent over and, with a motion of one shoulder, upset the kerosene lamp in the center of the table. The glass chimney shattered, and liquid flame snaked out in every direction.

Lily leapt back out of the way while Judd cursed and began beating at the flames with a blanket. He was too late, though, for the fire seemed to flow from the lamp like magic, and soon the blanket itself was burning.

Lily ran for the door and flung herself against it, momentarily panicked by the spreading fire. Then her good sense came back, and she turned around to work the latch with her bound hands. She was on the brink of freedom when Judd grabbed her by her hair and flung her backwards toward the leaping flames.

Behind her gag Lily screamed. The fire was all around her, catching at her dress, singeing her skin with its heat. She struggled to her feet and ran toward the gaping door, hurtling through it. Outside, she lay down in the muddy grass and rolled until she was sure her clothes weren't burning anymore.

The schoolmaster, a small, lithe man with thinning yellow hair and compassionate gray eyes, was the first to reach the scene. Lily was weeping in terror when he untied her gag and helped her free her hands from the length of rope Judd had used to bind her.

"In the name of heaven," gasped the teacher, "what happened here?"

Lily looked back at the cottage. Flames were roiling behind the windows; it was as though hell itself had somehow broken through the ground to show it wasn't bound to the bowels of the earth. Ignoring the schoolmaster's question, she ran toward the house; her mother's address, the temporary deed to the homestead, and every item of clothing she owned were inside.

Miraculously, despite the smoke and the heat, Lily managed to find her valise. There were no clothes in it, but it did contain the deed to her land and a few small personal items.

She collided with Corporal Pierce on the step, and he put strong arms around her and pulled her away. She heard the *clang-clang* of a fire bell and fainted.

When she awakened Caleb was there, and soldiers were everywhere, doing their best to contain the blaze. There was obviously no hope of saving the house.

"Oh, Caleb," Lily whispered, "my business is gone—my clothes—"

His face was rigid. Without a word of explanation to Lily or anyone around him, he lifted her into his arms, along with her charred, battered carpetbag, and started out of the yard. They were well down the street before he rasped, "What happened?"

Lily wanted a few moments to compose herself before she told him. "Where are we going?" she countered, reaching up to brush a stray lock of sooty hair from her face.

He crossed the street, moving rapidly toward the row of houses where the officers lived. Lily assumed they were going to the Tibbet house and didn't press.

But Caleb went right on past the Tibbet place, and past its neighbor, too. He kicked open the gate of the third house and started up the walk.

"Caleb," Lily said. She'd managed to calm herself somewhat once the immediate crisis of the fire was past, but now she was beginning to feel alarmed again.

He didn't stop, didn't even look at her as he carried her up the front steps, across the porch, and into his house. In the musty parlor, with its ghostly, covered furniture, he set her on her feet.

"How did it start?" he asked finally, turning away from her to stand facing the snapping fire on his hearth. Even the cloth of his shirt didn't hide the uncompromising rigidity of his back and shoulder muscles.

Lily looked around the shadowy room, stalling for time. If she told the truth, she knew Caleb would do something rash and probably ruin his career in the process, yet she didn't see where she had any real choice. "There was a man inside my cottage when you left. He gagged me and tied me up."

Caleb whirled. "What?"

Lily wet her lips, hating to go on, yet knowing that she must. That she would be forced to, if she refused. "I tipped over a lamp, and he panicked and ran."

Caleb's gaze swept over Lily's singed hair, her burned, soot-stained dress. "My God."

She started to approach him. "I'm all right, Caleb. Isn't that the important thing?"

He caught her shoulders in his hands. "Who?" he rasped.

Lily closed her eyes for a moment. God knew she had no desire to protect Judd Ingram from justice, but she didn't want Caleb dealing with him in this state of mind. "I'm not going to tell you," she said gently. Decisively. "Not until morning."

Caleb's jawline went taut, and his grasp tightened on her shoulders. His tone of voice was a warning. *"Lily . . ."*

She stood her ground. "Whatever our differences, Caleb Halliday," she said firmly, "I love you, and I won't see you court-martialed or hanged because of something you did in the heat of anger."

He freed her abruptly and turned away, and she knew a battle was going on between the reasoning part of him and the savage that all men and women harbor somewhere within themselves. Lily wandered over to a gun cabinet and assessed the rifles lined up behind the dusty glass.

"I want to practice my marksmanship," she said.

"Touch those rifles and I'll tan your hide," Caleb warned.

Lily squared her shoulders. "I'll just have to do it on my own, I guess. Though I daresay there are plenty of soldiers on this post who would be glad to help me."

Caleb had poured himself a drink, and the look in his eyes was deadly. "I'll personally horsewhip the man who tries," he said in a dangerous undertone.

Lily ignored the remark. "Well, I guess I'd better go and ask Mrs. Tibbet if I can rely on her kindness for somewhere to sleep tonight. Good night, Caleb." She started toward the hall, but she didn't even get to the parlor doorway before the major stopped her.

"You're not going anywhere," he breathed. And even though Lily knew it was fear for her safety and not cruelty that drove him, she was annoyed.

"Let me go, Caleb."

His grip tightened. "You'll spend the night here," he said.

Lily's eyes widened. "Caleb, it's bad enough that I'm alone with you under this roof right now. Can you imagine what people will say if I stay till morning?"

"I don't give a damn what they say," Caleb replied, and Lily knew he'd never been more serious about anything.

"I'll be ruined!" Lily protested.

"You're already ruined," Caleb said, letting her go so he could toss back the last of his drink and set the glass down on the sideboard with a clunk. "Besides, there's something I want to find out."

"Wh-what?" Lily asked, retreating a step.

"Whether you lied to me when you said you couldn't be carrying my child."

Lily's cheeks flushed crimson. "Caleb Halliday!"

He arched one eyebrow and drew nearer. In a motion Lily couldn't possibly have foreseen or prevented, he lifted her off her feet again, cradling her in his arms.

"I'll scream," she warned, for already he was starting to bewitch her with one of his mysterious spells.

His lips were a fraction of an inch from hers. "Maybe," he answered, "but not in pain or fear."

Lily whimpered as his mouth tamed hers. A fire as hot as the kerosene blaze in the cottage ignited in her loins. "Caleb," she gasped when he finally relented and lifted his head to look directly into her eyes.

"Only the beginning," he vowed, starting toward the darkened stairway.

"I won't let you do this," Lily protested, though she hadn't the faintest idea how she was going to stop him.

"Won't you?" He climbed the stairs, then moved swiftly along a hallway. Lily winced, her arms wrapped around his neck, when she heard a door fly inward and strike the wall.

She landed hard on a bed and started to scramble up, only to have Caleb press her back to the mattress. Her legs were dangling over the side, and they were separated because Caleb was standing between them.

He stretched to light a lamp on the bedside table, and the flame drove back the shadows just a little way, revealing Caleb's determined face and the carved mahogany of the bedstead.

He caught hold of one of her feet and began untying her shoelaces. The fingers of his left hand curved with a gentle possessiveness around Lily's calf.

"What are you doing?" she managed to demand.

"I told you," Caleb answered, tossing the shoe aside and starting to roll down her ribbed stocking. The process was slow and sensuous, and Lily drew in a sharp breath when she felt his hand caress her upper thigh.

She tried again, sounding very reasonable. "Caleb, this is madness."

He was taking off her other shoe, turning down her stocking. Again he moved with excruciating leisure. "What is love if not madness?" he countered. Now both her thighs were being petted, and his thumbs strayed lightly over the soft place hidden beneath her drawers.

Lily trembled, but when she tried to say his name it caught in her throat. She raised her arms high above her head and stretched as a feeling of anticipation swept over her, but she couldn't have spoken to save herself from the entire Sioux nation.

Caleb pulled her drawers down in the same languorous way he'd removed her stockings, then knelt between her legs. "You lied," he said softly, running a finger over the tangle of golden curls at the meeting place of Lily's thighs.

She twisted on the rough, nubby bedspread, her confession hardly more than a breath. "Yes."

His shoulders forced her legs wide apart. He kissed her lightly, just where she needed and wanted kissing, and her body convulsed, seeking greater contact. He put his hands under her smooth bottom and squeezed gently, as though testing fruit for ripeness. "You're badly in need of a husband," he scolded in a very low voice.

Lily could only utter a sharp "Oh!" as she felt his breath sweeping over her. She ached, and only Caleb could appease her.

He put one of her legs over his shoulder, then the other. Lily felt his tongue make a brief, heated foray into her curls and arched her neck and back at the same time, thrusting herself closer to Caleb.

"A husband could look after you properly," Caleb went on. Even the pressure of his words was a sweet torment against her throbbing, still-hidden flesh.

Lily clawed at the bedclothes. "Caleb," she whispered. *"Caleb."*

He chuckled at her eagerness and disciplined her lightly with his tongue. She cried out in response, then groaned her urgings, sounding primitive and wholly desperate.

He unveiled the hidden nubbin and kissed it in passing. "What do you promise in return for what you want?"

Lily gave a strangled cry of fury and need, and Caleb laughed again. She felt him withdraw, and she mourned, then rejoiced when she felt his fingers there, plying her. "Nothing!" she gasped. "I—promise—*nothing!*"

Caleb held her apart for a long, suspenseful moment, then lapped at her with his tongue.

"Oh, God!" Lily cried. Grasping Caleb's head in her hands, she tried to press him back to her, but he resisted.

"Tell me, Lily."

She was still his captive, though he refused her the conquering she desired so desperately. The very pressure of his breath was driving her mad, and so was the proximity of his lips and fingers to the center of her passion. "Anything," she gasped. "I'll say anything . . ."

Caleb laughed and touched her with his tongue, delighting in the way her hips flew at the fleeting parry. "That you'll marry me?"

"Yes!" Lily groaned. "Yes—oh, God—I'll marry you—"

Caleb's voice cajoled her; she could feel the motion of his lips against her intimate place as he spoke. "You're not just saying that?"

"No—it's true—I swear it!"

"Scamp," Caleb scolded, but then he settled down to enjoy her in earnest, and Lily's spirit soared as her body thrashed wildly on the bed. He brought her to a scalding climax that made her buck on the mattress like a frenzied mare being broken to ride, then soothed her with his hands and voice as she lay quivering in the aftermath, struggling to get her breath.

During that session she lost the rest of her clothes and had no memory of shedding them.

Caleb turned her on the bed so that she lay properly and gripped her ankles to spread her legs. She made no move to close herself to him as he slowly removed his uniform shirt, his belt and boots, his trousers.

Lily could see herself in the full-length mirror affixed to the inside of the bedroom door, lying there waiting so obediently, and although the sight angered her, she still didn't move. In that age-old way of women who want love when it's happening, if not before or afterward, she had suspended every instinct but one.

Caleb didn't trouble to blow out the lamp, and Lily didn't care about that, either. She spread her fingers over his chest as he lowered himself to her, not to push him away, but to fondle and caress.

She felt heat in every part of her body, her toes, her midsection, her breasts. Even her eyes were like pools of liquid fire in her head, sweet fire that consumed without burning. She reached down to grasp Caleb by his shaft and delighted in the gasp she elicited.

He arched his neck as Lily attended him with her fingers, and he held himself above her with the strength of his arms. She slid beneath him, loosing him for a moment to grasp the backs of his knees in her hands and pull. When he was kneeling she drew him down into her mouth and began to tease and torment him just as he had teased and tormented her.

Her hands were on his powerful buttocks, her shoulders between his knees. Now it was Caleb who was the beloved prisoner, and Lily cherished him with her fiery touch. He moaned loudly and soon began to plead with her.

She would not release him, for she wanted all that he was,

all that he would have withheld from her. She wanted tender vengeance.

His buttocks began to move rhythmically beneath her hands. His voice was as raspy as a rusty hinge on a gate; his words were senseless. Lily knew he was begging, and her triumph was delicious. She didn't know whether he wanted her to stop or to continue, and she didn't care. For now, Caleb belonged to her completely, and she would do with him as she pleased.

He surrendered with a hoarse shout and a swift stiffening of his body, and Lily stroked his buttocks and the muscular backs of his thighs tenderly as she received him. She held him captive for a few precious moments afterwards, and when she allowed him to collapse, exhausted, at her side, she kissed his belly and the front of his thighs and the delightful, hairy expanse of his chest.

Caleb lay with one arm across his face, still trembling from the force of his release. "If you ever do that again," he managed, in a mock-threatening tone of voice, "I swear to God I'll sign over everything I own and let you lead me around like a lap dog."

Lily circled one of his taut nipples with the tip of her finger. "Your warning has been duly noted—sir."

Caleb laughed. "Vixen."

She replaced her finger with the tip of her tongue. "Tit for tat, you might say," she teased.

He laughed again and entangled both his hands in her rich, tumbledown hair. In one deft and painless motion he brought her to lie on top of him, her chin touching his. Tilting his head to one side, Caleb kissed her.

As the seconds passed the kiss grew more demanding, and Lily marveled to feel Caleb growing hard against the soft flesh of her stomach.

Presently he turned her swiftly onto her back and placed himself between her knees. His shaft was straining to sheathe itself in her, and she closed her hands around it.

Caleb watched her face with a fierce expression in his eyes

as she let her fingers play over him. "This time," he said gruffly, "I'm taking no prisoners." He took both her hands in one of his and guided his manhood inside her with the other.

Lily felt a wave of sweet heat roll over her as he teased her, giving her only an inch of himself. He stretched her hands above her head, and wide of it.

"Say it, Lily," he whispered. "I see it in your eyes, but I want to hear you say it."

Lily turned her head from side to side, not in denial, but in fever. She desperately needed all of him, but he was still withholding all but an inch. "I want you," she gasped.

"And?" Caleb prompted.

"I need you, you bastard!"

He gave her another inch. "Is that all?"

"I love you," Lily whimpered.

Caleb was satisfied, and he treated her to a long, deep stroke, then nearly withdrew. She begged, with her body and her mouth, until he filled her again, and because he deliberately prolonged the process, Lily's release was a slow, searing explosion within her. It buckled her torso, stole her breath, and wrung a shameless cry from her throat, and it seemed to go on forever.

She felt Caleb finish and expected peace. Instead her climax heightened, flinging her high up on the backs of her heels and making her clutch at the bedding in an effort to keep from soaring away.

When she finally was permitted a tremulous rest, Caleb laid a hand on her stomach and with slow, lazy strokes let her know that more still would be asked of her that night.

"Let me sleep," she said, pouting.

"And interrupt the taming of Lily Chalmers? Absolutely not."

"I'm tame," Lily insisted in a whimper as the circle of his hand widened, and something deep within her began to stir from its stupor of satisfaction.

"Far from it."

"Caleb, it's late, and I've already had a difficult night."

"The night hasn't even begun," Caleb replied. He was caressing her breast now, his thumb shaping the nipple.

Lily summoned up enough defiance to try to rise off the bed, but he only brought her back with gentle force, and her small insurrection was punished by a series of moist nibbles at her breast. Her right knee drew up, and her hand went to his hair even as she protested. "Is this what I can expect if I marry you?" she demanded.

Caleb stopped his suckling long enough to reply, "Oh, no. When we're married I won't be nearly as careful about where I have you, or when."

Lily blushed, even though she'd already done so many scandalous things in this man's arms. "Where?" she asked, and the question made him laugh.

"On my table," he answered. "You'll bring my supper in, as any good wife would, but what I'll be having is usually served on a pillow, not a plate."

Lily flushed even harder. She wondered that even her hair didn't turn red. "You are utterly impossible!"

"And insatiable," Caleb agreed.

In the mirror Lily could see her legs parting at his silent bidding, see his fingers dancing up the inside of her thigh even as she felt them. "Oh," she groaned softly, bracing herself. "Caleb, I can't bear any more—I really can't."

He ignored her, settling down to enjoy her breast with a contented moan even as he played her private place like some rare and delicate instrument. He drew moist music from her, symphonies made up of sighs and whimpers and muted cries, and, true to his word, he kept her thighs thrashing upon his mattress until the first rays of sunlight cracked the broken black sky.

Lily awakened long past midday, climbing out of her stuporous sleep like a drunk ascending toward sobriety. Caleb was gone, though the sheets still bore his distinctive scent, as did Lily's flesh and hair.

238

She sat up, grumbling, and immediately fell back to the pillows. Every muscle in her body was limp as melting butter, and a lush feeling of well-being divested her of all ambition.

There was one need she couldn't ignore, however, and she got up and peeked behind a nearby door. To her vast relief, there was a commode inside, and she used it, but she still felt too languid to get dressed.

Lily washed herself at the basin on the stand across from the bed, then staggered back to bed and tumbled between the sheets. She was hungry, but her sated muscles would not carry her out of the room.

As if in answer to a silent summons, Caleb opened the door and stepped inside. He was wearing the usual uniform trousers and shirt, and his butterscotch hair glistened with cleanliness. In his hands he carried a tray.

"Sit up, sodbuster," he ordered with a broad grin.

Lily scowled at him, but she shimmied up so that the pillows and the mahogany headboard were at her back, and she pulled the covers over her well-tended breasts.

Caleb set the tray in her lap, and the scent that rose from it made Lily's empty stomach rumble in anticipation. He'd ladled chicken and dumplings into a big crockery bowl, and there was a cup of steaming tea, too.

He didn't need to tell Lily to eat; she was ravenous.

"You quite wore me out last night," she complained when she'd tucked away every scrap of food and sunk back against the pillows. "I feel as if I could sleep for a week."

Caleb grinned. "You can only sleep until I decide to come back to bed," he corrected her. He made a great business of pulling his watch from his trouser pocket and consulting it. "Which will be in six hours, approximately."

Lily glared at him and folded her arms across the part of the sheet that covered her breasts. "I'll be long gone by then, Caleb Halliday," she said. "You needn't think you're going to use me at your convenience, like some concubine in a harem!"

He laughed and gestured toward the door. "Go ahead and leave, Lily. Nobody's holding you captive."

Lily yawned. She still felt too languid to move, and the food had heightened her laziness, not dispelled it. Although she wouldn't have admitted it, she wasn't looking forward to walking out of that house and facing the rest of Fort Deveraux, either. "I'll go in a little while," she said as Caleb took the tray and set it on the washstand next to the pitcher and basin.

He watched her settle in, and she saw his throat move as he swallowed. "Be my guest," he said hoarsely.

Lily made a little crooning sound as she wriggled deeper into the pillows and the feather-filled mattress. A delicious weariness moved over her like a cloud covering a too-bright sun. When she turned onto her back she felt the sheets slip down, uncovering her breasts.

Before she could cloak them again Caleb bent over her and placed her own hands over them. They were warm and plump beneath her fingers, and she felt the nipples harden against her palms. She smiled, half-asleep, half-drugged from a night of almost ceaseless loving.

The covers moved down further and further, and Lily felt Caleb's fingertips coursing gently over the tops of her thighs. With a little sound of impish enticement she parted her legs.

Soon she was soaring again. She didn't know what Caleb was doing to her, and she didn't care. She only wanted it to continue.

She slept when he left her, a deep, consuming sleep, and when he returned she was once again in his power. She submitted joyfully, exulting in the feel of his driving shaft as he made her his own, and she became the temptress in her turn, sending Caleb into a delirium of surrender as she drew his essence from him.

When the clock downstairs struck midnight they were both asleep, entwined in each other's arms, their exhausted bodies clinging to one another in spent passion.

Chapter

❧ 16 ❧

*L*ily came suddenly and violently awake a few hours later, and she stared up at Caleb with wide eyes as he held her in place on the bed, her hands pressed into the pillows.

"Who was it?" he demanded.

Lily knew he was asking who had attacked her in her cottage the night of the fire, knew he wouldn't wait any longer to be told. Still she hesitated, not to protect Judd, but because she feared what could happen to Caleb if he took his revenge. "Judd Ingram," she said quietly.

Caleb swore, and the look in his eyes was murderous.

"He didn't hurt me, Caleb," Lily reasoned hastily, grabbing at his upper arm with both hands. She was under no illusion that she could restrain the major if he chose to pull away, but she held on with all her might just the same.

"Why are you defending the bastard?"

Lily sighed. "I'm not, Caleb—he can burn in hell for all I care. It's you I'm worried about."

Caleb relaxed a little and let his forehead rest against

241

Lily's. "I want to kill him," he breathed. "I want to gut him like a trout and feed his insides to the crows."

"I know," Lily said gently, her hands moving soothingly on his tense shoulders, "but you mustn't take the law into your own hands. We've got trouble enough, Caleb, without your being hanged for murder or confined to a federal prison for the rest of your life."

He kissed her lightly on the mouth. "You're right," he conceded after a long moment.

"You could have Judd thrown out of the army, couldn't you?"

Caleb nodded grimly. "Yes. But if I did that, he'd be free to hang around this part of the country. If you should end up on that homestead of yours, you'd be vulnerable to him."

Lily's face fell at the prospect.

"No," Caleb went on, "I'll have him transferred. Say, to Fort Yuma. He'll feel right at home there with all those other scorpions to keep him company."

Lily sighed. "Suppose he attacks somebody else, Caleb? Suppose they don't get away like I did?"

Caleb's hands were gentle on her shoulders. "I'll make sure Ingram's commanding officer knows what kind of man he is, Lily. Don't worry."

With that subject out of the way, Lily announced, "I have another problem."

Caleb's grin was at once endearing and obnoxious. "You're naked in my bed, and you don't own a stitch of clothing in the world," he agreed.

"You needn't look so pleased about it!" Lily snapped, drawing up her knees and wrapping her arms around them. She was very careful not to let the covers slip away from her breasts.

"Not only that," Caleb went on, as though she hadn't spoken, "but the whole fort is talking about us. Speculating on what's going on right here in this room."

Lily flushed. Now that she could see things in better perspective she was furious with herself for giving in to

Caleb the night of the fire. If she'd gone to Mrs. Tibbet and asked for a place to stay, she could have avoided this problem.

She let her forehead rest on her upraised knees. "I'm just like my mother," she despaired.

Caleb made her lift her head. "No," he said softly. "She gave up, and you don't have the first idea how to do that. I don't mind telling you that sometimes I wish you did." He paused. "You're still going to move onto your land, aren't you?"

Lily swallowed. "Yes," she said, because Caleb was right. She didn't know how to give up on her dream. She'd had to struggle for everything all her life, and she'd never learned to walk away from something she wanted.

The major rose from the bed, gazing distractedly toward the window. Lily knew he wasn't seeing the fluttering lace curtains, which needed washing, or the blue of the sky. Presently he spoke, his voice hoarse and so low that she had to strain to hear it. "I guess there's no point in talking about it anymore, then. I'll see what I can do about getting you some clothes."

Caleb's loving had affected Lily like a dose of opium, but now she was fully awake, and having to stay in bed was like being held prisoner. "Mrs. Tibbet may still have some of Sandra's things around," she suggested.

Caleb didn't so much as glance in her direction. "Right," he answered, crossing the room and pulling open the door.

"Caleb, wait!" Lily cried. "You can't just walk out and leave me here like this—I need to know how soon I can expect you back!"

He let his head rest against the doorjamb for a moment, and his shoulders, always so straight and strong, looked slightly stooped to Lily. "Half an hour," he said, and then he was gone, closing the door quietly behind him.

Lily scrambled out of bed the moment she heard his bootheels on the stairs and looked at herself in the tall mirror. She was a sight, with her hair all sooty and tangled, and there were even smudges of black on her skin. She went into Caleb's bathroom and started water running in the tub.

She washed her hair and bathed quickly, not wanting to be indisposed when Caleb returned. If he decided to make love to her again, she might still be lying around in bed come Judgment Day.

Lily wrapped one towel around her torso and twisted another about her head, turban fashion. Caleb was sitting on the edge of the bed when she stepped over the bathroom threshold. There was a parcel beside him on the rumpled covers.

"Here," he said. "I hope it fits."

Color spread from Lily's toes to the roots of her hair. "Oh, Caleb, you didn't! Tell me you didn't walk into the general store and ask for a dress that would fit me!"

He shrugged, looking as dispirited as before. "It's no secret that you're here," he reasoned.

"But you could have gone to Gertrude," Lily insisted, mortified.

"I wasn't in the mood for a morality lecture," Caleb answered. "Put these things on, and I'll go down and make something to eat."

Lily waited until Caleb had left the room, then tore open the package. It contained a simple blue and white calico dress, a muslin petticoat, and a camisole and drawers, along with a packet of hairpins. Lily's cheeks flamed as she imagined Caleb buying those things; by now everyone on post probably knew about the purchase and all that it implied.

Hastily Lily dressed herself, braided her still-damp hair, and wound it into a circumspect coronet. When she went downstairs Caleb was in the kitchen, stirring something at the stove. It smelled wonderful.

"I've never known a man to cook so well," she remarked, feeling strangely shy for a woman who had tossed and moaned as she had in Caleb's bed.

244

Caleb shrugged and grinned at her over one broad shoulder. "I like to avoid eating in the mess hall whenever possible," he replied, and his golden eyes moved over Lily with amused appreciation. "Pull up a chair."

Obediently, for she was hungry, Lily took a seat at Caleb's round oak table. He set a bowl of savory stew before her. Even though she felt like consuming the stuff in two bites, Lily waited politely until Caleb had joined her.

After a few spoonfuls, however, she stopped eating to gaze at Caleb. "What am I going to do?" she asked softly. "Where am I going to live?"

Caleb set down his spoon. "You already know my answers to those questions, Lily," he said reasonably. "And you don't like them, remember?"

Lily propped her elbows on either side of her stew bowl and covered her face with her hands for a moment. She sighed as she lowered them to look at Caleb. "You're so much smarter than I am, Caleb. So much stronger and so much more persuasive. If I married you, I wouldn't be myself for very long. I'd soon become the person you *want* me to be."

He sat back in his chair, his arms folded across his chest. "I wouldn't change you for the world," he protested quietly.

"Yes, you would," Lily insisted. "You'd make me into a china doll, overseeing tea parties and embroidering samplers and gazing at you in worshipful adoration. And eventually you'd get tired of me, Caleb, and take a mistress."

He glowered at her, as though insulted. "I would never betray you."

"Oh, no? What about when I'm pregnant, Caleb—all fat, with swollen ankles and a chronic case of the weeps. Can you honestly say you wouldn't turn to another woman for the comforts you so obviously need?"

"I'd find you more attractive than ever," Caleb answered with annoyed certainty.

Lily picked up her spoon, then set it down again. Her hands knotted into fists in her lap. "You weren't faithful to Sandra. Why should I fare any better?"

"Because I love you, for one thing. And I explained before—I didn't sleep with Sandra."

"I might not feel like sleeping with you, either—if I happened to get pregnant, that is. What would you do then, Caleb?"

"Wait," he answered. Then a slow grin spread across his face. "And do my damnedest to seduce you. In case you haven't noticed, I'm pretty good at that."

Lily flushed and squirmed a little, remembering. There was no denying his assertion: Caleb could practically tumble her onto her back with a look or a touch. The fact tormented her, for she couldn't discern whether it was because of some special skill on his part or because she was basically a loose woman like her mother. "I've noticed," she admitted.

Caleb gazed at her for a long time, then went back to eating his stew. His silence was eloquent.

Lily finished her own food and rose to put the bowl in the sink. "Did you have Judd Ingram transferred?" she asked, because she needed the sound of Caleb's voice, whether it was kind or indifferent.

"He's in the stockade," Caleb answered, pushing away his empty bowl. "The colonel's considering making an example out of him."

Lily felt the hair stand up on the back of her neck. "By doing what?" she asked.

"The law provides ways to discipline a soldier, Lily."

She came to stand beside Caleb's chair and looked directly into his eyes. "Such as?"

Caleb sighed heavily. "Such as a public whipping."

Lily was horrified. Even though she despised Judd Ingram, she would never have wished him such a brutal fate. "Without a trial?" she demanded.

"Colonel Tibbet has the power to pronounce him guilty or

246

innocent, and it turns out that there are other incidents in his record."

Lily laid a hand on Caleb's shoulder, but it wasn't a gesture of affection. "If you permit such a barbarous thing to happen, Caleb Halliday, I vow that I'll never speak to you again."

He pushed back his chair, and Lily's hand in the process, to stand. "If you have your way, we'll be apart soon anyway. What do I have to lose?"

"Your honor," Lily argued.

He crossed the room to take his campaign hat from one of the pegs beside the kitchen door. "When it comes to letting another man lay his hands on you, I have no honor," he said bluntly.

She grasped the back of a chair as he put his hat on and reached for the doorknob. "Where are you going? You can't just leave me here—"

"I need to think," Caleb replied. "I'll be at my office if you want me."

"Well, I won't be here when you get back."

He grinned at her, but there was no fondness in the expression, no light in his eyes. "You won't get far, will you?" he asked, and Lily saw mockery in the curve of his lips and the set of his shoulders. "I'll wager you don't want to face even Gertrude without my wedding band on your finger."

He was right, and the knowledge stung Lily like the venom of a snake. She had no place to go now that her cottage had burned.

Slowly she turned away from Caleb and started out of the kitchen, but she flinched when she heard the door close. Lily had been lonely many times in her life, but nothing had ever weighed on her like Caleb's absence, and his anger.

She ventured through the spacious house, eyes brimming with tears as she explored it. In the study she found books, shelf after shelf of them, and their presence assuaged her aching spirit somewhat. When life became too complicated for Lily to bear, she always took refuge in a book.

After considerable deliberation she chose a novel translated from the French, and, having built a fire on the study hearth and lit the wick in a china lamp, she settled into a large leather chair to read.

The book was considerably spicier than any of the dime novels Lily had devoured over the years, and her eyes were wide as she turned page after page. The heroine was having some very naughty adventures, and Lily knew she shouldn't be enjoying them so. Still, she couldn't put the volume down.

The clock on the mantelpiece was striking twelve when she finally finished the rollicking novel and set it aside. The instant Lily left the story world for reality her problems crowded around her like invisible specters.

She thought of her sisters and wished them well, wherever they were, but something else was distracting her tonight. Caleb had gone out to "think," and he wasn't home yet.

Had he ridden to Tylerville, through the dark of night, to take solace in the arms of some new mistress?

Lily wrapped her arms around herself and bit down on her lower lip in an effort to hold in her despair. She reminded herself forcefully that she had no say over what Caleb did, since she wasn't his wife.

Because she was too proud to let him find her waiting up, Lily turned out the lamp and banked the fire, then felt her way upstairs in the dark. On the second floor the rooms were flooded with the light of a bright spring moon.

She selected the one furthest from Caleb's and slipped inside. After sitting at the window, looking down at the silver-bathed yards of the houses around her for some time, Lily finally stripped to her camisole and drawers and got into bed.

There was no scent of Caleb on the sheets, and that was both a relief and a torment to Lily. She snuggled down into the musty covers and waited in pained silence for the sound of a door opening and closing in the distance.

When Caleb arrived home from his office, where he'd sat thinking in the darkness for hours, Lily wasn't in his bed. While the discovery certainly didn't surprise him, it was painful. For one wild moment he thought she'd gone— maybe even persuaded the guards to let her ride out of the fort.

His panic subsided when his senses told him Lily was nearby.

He found her sleeping soundly in the spare room, arms and legs akimbo, blankets tossed aside. Gently he covered her, bent to kiss her forehead as he might have kissed his sister, and then left the room.

Despite his relief at finding Lily safe, Caleb was still troubled. There were so many things he and Lily hadn't resolved, might never resolve. At one time he'd been so certain about the course his life was taking, so sure that he was doing what he wanted to do. Now he felt more confused with every passing day.

All he was sure of was that he wanted Lily and needed her, not just in his bed but in every part of his life.

Alone in his room, he sat down in a chair to pull off his boots. After tossing them aside he stripped away his shirt and belt and trousers, climbing naked into a bed perfumed by Lily's presence.

He ached, not just to have her beneath him, but to have her beside him. He wanted to tell her why he needed to go home and face Joss, why he was tired of the army, why he wanted sons and daughters. He wanted her to hold him in her arms and tell him that everything would be all right, that they would work out all their differences and learn to live together in peace.

It seemed impossible. Turning onto his stomach, Caleb pounded his pillow into shape and collapsed into it. The erection he'd gotten, thinking about Lily, forced him to flip over onto his back again. If that woman had the sense God gave a gopher, she'd have been in that bed, warm and willing. She'd have taken him to her, burned him with her gentle fire, made him cry out in the night.

Caleb's shaft seemed to double in size.

Cursing, he got out of bed, walked into the bathroom, and, without lighting the kerosene-fed heater under the water tank, began filling the tub.

He gasped and bared his teeth when he settled into the frigid water, but it did its work. Ten minutes later he was in bed, shivering even in his sleep.

When Lily awakened the next morning she quickly discovered that Caleb had already left the house. After washing she dressed and groomed her hair, then squared her shoulders and went out. It was time she stopped hiding under Caleb's roof.

She was halfway up the Tibbets' front walk when Velvet came bursting out to greet her.

"Lily!" she whispered, as though she'd never expected to see her friend again.

Lily smiled wanly. "Hello, Velvet. Have you come to warn me that the Scarlet Letter Society is out to put an 'A' on my chest?"

Velvet looked baffled. "The who is about to do what?"

"Never mind," Lily replied. "Is Mrs. Tibbet at home?"

Velvet shook her head. "She's at a special meetin' over at the church."

Lily sighed. "They're probably casting lots to decide whether to tar-and-feather me or hand me over to the Indians."

Eyes rounded, Velvet shook her head. "No, they're jawin' about what to do with the women and kids that still live down on Suds Row." Hesitantly she gripped Lily's hand. "I've been worried ever since I heard about what Judd done. You didn't set foot out of the major's house, and I was afraid you'd been hurt bad in the fire."

"I'm sorry, Velvet," Lily said softly, touched at her friend's obvious concern. Her cheeks stung a little as she remembered what she'd been doing, with and for Caleb. "I didn't think anybody would be concerned."

Velvet was starting off down the walk, and she clearly wanted Lily to go along. "They're going to knock down my shack and chop it up for firewood, and I don't want to miss that!"

Lily laughed, but before the sound had died away an idea came to her. A stunning, daring, wonderful idea.

"Come on, Velvet!" she cried, lifting her skirts and bursting into a dead run. "We've got to get there fast!"

Lily ran breathlessly down the street, her skirts still clasped in her hands, Velvet hot on her heels. She was gasping when she reached Suds Row just in time to see the last wall of Velvet's weathered hovel topple inward.

"Stop!" she screamed as one of the half dozen men assigned to the detail hoisted an ax to begin breaking a wall into manageable pieces.

Although Lily had no power to give orders and expect to have them obeyed, the soldier lowered the ax to his side.

Corporal Pierce approached, with a touch to the brim of his cap and an embarrassed aversion of his eyes. "Begging your pardon, Miss Lily," he said uncomfortably, "but we've got orders to follow here."

By then Lily had almost caught her breath. "I—want it—" she gasped out.

Wilbur looked patently horrified. "Surely you wouldn't consider living on Suds Row," he said. Then he lowered his voice. "If the major won't marry you, I will."

Lily was now exasperated as well as winded. "Of course I don't mean to live on the Row," she answered, ignoring Wilbur's whispered offer to make an honest woman of her. "I want to haul that building onto my land and nail it together again."

A buzz went through the small company of men, then spread to the women looking on, children clinging to their skirts. Their eyes were flinty with hardship and perpetual suspicion.

Lily put her hands on her hips. "I have a homestead a few miles from here," she explained. "In order to prove up, I've got to have a house, and I don't see why this one wouldn't do until I get my lumber."

Wilbur sighed. He clearly wasn't much fonder of Lily's homesteading notions than Caleb was, and he had even less room to say so. "This shack is government property," he said, "and the colonel told us to chop it up for the mess hall stove."

"It's such a waste just to burn it," Lily reasoned, her voice carrying through the small crowd.

"How would you get it out to your land anyhow?" one of the laundresses inquired. She sounded curious rather than hostile.

"You'd need lots of help," observed another.

Three of the soldiers volunteered to haul the four downed walls to Lily's homestead by mule team. Corporal Wilbur Pierce, not to be outdone, insisted on leading the expedition.

"Wait a minute," Velvet called out. "What about your orders? How are you going to explain this to Colonel Tibbet?"

Lily glared at her friend. "He doesn't care what happens to this pile of old boards," she insisted. "He just wants it cleared away."

The soldiers discussed this, and Wilbur allowed as how he couldn't turn a wheel without speaking to the colonel first. He set off to do so while Lily walked around and around the fallen building. She'd live in it until her other house was built, then turn it into a chicken coop or a stable for Dancer.

It never once occurred to her that Colonel Tibbet might have an objection, and, as it happened, he didn't. Wilbur returned within fifteen minutes, beaming.

"He said he didn't give a damn what I did with the thing as long as I got it out of here so Mrs. Tibbet would stop pestering him about 'flourishing sin,'" Wilbur confided, reaching Lily's side. His smile faded. "There's no telling what the major'll have to say when he hears about this, though."

"Nothing," Lily said confidently. "Caleb's under Colonel Tibbet's command, same as you are."

"He's going to tan your hide, that's what he's going to do," Velvet fretted, fidgeting at Lily's side.

"He wouldn't dare."

Wilbur cleared his throat. "Don't be too sure of it. The major isn't afraid of anybody or anything. He probably wouldn't think twice about walloping one puny little woman."

Lily gave the corporal a quelling look, causing him to blush to his ears. "When can we move this building?" she asked practically.

The soldiers consulted with one another and agreed that Sunday would be the day, since they'd all be off duty then.

Lily would have liked to undertake the project that very morning, but she knew she wasn't going to get her way, so she thanked the men graciously, and they left. Wilbur hesitated, but in the end he followed the others.

Assessing the women around her, Lily approached the one with the most threatening countenance. She held out her hand in a gesture of friendship but said nothing.

The woman, not big like Velvet but wiry and hard-looking, ignored Lily's hand. "Are you like them church ladies?" she demanded. "You wantin' to see us run off for good?"

Lily drew a deep breath, then let it out again. Although she could be devious if the situation called for it, she didn't make a habit of telling lies. "I don't approve of what you do," she answered, "but I'm not part of any crusade to send you away. The ladies of Fort Deveraux aren't any fonder of me than they are of you."

At this, the woman spat into the dirt, then beamed and returned Lily's handshake.

With great personal effort Lily kept herself from cringing. "Thank you," she said.

She would have turned and walked away, but the woman engaged Velvet in conversation.

"How're you doing over there at the Tibbet place? They treatin' you right?"

"I've got use of the family bathroom," Velvet replied proudly.

There was a collective gasp of wonder at this, and Lily felt an aching sorrow to think that most of these women envied Velvet her fresh start in life. They weren't prostituting themselves and ruining their hands with lye soap by choice, after all. They were just trying to survive.

Velvet took Lily's arm and started pulling her back in the direction of the officers' houses. "We've got a lot to do," she called to her friends, in explanation.

"Did Hank come to call yet?" Lily asked eagerly as she and Velvet hastened along the hard-packed road.

"No," Velvet answered, looking crestfallen. "I figure he's probably heard about me and Judd. Couldn't have helped it, with everybody yammering about whether Major Halliday's going to horsewhip that little two-peckered cuss or not."

Lily felt herself go pale, and not because of Velvet's language. She'd hoped she'd dissuaded Caleb from having Private Ingram whipped, but it appeared that he was still entertaining the idea. She drew a deep breath to steady her nerves. "Do you still love Hank?"

"Never loved nobody else," Velvet said firmly.

"Well, then, why don't you go to him before he gives up and leaves the fort forever?"

Velvet's voice was hushed. "You don't think he'd really do that, do you?"

Lily shrugged, wondering why she couldn't set aside her misgivings and take her own advice. She ought to go to Caleb with a white flag in one hand and let him marry her. "Men get discouraged, just like women do," she answered.

Velvet looked delightfully worried. "Oh, my. I just naturally figured he'd come to me, since he was in the wrong and all."

With a smile Lily took Velvet's hand for a moment and squeezed it. "If I were you, I'd go to him and tell him just how wrong he was."

A touching eagerness showed in Velvet's face, but then she gave Lily a stern look. "If I were you," she countered, "I'd get the major's weddin' ring on my finger, and his baby in my belly, and I'd forget this whole stupid idea of homesteadin'!"

Insulted, Lily lifted her chin and quickened her pace, as if to leave Velvet behind. "Well, you're not me," she said stiffly.

Velvet's sigh was a little forlorn. "No," she agreed. "I ain't you."

Chapter
❧ 17 ❧

When Lily arrived at Caleb's house prepared to tell him that she refused to spend another night under his roof, no matter how he might protest, she got a surprise. He'd left a note in the center of the kitchen table, brusquely informing her that he'd taken some of his troops on patrol and that he'd be gone about a week. His crisp order that she behave herself was followed by a hastily scrawled "Regards, Caleb."

"Regards!" Lily muttered, the note rattling a little in her hand. "The man steals my virtue, holds me prisoner in his bed like some harem girl, and then he has the *temerity* to offer me his regards!"

It was only after time had soothed her nettled pride that Lily realized what a stroke of good fortune it was, Caleb's being gone a full week. By the time he got back she'd be settled on her homestead, living in the house the United States Army had so conveniently discarded.

Humming, Lily went about straightening up Caleb's house, that being the least she could do in return for his hospitality—however selfishly motivated it was. She'd made very good progress by the time Mrs. Tibbet came to call that afternoon.

"Would you like tea?" Lily asked, straightening her dusty apron as she admitted her friend.

Gertrude beamed. "So you've married him after all. Oh, Lily, that's grand!"

Disappointing Mrs. Tibbet was one of the most difficult things Lily had ever done. "But I haven't, you see," she said, lowering her eyes. "The place needed cleaning, and I didn't want to be obliged—"

"Oh, dear," sighed Mrs. Tibbet. As she entered the house she tugged off her gloves and shook her head. "I don't mind telling you that it's a blow," she said. "I was so sure you'd come to your senses."

Lily bit back a sharp reply and forced herself to smile. "About that tea . . ."

"I couldn't swallow a thing," said Gertrude, and she did indeed look a little peaked. She moved unsteadily into the parlor and collapsed into a chair. Her manner was quite resolute when she spoke again, however. "Lily, I simply cannot tolerate this situation. It absolutely will not do. You are not only ruining your own reputation, my dear, but Caleb's career as well."

Lily was dejected. "I'd never hurt Caleb on purpose," she said.

"I don't know about that," Mrs. Tibbet replied, her blue eyes sharp and uncompromising as they swept over Lily's person. "You've quite bewitched him, and you've as much as admitted to me that you and Caleb have been intimate. And yet you refuse to marry the man. Do you think that doesn't hurt him?"

Lily swallowed. "I suppose it does," she confessed. "But I do love him—that's why I can't resist when he wants"—she hesitated and blushed furiously—"when he wants me. And I'm only here because the cottage burned and I had no place to stay."

"You know very well that you could have come to the colonel and me!" Mrs. Tibbet flared, shaking her finger at Lily.

Lily swallowed again, and her eyes were burning with unshed tears. "I know. Caleb has only to touch me, or look at me in a certain way, and I lose my head."

Mrs. Tibbet relented a little in the face of Lily's abject repentance and spoke more gently. "Believe it or not, I do understand—it was the same with the colonel and me, once upon a time. The difference is that I couldn't wait to marry John—the moment he asked me, I set a date."

It was hopeless trying to explain why she couldn't marry Caleb. Nobody understood—sometimes Lily didn't understand it herself. "I'll be leaving the fort on Sunday," she said finally, "if all goes well. May I stay with you until then?"

"Certainly, though it's a little late if you're hoping to save your reputation. Nothing will do that but a wedding!"

Lily bit her lower lip. Her reputation be damned, then, for there would be no wedding—not unless Caleb decided to live with her on the homestead. And he'd have to give his word that he wouldn't drag her off to Pennsylvania, either. "Thank you," she said, leaving her other thoughts unspoken. Since she had no things to gather, she and Mrs. Tibbet left the house at once.

The soup tureen nearly slipped from Velvet's hands when she walked into the Tibbets' dining room that night and found Hank Robbins sitting at the table, bold as you please. His brown eyes seemed to strip away her dress as she stood there, and suddenly she felt as delicate and attractive as Lily.

"Hello, Velvet," he said.

Velvet glanced at Lily in desperation. Her friend was smiling, a sure sign that inviting Hank for dinner had been her idea. "Hello," she managed to croak, setting the tureen down in the middle of the table with a clunk. Hank's hair brushed the underside of her breast as she reached, and she felt as though she'd stepped into a lake just as lightning was striking the water.

Somehow she got back to the kitchen, where she used up a good five minutes trying to figure out what to do. The only thing she could think of was strangling Lily.

Just walking in there and serving the roast beef, once the first course was over, took all the fortitude Velvet possessed. She gave Lily a look that would have ignited a wet blanket even as she carefully avoided Hank's gaze.

"Mr. Robbins was just telling us that he didn't mean to leave you at the altar at all," Lily announced with a bright smile. "He was hurt in an accident—you've noticed, of course, that he limps—and when he was supposed to be at your wedding he was laid up in the hospital in the next town."

Velvet scowled at Hank as the pain of that day came back, fresh as ever. "He could've sent a message," she said.

"I did," Hank replied quietly. "My guess would be your dear old daddy just didn't pass it on to you. He wanted you to go west with him, remember, so he'd have somebody to cook his meals and wash his clothes."

Velvet reflected that that was just the kind of nasty, underhanded thing her pa would have done, God rest his soul. "You sent a message?" was all she could say, even though she knew it sounded stupid.

Hank nodded. "I told you I loved you," he said. "I've been searching for you ever since, Velvet."

"Do we get any dessert?" the colonel boomed.

Lily was immediately out of her chair. "I'll finish serving dinner and clean up afterwards," she volunteered. "Velvet, why don't you and Mr. Robbins go out for a walk?"

Tears slipped down Velvet's cheeks, and she wiped at them with the corner of her apron. "You don't know what I've been doing all this time!" she wailed to Hank, and then she turned and fled back to the kitchen.

She dashed out the back door and down the steps, but she found she could go no further than the rear gate. She was consumed by grief and stood sobbing into her palms.

Hank stood behind her at a little distance—she was aware of him long before he touched her shoulder and said her name.

She forced herself to turn and face him, but she still couldn't speak.

"What is it?" he asked quietly, his eyes full of concern. "What have you been doing that's so terrible?"

A great shudder of anguish moved through Velvet. Once he learned the truth Hank would never forgive her, but there had been enough running away, and she couldn't bring herself to lie. Not to this man. She accepted the handkerchief he offered and dried her face.

"Things was hard after Pa and Eldon died," she managed to say, mopping at her eyes again.

Hank nodded, his gaze tender, silently urging her to go on.

Velvet drew in a deep breath and gripped a picket of the gate in one hand. For the first time in her life she thought she might faint. "I did cleanin' work mostly till I came to Fort Deveraux. I'd heard I could make a lot of money here, washin' clothes for the soldiers." She paused and looked away for a moment, drawing strength from the orange and crimson blaze of the setting sun. "I found out soon enough that there were a lot of other women here lookin' to wash clothes—there just wasn't enough work to go around. I—I ended up takin' money from men."

For a moment Hank just stood there, the color draining out of his skin. "For what?" he asked, his voice a low rasp.

Velvet felt as though she was being torn apart piece by piece, organ by organ. She lowered her eyes for a moment, then met Hank's gaze squarely. He knew—she could see that—but he was going to make her tell him. "For sleepin' with me," she said.

With a muttered exclamation Hank turned away, his

broad shoulders stiff beneath the rough, plain fabric of his shirt.

Velvet reached out her hand, then let it fall helplessly to her side. She'd lost him a second time, and the experience was a cruel one. She doubted she'd ever recover from it. "I'm sorry," she whispered.

He whirled so suddenly that Velvet was startled and leapt backward. His face was taut with anger and pain.

"You were my woman," he whispered with hoarse fury. "How could you have let another man touch you?"

The resilience that had allowed Velvet to survive the many hardships life had dealt her surged to the fore. She advanced on Hank, raging. "I wasn't your woman. I wasn't *anybody's* woman. I was all alone in this world, and I did what I had to do!"

Hesitantly Hank lifted his hand to her face. His thumb brushed away a tear. "There wasn't a day or a night that I didn't think about you, Velvet."

She hugged herself, afraid to hope or trust. "I didn't love none of those men," she said miserably. "I could only stand lettin' them touch me because I pretended they was you."

Hank's smile was soft and infinitely sad. "I'm not going to lose you again because of pride," he said. "I don't like that you took money from those men, but I figure I love you enough to get by that in time. All that really matters to me is now, Velvet. Now and next week and next year, and all the years after that, when you and I are going to be together."

Velvet hardly dared to believe her ears. She'd had very little good fortune in her life; she didn't know how to deal with much besides trouble. "Folks around here won't ever forget—there'll be talk—"

He laid two fingers to her lips, silencing her. "I don't care," he said. "I've found you. That's all that's important."

With a sob, Velvet let her head drop against Hank's sturdy chest. Tenderly he enfolded her in his arms.

"Hush, now," he said. "Things are going to be different after this. Very different."

An hour later Velvet and Hank were married in the Tibbets' front parlor, and Lily and Mrs. Tibbet cried throughout the ceremony. Velvet figured Lily was touched by the romance of it, and Mrs. Tibbet was probably grieving because she'd lost another housekeeper.

Velvet didn't care about anything but the man at her side.

The sun was just setting when he handed her up into his rig, parked out behind the Tibbets' house. The inside was cool and dark and smelled of chemicals, but it might as well have been a palace as a photographer's wagon, for all Velvet cared.

As Lily looked down on the photographer's wagon from an upstairs window that night she was almost overcome with loneliness. She pictured Caleb spreading his bedroll out on the ground and remembered how it had been that night when the two of them had slept on her land, with the creek flowing by in the darkness.

She recalled that first release, brutal in its force. The stars had seemed to melt in the sky. . . .

Resolutely Lily turned away from the window and began undressing. It was Velvet's wedding night, not her own, she scolded herself, so she might as well stop having such wicked thoughts.

Of course, thoughts don't go away just because a body decides they're wicked—sometimes that makes them all the more tenacious. Lily stretched uncomfortably, her body tensed in a way that only Caleb could relieve.

She bit her upper lip. Once Caleb returned from patrol and found out she'd moved onto her land, he'd probably wash his hands of her once and for all and take up with a woman who was less of a trial. Bianca, for instance.

Pain speared Lily as she imagined Caleb leaving Bianca's house in Tylerville, whistling under his breath. Maybe Velvet and Mrs. Tibbet were right; maybe she should just get Caleb's wedding band on her finger and his baby growing inside her, if it wasn't already, and put homesteading straight out of her mind.

A burning ache settled between Lily's legs. If she didn't marry Caleb, what was she going to do when she felt like this? And she knew she would, over and over again, night after night and year after year.

"Caleb," she whispered, and the May breeze flowing into the room through her open window seemed to whisper back.

She shook his name off with a toss of her head. She knew better than to depend on anybody else, especially a man, for anything she needed. Lily spread her legs and arched her neck, and after a few feverish minutes the tension in her came unsprung, like a watch too tightly wound.

It wasn't the same as it would have been with Caleb, though, and Lily cried a little as she settled down to sleep.

On Sunday morning, while the church service was going on, the pieces of Lily's house were loaded onto two drays, which were drawn by teams of sturdy army mules. Lily thought the Lord might be against the project—it being the Sabbath day—when a wall slipped its rope bindings and slid onto the ground before they'd even reached the gates.

Behind the drays was a wagon carrying the wood stove and furniture that had been in Velvet's house. Lily wasn't looking forward to sleeping on the mattress where so many men had been entertained, but she supposed it was better than stretching out on the floor. The things she'd ordered in Spokane would start arriving soon anyway. She could make do until then.

At noon the small party reached Lily's plot of land.

She got out a hand-drawn map that she'd made herself and carefully showed Wilbur where she wanted the shack to be erected. Her permanent house would be built with the back wall on the very edge of the property line so she could look out her front window and watch her crops growing.

Lily had been in Mrs. Tibbet's kitchen since before the

sun rose, making doughnuts for the men. These she'd carried in a picnic basket strapped on top of one of the loads. A keg of nails and a collection of tools had been brought along, too, and soon the battered walls were going up.

Using a borrowed ax, Lily went to the woods at the far side of her property and found a fallen tree. She began chopping at it, meaning to secure wood for her stove, and before she'd made more than a dent in the thick bark she was sweating like a field hand.

Lily decided she was going to need a saw and went back to get one from the supply wagon.

The walls of the shack were up, and the dedicated young soldiers were hoisting the roof into place. Lily stopped to watch as the other men started carrying things inside.

When they got to the small cook stove she remembered her mission and began plundering for a saw. She found one and started back toward the woods, only to have Corporal Pierce fall into step beside her.

"Here," he said, taking the saw from her in an undeniably arbitrary way.

Lily was too grateful for Wilbur's help to point out that he was being high-handed. "I'll have to learn to cut my own wood sooner or later," she reasoned.

Wilbur pushed his blue cap to the back of his head and looked patently annoyed. "Maybe so, but I've got leave coming this month, and I mean to see that you're set up proper. Some of the men will help."

On impulse Lily linked her arm with Wilbur's. "No," she protested. "I know you've been looking forward to this leave—you had plans for it."

Wilbur favored her with a bright grin, and Lily reflected that if it hadn't been for Caleb, and their differing dreams, she might have fallen in love with this young soldier. "Sure I have plans for it. Chopping wood and putting up a new house, once that lumber arrives."

Lily laid her head against the rounding of his shoulder for

a moment. "I'm grateful, Wilbur," she said. When she looked up at him again she saw bewilderment in his eyes.

When they reached the fallen tree Wilbur set to work, sawing with a vengeance. Lily couldn't just stand still and watch him, so she took up the ax she'd left behind and did her best to cut away some of the larger branches.

There was a neat pile of firewood on the ground within an hour, and Lily was about to gather up an armful to carry back when Wilbur gripped her gently by the shoulders and made her stand up straight again.

"You're so beautiful," he said, as though the fact troubled him terribly.

Lily felt uneasy. "Wilbur—"

Before she could get out more than his name he dragged her against him and kissed her soundly on the mouth. It was over before Lily gathered the impetus to push away, and it left her stricken. She hadn't expected to enjoy another man's kiss, but there had been definite stirrings deep down inside her, and Lily was horrified.

She'd been right, she realized, in fearing that she was like her mother. She squatted hastily to gather up the firewood again, her vision blurred by tears of pure shame. "Don't you ever do that again, Wilbur Pierce," she whispered. "Do you hear me? Not ever!"

"I'm sorry," Wilbur said, crouching to face her and pick up chunks of wood from the small tree.

Lily thrust herself to her feet and started back toward her little house, which was now completely assembled. The photographer's wagon was sitting down by the creek, and the horses, unharnessed, were drinking.

Velvet and Hank had come to visit. Lily was so delighted that she put the episode with Wilbur out of her mind, dashed away her tears with the back of one hand, and quickened her pace. After dropping the wood by the front door she embraced Velvet, who had been watching Hank set up his camera.

"Mr. Robbins thought you might like a few pictures,"

Velvet informed her friend. "To commemorate the occasion."

Lily was delighted by the idea, and she posed, looking suitably serious, beside the front door. A tremendous flash exploded from the bar Hank was holding high above his head, and she started.

"Someday you'll show these photographs to your grandchildren," Hank enthused, coming out from beneath the black cloth that draped both himself and his camera.

I'm probably never going to have any, Lily thought sadly, but her smile was unwavering.

Wilbur and his friends went back to the trees with a wagon for the rest of Lily's firewood, and Lily and Velvet walked down to the creek with water buckets.

"Hank and me, we're probably going to be your neighbors," Velvet confided. "We got our eye on a piece of land over yonder, on the other side of them trees. Matter of fact, we're on our way to Tylerville to file a claim."

"But what about his photography business?"

"Hank says he can still take pictures now and then. What we really want is a piece of land, so we can make a place for our sons and daughters to grow up."

Lily put down her bucket and flung her arms around her friend for a brief hug. "Oh, Velvet, that's wonderful! I won't feel so lonely, knowing you're nearby."

Velvet returned the embrace somewhat awkwardly, and she didn't look all that enthusiastic. "I don't understand why you'd want to live out here all by yourself anyway, especially when you could be with the major."

Lily didn't want to talk or even think about Caleb. Or the kiss she and Wilbur had just exchanged under the fragrant pine trees. "A woman doesn't need a man to live, Velvet. And I'm living proof of that."

"Oh, no?" countered Velvet. "Well, what about all these blue-suited monkeys fetchin' and carryin' and nailin' and sawin'? Where would you be without them, Lily Chalmers?"

Lily picked up her bucket again and started toward the

house. "They'd have helped a man as willingly as they're helping me," she said.

"In a pig's eye," Velvet retorted. "They know you're going to be out here all alone, Lily, and some of them just may expect somethin' in return for all this neighborliness!"

Lily raised her chin. "Any unwelcome callers will find themselves looking down the barrel of a twelve-gauge shotgun."

They had reached the makeshift cabin, and Lily led the way over the threshold. There were gaps in the floor, and all the glass had broken out of the windows except for a few jagged shards. "What do you know about shootin'?" Velvet demanded, shuddering a little as she glanced around the one-room shack. Just being there probably brought back unpleasant memories for her.

"I used to hunt grouse with my brother," Lily said firmly, "and I've got a gun. See? It's right over there, in the corner."

Velvet put down her bucket beside the stove and walked over to inspect the shotgun. She let out a long, low whistle. "Where did you get this?"

"I . . . borrowed it from Caleb."

"Without him knowin', I reckon," Velvet added. "You'd better aim good when you fire this, Lily, because it's only going to shoot one shell at a time. You'll have to stop every time and reload."

Lily was distinctly uneasy. "Put that thing down, for heaven's sake. You're making me nervous!"

"You ain't smart enough to be nervous," Velvet countered.

"If you weren't practically the only friend I have," Lily returned, her cheeks flaming with anger, "I'd be insulted right now."

Velvet shook her head. "They say the good Lord looks after fools and drunks. I hope He's keepin' an eye on you."

"I'm no drunk!" Lily flared.

"That's so," Velvet replied meaningfully.

Lily decided to change the subject before she found

herself friendless. "If you and Hank are going to Tylerville, you could do me a big favor."

"What's that?" For the first time Lily noticed how Velvet's eyes were sparkling, and how her skin had a pretty pink blush behind it.

"I've ordered some things from Spokane. I expect they've arrived by now, and I'd like you to tell the man at the freight office to ship them on out here."

Velvet nodded. "That's easy enough."

Hank was calling her name from outside.

"Time to go," Velvet said, beaming. She not only jumped at Hank's command, it seemed to Lily that she liked being ordered around.

Lily shook her head in disgust. Now that Caleb was probably out of her life for good, she was never going to fall into that kind of trap again. She'd be beholden to no man.

In five minutes Velvet and Hank were rolling over the hillside toward Tylerville in their big wagon. Lily devoutly hoped they would be back soon.

Presently the soldiers returned to the fort, including a distracted Wilbur, and Lily was alone on her land, in her own house, for the first time. She immediately took up the shotgun and carried it outside.

After taking a shell from her apron pocket and putting it carefully into the weapon's chamber, she pointed the shotgun away from the house and Dancer, who was tethered nearby, and drew back on the trigger. There was a deafening explosion, and Lily was flung backwards onto the ground, the butt of the shotgun striking her square in the stomach as she fell.

It sure wasn't anything like using a .22 caliber to hunt grouse.

"Damnation!" she shouted, struggling back to her feet. Dancer was whinnying and pulling at the stake Wilbur had tied him to, trying to escape.

Lily decided to master the shotgun another day and

carried the weapon back inside. She made a fire in the stove with the fresh, pitchy wood she and Wilbur had cut, and as she permitted herself to remember the kiss, her cheeks were as hot as the flames she'd just ignited.

With a little wail of despair she went over to the rough board table that had been Velvet's and collapsed into a chair. While she hadn't wanted to make love with Wilbur, she hadn't been repulsed, either. That kiss had made her feel all warm and achy inside—there was no denying it.

Lily wondered how such a kiss would affect her in a month, or a year, when she didn't have Caleb around to ease the strange tensions that rose constantly within her. Would she be drinking brandy then, the way her mother had, and welcoming men into her bed?

She paused and laid her hands on her abdomen. If there was indeed a baby growing inside her, would she eventually decide the child was in her way and send him or her off into the world alone to make its own way?

"No," Lily insisted out loud. "No!"

With resolution she went about putting boards over the holes where the windows had been so that the cold air wouldn't get in come nightfall. When that was done she fixed herself an early supper of scrambled eggs and fried pork from the few provisions she'd brought along.

After heating water on the small cook stove and washing the dishes she decided to make up the bed with the blankets, sheets, and pillows she'd borrowed from Caleb's house. She had a few books of his, too, as well as a number of kitchen utensils, but she was confident he wouldn't miss the items before she could return them.

The mattress was lumpy, and there was a great canyon in the middle where Velvet and her lovers had probably met in unbridled passion. With a great deal of effort, for it was an awkward task, Lily turned it over.

There were stains on the other side.

Wrinkling her nose, Lily shifted the mattress again, then

briskly made it up with starched linen sheets and heavy blankets. She couldn't afford to be fussy until her own bed arrived.

Nightfall brought strange animal sounds from the woods, as well as a persistent breeze that seemed to flow up through the cracks in the floor and seep right through the bottom of Lily's bed. Since she'd forgotten to borrow lamps from Caleb, or even candles, there was no light at all; the shack was as dark as a bank vault in hell.

Lily settled down between the sheets, reminding herself that Velvet and Hank would be back from Tylerville in a couple of days. It would be much easier to sleep then, knowing she had neighbors.

Chapter
❧ 18 ❧

There had to be some mistake.

Caleb lifted his right hand in a weary signal, and the troops behind him came to an obedient halt.

"What the hell?" muttered Sergeant Fortner, who rode beside him, standing up in his stirrups to squint at the smoke rising in a neat gray plume in the distance. "Indians?"

"More likely settlers," Caleb answered with a shake of his head. He wondered what Lily would say when she found out there were squatters on that precious three hundred and twenty acres of hers. "We'll take a closer look."

The men riding behind Caleb were hot, dusty, and saddlesore, but there were no murmurs of protest when he led the troops off the direct route to Fort Deveraux. They were aware, down to a man, of Judd Ingram sweating in the stockade, wondering whether he was going to be whipped or not, and none of them were willing to cross the major.

271

Caleb allowed himself a grim smile at this realization and spurred his gelding to a quicker pace. Fact was, he wanted to get back to the fort, too. He wanted a hot bath, a steak dinner, and Lily, in that order.

He shifted in the saddle to accommodate the discomfort thoughts of Lily always aroused. This time he wasn't going to stop making love to her until she begged him to marry her, until she admitted she belonged at his side.

Lily's lumber and other supplies had arrived two days before, and thanks to the industry of Wilbur and his colleagues, her new house was going up rapidly. There was already framework and a floor, and soon there would be a roof and windows.

Lily had made plans to convert the shack into a chicken coop, reserving part of it for a stall for Dancer, and she was busily hoeing out a plot for her garden when the cry went up.

"Troops!" one of the men yelled, pointing.

Lily turned her head, and sure enough, there was a cavalry patrol approaching—led by Caleb Halliday. She drew a deep breath and closed her eyes for a moment, composing herself.

She was watching intently when Caleb halted the patrol and spoke to the man at his side. The sergeant saluted, then turned his horse and shouted a command to the men. Soon they were all riding toward the fort, and Caleb approached alone.

His glittering golden eyes swept over Wilbur and the others with all the friendliness of scalding hot butter. Wilbur, who had been nailing in a window casing, was the only man brave enough to approach the major.

"Major Halliday, sir," he said, with a crisp salute.

Caleb didn't bother to return the courtesy. "What's going on here, Corporal?" he demanded.

"We're building a house, sir."

"At ease, Corporal. I can see that for myself. You and your men are dismissed."

If he'd been talking to Lily, she would have wanted to know why he'd asked in the first place, since he could see what was going on with his own eyes, but Wilbur just cleared his throat and said, "Excuse me, sir, but I'm on leave, and the other men are off-duty."

"Does that mean you don't have to follow my orders?"

"No, sir."

"That's correct, Corporal. I repeat, you are dismissed."

"Yes, sir." After casting one beleaguered look in Lily's direction Wilbur turned and strode back to the men to relay the order.

Lily was now too angry to be intimidated. She stormed over to where Caleb sat, still mounted on his horse, and looked up into his face. "It just so happens that I need these men to help me finish my house," she pointed out.

Caleb swung one leg over his saddle horn and dismounted. "As you were, Corporal," he called to Wilbur and the others. Then he took Lily by the arm and hustled her away. They were nearly to the trees before he stopped.

"What did that mean," Lily asked with hopeful defiance, "when you said 'as you were'?"

"See for yourself," Caleb bit out, gesturing angrily toward the house. The soldiers were picking up their hammers and saws and going back to work.

Lily folded her arms. "Thank you," she said in a saucy tone of voice. "Now, if you'll just get back on your horse and ride out—"

"I'm not going anywhere," Caleb informed her coldly. His jaw ground when he closed his mouth, and he was glaring at Lily's house as though he could set it on fire with a look.

Fury flushed through Lily's system, turning her pink. "I beg your pardon."

"If you want to play this game, then so be it," he snapped. "We'll play settler until you finally learn what a miserable, hardscrabble life it really is!" He'd swept his hat off his head, and when he slapped it against his thigh, dust flew.

273

"You mean you're going to marry me?" Lily dared to ask, coughing.

"Hell, no!" Caleb retorted in a raspy whisper. "I wouldn't marry a stubborn, sneaky little chit like you for anything!"

Lily might have slapped him if she hadn't been so aware that Wilbur and the others were looking on, no matter how disinterested they might pretend to be. "Well, I know I'm stubborn," Lily admitted grudgingly. "But *sneaky?*"

"Yes, sneaky!" Caleb hissed, whacking his hat against his leg again. "I turn my back for a week, and here you are, charming my men into building your damned house for you!"

Lily was staring up at him in confusion and concern. "Caleb, just what is it you plan to do?"

He stormed past her toward the new house, and Lily was compelled to follow. Clasping her skirts in her hands, she scrambled alongside him in an effort to keep up with his long strides.

As he passed the tool wagon Wilbur had brought out that morning from Fort Deveraux he snatched up a pick.

"Caleb!" Lily cried, terrified that he meant to destroy her cabin.

But he went around the cabin to the land behind it and plunged the pick into the ground with a mighty swing.

"Right here!" he bellowed, no longer caring, evidently, that some of his troops were there to witness his fit of temper. "I'm building my house *right here!*"

Lily stared. "But you can't, Caleb. Someone else has claim to that land."

"The hell I can't," he barked back. "I filed before I ever had the misfortune to meet you!"

Lily's eyes went wide. *"You've claimed the land adjoining mine?"*

Caleb grinned, but his gaze fairly crackled with fury. "I have indeed."

"Well, I don't want your house so close by," Lily fussed,

folding her arms again and stomping over to look up into his face.

Caleb pointed to the ground. "Get off my land," he ordered.

"Everybody else around here might jump when you give an order, Caleb Halliday," Lily told him, "but I'm not afraid of you."

"You'd better be," Caleb drawled, advancing on her so that she was forced to retreat.

Lily went inside her shack, wildly embarrassed that Wilbur and the others had witnessed the scene, and slammed the door. Before she could shoot the bolt, however, Caleb came in. Seething, he flung his hat aside so that it landed on Lily's new bed.

"Now you're on *my* land," Lily pointed out, inching backwards. The shack was mostly in shadow, though shafts of light struggled inside through the cracks in the boards over the windows.

Caleb's eyes shifted to something in the corner and went narrow, and a dangerous calm replaced his outrage. "My shotgun," he said disbelievingly. "Isn't that my shotgun?"

"I only borrowed it," Lily said, squaring her shoulders. "You shouldn't make such an issue of a little thing like that."

"Have you fired it?"

Lily thought of the large round bruise on her stomach where the butt of the weapon had struck her when she pulled the trigger. She wasn't about to talk about that, or the fact that the force had thrown her ignobly to the ground. "Yes, sir," she said, putting a pointed and mocking emphasis on the word "sir."

Caleb let out a long sigh and shoved splayed fingers through his dirty hair. "Lily, you could hurt yourself with that thing. You've got no damned business being out here without a man to protect you."

Lily ladled water into her shiny new enamel coffeepot and set it on the stove with a bang. "Well, I won't have to worry anymore, will I? Now I'll have *you* for a neighbor!"

Linda Lael Miller

"You could be a little happier about it."

"Why should I be? Velvet and Hank are settling just over the next hill. What do I need with a man who won't marry me, who thinks I'm sneaky? Besides, you're not interested in settling here—you just want to be handy so you can gloat every time I make a mistake!"

Caleb chuckled ruefully and shook his head. "To think I actually imagined you'd be waiting for me at home."

"This is home," Lily said tautly, spooning coffee grounds into the pot.

"We'll see how you feel when the snow is six feet deep and you've been eating beans for two months straight," Caleb replied. He drew back a chair and sat right down at Lily's new table without even waiting for a nod. "God, I'm tired."

Lily felt sympathy for Caleb even though she resented him heartily for refusing to marry her. "Did you really file a claim on the next half-section?" she asked in a more moderate tone.

"Yes," he answered, running the fingers of both hands through his hair again.

Lily imagined him as her husband, stretched out in his bathtub at the fort, imagined herself washing his back, and she had to turn away again and pretend an interest in the coffee to hide her expression. "You can't just leave the army and start up a farm," she reasoned in a small voice.

"Yes, I can. My tour of duty is finished next month, and I've got plenty of leave saved up. Colonel Tibbet won't like it, but I'll be back here tonight, Lily."

"Tonight?" Lily's voice was a squeak, and she couldn't help turning around to look at Caleb. "Where would you sleep?"

His cleft chin was set at a stubborn angle. "In a tent," he answered flatly.

Lily swallowed, filled with the small, warm aches that Caleb's presence always engendered in her. "It looks like it might rain. Maybe you should sleep in here."

His gaze practically flayed her alive. "Not on your life. I'm not going to marry you, Lily, and I'm not about to share your bed, either."

It was humiliating to make such an offer and be rejected. "If you feel that way, then perhaps it would be better if you just went on with your life and forgot all about me."

"I'm sure it would be better," Caleb agreed, "but I'd never get a moment's peace for wondering if you were being carried off by rogue Indians or raped by outlaws."

Lily felt a little better. "Then you do care?"

"Yes," Caleb admitted grudgingly, "but if I can find a way to put you out of my mind, I'm going to do it. That will be the day I ride out of here and never look back."

Lily suffered a chill, envisioning that. "Good riddance, that's what I'll say," she bluffed.

Caleb pushed back his chair and fetched his hat from the bed, but not before he put his hand on the mattress and pressed to make the bedsprings squeak.

The sound was so loud that Lily cringed, knowing what Wilbur and his men would think. "Caleb, stop!" she cried angrily.

Caleb only grinned at her and repeated the process, once, then again, then again and again.

"Damn you," Lily whispered, "stop it."

He paused, watching the color climb her face. After deliberately stalling for several minutes he put on his hat, swatted Lily on the bottom as he passed her, and left the shack whistling. Loudly.

Lily was so mortified that she could not bring herself to go outside, even after she heard Caleb riding away. She was sitting at the table, holding a coffee mug in both hands and sipping the brew like a survivor of some cataclysm, when a knock sounded at the door and Wilbur put his head inside.

"You all right, Miss Lily?" he asked, and Lily could see in the stream of sunlight he'd let in that his face was red as a ruby.

Lily swallowed hard. "I'm perfectly fine," she lied. "Why wouldn't I be?"

Wilbur was plainly too polite to answer that question. "Looks like it might rain later on," he said after clearing his throat. "Think this roof is sound?"

Lily sighed. She wanted to ask Wilbur to come in and sit down, but she didn't dare ask him. After that little exhibition of Caleb's, heaven only knew what the other men would think if she and the corporal were alone for any length of time. "I guess I'll find out pretty soon," she said. "Why don't you and the others just call it a day and go on back to the fort? I'll be fine."

Wilbur looked tremendously relieved, if slightly torn. "You keep that shotgun handy now," he said, "just in case."

"I will," Lily promised wearily.

When she was sure the soldiers were gone Lily went outside to assess the sky. Sure enough, there were dark clouds gathering on the horizon, roiling and angry-looking.

Lily carried firewood into the house—she noted with discouragement that she was going to need more soon—and then went out to see what could be done with Dancer. In the end she untied him and led him into the woods, where he would have at least some shelter. She tied his halter to a low-hanging tree branch and went back to the house for a bucket of water and some grain.

Once the horse was taken care of, Lily ventured on through the woods to the opposite side, where, down at the bottom of a little hill, Velvet and Hank had stopped their wagon beside a natural spring. There was no sign of either of her neighbors, and Lily was too shy to go and knock on the wagon's door. Feeling incredibly lonely, she turned around and walked back toward her own place.

The dark clouds were much nearer now, and there was a chilly wind blowing. The grass on Lily's land and Caleb's waved like an ocean, and there were little whitecaps of foam on the creek. Her skirt clinging to her legs, Lily stood with one hand shading her eyes, watching the storm approach.

Its harbinger was a light, warm, pattering rain that sent

her scurrying for the shack. Inside, Lily stoked up the fire, lighted the lamp in the center of the table, and got out one of the books she'd purloined from Caleb's library. She was sitting at the table, happily reading and sipping coffee, when the rain came in earnest.

It hammered at the old roof with frightening fury, then began creeping in through cracks and crevices. It fell over the bed, and over the flour sack, and over the hooked rug Mrs. Tibbet had given Lily as a housewarming present. It fell until Lily had run out of pots and kettles to catch the drips, and then it cascaded like water from a broken dam.

Lily sat wretchedly at her table, watching droplets sizzle and dance on the stove top, her book forgotten. A hammering at the door made her start and then beam. Caleb was back! What would a little rain matter if he was there to tell her he was sorry for behaving so badly, to take her into his arms and make love to her?

She yanked open the door, and her smile faded. The same Indian who had wanted to trade two horses for her was standing on the apple crate that served as a front step, his black hair dripping with water, his calico shirt so wet that his copper skin showed through in places.

"No house!" he said.

Lily was paralyzed for a moment. Here it was, she thought, the moment she'd been warned about. She was going to be scalped, or ravaged, or carried off to an Indian village. Maybe all three.

She cast a desperate glance toward the shotgun, at the same time smiling broadly at the Indian. "I'm terribly sorry," she said, "but of course you can see that there *is* a house."

"Woman go away!" the Indian insisted.

Lily's heart was flailing in her throat like a bird trapped in a chimney, but she squared her shoulders and put out her chin. "I'm not going anywhere, you rude man," she replied. "This is my land, and I have the papers to prove it!"

The Indian spouted a flock of curses; Lily knew the words for what they were only because of their tone.

She started to close the door. "If you're going to be nasty," she said, "you'll just have to leave."

Undaunted, the red man pushed past Lily and strode right over to the stove. He got a cup from the shelf, filled it with coffee, and took a sip. He grimaced. "You got firewater?" he demanded. "Better with firewater."

Lily had never been so frightened or so angry in her life. With one hand to her bosom she edged toward the shotgun. "No firewater," she said apologetically, "but there is a little sugar. There"—she pointed—"in the blue bowl."

When her unwanted guest turned around to look for the sugar, Lily lunged for the shotgun and cocked it. There was no shell in the chamber; she could only hope the Indian wouldn't guess.

"All right, you," she said, narrowing her eyes and pointing the shotgun. "Get out of here right now. Just ride away and there won't be any trouble."

The Indian stared at her for a moment, then had the audacity to burst out laughing. "The major's right about you," he said in perfectly clear English. "You are a hellcat."

Now it was Lily who stared, slowly lowering the shotgun. "So that's why Caleb wasn't alarmed that day when you and your friends rode up and made all that fuss about the land. He *knows* you."

"The name's Charlie Fast Horse," the man said, offering his hand.

Lily's blood was rushing to her head like lava flowing to the top of an erupting volcano. "Why, that polecat—that rounder—that son-of-a—"

Charlie Fast Horse set his coffee aside and held out both hands in a plea for peace. "Calm down, now, Miss Lily," he pleaded. "It was just a harmless little joke, after all."

"When I see that scoundrel again I'm going to peel off his hide!"

Charlie was edging toward the door. "Lord knows I'd like

to warm myself by your fire, Miss Lily, but I've got to be going. No, no—don't plead with me to stay."

"Get out of here!" Lily screamed, and Charlie Fast Horse ran for his life. Obviously he didn't know the shotgun wasn't loaded.

The moment he was gone Lily bolted the door and collapsed against it. Her heart was beating so hard that it felt as if it would jump right out of her chest at any moment, and she was shivering from head to foot with both fury and lingering traces of fear.

At sunset Lily heard a wagon roll up, but this time she wasn't so rash as to open the door. She peeked out through one of the broader cracks in the wall and saw Caleb passing by on his way to his land.

Not caring about the pounding rain, Lily loaded the shotgun and marched outside and around behind the framework of the new cabin to confront Caleb. He was unloading a canvas tent from the back of his wagon, and there were other things secured there under a tarp; Lily could see the outlines of them.

She pointed the shotgun and fired, blowing the spokes out of the rear wheel of Caleb's wagon. The vehicle promptly collapsed, sending boxes and crates sliding into the muddy grass, and the horses screamed in terror and strained wildly at the harness.

Caleb took the time to settle them before approaching Lily. Rain dripped off the brim of his campaign hat.

"I'm willing to put up with a lot from you, Lily," he shouted, in order to be heard over the driving rain, "but I won't be shot at!" Having imparted this information, he wrenched the shotgun out of Lily's grasp with one hand and took a painless but inescapable hold on her arm with the other.

She found herself double-stepping around to the front of the shack and inside.

"I had a visit from your friend Charlie Fast Horse a little while ago!" she yelled, too angry to be afraid of any reprisals for shooting up Caleb's wagon. Besides, any fool would have known she wasn't trying to hit him—she'd missed by a country mile.

Caleb stood the shotgun in a corner by the door, took off his hat and threw it, then yanked off his gloves. After that he shed his canvas raincoat, tossing it casually over the back of a chair. "I've been wanting to do this for a long time," he said in a dangerous drawl, "and you just gave me the excuse I needed."

"What—what are you talking about?" Lily demanded, stepping backwards. A drop of rainwater from the leaky roof landed with a disconcerting *ker-plop* on the top of her head.

Caleb was unbuttoning his cuffs, rolling up his sleeves. "I'm talking," he replied evenly, "about raising blisters on your sweet little backside."

Lily was careful to keep to the opposite side of the table. "Now, Caleb, that wouldn't be wise."

"Oh, I think it would be about the smartest thing I've ever done," Caleb answered, advancing on her again.

Lily kept the table between them. "I might be pregnant!" she reasoned desperately.

"Then again," Caleb countered, "you might not." The muscles of his forearms were corded, the skin covered with maple-sugar hair.

"I wasn't going to shoot you—I only wanted to scare you away." Lily dodged him, moving from one side of the table to the other, always keeping it between them. "Caleb, be reasonable. I wouldn't shoot you—I love you!"

"I love you, too," Caleb returned in a furious croon, "and right now I'd like nothing better than to shoot you!"

Lily picked up a chair and held it as she'd seen a lion tamer do in an illustration in one of her beloved dime novels. *Helga of the Circus,* if she remembered correctly. "Now, just stay back, Caleb. If you lay a hand on me, I assure you, you'll regret it!"

"I doubt that very much," Caleb replied. And then he gripped one leg of the chair, and Lily realized what a pitiful defense it had been. He set it easily on the floor even as his other arm shot out like a coiled snake and caught Lily firmly by the wrist.

Like a man sitting down to a cigar and a glass of port after a good dinner Caleb dropped comfortably into the chair. With a single tug he brought Lily facedown across his lap. Quick as mercury he had her skirts up and her drawers down, and when she struggled he simply imprisoned her between his thighs scissor fashion.

"Caleb Halliday," Lily gasped, writhing between his legs, "you let me go this instant!"

"Or else you'll do what?" he asked evenly. Lily felt his hand caress one cheek of her bottom and then the other, as though charting them for assault.

"I'll scream, and Hank Robbins will run over here and shoot you for the rascal you are!"

Caleb laughed thunderously at that.

"You've had your little joke," Lily huffed, "now let me up!"

"No," Caleb replied.

Lily threw back her head and screamed as loudly as she could.

"You can do better than that," Caleb said. "Hell, nobody would hear a whimper like that in this rain."

Lily filled her lungs to capacity and screamed again.

She was as surprised as Caleb when the door flew open and Velvet burst in, ready for battle. Color filled her face when she understood the situation.

In no particular rush, Caleb released Lily, and she scrambled to her feet unassisted, blushing painfully as she righted her drawers and lowered her skirts.

Caleb chuckled at her indignation and then stood up respectfully. "Hello, Velvet."

Velvet's embarrassment had turned to amusement, and

she was doing a very poor job of concealing it. Her lips twitched as she looked at Lily, who glared at Caleb before she said, "Would you like a cup of coffee?"

"Good Lord," Velvet complained, laying one hand to her breast and sinking into the other chair. Her clothes and hair were dripping wet. "I thought there was an Indian in here killin' you, the way you was carryin' on."

"I was, after all, being assaulted," Lily pointed out, with a cold glance at Caleb. "Thank you for rescuing me before this fiend could do bodily harm."

Caleb grinned. "Velvet can't stay forever," he reminded Lily.

"Neither can you," Lily rejoined.

"You might be surprised," Caleb said.

Velvet cleared her throat. "Maybe I shouldn't have come," she said. "I was just feelin' lonesome, since Hank is out huntin' somewhere, and I decided to pay a call, rain or no rain."

It was obvious to everyone that Velvet was running on because she was uncomfortable.

"Don't you dare leave me alone with this brute," Lily said, filling a coffee cup for Velvet and ignoring Caleb entirely.

Caleb pushed back his chair and stood, tilting his head back to inspect the roof as the rain continued to seep through in a thousand places.

"I see the roof ain't changed," Velvet commented after taking a loud slurp of her coffee. "Got more holes in it than a sieve."

Lily sighed and sat down in the chair Caleb had vacated, warming her hands around her cup of fresh coffee. "In a few days that will be a worry to the chickens, not to me."

Caleb took his coat from the floor, where it had fallen in the scuffle with Lily, and shrugged into it. "Rain's letting up," he commented. "Guess I'll go out and put up my tent."

Lily pretended he hadn't spoken—that he wasn't even

there, for that matter—but the moment the door closed behind him Velvet burst out in uproarious laughter.

"If this don't beat anything I've ever seen!" she cried between yelps of mirth.

Lily relived the incident in her mind and reddened accordingly. "He wouldn't really have struck me," she insisted. "He wouldn't have dared."

Velvet's guffaws became giggles. "His hand was about this far from your bottom when I stepped through the door," she said, showing an inch of space between her thumb and index finger. "Yes, sir, if I'd been a second later, he'd have walloped you one."

"I don't want to talk about it," Lily said. "I don't even want to *think* about that man." But when the rain stopped she couldn't resist going to the wall to peer through a crack.

There was a tent standing just on the other side of the property line, but Lily could see no sign of Caleb.

She could only hope he'd slipped in the mud, landed face first in a puddle, and drowned.

Chapter
❧ 19 ❦

When Lily awakened in the morning Caleb's tent was still standing directly behind the framework of her new house, along with his broken wagon, but his horse was gone.

A smile curved her lips. It would serve him right if the gelding had run off during the night.

After washing, dressing, and pinning up her hair, Lily went out to the woods to fetch Dancer. Now that the rain was over the air smelled deliciously fresh, and the grass was beaded with moisture. The creek sparkled in the sunshine like a liquid gem, singing its restless song as it tumbled along.

Lily tethered Dancer near the water so he could drink when he wished, then approached the front of Caleb's tent.

"Hello," she called cheerfully.

There was no answer.

Lily tried again. "Your horse got away," she said with pleasure.

No reply.

LILY AND THE MAJOR

Exasperated, Lily pulled back the tent flap and peered into the dank, shadowy interior. The bedroll was not only empty, it was neatly tucked away in a corner and tied with string. There was a lantern nearby, along with a book and a mess kit.

Lily lowered the flap and stepped back, frowning. She wondered where Caleb had gone so early in the morning—the sun hadn't been up longer than half an hour—but she knew she would be too proud to ask if he didn't volunteer the information. And he wasn't likely to do that.

Resigned, Lily made herself a light breakfast from her small store of provisions and ate. During the night she'd had to push the bed away from the wall to escape the dripping rain; now she put it carefully back into place.

When she'd washed and dried her single plate and fork she went outside, shiny new hoe in hand, to begin turning up the ground for a garden. It was too late for planting most things, but if the summer was long and hot, she'd be able to grow corn, at least.

Lily was hard at work when Wilbur appeared with his small but dedicated band of soldiers. As before, the men were not dressed in military garb, but in plain trousers and shirts.

Wilbur approached Lily as the others went immediately to work. "Morning," he said in an awkward way, his eyes averted.

"Good morning, Wilbur," Lily replied, stopping her work to lean on the hoe handle.

Shifting from one foot to the other, Wilbur looked uncomfortable in the extreme. "About yesterday in the woods . . . I'm sorry I kissed you, Lily. I shouldn't have done that, considering our agreement and everything."

Lily sighed and smiled wearily. What with moving the bed from place to place most of the night, she hadn't gotten much sleep. "I don't see how I could possibly hold a grudge, Wilbur, when you've been so kind and so generous with your time."

His eyes met hers, and he smiled shyly. "I guess you know I'd do just about anything for you, Miss Lily. Even farming, if it came to that."

There was a rider coming over the rise, and Lily knew in an instant that it was Caleb. Given his direction, he'd been to Tylerville. She wanted to share that farm with just one man, and he was riding arrogantly across the creek at that moment. "Thank you, Wilbur," she said gently. "But I'm not the right woman for you."

Wilbur, like Lily, was looking in Caleb's direction. "I understand," he said quietly, and then, without another word, he turned and walked away to help with the house.

"I suppose you're wondering where I've been," Caleb said, sounding damnably pleased with himself as he climbed down from the gelding's back.

"I wasn't wondering any such thing." Lily's arms were folded, and her chin was thrust out. She couldn't help noticing that Caleb wasn't wearing his uniform—he had on dark trousers and a cotton shirt. On his head in place of the tasseled campaign hat was a slouchy leather one. Although he wasn't wearing a holster and pistol, there was a rifle in the scabbard on his saddle.

Caleb grinned as he reached up for his saddlebags. "That being the case, you probably wouldn't be interested in the presents I brought you."

Lily took a reluctant step nearer. "Presents?"

He slung the bulging saddlebags over one sturdy shoulder and gave a long-suffering sigh. "You won't want to see them, of course."

Lily bit her lower lip. "That would depend," she said.

Caleb laughed. "On what?"

There was no helping it; Lily had to smile. "On what they are, silly."

He tossed the saddlebags to Lily, and they nearly knocked her over. "Go ahead, sodbuster. Have a look."

Feeling self-conscious, Lily opened the flap of one saddlebag and peeked inside. It was bulging with fragrant, tangy oranges, and Lily's mouth watered at the prospect of such a treat.

In the other saddlebag she found two dime novels, *Wilhelmina and the Wild Indians* and *Evelyn and the Mountain Man,* along with a bar of chocolate and two pretty tortoiseshell combs for her hair. "I don't know what to say," Lily whispered. She'd never received so many wonderful presents at one time in her life. "Except for thank you, of course."

Caleb kissed her forehead. "Am I back in your good graces now?"

Lily looked up at him, clutching the saddlebags to her chest. "That depends on whether or not you've decided to marry me."

His jawline tightened, and for one terrible moment Lily was afraid he meant to take back the oranges and the books and the chocolate and the combs. "I've decided," he answered. His voice was so cold that Lily didn't need to ask what that decision was.

She flung the saddlebags with their cherished contents back into his arms, whirled on one heel, and strode back to the garden plot, where she began hoeing again with a vengeance. She was aware without looking that Caleb had followed her, but she was determined to ignore him.

"I had a letter waiting for me at the fort today when I went to talk with Colonel Tibbet," he said.

"I'm happy for you," Lily replied, breaking a clod of dirt into fine grains with a lethal swing of the hoe.

"It's from my sister Abbie," Caleb went on, just as though Lily had asked him to elaborate. "She said Sandra went ahead and married her lieutenant."

Lily swung her hoe again, making no comment. Her eyes stung, and her vision was a little blurred. Next Caleb would say he was going back to Fox Chapel and give her an ultimatum. Go or be left behind.

He sighed. "There was a letter for you, too."

The words seemed to echo in the warm, sun-brightened

air like the blows of the men's hammers and the rasps of their saws as they worked on Lily's house. She dropped the hoe unceremoniously and stumbled toward him through the upturned dirt. "Why didn't you tell me?" she demanded. "Where is this letter? Did you bring it?"

Caleb took a blue envelope from the back pocket of his trousers and held it out.

The letter was postmarked Bolton, Wyoming, and there was no return address. Lily opened it with trembling hands and shook out the single piece of paper inside.

It was dated only a week before, in a spare but tidy hand, and read,

> *Dear Miss Chalmers,*
> *Your sister, Caroline Chalmers, lived in our town for some time. About two weeks ago she disappeared from here, and her aunts are quite distressed, as you can well imagine. Should you have word from Miss Caroline, please ask her to write or wire home.*
> *Sincerely,*
> *Mrs. Daniel Pride*

Lily crumpled the paper and would have sunk to her knees in the loamy dirt of her potential garden if Caleb hadn't reached out immediately to steady her.

"What is it, Lily?"

Lily wet her lips. "It's Caroline—my older sister. She's— she's disappeared."

Without a care for the soldiers, who were probably looking on, Caleb swept Lily up into his arms and carried her inside her shadowy cabin. There he set her gently in a chair and, after tossing the saddlebags onto the table, went to the bucket by the stove to ladle cold water into a tin cup. He gave the cup to Lily, and she drank thirstily, with her eyes closed.

Caleb took the letter from her hands and read it. "Maybe there's a good explanation," he reasoned.

"I finally found one of them," Lily mourned, "only to be told that she's gone away, and no one knows where."

"She may be back by now, for all you know. Why don't you write her in care of the Bolton postmaster?"

Lily nodded as hope surged within her again. Caleb was right. If Caroline had left Bolton without telling anyone of her destination, she'd probably had very good reasons. She might even have returned by now.

Glancing about her until she sighted her valise, where she'd tucked her writing paper to keep it from getting wet, Lily started out of her chair only to have Caleb press her back.

"Just sit there a minute," he ordered quietly, "until you get your breath. Tell me what you want, and I'll get it."

"The valise," Lily answered, and Caleb fetched it for her.

She opened it and pulled out the writing paper, her ink bottle, and the wooden box that contained her pens. While she was preparing to write Caleb emptied his saddlebags in the middle of the table and started toward the door without a word.

Lily stopped him. "Caleb."

His back stiffened, and he didn't turn to face her. "What?"

"Thank you for bringing this letter, and these lovely presents."

"It was nothing," he said, and he went out, closing the door quietly behind him.

She wrote a short letter to Mrs. Pride, thanking her warmly for her response. She asked the woman to write again if she learned anything new about Caroline's whereabouts, and she left the envelope unsealed so that she could enclose mailing expenses.

Following that, she wrote to Caroline herself, praying her elder sister was back in Bolton with her "aunts" to receive Lily's letter. It was a long letter, detailing Lily's experiences after she'd left the orphan train, her time at Fort Deveraux, and her homestead. She even mentioned Caleb, though she made it sound as though he was just a crotchety neighbor.

After sealing the letter she tucked it into the pocket of her apron with the one directed to Mrs. Pride and went outside to find Wilbur. He was up on the roof of the new place, nailing down shingles.

Caleb, Lily noted, was just mounting his gelding.

She turned to him. "Are you off to the fort?"

"Yes," he answered, his face revealing no hint of his emotions. "Want to go along?"

Lily thought it would be nice to pay a call on Mrs. Tibbet, but she wasn't ready to face the other women of the fort just yet. Now that Caleb had moved out here onto the section behind hers, the gossip was probably flying.

She shook her head. "If you'd just mail these letters for me . . . I have an account at the general store, so they'll put the postage on my bill."

Caleb smiled, but his expression showed no humor. He took the envelopes from Lily and tucked them into his shirt pocket. "I'll bring something back for supper," he said, and then he rode off.

Lily went back inside the cabin and read the letter from Mrs. Pride all over again. Then she mixed bread batter, set the dough in the sun to rise, and stoked up the fire in her cook stove. By the time the sun was high in the sky she'd made a midday meal of salt pork and fresh bread, and she carried plates out to Wilbur and his men.

They ate with gratifying appetite, and Lily was feeling pleased when she carried the dishes back into the cabin and then went out to hoe again.

She was intent on her work, backing along the row, and it startled her when she suddenly collided with a hard, masculine body. She looked up to see Private Matthews, one of the young men helping to build her house.

"Was there something you wanted?" she asked, shading her eyes from the bright sunshine.

Matthews was taller than Lily by about six inches, and his blue eyes swept over her in a way that could only be called suggestive. "I reckon I want what the major was havin' yesterday when the bedsprings was creakin' fit to wake the dead," he told her.

Lily retreated a step, cheeks flaming. She clasped the hoe handle in white-knuckled fingers. The affront was so brazen and so unexpected that she had no ready idea how to deal with it.

"Such a saucy little thing," Private Matthews went on, reaching out to touch Lily's hair. He only smiled when she flinched away, and after a moment he went on. "I'll bet you're a real wildcat."

Lily held up the hoe in both hands as a warrior might hold a shield. "You just stay back," she warned, her heels sinking into the loose dirt as she retreated from him.

"What's the matter, pretty Lily?" the young soldier crooned.

"Get out of here," Lily managed to choke out. "Get off my land and stay off!"

He advanced on her. "I figure riding you would be *worth* takin' a horsewhip across my back. That's what Judd's tellin' everybody. That it was worth all the trouble he got into."

Lily swallowed, then screamed out, "Wilbur! Help me!"

Matthews spat contemptuously into the dirt and kept right on coming toward her. "You think I can't handle the corporal, little lady?" He laughed. "Hell, you can just bet it'll be him against the rest of us."

Lily felt the color seep out of her face. She swung the hoe at the soldier, meaning to scare him, but he smiled as he sidestepped the glistening blade. "You stay away from me," she warned.

Matthews leapt forward suddenly and wrenched the hoe out of Lily's hands, hurling it aside so that it landed against a large rock with a clatter. He was gripping Lily by the shoulders, trying to force her toward the deep grass on the other side of the garden, when Wilbur rounded the corner of the cabin.

The moment he dragged Matthews off Lily and threw a punch, Lily ran for the house to get the shotgun. She didn't know Wilbur's friends very well, for all that they'd been helping her for several days, and she was taking no chances that they shared Private Matthews's opinion of her. Inside the cabin she snatched up the twelve-gauge shotgun she'd purloined from Caleb's house, took a shell from the box stored under her bed, and shoved it into the chamber. Having done that, she dropped half a dozen more shells into her pocket and bounded outside again.

The others had gathered to watch the fight, and Lily was relieved to see that Wilbur was more than holding his own. All the same, she kept the shotgun at the ready as the battle progressed, prepared to defend herself and her friend if the need arose.

Finally, Wilbur prevailed. Private Matthews lay in the furrowed dirt of Lily's garden, his nose and lip bleeding. Sitting astraddle of the man's hips, Wilbur looked around at his companions. "Anybody else want to try his luck?" he asked.

The men only murmured and shook their heads. Lily's hands were wet when she allowed the butt of the shotgun to rest on the ground, gripping the barrel in both hands.

"Go on back to work, then," Wilbur said, wiping blood from his mouth as he stood. He kicked a clod of dirt over Private Matthews's middle. "As for you, friend, we don't need your kind of help around here. Ride out."

After flinging one poisonous look at Lily the private scrambled to his feet and staggered toward his horse, which was tethered, with the others, near the creek.

Lily was shaking when Wilbur came and wrenched the shotgun out of her hands.

"Good God," he bit out, "don't ever hold a weapon like that, Lily. You'll blow your face clean off!"

Lily ran her tongue nervously over her lips and nodded. "Thank you, Wilbur."

Wilbur watched as his former friend rode off toward the post at top speed. "You might have more trouble with Ethan—he can be a persistent bastard. The major is coming back here, isn't he?"

Lily nodded again. "I'll be safe," she promised.

Wilbur carried the shotgun back inside, refusing to let Lily so much as touch it and, after removing the shell, set it in a corner. "I'll get back to work now," he said shyly.

Lily took a chair from the table and carried it out in front of the cabin, setting it down in the full sunshine. "Sit down, Wilbur," she ordered. "I want to have a look at your face."

She was bathing his bruises and cuts with a cloth dipped in cold creek water when Caleb rode up. Despite the shading effect of his floppy leather hat, Lily could see that the sight of her tending Wilbur's wounds didn't please him.

"What happened?" he demanded.

"There was a fight," Lily began.

Caleb immediately cut her off. "I think the man can speak for himself. Were you discharged from the army without my knowledge, Corporal?"

Poor Wilbur bounded to his feet, nearly upsetting the basin Lily was holding. He saluted. "No, sir," he answered earnestly.

Lily suppressed an urge to throw the basinful of water all over Caleb, but she didn't quite dare. She hadn't forgotten her experience of the day before, when he'd imprisoned her across his lap and come within an inch of smacking her bare bottom. "Caleb, he was defending me," she said evenly.

Caleb raked Wilbur with his stern gaze, then barked, "You're dismissed, Corporal."

Wilbur saluted again and hastened away.

"I do believe you *enjoy* bossing people around like that," Lily accused in an angry whisper. "I'll have you know that I might have been raped if he hadn't been here!"

"So that's why Private Matthews came riding through the gates as if the devil himself were chasing him," Caleb said, and his eyes narrowed. He started to turn back toward his horse, but Lily stopped him by grasping his arm.

"Did you mail my letters?" she asked softly.

She felt some of the tension and fury drain out of him. "Yes," he answered, his voice taut as stretched rawhide.

"What did you bring for supper?" Lily didn't really care what the answer was; she only wanted to give Caleb a chance to get his temper under control before he went chasing off to the fort and did something he'd later have cause to regret.

He sighed and walked away to untie a burlap bag from the horn of his saddle. He handed the bag to Lily, a muscle working in his jaw, and gazed toward Wilbur and the others. They were making very good progress on the house; in another few days Lily would be able to move in.

"Judd Ingram's on his way to Yuma," Caleb said. He paused to sigh. "Maybe I should have made an example of him."

"That would have been wrong," Lily responded quietly, "and you know it." All of a sudden the burlap bag in her hands started to squawk and bulge wildly. "What is this?"

Caleb's good humor was apparently restored. "It's a chicken, sodbuster. After you chop off his head, gut him, and pluck out all his feathers, he'll fry up real nice."

Lily felt her lunch boil up into her throat. She'd fed plenty of chickens in her time, and certainly fried a few, but Rupert had usually been the one to kill them. "He looks delicious," she said in a small voice.

Caleb, who had been about to lead his horse back to his grazing place, stopped in midstride and grinned at her.

Not for another three sections of land would Lily have let him know she dreaded the task. "Was there something you wanted?" she asked a little stiffly.

He shrugged. "Just a chicken dinner."

After squaring her shoulders and giving Caleb a look that

clearly said he wouldn't be welcome in her cabin once supper was over, Lily turned and marched stoically off to the chopping block.

There she let the rooster out of the bag. He gave a loud squawk and tried to fly away, and it took Lily at least five minutes to tackle him and wrestle his head onto the block. When she'd done that and was holding the doomed bird by the base of his neck, she took the ax into her right hand and swung.

When the awful job was done Lily's skin was slick with perspiration. The rooster's head was staring up at her from the block, while his body flapped around at her feet. Although she'd seen this phenomenon many times before, that day it took away her appetite.

Finally the contentious bird gave up the ghost and collapsed. Lily separated him from his insides with a knife and, nose wrinkled, carried the filthy, feathery carcass around to the front of the cabin.

Someone—probably Caleb—had thoughtfully set a large kettle on the stove to boil, and it was still bubbling when Lily carried it outside. She plunged the rooster's motionless body into the hot water, then quickly pulled it out again. Her eyes narrowed, her nose crinkling, she began the laborious job of plucking feathers.

The smell was almost too odious to be endured, and by the time Lily had finally denuded the bird, and fried him, and set him on the table with mashed potatoes and gravy and some of Mrs. Tibbet's canned peas, all she wanted was a walk in the fresh air. Caleb, Wilbur, and the others ate with zest, not even noticing when she left.

Presently, long after Lily had returned from her walk, Wilbur and the others went back to the fort. She sat brooding on the apple crate that served as a step, her chin in her hands.

Caleb edged around her and stepped down from the high threshold. "Of course," he said, as though they'd been carrying on a conversation for some minutes, "if you lived in Fox Chapel, you wouldn't have to pluck chickens. You'd have servants to take care of things like that."

Lily knew she still smelled of wet feathers. "I'd settle for a hot bath," she said wistfully.

Twilight had fallen, and the horses—Caleb's gelding and Lily's Dancer—were snuffling contentedly by the creek.

"Fill some buckets at the creek and heat the water," Caleb said offhandedly. He was looking up at the first stars, popping out here and there like silver fireflies, near enough to touch.

Lily didn't move. She was too tired to prepare a bath, and it was all she could do not to cry. She'd come so close to making contact with one of her sisters, then lost her again, and she'd nearly been raped. All in all, it hadn't been a very good day.

Caleb went back inside the cabin and returned a moment later with one of the oranges he'd brought her from Tylerville. He peeled it with deft strokes of his pocket knife.

"Here," he said when he'd finished, handing the fruit to Lily. "You need to eat something."

Lily accepted the orange and broke it into juicy sections. The brisk taste restored her a little, and she even offered a piece to Caleb.

He declined with a shake of his head. "Have you got a tub, Lily?"

She pointed to a nearby mound of household goods covered by a big canvas tarp from the fort. All these things were reserved for the new cabin. "It's under there somewhere, with the stove and all the other things."

To her surprise, Caleb walked over, threw back the tarp, and rummaged through fixtures and household goods until he found the big tub. Lily intended it to serve for both washing and bathing.

After setting it right out in the middle of the grassy yard under the stars, Caleb disappeared inside the cabin to fetch Lily's water buckets. These he carried to the creek, where he fillcd them, then he hauled them back and dumped them into the bathtub.

Lily watched him in silence, wondering if he planned to bathe right out there in front of God and everybody, and in cold water, too. *She* certainly had no intention of doing any such thing.

Once Caleb was satisfied that there was enough water he stacked wood around the base of the big vat, along with twigs and dry grass, and struck a match to the lot. Lily drew in a sharp breath as the flames encircled the tub, racing around it in a flickering orange circle.

"What are you doing?" Lily called from the apple crate, unable to keep her silence any longer.

She saw Caleb's teeth flash in the semidarkness as he grinned. There was a moon out, and it gilded him and shimmered on the water in the bathtub and the creek.

Presently, after testing the water with his hand, Caleb announced, "Your bath is ready, sodbuster."

Lily stood. "I'm not going to bathe in the open," she said.

"All right, then," Caleb answered, pulling his shirt from his trousers, "I will. No sense letting all this nice hot water go to waste."

Lily might have loved Caleb Halliday, but she begrudged him that clean, steaming bath water in the worst way. "Don't you dare step into that tub," she said, marching over to where he stood. "It's mine."

Caleb smiled and folded his arms. "Fine," he said. He didn't show any sign of moving, and the fire around the tub was getting low. Soon the chilly evening air would cool the water.

"You could at least give me some privacy."

He smiled and sat down on the nearby stump of a long-gone maple tree. "I could," he said. It was perfectly clear that he didn't intend to, however.

Lily looked with longing at the water, then turned her back on Caleb and pretended he wasn't there. Quickly, before her courage could desert her, she removed her clothes and stepped into the tub. The feel of the hot water closing around her tired, achy flesh was so delicious that she made a little crooning sound as she settled in.

She was caught completely by surprise when Caleb joined her, naked as the day he'd left heaven, and sank into the water. Some of it splashed over the edges of the oblong tub and sizzled as it met the fire.

"I suppose it would be a waste of breath to ask you to get out of this tub," Lily said.

"Absolutely," Caleb replied.

Chapter
❧ 20 ❦

*C*aleb leaned back in the bathtub, apparently unabashed by his nakedness. His long, muscled legs were entwined with Lily's softer ones, and she felt a toe touching her in a most private place. She sank a little deeper into the water, at once hiding her bare breasts and warming herself against the chill of a May night.

"Why did you go to Tylerville this morning?" she asked, as though it was perfectly normal to be sitting in a brimming bathtub in the middle of a meadow with a man she hadn't married. Safety, it seemed to Lily, lay in ordinary topics.

Caleb smiled. He'd gotten a bar of soap from somewhere, and he began lathering his hands with foamy suds. "I wanted to order lumber for my house," he answered at his leisure.

Lily shifted in an effort to escape his toe. "Why are you doing this, Caleb?"

"Doing what?" He was washing industriously under one arm.

"Going to all the trouble to homestead and build a house when you have no intention of staying here."

Caleb soaped the other armpit, then cordially handed the bar to Lily. "I can't leave you out here alone, can I?" he reasoned in pleasant tones. "I haven't resigned my commission yet, so I can't board a train for Pennsylvania either. I might as well do something constructive while I'm waiting for you to come to your senses."

Lily sighed. There was no point in trying to convince Caleb that she was never going to leave the homestead if she could help it. At long last she had something of her own, and through her mother and Mrs. Pride of Bolton, Wyoming, she had a chance, however remote, of finally finding her sisters.

"Turn around," Caleb said gently when she didn't speak, "and I'll wash your back for you."

The experience sounded too pleasant to refuse, and Lily shifted until she was kneeling, facing away from Caleb. The breeze made her nipples stand taut, and she was glad he couldn't see. "I have another bone to pick with you," she said as he began a delicious process of washing and massage combined.

"Umm?"

There had been so many things happening that Lily hadn't had a chance to pursue this particular subject. "Charlie Fast Horse."

Caleb's tone was sober. "Oh."

"Yes," Lily said, looking back over one soapy shoulder, "oh. Caleb Halliday, that was a nasty trick you pulled, pretending that Mr. Fast Horse might buy me for two horses and carry me off to his camp. I was terrified."

He began rinsing away the soap, and when he spoke he didn't sound the least bit contrite. "It wasn't prearranged, if that's what you think. Charlie and his friends just happened by, and there was sort of a tacit agreement to have a little fun with you. You must know that I wouldn't let anybody hurt you."

LILY AND THE MAJOR

Lily started to turn around, meaning to lecture Caleb on the perils of such pranks, but he stopped her by grasping her shoulders in his hands. His fingers were slick with soap, and they slid down to encompass her sumptuous breasts. She gave a trembling sigh and ceased her resistance before it could begin.

She arched her back, letting her head rest against his shoulder as he made free with her breasts. His lips moved along the sensitive flesh of her neck, where tendrils of her hair were starting to slip from their pins.

Lily closed her eyes as he cupped water in his hands and rinsed the soap from her breasts; in some ways, the sensation was as delicious as a caress.

Caleb nibbled lightly at the place where her neck and shoulder met. "Shall I make love to you, Lily? Right here and now?"

"Yes," she whispered. "Oh, yes."

Caleb turned her, causing her to kneel astraddle of his lap. She could feel his powerful shaft between her thighs as he bent his head to take one aroused nipple between his lips.

Unashamed, Lily gasped with pleasure and wove her fingers through his hair. Whatever it was he drew from her so hungrily, she delighted in giving it.

Water began to splash over the sides of the tub as Lily moved in response to Caleb's ministerings, seeking the thing that evaded her so persistently. "Not yet," he said against her breast, but his hand pushed back the velvet shelter to fondle her.

Lily was soon desperate. Her hands left Caleb's hair to grasp his shoulders in an attempt to persuade him, but he continued to feast upon her, and to tease her with beginnings that did not progress to an end. She let go of his shoulders to grip the sides of the tub, her head back and twisting from side to side as he tongued and suckled her nipples.

When his finger slipped inside her she tensed violently, feeling her body clutch at it, try to draw it in. Caleb

303

withdrew the finger and positioned Lily to receive him. "All right," he whispered, and, laying his hands on her shoulders, he pressed her slowly down onto the length of him.

Lily was in a fever; she sought to move upon Caleb, but he grasped her hips and stilled their motion. She knew he would make her glory in his possession of her, make her savor it.

She longed so for the friction he denied her that she raised his head from her breast to receive her kiss. He was as hungry at her mouth as he had been at her nipple, but he wouldn't allow her a single stroke of his rod.

Lily was not without recourse, for she knew how to break Caleb's resolve. She found his ear and traced its outer rim with the tip of her tongue, and he shuddered in her arms and within her. With a groan he raised her slowly to a point of near abandonment, then took her again.

It was easy to increase his pace after that; Lily had only to whisper wicked little promises to him. Soon he was no longer restraining her, but using his hold on her hips to propel her along his shaft. Lily shouted to the stars and spasmed repeatedly as she climaxed, and Caleb soon joined her in the sweet inferno.

When it was over, and they'd both settled back to earth, Lily reached for the soap and gently washed the warrior that had conquered her. He came to smart attention in her hands in the process, and Lily knew there would be another tender battle, perhaps less urgent than the first, but no less satisfying.

After Caleb had reciprocated by cleansing Lily, the moment calling for supreme bravery arrived. She snatched up her discarded clothes and rose out of the relative warmth of the tub, shivering as the night chill savaged her. Not waiting to dry herself, Lily ran naked into the cabin and poked the last of her firewood into the stove in a desperate bid for warmth.

Caleb entered minutes later. He was wearing his trousers and carrying his boots and the rest of his clothes. He dropped the boots beside the stove and held out his hands to the hidden blaze.

Suddenly self-conscious, Lily picked up his shirt and put it over her, buttoning it carefully so that only the sides of her thighs and her knees, ankles, and feet showed.

Caleb chuckled at that. "I emptied the tub and put it back under the tarp," he said, "so Corporal Pierce and the others won't get any wild ideas about you bathing in the middle of the prairie."

Lily blushed, embarrassed by what she'd done. She wondered why she never suffered these agonies *before* the fact, when it might do some good. "Corporal Pierce is a gentleman," Lily said stiffly.

"And I'm not?"

Lily shook her head. "No gentleman would do what you just did."

"And no lady would howl like a she-wolf while riding a man," Caleb retorted.

Lily guessed they were even, and she didn't want to fight with Caleb. She was tired and a little discouraged, and that would give him an unfair advantage. She averted her eyes and let the remark pass.

Caleb caught a finger under her chin and made her look at him. "Do I have to sleep in the tent tonight?" he asked quietly.

Lily swallowed and shook her head from side to side. "No."

They took their time in retiring to Lily's bed, but when they did, Caleb unbuttoned the shirt she was wearing and laid the fabric aside. She spent most of the next hour pitching breathlessly from star to star, unable to hold back the cries of pleasure Caleb extracted from her.

When she awakened in the morning, Caleb was gone from her bed, and there was a fire blazing in the stove and water heating on top. Lily tossed back the covers and rose, naked—Caleb had reclaimed his shirt—to wash and put on underthings. She wore her bright yellow dress that day, because there was sunshine seeping through the cracks in the walls, and that was reason to celebrate.

For the next week Lily was content. She worked on her garden in the daytime and watched the steady progress Wilbur and the others made on her house. At night, when Caleb returned from the fort, they read or played cards or talked, then slipped into Lily's bed and made love until the last dregs of energy were drained from their resilient young bodies.

Perhaps it was the knowledge that this idyllic time would soon pass that sweetened it for Lily; she was under no illusions that Caleb meant to stay with her. He was only trying to bind her to him, using his body and the everyday difficulties of a homestead. But even if that had not been the case, even if Caleb had married her and promised to stay right there on the land until the day he died, there would still have been an empty, bruised place in Lily's heart.

She wanted, needed, to find her sisters. In fact, with each passing day the dream seemed more compelling, more urgent, as though there was some terrible danger looming over Caroline and Emma that might destroy them.

The day Lily's house was finished, the lumber for Caleb's arrived. Lily thought it was stupid of Caleb to build a house at all, and obnoxious of him to insist on putting it just on the other side of her property line so that it would come within inches of adjoining hers.

Once her stove had been carried inside her new house, and her bed had been set up, and her bright new dishes unpacked from their sawdust-filled barrels, Lily decided it was time for a party. She invited Colonel and Mrs. Tibbet, and Velvet and Hank, and Wilbur and all his friends. She served a large beef roast for supper, having held her breath for a moment when Sergeant Killoran told her its price, and Hank played a fiddle for their entertainment and took photographs of everyone before the sun set in a majestic blaze.

There was much merriment that night, with everyone laughing and talking and dancing to the spirited measures of Hank's fiddle, but as the evening drew to a close Gertrude Tibbet took Lily aside and whispered, "This is all very nice, dear, but why haven't you married Caleb?"

Lily looked down at the diamond engagement ring still glittering on her finger. She'd given up trying to remove it days before, though this was the first time she'd truly admitted the defeat to herself. "We still can't agree on the important things."

Mrs. Tibbet glanced pointedly at Lily's waistline, which seemed to be expanding of late. "I have a feeling it's the future you can't agree on. The present is quite another matter, though, isn't it?"

Lily sighed. The nights she'd spent with Caleb in the past week had been the most pleasant of her life, and not just because of the lovemaking. They'd talked together, and Lily had read whole chapters from her beloved dime novels for Caleb's enlightenment. They'd played games of gin rummy, Lily usually coming out the winner, and best of all, they'd laughed. She was going to miss those things even more than she'd miss the feel of Caleb's hands on her body, once he was gone.

And she knew he would leave soon, even if he had ordered lumber and laid out a foundation for a sizable house.

Mrs. Tibbet put a gentle hand on Lily's shoulder. "I've given up tendering advice, my dear, since you never take it anyway. I'll only say, do come to the colonel and me if things get too difficult."

On impulse Lily embraced her friend. "I promise I will," she said gratefully.

When everyone had gone but Velvet and Hank, Lily and her friend sat in the light of the bonfire Caleb had built in the yard and talked. The Robbinses had started building their house, too, and with both of them working on it the walls were rising rapidly.

Velvet laid modest hands on her stomach when she was

sure Caleb and Hank were still occupied smoking their cheroots a little distance away, talking about whatever things men talk about. "I'm going to have a baby 'long about Christmas time I think," Lily's neighbor confided. "I'm always real regular, and I haven't bled since before Hank came back."

Lily reached out and clasped her friend's hand. "That's wonderful," she said sincerely, but then her smile faded. "I think we'll probably become mothers right about the same time."

Velvet's grip on Lily's hand was so tight that it pressed her knuckles together and made them ache. "That decides it, then. You've got to marry the major while he's willin', Lily."

She lifted her chin to an obstinate angle. "Don't you think I would, Velvet, if the man would only be reasonable?"

Velvet's eyes rounded. "You mean he wants the cream without buyin' the cow? But what about this ring?"

Lily sighed. "Caleb would marry me—if I would agree to follow him to Pennsylvania."

"Isn't that what the good book says?" Velvet asked. "Weather thou goest, or something like that?"

The trace of scripture was like a painful barb to Lily. She supposed by now even God was against her, and she was too weary to repeat all her excuses. The truth was, for all of it, she was just plain scared. "What's it like for you, Velvet? Being married, I mean?"

Velvet permitted herself a dreamy sigh and gazed into the bonfire as though she saw some wonderful pageant being played out there. "It gets better every day," she answered after a long time. "Hank and me, we work together, side by side, all day through. And come night, we—well, we're together then, too."

Lily was touched, and a little amused, to see that her worldly friend was blushing. "Do you think that's enough, though—liking what a man does to you in bed?"

Velvet shook her head. "Wouldn't be enough by itself, I reckon. It's if you can laugh and talk together, and if you know you'd stand by him no matter what, and he'd stand by you."

Glancing toward Caleb, Lily let out a long sigh. "I just don't know. That man is so stubborn, sometimes I think I'd better just give in and marry him."

"Why don't you?"

"He'd own me then, just like he owns his horse and his land and his shotgun."

Velvet smiled. "I don't mind Hank ownin' me," she said.

"That's silly, Velvet," Lily protested. "You're a human being, not a saddle blanket or a wheelbarrow. Nobody can own you."

"Can if you let 'em," Velvet insisted.

Lily gave up.

Soon Hank came over to Velvet—it struck Lily again how agile he was for a man with a twisted limb—and they said their farewells for the night. Then, with Velvet carrying a lantern in one hand, they set out for their place on the other side of the timber.

Lily watched them go in silence, her arms folded.

"What are you thinking?" Caleb asked, coming up behind her. She could feel his breath on her nape, warm and gentle. His arms slipped around her, pulling her close.

"That I envy Hank and Velvet," Lily said honestly. "It's so simple with them. They're just—well—together. And they're not sure but they think they're going to have a baby."

Caleb turned Lily to face him. "And so are we," he reminded her, his arms around her again.

She looked up at him. "Yes," she answered, "it would seem so." She drew a deep breath and let it out again. "I don't think we should make love anymore, Caleb."

"Why not?"

"Because we're not married, and we don't have any intention of *ever* being married. That's sinful."

Caleb bent to taste her lips. "I couldn't agree more. That it's sinful for us not to be married, I mean."

Lily stiffened when she felt herself beginning, already, to

respond to Caleb's touch. "But you aren't willing to concede anything, are you?"

"I won't promise to stay here for the rest of my life, if that's what you mean."

An overwhelming sadness filled Lily. What wild impulse had made her hope that tonight would be different? She pulled out of his arms. "Good night, Caleb," she said, turning and starting toward the new house, where Lily would sleep for the first time.

Caleb did not follow, and even after Lily had done up the dishes and banked the fire there was still no sign of him.

It was at once ironic and fitting, she reflected later, when she was lying alone between her crisp, clean sheets, that she should spend this night by herself.

Tears burning in her eyes, Lily turned her face to the wall, huddled down in the covers, and tried to sleep.

She was awakened in the early morning by the steady *smack-smack-smack* of a hammer. Lily got up, made her bed, left her room, and crossed the cabin to pour a cup of coffee. But since Caleb had not slept in the house there was no fire in the stove and no coffee brewing in the pot.

Resigned, Lily dressed in the trousers and shirt she'd bought in Spokane for riding and strode outside to rinse and fill the coffeepot at the creek.

Caleb was making good progress on his house, even though he could work on it only in the morning hours, before he went to the post to carry out his duties, and in the evenings after supper. He had put up the framework—it was five times the size of Lily's place, that house—and laid the floor.

Lily stood looking up at him, the coffeepot full of water in her hands. "Good morning, Caleb," she said.

He looked down at her, nails jutting from his mouth, and nodded in an abrupt fashion.

"I thought I'd go to Tylerville today," Lily said, "after I water that corn I planted, of course."

Caleb didn't look at her again, but he did speak around

the nails in his mouth. The words were garbled, but Lily translated them to: "Why would you want to go there?"

"I'd like to do some shopping. There are some things I need."

He pulled the nails from his mouth and dropped them into his shirt pocket. "You're going like that? In trousers?"

Lily nodded. "They're much handier for riding than a skirt," she informed him, though she privately thought any idiot would have been able to figure out such an obvious thing on his own.

"You'll be arrested," Caleb fretted, climbing down from the framework of his house to stand on the ground facing Lily.

"I don't believe it's against the law for a woman to wear trousers, Caleb."

"Don't be too sure of that. If they can throw you in the hoosegow for wearing lip paint—and they can—I figure trousers probably won't endear you to them either." He paused, grinning, to turn Lily around once, and then back to face him. "They do look pretty good on you, though."

Lily glared at Caleb, but not out of any real ire. If she didn't keep him at a distance, he'd soon have her sprawled on the bed or bent over a sawhorse, and she'd be carrying on fit to shame Jezebel herself. "I didn't ask for your opinion, Caleb Halliday," she said.

He laughed and caught his hands under her bottom, lifting her against him. "If you're going to strut around in pants, sodbuster, you have to be prepared to face up to the consequences."

Lily hated herself for the way her blood was heating and her heartbeat quickening. "Put me down, Caleb," she fussed.

She was mildly disappointed when he did. "All right," he agreed. "But if you're going to town, change your clothes first."

Lily started to speak, then closed her mouth. She went into her house and closed the door.

When she came out of the bedroom Caleb was standing by the table. Lily was wearing the obligatory dress, but she didn't once meet Caleb's gaze because she didn't want to see the satisfaction there. "May I use your buggy?" she asked.

Out of the corner of her eye she saw him set a coffee cup in her new porcelain sink. "I'll hitch it up for you," he answered. Then, without another word, he left the house.

Lily waited until he'd had time to harness Dancer to his buggy, then went outside. She managed to avoid looking directly into Caleb's eyes when he handed her up into the seat of the rig.

"When will you be back?" he asked.

It was an odd question, Lily reflected, coming from a man who usually went wherever he wished without so much as a word to her. She shrugged. "I don't see where that's any of your business, Major Halliday," she replied primly.

Caleb touched the brim of his hat, and it seemed to Lily that he was struggling to hold back a smile. "I'd like to make it my business, but you insist on living in sin."

Lily barely restrained herself from slapping him. Without speaking at all she brought down the buggy reins on Dancer's back and was off. Her cheeks didn't stop throbbing until she was halfway to Tylerville.

Arriving there, she immediately went to the general store and asked the storekeeper to wire Spokane for the rest of her money. The bank there promptly wired back that the funds would be on their way to her in the next mail.

Because the storekeeper had been a witness to all this, Lily was allowed credit in his store. Since she'd brought the buggy, she bought food mostly—beans and dried pork, canned vegetables, and staples like flour and sugar and coffee.

Heaven knew Caleb wasn't in her best graces that day, but she chose a pipe and tobacco for him anyway. She told herself she was only repaying him for the gifts he'd given her, so she wouldn't be obliged to him.

She was making her most ambitious purchase, a crate containing two dozen chirping yellow chicks, when the storekeeper suddenly remembered something. "There's a letter for you, Miss Chalmers. We was holding it to send out to you on Monday's stage."

Lily snatched the envelope hungrily from his hands. It was postmarked Chicago, but the handwriting was not her mother's.

She tore it open and skipped over the salutation and greetings to read, ". . . regret to inform you of Mrs. Harrington's untimely death. We have no knowledge of your sisters' whereabouts, though of course it is possible that your mother knew. Sincerely . . ."

Lily crumpled the letter in one hand and sank into a rocking chair next to the store's potbellied stove. This new defeat in the face of the secret hopes she'd held was devastating. Her mother had died and taken with her all knowledge of Emma and Caroline.

"Miss Lily?" the storekeeper asked worriedly. "Are you all right?"

Lily nodded and forced herself up out of the chair. "Y-yes," she said, smoothing her skirts. "Tell me, is there any mail for Mr. Hank Robbins or Major Caleb Halliday? They're my neighbors."

The portly man rushed to check the pigeonholes allotted to the mail and returned with a letter for Caleb, addressed in a strong and forceful hand and postmarked Fox Chapel, Pennsylvania.

Lily could think only of her mother. Had she died alone, with no one to love her? Had she suffered pain?

Kathleen was gone, and so were Lily's hopes of ever finding her sisters. She'd been silly and naïve to think she'd ever be able to track them down. It was time to stop dreaming and face reality.

She had to stop thinking of lives that were over and turn her mind to one that was just beginning. After splaying the fingers of one hand over her belly and biting down hard on her lower lip to keep from weeping, Lily made one more sizable purchase and dropped it into her handbag.

The storekeeper managed to load all Lily's purchases beneath, behind, and on top of the buggy seat, barely leaving room for her. She set off for home in something of a daze.

She had no mother.

Lily's mind kept coming back to that fact, and even though she felt no crushing sense of grief, it was difficult to accept that she would never be able to ask Kathleen the million and one questions that had arisen since the day she and Emma and Caroline were put on the orphan train. Apparently she'd married the soldier who'd made her send her daughters away. Had she been happy? Were there other children by him?

Tears slipped down Lily's cheeks; they dried in the bright sunshine and the fresh wind. When she arrived at home Caleb was gone.

Lily took the chicks inside first, setting their crate near the stove so they'd be warm. After giving them water and a handful of the chicken feed she'd bought, she carried in all the other supplies and put them away.

When it was all done she took the last item she'd purchased from her bag and held it up to the light. It was a man's golden wedding band, and it glinted in the sunshine.

Lily looked around the little cabin she'd fought so hard to have and sighed. When Caleb returned from Fort Deveraux that evening she meant to propose.

Chapter

❧ 21 ❦

*C*aleb was surprised and a little worried when Lily met him almost halfway between the homestead and Fort Deveraux. She wasn't carrying a gun or even riding Dancer, just striding along with her skirts hiked up, an intent expression on her beautiful face.

He was struck, not for the first time, by the magnitude of his love for her. It was an enormous thing, and frightening in its power. He reined in the gelding he had ridden for three years and never bothered to name.

She let her skirts fall back into place around her ankles as she stopped and looked up at him. "I've decided to marry you, if you'll still have me," she said matter-of-factly.

Caleb was an astute man, and he knew something was very wrong, but he wanted Lily too much to question her sudden change of heart. There would be plenty of time for working out details after he'd gotten his wedding band on her finger and bedded her as his wife. Without a word he

315

reached down for Lily's hand, and when she gave it he hoisted her up onto the horse, positioning her between the saddle horn and his abdomen.

He kissed her thoroughly and turned the gelding back toward Fort Deveraux.

It was no trouble getting the special license; Colonel Tibbet took care of that. Caleb had a ring for Lily at his house—he'd bought it when he followed her to Spokane—and he went to fetch it while Gertrude was fussing over the bride.

Caleb had once dreamed of bringing Lily to his house, of having her fill it with flowers and laughter, of showing her off to his friends, of pampering and spoiling her. Now that he meant to leave the army, he would do those things in some other house.

Preferably the house he'd grown up in, outside of Fox Chapel.

Hastily Caleb bathed and shaved and put on his best uniform. He didn't let himself think about that troubling expression in Lily's eyes; he considered, instead, as any bridegroom might, the pleasures of the coming night.

The dress was old, since Mrs. Tibbet had been married in it herself, but it was still very beautiful, and it fit Lily after only a few tucks had been taken. It was ivory silk, of the finest quality, and there were tiny cream-colored pearls stitched to the fabric. Although the neckline was high, much of the bodice was sheer lace, showing a tantalizing amount of skin, and the sleeves were filmy, revealing the flesh of Lily's arms.

"You look wonderful," Gertrude Tibbet said with satisfaction.

Lily inspected herself in the mirror and sighed. "Thank you," she said. "Has anyone sent for Velvet and Hank?"

Mrs. Tibbet nodded. "I'm sure they'll be here soon. The chaplain is already downstairs having a brandy with the colonel, and his wife is going to play the organ." She took a flowing, gossamer veil from a box on the bed. "This will provide the finishing touch," she said.

Lily sat patiently in the chair in front of Mrs. Tibbet's vanity table while that lady pinned the veil carefully in place. When it was done she laid gentle hands on the bride's shoulders. "You do love Caleb, don't you, Lily? He's a fine man, and he deserves a wife who loves him."

"I love him," Lily answered truthfully, "very much."

"You don't seem very happy about this wedding, though."

Lily lowered her eyes. She supposed she should tell her friend that it wasn't marrying Caleb she was unhappy about, but the death of her mother and the loss of her dream of finding her sisters. She couldn't bring herself to talk about those things, however. Not then.

"Lily?" Mrs. Tibbet prompted kindly.

Lily found a radiant smile somewhere inside herself and lifted her face to show it. "You needn't worry. Caleb will never regret marrying me."

The older woman looked mildly exasperated, but she patted Lily's lace-covered shoulder and changed the subject. "Will you be going on a honeymoon?"

Lily hadn't thought that far ahead. "I don't think so," she said. "Who would feed my chickens?"

In the vanity mirror she caught Mrs. Tibbet rolling her eyes. "Lily, Lily—there isn't another girl like you in all God's creation."

The remark made Lily feel sad again, since there *were* two, somewhere, who could be expected to have similarities. She put Emma and Caroline out of her mind for the moment and laid a hand on top of Mrs. Tibbet's be-ringed fingers. "I'm grateful to you and the colonel for all you've done. You've been so very kind."

"Caleb has practically been a son to us," Mrs. Tibbet replied, "and now you'll be a daughter."

"But you'll be returning to Fox Chapel once the colonel retires," Lily pointed out.

Mrs. Tibbet's expression said she expected Lily would be

living in Pennsylvania as well, but she was far too polite to make such a statement outright. "I'll just go downstairs and see how the bridegroom is bearing up. Can I bring you anything, Lily? A cup of tea, perhaps?"

Lily's taste ran more toward the brandy the men were having, though she wouldn't have indulged because of her fear of turning out like Kathleen. She shook her head and said, "No, thank you," and Mrs. Tibbet left the room.

Rising from the little stool in front of the vanity, Lily went to the window. It was light, but soon there would be stars in the sky, and the birds, now twittering in their elms and maples, would be still. This night would be different from all other nights before it, for even though Lily had given herself to Caleb, she had never lain with him as an honest-to-goodness wife.

Standing there, gripping the lace curtain in one hand, Lily wondered why she had resisted marriage so strenuously. It seemed the most natural thing in the world to marry Caleb, to give the child growing within her a name and a home. There was a certain sweet resignation in it, a peace that comes of accepting the inevitable.

The door opened behind her, and Lily looked back over her shoulder to see Velvet standing there, smiling as happily as she had on the occasion of her own wedding.

"You've made the right decision, Lily," she said. The two women embraced briefly, then Velvet straightened Lily's veil. "My, what a lovely thing you are."

Lily smiled. "All brides are beautiful, aren't they?"

Velvet nodded. "When they're marrying the right man, I reckon they are. Hank's going to take photographs of you and Caleb—that's our gift to you."

"I couldn't think of a better present," Lily said. Hank had already developed the images of Velvet and Lily standing together in front of her transported house, and the ones of the party, and they were among her most cherished possessions.

Soon the sound of Mrs. Tibbet's parlor organ came up the

stairs, and there was a firm rap at Lily's door. She opened it to find Colonel Tibbet standing there, looking very handsome in his uniform, his white hair and mustache gleaming.

"Are you ready, Miss Lily?" he asked and, when Lily nodded he offered his arm and escorted her to the top of the stairs. Velvet stepped down ahead of them to take her place as matron of honor, and when the wedding march began they descended at a stately pace.

Caleb was standing next to the chaplain, in front of the parlor fireplace, and he looked magnificent to Lily in his long blue coat with its glistening braid and epaulets, and the trousers striped in gold on each leg. He smiled and extended one hand, and Colonel Tibbet surrendered Lily with a gracious nod and a subtle clearing of his throat.

The ceremony passed very swiftly, it seemed to Lily. She promised to love, honor, and obey, and Caleb promised to love, honor, and cherish. It didn't seem right, but Lily was too dazed to weigh the inequities. She simply made her vows, and when Caleb kissed her her knees weakened, as always, and her spirits lifted a little.

There was cake, albeit a raisin cake Mrs. Tibbet had baked for her husband, being bereft of a housekeeper again, and afterwards Hank took the photographs. Lily was only sorry that Rupert wasn't there to give his blessing.

Once the union had been adequately celebrated Caleb caught Lily by the arm and ushered her out the front door and down the steps. The stars were out in legions by then, glimmering against the sky.

Looking up at them, Lily sighed with contentment. "Have you borrowed a buggy?" she asked her husband.

"We're not going home tonight, Lily," Caleb answered, opening the gate for her. His touch was light on her elbow, but forceful, too.

Lily bristled. "Don't I have a choice in the matter?"

"Not really," Caleb replied with amusement in his eyes.

"I have baby chicks to think about," Lily protested. "Twenty-four of them."

"They'll be all right until tomorrow," Caleb replied, urging her down the wooden sidewalk toward the house he had been assigned as a concession to his rank.

Lamps burned in the windows of Caleb's parlor, and there was smoke curling from the chimney. Lily was pleased that he'd been there and made preparations. It meant he loved her.

When they reached the porch, and Caleb had opened the door, he swept Lily up in his arms and carried her across the threshold. The moment they were inside, away from the eyes of interested neighbors, he covered her mouth with his in a consuming kiss.

Lily felt her bones melt within her, along with all her misgivings. Her arms wrapped around Caleb's neck, and she responded wholeheartedly to the kiss. When it was over she took his hat from his head and tossed it away.

"I love you, Major Halliday," she said boldly.

"How much?" he teased in a low, husky voice.

"I couldn't possibly tell you."

He nibbled at her lower lip for a moment, still holding her in his arms. "Will you show me?"

"Oh, yes," Lily whispered, kissing him lightly.

Caleb carried her up the stairs and along the hallway to the master bedroom. There was a fire snapping on the hearth. The bed was made up with crisp, clean sheets turned back in a welcoming fashion.

The major set Lily in a chair near the fire, and he dropped to one knee in front of her, took her hand in his, and kissed it. He looked so like a prince from a fairy tale that Lily was nearly overcome.

"I didn't make a proper proposal before," he said quietly.

"Oh, Caleb."

"There's never been anyone else for me, Lily," he went on, "and there never will be again. I'm promising you right now that your happiness will always be as important to me as my own."

Lily's eyes brimmed with joyous tears. Why had she

waited so long? She put her arms around Caleb's neck and embraced him, and his head was cradled against the plump cushion of her breasts. "I love you so much," she whispered.

He looked up at her, a glint dancing in his eyes. "Show me, Mrs. Halliday."

Lily sat up very straight in the chair. "Very well, then, Major, I will," she said in a most proper tone of voice. "If you'll just unfasten the back of my dress . . ."

Caleb reached behind her to comply, and his usually deft fingers fumbled at the task. It touched Lily to know that he was nervous on this special night, even after all that had gone before.

When he'd finally managed to work the last button Lily slowly lowered the gossamer bodice of her borrowed wedding gown. She was bare beneath it, since it wouldn't have accommodated a camisole, and Caleb drew in his breath at the sight of her breasts, as though he'd never seen them before.

Lily traced his mouth with the tip of her index finger, then brought him gently forward to her nipple, and he took it hungrily. While he suckled she ran her hands through his soft, wheat-colored hair, encouraging him. Presently he took sustenance at the other breast, and Lily relaxed her hands and let her head fall back in sheer contentment. She could have gone on nourishing Caleb like that for hours, the sensation was so piercingly blissful, but eventually he had his fill.

Without rising from his knees he lifted Lily's skirts and petticoat, letting the froth of lace and silk fall over the sides of the chair. Then he untied the ribbons that held her drawers closed.

Lily moaned as he drew them down over her legs and thighs and feet, then tossed them away.

He lifted one of her knees over one arm of the chair, and the opposite knee over the other. His hands caressed Lily's inner thighs. "Show me how much you love me, Mrs. Halliday," he said.

Lily was filled with sweet despair. Never had she been so totally vulnerable to Caleb, never had she enjoyed it more. She parted the silken veil for him and started, with a whimper, when he touched her treasure with his tongue. She tried to draw her knees together—the pleasure was too keen to be borne—but Caleb held them firmly over the arms of the chair.

He laved her once, lightly, and her fingers went back to his hair, knotting there, trying to press him closer.

Caleb chuckled against her spicy warmth. "This one is going to take a lot out of you, sodbuster," he promised.

Lily was writhing slightly, but she couldn't go far because Caleb was holding her knees. Her vision blurred and her breath quickened as he sampled her again, and she gasped his name.

"Do you like that, Lily?"

"Oh," she whimpered. "Oh, Caleb . . ."

"Do you?"

"Yes! Oh, yes!"

He took her full into his mouth, and he was greedy. Lily rocked wildly with pleasure, her hands clawing at his shoulders.

Caleb brought her to the very brink, then nipped her lightly with his teeth. With a lusty cry she gave up in an explosive surrender, her hips buckling as he wrung every last response from her.

When it was over she sagged in the chair, too dazed to speak. Caleb gently brought her legs back together, lifted her from the chair and set her on the bed. There he tenderly undressed her, and when she lay naked before him, her legs spread wide as he wanted them, he took off his own clothes without ever looking away from her face.

When he was as bare as she, he mounted her.

Lily was ready for him; her satisfaction had only made her long to be filled with Caleb, to be a part of him, to extract cries of pleasure from him as he had done with her.

322

LILY AND THE MAJOR

But Caleb, as usual, was stubborn. He came back to Lily's mouth and kissed her, and his shaft was positioned to enter her. Lily tried to enclose him with a thrust of her hips and instead got just an inch of him, enough to tease her.

She begged him to take her, but he only kissed her again and gave her another inch. Wild with need, Lily clasped his buttocks in her hands and pressed him to her with all her might. This time he allowed her to prevail, giving her his full length.

Pressing his hands into the mattress, he raised himself upon her and began to thrust and withdraw, his pace slow and steady and calculated to drive Lily mad. Finally, in desperation, she flung her legs around his hips and would not let him leave her.

"I love you, Lily," he groaned against her neck, and then he lunged deep.

She arched her back and cried out for joy, and from that moment on they were both lost. The tempo increased second by second until they were heaving their bodies together in unreasoning need. The crescendo of their two quests tore cries from both their throats and hurled them back to the mattress in utter exhaustion.

Lily had promised herself that this would be the time she would tell Caleb about the letter that had prompted her decision to marry him, but she was too spent to shape the words. She snuggled close to him beneath the covers and slept until desire shook them awake again, demanding every scrap of energy they'd regained through rest.

The next day, at midmorning, Caleb and Lily went home again, because Lily was worried about her chickens.

When they reached the homestead the chicks were still chirping merrily in their box. When Lily had fed and watered them and caressed a few lightly with her fingertips, she was happy again.

Laughing, Caleb gave her a long kiss and a swat on the bottom, and he warned her that he intended to have her well

323

and truly that night when he returned from the post. Lily didn't much mind the prospect; so far, it had been easy to love, honor, and obey.

Once Caleb was gone she made sure Dancer was all right, then ventured to the old house to see what could be done to make it habitable for the chicks. They would need heat, since they were so small, but that was no problem. There was still a rickety old cook stove there, and Lily filled it with kindling and got a nice blaze going.

After that she put the chicks close by, still in their crate, since she had no chicken wire to contain them, and made sure they had food and water. When that was done she dragged the big tub from its peg on the rear wall and carried it to the new house, where she set it in the yard, in the very place where she and Caleb had bathed.

Once she'd filled it with creek water she built a fire around the base of the tub. When Caleb returned early that afternoon she was industriously washing clothes. She had a smaller tub for rinse water, and a line, bought in Tylerville the day before, stretched from the corner of the new house to the corner of the old one. Clean shirts, petticoats, dresses, trousers, and drawers all flapped in the fresh May breeze.

Lily stopped her work to throw her arms around Caleb's neck. "Home so soon, Major?"

He gave her an energetic kiss. "I couldn't stop thinking about you, sodbuster."

Lily delighted in being held so close to him, but her pleasure faded a little when she remembered that there had been a letter for him from someone in Fox Chapel, as well as the one from her mother's lawyer.

She left Caleb's arms and rolled down her sleeves.

His eyes held a bewildered expression. "Lily, what is it?"

"Yesterday, when I went to Tylerville, there was a letter for you. I forgot to mention it, with all the excitement."

Caleb's eyes cleared a little. "Where is it?"

She fetched it from the table beside her bed and brought it outside to him.

He frowned as he assessed the handwriting on the envelope, and Lily turned and walked toward the house as he opened it. Somehow she knew it was going to change things for them, just as the letter about her mother's death had done.

"W-would you like something to eat?" she asked, aware that he'd followed her. She busied herself stoking up the fire in the stove and ladling water into the pot to brew coffee.

"Nothing you're prepared to serve right this moment," Caleb replied in a distracted voice. Then he was silent.

When Lily could bear that silence no longer, when it had stretched on and on for what seemed like an eternity, she turned to face him. "Caleb, what is it?"

"It's from my brother Joss," Caleb answered. The letter lay on the table beside him, and he was staring out the window as though he could see some long-ago scene just beyond the glass.

Lily drew a deep breath, then let it out again. She wondered why she hadn't seen it in Caleb before, this desperate wish to go back to Pennsylvania and confront his past. It was probably every bit as consuming as her own need to see her sisters again.

"He wants you to come home to Fox Chapel," she said.

"No," Caleb answered without even looking at her, his tone gravelly. "He wants to buy my share of the farm so he can forget he ever had a brother."

Although Caleb's expression and bearing were unreadable, Lily knew he was wounded. She went to him and laid a gentle hand on his shoulder. "Can he do that?"

At last Caleb looked up at her. The reflections of a thousand yesterdays were visible in his golden eyes. "I suppose. Joss is a powerful man, and he has a lot of influence in Pennsylvania."

Lily caressed her husband's cheeks. She longed to comfort Caleb, but she wasn't sure how to go about it. "What will you do?"

"I don't know," he answered, and Lily's hand fell away

when he rose from the chair. He crossed the kitchen and opened the door, and Lily felt as though a great and terrible distance had opened between them.

"I'll make biscuits for supper," she said, because she didn't know what else to offer him.

"Good," Caleb replied, and then he left the house.

Soon Lily heard the steady bang of his hammer, and she knew he was working on his house again. She mixed up the biscuit dough, then set it aside, since it was still too early to start supper.

When she figured Caleb had had enough time to assemble his thoughts, she went outside.

He was on the roof of his house, hammering down shingles. He'd taken off his shirt, and his muscled chest glinted in the late afternoon sunshine.

"I'm going over to see Velvet," Lily called up to him in a casual tone. She wanted him to say she should stay, wanted him to climb down from the roof and let her take him into her arms, but he didn't so much as look at her.

"All right," he answered.

Feeling bereft, Lily started toward the woods, stopping off at the old house to check on the chicks. The laundry was nearly dry, too, and she still had a few pieces to wash.

She found Velvet chasing a spotted cow around the corner of the new cabin she and Hank had been building almost since the day of their wedding. It wasn't finished by any means, but the roof was up and the walls were enclosed, so they were living inside. No doubt it felt like a palace after residing in an enclosed wagon.

"Come back here, you!" Velvet shrieked, unaware of Lily's presence.

Lily laughed, forgetting her own worries for a moment, and ran to help her friend corral the renegade. She'd had some experience with the animals, since it had been her job, when she was living with the Sommerses, to hunt down the milk cow every evening and bring her home.

Together Lily and Velvet managed to corner the testy bovine between the wagon and the newly constructed outhouse, and Velvet threw a rope around the beast's neck.

"Mule-headed rascal!" Velvet scolded, giving the cow a slap across the nose.

"Where did you get her?" Lily asked, delighted.

"Hank bought her off an Indian," Velvet answered, wiping one arm across her forehead. "I say that Indian got the best part of the deal."

Lily was petting the cow's heaving side, trying to calm her. "You won't think that when you have milk and butter and cream," she said.

"If I have to catch her every time I want them things," Velvet replied, "well—I'd sooner go right on buyin' 'em at the post store."

"I've got chickens now," Lily volunteered proudly. "In a few months, when they're big enough, there'll be plenty of eggs for all of us."

Velvet was calmer then. "Excuse my bad manners," she fretted. "I didn't even ask how the wedding night went!"

Lily's blush was answer enough.

"Come in," Velvet said, tying the cow to the left rear wheel of Hank's wagon. "I got some coffee left from breakfast."

"Where's Hank?" Lily asked as she followed her friend into the little house. Like her own place, it smelled delightfully of freshly sawed wood.

If Velvet sensed that something was wrong, she'd also discerned that Lily wasn't ready to talk about it. "He's plantin' some fruit trees up on the rise." She poured hot, strong coffee for herself and Lily and joined her friend at the table. "That sure was a pretty weddin' you and Caleb had," she said dreamily. "Him so handsome in that uniform and all, and you so lovely in that lacy dress."

Lily wanted to lay her head down on her arms and weep, but she didn't. She was a pioneer, a homesteader, and she had to be strong. "Caleb had a letter from Fox Chapel," she began, and as she listed her worries and her fears Velvet listened closely.

"He's not going to want to come back once he's there with his own people around him, and I'll have to choose between Caleb and my land."

Velvet leaned forward slightly in her chair. "You'd choose Caleb, wouldn't you?"

Slowly, Lily nodded. "But there'd be bitterness between us, Velvet. I'd give up the homestead for him, but that doesn't mean we'd be happy together."

With an awkward, work-worn hand Velvet reached out to touch Lily's arm. "I thought things could never turn out right for me, and they sure enough did. Don't give up now, Lily. You've got to hold on."

Lily tried to smile, but she couldn't quite manage. She'd run out of hope.

Chapter

❧ 22 ❧

*E*ven though nothing had really been resolved, Lily felt better for having shared her burdens with Velvet. She returned home in the last blaze of sunshine to find that Caleb was still on the roof of his silly, spacious house, hammering and hammering.

Lily squared her shoulders and set to work finishing up the last of the wash—it could dry inside, by the stove—and taking the clean garments down from the clotheslines. After that she looked in on her chickens and was stricken to find that two of the downy little creatures had perished. Even though this was only to be expected in the raising of chicks, Lily mourned them.

She buried the feather-light bodies solemnly, well behind the privy Wilbur Pierce and his friends had erected while they were building Lily's new house, and went to the creek to wash her hands. The hammering ceased, and she turned to look back over one shoulder.

Caleb was regarding her in a strange way, as though he could see straight through her.

Drying her hands on her apron, Lily got to her feet and walked slowly over to stand within the shadow of Caleb's house and look up at him. He was ablaze with the golden fire of the struggling sun.

Lily put her hands on her hips and tilted her head to one side. "Why are you building that house, Caleb Halliday, when we both know you're going to hightail it back to Pennsylvania and drag me right along with you?"

She couldn't read his expression, but she saw that he was climbing deftly down the roof. He reached the ladder and descended to stand facing her, his shirt in one hand, his muscular chest glistening with sweat even as the first chill of twilight came up from the creek.

"Half of that farm is mine," he said.

Lily sighed. "So go back to Pennsylvania and fight for it," she said, exasperated. "You're not the only one with problems, you know."

Caleb looked at her closely as he shrugged back into his shirt and began doing up the buttons, but he didn't speak. He seemed to know that Lily was going to go on talking without any urging from him.

"It just so happens that my mother is dead, and I'll probably never find out where my sisters are."

"So that's why you were willing to marry me all of a sudden—you've given up. I don't know as I like that very much, Lily."

"What you like is of no concern to me," Lily said briskly. She started to turn away, but Caleb caught her by the arm and made her stay.

"You can't just up and quit like this. It isn't like you."

"You've said it yourself, Caleb: The West is a big place. My sisters could be married, with no time in their busy lives for a lost sister they haven't seen in thirteen years. They might even be dead."

Caleb's mouth fell open, but he recovered himself quickly. "I don't believe I'm hearing this. You've fought me from the day we met because you wanted to find your sisters, and now you're standing there telling me that it's no use looking for them. What about that letter you had from Wyoming?"

"It said Caroline had disappeared, Caleb. That's hardly reason for encouragement."

"Maybe we'd better go there and find out."

Lily had never dared to think such a thought. "Travel all the way to Wyoming? But what about the chickens?"

"What's more important to you, Lily—your sister or those damn chickens?"

Despite herself, Lily was beginning to believe her dreams might come true after all. "My sister," she said quietly.

Caleb reached out at long last and laid his hands on Lily's shoulders, drawing her close. "Lily, come to Fox Chapel with me," he said hoarsely. "I'm going to need you."

Lily looked up at her husband. He was, for all practical purposes, the only family she had, and she couldn't imagine living without him. "What if I hate it there?" she asked, her voice very quiet. "What if I miss my house and my chickens so much I can't stand it?"

He gave her a light, undemanding kiss, and his lips were warm and soft as they moved against hers. "If you hate Fox Chapel, I'll bring you back here."

"Is that a promise?"

"Yes."

"Even if you work things out with your brother and want to stay?"

Caleb sighed. "I told you—your happiness is as important to me as my own."

Lily was not a worldly woman, but she'd seen enough to know that such an attitude was rare in a man. She hugged Caleb. "In that case, maybe you won't be mad that there's nothing for supper but biscuits."

Although his lips curved into a slight smile, Caleb's eyes were serious. He lifted one hand to caress Lily's cheek. "I'm sorry about your mother," he said quietly.

Lily straightened in his arms. "I didn't even know the woman, really," she said lightly. "So it's not as though I'm grieving." She would have walked away toward the house, but Caleb held her fast.

"I think you are," he said.

Lily swallowed. Damn the man—now he had her on the verge of tears. She struggled all the harder to maintain her composure. "If I wept for her, Caleb, I'd be weeping for a woman who never existed—the woman I needed her to be. She was never a real mother to us."

At that, Caleb let Lily go free and followed her into the small, stove-warmed kitchen. While Lily was washing her hands to roll out the biscuit dough Caleb got eggs and cheese from the larder and onions from a bin under the sink. By the time the biscuits were ready to go into the oven he had an impressive omelette steaming in a pan.

"You're a remarkable man," Lily allowed.

Caleb smiled at her, his gaze sliding over her figure, making silent promises for the night. "And you're a remarkable woman."

Lily felt a little tug in her heart.

All during supper Lily was conscious of being drawn toward Caleb. She squirmed, all too aware that she hadn't any defense against him.

When the meal was over and the dishes were done Caleb began yawning. "It's been a long, difficult day, Mrs. Halliday," he said, reaching out to trim the lamp. "Let's go to bed."

Lily's face flushed hot. "My chickens—"

He shrugged. "Your chickens are just fine. In fact, they'd probably appreciate it if you gave them a little peace."

"Suppose there's a coyote, or a fox?"

Caleb had caught her by the elbow, and he was ushering her toward the door of their tiny bedroom. "No animal in its right mind would try to get past your shotgun."

The door closed behind them, and Lily was suddenly as shy as if she'd never shared her body with this man. She turned her back and filled the basin on the washstand from its matching pitcher, then started unbuttoning the front of her dress. She heard the bedsprings creak and risked a look back at Caleb.

He was sitting on the edge of the mattress, pulling off his boots, and he gave a great yawn, like a bear settling down to hibernate.

Lily took up her basin and moved toward the door. Despite her intimacy with Caleb, there were certain things she liked to attend to alone. She slipped out into the main part of the cabin, darkened now that the sun was set and the lamps had been extinguished.

There was still a fire burning, and Lily undressed nearby, remembering long-ago winter mornings when she and Emma and Caroline had jumped from their beds, squealing, and rushed to warm themselves by the coal stove. Her eyes filled with tears as she recalled her sisters' faces and heard their voices, and she knew she had never truly given up on finding them—she had only taken a rest from hoping when it had become too painful.

When Lily had finished her makeshift bath she opened the cabin door and tossed the water out. She nearly dropped the basin when she turned and found Caleb watching her, leaning against the bedroom doorjamb. He was wearing trousers, but nothing else, and his eyes moved over Lily's naked curves like molten gold.

Idly, he straightened and held out one hand to her. "Come here," he said, in a husky voice.

Lily was struck yet again by the power of the love she felt for him. Smiling through her tears, she closed the door, set the basin aside, and went to him.

Caleb laughed and reached out to claim her. He carried her into their bedroom, kicking the door shut behind him. Somewhere close by a coyote barked and howled, giving his lonely benediction, but Lily didn't give a thought to her chickens.

* * *

Caleb didn't speak of his brother for a full two weeks. He went to the post in the mornings, remaining there until midafternoon, and then he worked on his house. Lily stopped asking why he wanted to build it when he didn't plan on staying in Washington Territory. She finally understood that while Caleb's hands were occupied his mind and spirit worked at the dilemma that troubled him.

Late in June Caleb left the army for good, over Colonel Tibbet's loud objections, and to celebrate he made Lily put the chicks in Velvet's care and took her to Spokane.

Caleb's house was much larger and much grander than Lily's, and when they reached the city he went straight to the mercantile and started ordering things for it. He sent away for a piano, and a big cook stove with a hot-water reservoir, and an icebox with a brass handle. He selected Oriental rugs, too, and a clock that stood as tall as he did.

Lily was baffled, but she kept her questions to herself. Caleb had told her to buy anything she wanted or needed, and she wasn't too shy to comply. She selected dress patterns, thread, and a number of lengths of fabric. She chose muslin for drawers and camisoles and petticoats, and lace for trim.

At midday she and Caleb went to lunch in the hotel dining room, and in the evening they paid a call on Rupert. The yard surrounding his small house was sweet-scented with lilacs, and they sat on the porch in worn wicker chairs.

Lily's adopted brother was obviously pleased that she'd married Caleb; he kept beaming at his new brother-in-law.

Lily wondered when somebody was going to notice that she hadn't been the only one to make a good match, but she didn't complain. She and Caleb had spent the afternoon making love in their hotel room, and that sweet violence had left Lily feeling generous and very patient.

"When are you going to marry Winola?" she asked directly.

Rupert "ahemed," took his pipe from the pocket of his worn coat, filled it with tobacco, and tamped down with a practiced thumb. "She and I were married a week ago," he confided in a low tone of voice, "but we're keeping it a secret for the time being."

A secret marriage! Lily was delighted, but she was also curious. "Why don't you tell the world?"

Rupert sighed. "Winola wants to keep on teaching. If the school board finds out she's married, she'll lose her job."

Caleb, who had been listening thoughtfully, spoke for the first time. "If it's so important to her, why don't the two of you start a school of your own?"

"We've thought of that," Rupert replied. "There are a lot of children growing up uneducated because they live so far from town. Winola and I would like to start a boarding school for young men, but it takes money."

Lily was reminded of the Reverend Sommers, who had never permitted her to go to school. She'd been allowed to sit in on Isadora's lessons with Rupert only because Rupert had insisted. "Why young men," Lily demanded, "and not girls?"

Caleb put a hand over hers in a gesture that had become familiar. She knew he wasn't silencing her, but merely asking her to wait. "I'd be willing to invest in something like that," he said.

Rupert looked embarrassed and chagrined. "I couldn't take money from you."

"Why not?" Lily wanted to know. She was still ruffled and spoke peevishly. "He must have piles of it, the way he throws it around."

In that instant the tension was broken and both men laughed.

"Perhaps I should discuss this with Winola," Rupert conceded.

"I still want to know why it's going to be a boarding school for boys," Lily put in.

Rupert smiled at her and took her hand. "Lily, dear, so many people don't believe in educating girls. Boys, now, they have to make their way in the world—"

Lily was outraged. "And girls don't?" she snapped, looking from Caleb to Rupert. Caleb was distinctly uncomfortable, while Rupert wore his prejudices and complacency as easily as a pair of old slippers.

"You and Winola are both notable exceptions, of course," Rupert allowed with a benevolent smile. "Mostly, though, girls just need to be taught to cook and sew and care for children, and they can learn those things right at home."

Caleb closed his eyes as though bracing for an explosion.

Lily leapt to her feet, waggling one finger in her brother's face. "Is that what you'll want for daughters of your own?" she sputtered. "Nothing but babies, and slaving for some man?"

Rupert's expression was one of kindly bafflement. Obviously Winola's progressive ideas had not affected him. "It's what a woman wants—"

Lily wouldn't have begrudged Rupert a penny if it hadn't been for his narrow and unfair views. "If you give this man money for a school that admits only boys, Caleb Halliday," she railed, "I'll make you sleep in the chicken house!"

"Sit down," Caleb said quietly.

Lily sat, but grudgingly.

"I'll be happy to give you the money you need," Caleb told Rupert.

Lily favored him with a horrified glare. "You mean you would *support* such a prejudice?" She was back on her feet again. "Tell me this, Caleb Halliday—do you want *your* daughters to be ignorant? I can assure you they won't be, because I will not permit it!"

"That," said Caleb evenly, "is enough. You and I will discuss this later, in private."

Lily's cheeks were flaming, but she resisted an impulse to storm off to the hotel in high dudgeon because she knew Caleb would not follow or try to assuage her anger in any way. "Yes, Major," she said sweetly.

Caleb narrowed his eyes at her but said nothing.

Rupert looked concerned. "I can't be the cause of trouble between the two of you," he said. "Winola and I will think of some other solution to the problem."

"You could at least include girls in the classes," Lily said stiffly.

But Rupert shook his head. "Their parents would never permit them to live in such close quarters with young men, Lily," he reasoned, "and rightly so."

Lily still felt as though her entire gender had been insulted, but she kept silent.

Finally, after a half hour had passed, Caleb stood. "We'll be having dinner at the hotel at seven," he said to Rupert. "Lily and I would enjoy having you and Winola join us."

Lily didn't look at her brother. "I presume Winola will be able to read the menu for herself, even though she is female," she observed.

Caleb gave her a little jab with his elbow. "Don't mind your sister, Rupert," he said. "If she can't behave herself, she'll have to eat alone in the room."

"I will not be sent to my room like a child," Lily hissed when she and Caleb were walking along the sidewalk toward the center of town.

Caleb smiled down at her. "If you don't enjoy being treated like a child, maybe you should stop behaving like one."

Lily drew a deep breath and let it out. It was still light outside, since summer was near, and the scents of early flowers and freshly turned earth took away some of the pungency of the horse manure dappling the street. "You are completely ignoring the fact that I have a valid point," she said formally.

"When we have daughters," Caleb conceded generously, "they can go to school. Now are you happy?"

"It will have to be a real school, Caleb. Not a place where they are taught to embroider and pander to some man's every whim."

"What would you have them learn? Military strategy?"

"Higher mathematics," answered Lily, who had always found numbers fascinating. "And science."

"Those subjects are useless to a girl," Caleb objected.

Lily quickened her pace. "It's a wonder anyone was ever able to teach them to *you*, Major, given the fact that your head is so hard."

He chuckled. "You know, Lily, when we reach Fox Chapel you'll be assured of at least one friend—my brother Joss. He has the same low opinion of me as you do."

"I'm sure he's even more bullheaded than you are," Lily said, folding her arms. "Therefore, I don't expect to like him at all."

They'd reached the hotel, and Caleb led the way through the lobby to the stairs. Soon they were in their room.

Lily took a hat she'd bought that afternoon from its pink and white striped box and perched it atop her head. It was a delightful creation, with a narrow straw base and a plume of scarlet ostrich feathers, and it tied with a ribbon beneath her chin. She turned from side to side to admire her reflection in the mirror.

"You look beautiful," Caleb said softly, laying his hands on the sides of her slender waist.

Lily smiled at his reflection in the glass. "Don't you try to flatter me, Caleb Halliday," she warned. "I think you're a brute with a despicable attitude toward women."

He cupped her breasts in his hands. "I love women," he said, bending to nibble at the exposed flesh of her neck.

"When they obey, of course."

"Of course," Caleb replied. He was untying the ribbon of Lily's hat, taking it from her head, setting it back in its box.

"You needn't think you're going to take me to bed," Lily said airily. "Not, that is, until you apologize to me and tell Rupert you won't lend him the money to build a boarding school unless he allows girls to attend."

Caleb turned Lily to face him. "You're free to disagree

with my opinions any time you like, Mrs. Halliday, but you will not refuse me your bed. Is that understood?"

Lily's cheeks heated. "I don't guess you give a damn about my opinions," she said, "but you'll come around soon enough."

"Sometimes I think you enjoy baiting me. It makes the pleasure more intense when I lay you down and take you, doesn't it, Lily?"

She raised her hand to slap him, then thought better of the idea. "You are reprehensible."

Caleb dragged her close and kissed her. Lily struggled for a few moments, but her instincts betrayed her, and she ended up returning the kiss wholeheartedly. When she was practically dissolving against him, Caleb set her away from him.

"I've got some business to attend to," he said brusquely. "I'll see you later, at supper."

Lily couldn't believe he was going to leave after the way he'd just kissed her. "What kind of business?" she asked, smoothing her tumbledown hair as she followed her husband to the door.

"If you must know," Caleb answered patiently, "I'm going to answer my brother's letter with a wire."

Even though Lily had accepted the idea of leaving the homestead to travel to Fox Chapel, she still tensed at this announcement. "What are you going to say?"

Caleb reached out to caress Lily's left breast, making the nipple pulse beneath the fabric of her camisole and dress. "I plan to tell him to go straight to hell," he answered. With that, he went out of the room and closed the door behind him.

Lily loved her husband, but in that moment she longed to murder him. He'd deliberately aroused her, just to put her in her place, and now she would suffer until he chose to relieve her. It was a punishment, and Lily resented it heartily.

After several minutes she took one last furious look around the room meant to be her prison, opened the door, and went out, carrying her dress patterns and fabric in a valise. If Caleb expected her to stay put like a naughty child pondering her transgressions, he was in for a surprise.

Finding the livery stable, Lily hired a surrey and a pair of horses to pull it, charging the cost to Caleb. Then, with her purchases, she set out for Rupert's house.

He was there, but it took him a long time to answer her knock. From his rumpled appearance Lily guessed that Winola, her brother's secret wife, was hiding out in the bedroom.

"I came to tell you good-bye," Lily said in a straightforward voice, "and that I bear you no ill will for your appalling prejudices."

Rupert stared at his sister, then looked beyond her to the surrey. "You don't mean you're *leaving?* Does the major know?"

Lily shook her head. "Caleb thinks he can be arbitrary, not to mention arrogant, and order me to stay in our room like a child. He believes women should be raised expressly to care for the needs of a man. For the sake of any daughters we might have, I'm going to teach him a lesson."

"It's you that'll be learning a lesson, I think. Don't do this, Lily. It's rash, and you'll have cause to regret it."

"It's not as if I'm going to New York or somewhere," Lily pointed out. "I'm only returning to the homestead, where I belong."

"You know damned well that Caleb will be furious!"

"I don't care," Lily answered, and she meant it. "I mean to bear that man girls as well as boys, and I won't have him treating my daughters like idiots."

Rupert looked as though he might be suffering from a headache, and he sighed. "What a fine kettle of fish this is," he muttered. "Lily, you can't leave like this. It isn't safe."

Lily remembered the last time she'd left Spokane without Caleb. She'd ended up with ants crawling all over her body, and she hadn't thought to bring matches for a fire. If Caleb hadn't come along when he had, she'd have spent a long, cold, and hungry night. Her conviction wavered for a moment until she settled on the idea of finding another place to stay until morning.

Her pride would not allow her to go back to the hotel like a meek little wife now that her course had been set.

"Do come and visit us soon," she said, patting Rupert's cheek. "I'm sorry I couldn't be with you at the hotel tonight for supper."

"You are impossible," Rupert said. "I have half a mind to take you straight to the woodshed and blister your behind."

Lily wasn't worried; she knew her brother didn't have a violent bone in his body. "Good night, Rupert," she said, and then she turned and walked down the path to the gate.

"Lily!" Rupert shouted after her. "You come back here this instant!"

"Do give my regards to Winola!" she called back, practically singing the words.

Finding a boarding house took time, but Lily managed. When nightfall came she was seated at the table of a Miss Hermione Cartworth eating lamb stew, her hired horses and surrey safely stowed in that lady's backyard.

Several times during the night Lily had cause to regret her decision, but she was too stubborn to go back to the hotel and face Caleb. Besides, she wanted him to know that he couldn't treat her like a brainless concubine and get away with it.

Early the next morning Lily hitched horses and surrey together and started out for home, carefully avoiding the center of town. It was a bright, sunny June morning, and as she traveled she thought happily of the new dresses she would make.

She was a little surprised to find that Caleb had reached home ahead of her, and she had to gather up all her courage to drive the surrey across the creek and face him, but she did those things.

Caleb's expression was thunderous. *"Where the hell have you been?"* he growled, his arms folded across his chest.

"I stayed the night in a boarding house," Lily answered as she climbed down from the surrey. "Did you and Winola and Rupert have a nice dinner together?"

He glared at her. "Get in that house!"

"And do what?" Lily retorted. "Write 'I will not disobey my husband' a thousand times?"

"Move!" Caleb roared.

Lily's aplomb fled in an instant, and she dashed toward the door of the cabin. "I'll thank you to remember that I'm in the family way," she was quick to say. She was recalling that other time, when Caleb would have paddled her if Velvet hadn't happened along just in time to prevent it.

Inside the cabin Caleb set Lily in a chair and proceeded to deliver a lecture that was, in many ways, worse than a spanking. He shouted, he listed the perils of traveling alone, he swore by all that was holy that if Lily ever did such a stupid thing again he'd wring her neck.

Lily's eyes were wide by the time he began to wind down, and when he sent her to the bedroom she went.

When Caleb came to her it was from a different direction than expected. A terrible racket arose on the other side of the bedroom wall, and Lily watched in horrified amazement as an ax bit through the new wood.

Furiously Caleb shaped a rude door. "Now," he said, tossing the ax behind him, "it's all one house. Welcome to our bedroom, Mrs. Halliday."

Lily was convinced she'd married a madman. "You stay away from me," she said, scooting backwards on the bed.

She didn't move fast enough. Caleb caught hold of one of her legs, lifted it high, and began untying her shoelace. "There isn't a chance in hell of that, sodbuster," he said, and then he began rolling Lily's stocking down. She trembled as his hand caressed her inner thigh for the briefest moment. "Not a chance in hell."

Only when the lovemaking was over and Caleb had risen from the bed did Lily's pride come back into its own. The moment he stepped through the hacked-out opening into his side of the house she moved the bureau in front of the opening.

"You stay on your side," she said when she saw him through the opening above the chest of drawers, "and I'll keep to mine."

As usual, Caleb had expected his romantic attentions to make everything all right between them. "Damn it, Lily," he growled, bracing his hands on the bureau top and leaning forward ominously, "we're married!"

"As far as I'm concerned, we can just forget that unfortunate fact."

"That's fine with me," Caleb snapped. And then he turned and stormed away.

Lily returned to the kitchen and began washing dishes. When she finished she carefully carried the dirty water outside and flung it over Caleb's property line.

Since he was saddling his horse in the side yard, he saw the gesture. Although he glared at her, he didn't speak; he simply mounted his horse and rode off toward Fort Deveraux.

He probably meant to reenlist, Lily thought contemptuously. Heaven knew the major wasn't happy unless he had somebody to boss around.

At noon a freight wagon arrived, bringing Caleb's new stove and a number of other things in boxes and crates. Without setting foot on Caleb's side of the property Lily explained to the men where to put things.

When Caleb returned from the fort hours later he was carrying another wriggling burlap sack. He frowned at Lily, daring her to object, as he led the horse across her part of the land and into the combination stable and chicken coop.

After he came out he carried the burlap sack to the chopping block.

Lily was sewing—cutting out the pattern had been a far more difficult task because she'd had to give up the use of Caleb's dining room table—when he began rattling and banging next door. He was setting up the stove, Lily figured, and she got a little wistful when she thought of that big hot-water reservoir. Why, a person would be able to take a hot bath any time she wanted.

The pounding soon subsided, only to be replaced within a short time by the delectable smell of boiling chicken.

Lily put aside the dress she was stitching to go and close the door of her bedroom, but the delicious aroma still wafted through.

By then it was late afternoon, and the bread and butter Lily had eaten for lunch had definitely worn off. She wondered what to fix for supper.

She was putting away the dress, too hungry and tired to sew anymore, when she saw Caleb through the bedroom window. He had a fishing pole in one hand, and he was headed down the creek.

Lily's stomach grumbled in accompaniment to her thoughts. Here was her chance to raid Caleb's kitchen.

After taking one more look to make sure he wasn't doubling back Lily scrambled over the bureau she'd used to bar the door and entered enemy territory.

There were soft, colorful rugs rolled out on the floor, and in the kitchen chicken and dumplings bubbled on the surface of that wonderful stove.

Lily sneaked up and lifted the lid of the reservoir to look inside. Sure enough, Caleb had filled it with water, and it was steaming now. She thought with a sigh of the luxurious bath she might have taken that night, using that very water.

Dishes lined the shelves of Caleb's well-organized kitchen, so Lily helped herself to a large bowl. She filled it with chicken and dumplings—whatever else he might have been, Caleb was a creditable cook—and sat down at his table, bold as brass. The luscious delight of sampling the forbidden filled her as she began to eat.

She consumed two bowlfuls of the delicious food; then, leaving her dish on the table to let Caleb know she'd flouted his property line, she started back through the house.

She had one knee up on the bureau and was just about to crawl through when she felt two hands close around her waist and pull her down. She turned her head and saw Caleb grinning at her.

"Trespassing, were you? Well, sodbuster, there's a penalty for that, you know."

Lily put out her chin and turned to crawl over the bureau. She wasn't about to dignify his remark with an answer.

"If that's how you want it, fine," he said, and he pinned her right to that bureau, with her bottom making a plump cushion against his masculinity.

"Caleb Halliday," Lily sputtered, "you let me up!"

Caleb was lifting her skirts. "I don't deal lightly with trespassers," he said in a conversational tone of voice. "Give 'em an inch, and pretty soon they're swinging from the rafters."

Lily felt her drawers begin to slide downward. She squirmed, but she was stuck between Caleb's thighs. "Caleb," she said, "I am not amused."

He laid a brazen finger to the rosebud between her legs and chuckled when she started with a little moan. He continued to caress her, making her go all warm and moist. Considering that he'd already had her, and well, earlier that day, her involuntary response was doubly humiliating.

"You know," he remarked, "in some places they hang a chicken thief. I think the penalty's probably even stiffer when dumplings are involved."

"I hate you!" Lily sputtered, her hips twisting.

His fingers slid into her femininity in one deft move. "Do you?"

"Oh, Caleb—"

"Yes, dear?"

Lily didn't want to like being touched, and she definitely didn't want to love Caleb. She didn't get her way in either case. "Take me to your bed."

His answer was immediate. "Oh, no. I'm going to take you right here, Mrs. Halliday. And right now."

Lily imagined what a picture she must make, doubled over that dresser with her skirts up. "That's awful!"

"No worse than some of the other places we've made love," Caleb sighed. He removed his fingers and replaced them with just the tip of his shaft.

"Oh, my God," Lily gasped, clutching the edge of the bureau in both hands.

"It's a religious experience for me, too," Caleb commented, giving her another small ration of what she craved.

"You—are—reprehensible!"

"And what else?"

"Hard. Oh, God, Caleb, you are so hard."

He chuckled and gave her most of his length in a gentle stroke.

Lily whimpered as he parted her legs to enter her even more deeply. A sweet tingle, stemming from the core of her womanhood, fanned out into her thighs and torso. Her breasts ached for his touch. "Faster," she whispered. "Oh, Caleb, please—do it faster."

For once Caleb complied with her request instead of making her wait until the waiting became unbearable. He gave himself to her in hard, fast strokes, and she flung her head back, her back arching with each powerful tremor of release.

Caleb made a ferocious thrust and emptied himself into her, groaning. When it was over he stood trembling against her, squeezing her bottom gently in his hands. Within a matter of minutes Lily felt him growing hard inside her again.

"I'll want you in my bed, Mrs. Halliday," Caleb said formally, pulling back just when Lily wanted more of him. "Go there and wait for me."

Lily's brief rebellion was over, and she knew it, but since defeat was so delicious, she unbent herself from the bureau, pulled up her drawers, and crossed the large room to Caleb's bed. Her knees were so pleasure-weakened that they would barely support her.

When he came to her, she held out her arms to him.

Chapter
❧ *23* ❧

*L*ily's corn stood a head taller than she did on that hot day in early July when she and Caleb were to leave for the east. Dressed in her traveling clothes—a green and white striped shirtwaist with an emerald skirt—Lily walked up and down the rows, inspecting the rich green stocks and touching the tassels of yellow-white silk. She'd planted and weeded and watered this corn, and she wasn't even going to eat any of it.

Deciding there was no use in fussing, since she'd made up her mind to go with Caleb wherever he went, Lily strode resolutely back between the rows, moving toward the house. She almost screamed when she encountered Charlie Fast Horse among the whispering stalks. He was backing toward her, and when they collided he gave a yelp.

"If you're looking for the major," Lily said stiffly, "he's gone to the post to say his farewells."

Charlie put a finger to his lips. "Keep your voice down, missus," he said. "There's outlaws on the way. They aren't more than a mile or two down the road, and sound carries on a day like this."

Lily felt the color drain from her face. "Well, a lot of use you'll be, hiding in a cornfield!" She grasped her skirts and started for the house. She meant to get a rifle from Caleb's gun cabinet while there was still time.

Charlie followed, whispering and gesturing. "It's best we just stay here, missus—let them take what they want and move on. If they get a look at you, there's no telling what'll happen."

They were going to get a look at Lily, all right. They'd see her staring back at them, right down the barrel of a gun. "How many are there?"

"Five, six," Charlie responded. "Too many."

"Some Indian you are," Lily complained. She raced up the steps of Caleb's fancy veranda and through the side door, with Charlie right behind her. "Can you shoot, at least?"

"Of course I can shoot," Charlie grumbled.

"Then where is your rifle?"

The Indian sighed. "My horse ran away, and the rifle was in the scabbard."

Lily found the key to the gun cabinet, unlocked it, and took out a shotgun. She'd been practicing her shooting, and while she was never going to be invited to perform in wild west shows, she could at least fire without falling down. "Here," she said, shoving the shotgun at Charlie. She gave him some shells from a drawer before selecting a thirty-thirty for herself and loading it the way Caleb had taught her to do.

"How do you know these men are outlaws, and not just men out riding?" she asked practically, marching to the window to scan the horizon. She wondered if Caleb was nearby, and if he'd spotted the riders.

"They've got a look about them," Charlie answered. "Besides, white men don't ride in groups bigger than two, usually, unless they're part of an army detachment."

Lily could see the visitors in the distance, beyond the creek. The hooves of their horses raised dust, which swirled in the hot July breeze. Counting five of them, Lily cocked her rifle. "You'd better ride to the fort and fetch Caleb," she said without looking at Charlie. "If these men are outlaws, they should be arrested."

"I told you," said Charlie. "My horse ran off."

"Then take mine. He's in the shed."

Still Charlie hesitated. "I don't like leaving you here alone, missus. You'd better come with me."

"And let those rascals rifle my house? Not on your life, Charlie Fast Horse. Now get out of here."

Reluctantly Charlie left, hurrying noiselessly out through the part of the house that had been Lily's. It was mostly used as a storage room now, and she hoped to change her bedroom into a newfangled bathroom one day, provided she and Caleb ever returned to Washington Territory.

The sun was bright, but Lily didn't let herself squint as she watched the five riders approaching at a steady pace. She tensed a little when one of them pointed—having spotted Charlie dashing for the fort, no doubt—but none of them gave chase.

Lily gnawed at her lower lip as she waited. What did Charlie know? These men probably weren't outlaws at all. They could be a posse, for one thing, or a band of politicians going to visit the fort.

Perspiration tickled between Lily's breasts as she waited.

Finally they were crossing the creek. The leader, a fair-haired man riding a pinto gelding, swept off his broad-brimmed hat and assessed the homestead.

"Hello the house!" he called.

After drawing a deep breath Lily opened the door and stepped outside, the thirty-thirty in hand.

The men chuckled and grinned at the sight of the rifle.

Lily cocked it, just to show them she wasn't some green-horn trying to bluff her way out of a bad situation. "What's your business?"

The leader rode forward a little way. "We're just looking to water our horses and rest a spell, ma'am. That's all."

"Go ahead, then," Lily said, and soon the horses were drinking thirstily from the creek while four of the men splashed their dusty faces and the backs of their necks with the cold water.

"You alone here?" the leader asked.

Lily managed a taut smile. "For a little while, yes."

The stranger took a step closer, and Lily responded by training her sights on him. He held both hands out from his sides in a nonchalant gesture of peace. He was a slender man clad in dark trousers, a vest, and a shirt that had once been white.

"Don't shoot, little lady. We ain't here to hurt you."

Lily didn't lower the rifle. "I've heard you're outlaws. Is that true?"

"Word gets around fast in these parts," one of the other four seedy travelers put in. He was fat, and he wore a Chinese mustache and a dusty top hat that might once have graced a gentleman's head.

"Shut up, Royce," said the man in the vest.

"Your horses have been watered," Lily put in. "I think it would be best if you just moved on now."

They all laughed as though Lily had made a joke, and in the next instant someone grasped her from behind, covering her mouth with one hand and wresting the rifle away with the other.

Lily struggled, but it was useless. Her attacker encircled her waist with one manacle-like arm and held her tightly. He smelled of whiskey and dust and the sweat of many days on the trail, and Lily was revolted.

The leader grinned at her. "Seems like we'll want more than just water for our horses," he said, approaching. His gaze shifted to the man grasping her from behind. "Did you see the Indian? He was on his way somewhere, hell-bent for leather."

"The fort, I reckon. Trouble is, most of the troops are out on patrol. We saw 'em hours ago."

Lily knew the odious man holding her was speaking for her benefit, not for that of his friend. Even so, her heart sank. Charlie would bring Caleb back if he made it to the fort at all, and Caleb would be outnumbered. These men would probably set a trap for him and kill him.

"We oughta take her with us," one of the men by the creek said. "She's a pretty little thing—be mighty entertainin' of an evenin'."

"Bet she can cook, too," said the fat man in the top hat.

"Let her go," said the leader.

The moment the other man's hand left her mouth Lily let out a long, shrill scream. There was another hope—that her cry would echo through the trees to Velvet, as it had once before.

"We'll just go inside a while, you and I." The leader ignored Lily's scream and took her arm, forcing her back through the front door. "You men surround the house and keep a lookout."

There was grumbling, but the outlaws did as he told them, and Lily was filled with a new fear as she found herself alone in the parlor with the stranger.

"Name's George Baker," he said. "What's yours?"

"This isn't a church social, Mr. Baker," Lily pointed out calmly. "I don't want you here, or your men all over my yard."

He went to the mantelpiece over the stone fireplace Caleb had built with his own hands and looked at the framed photographs displayed there. "This your husband?" he asked, pointing to a portrait of Caleb seated, wearing his uniform, while Lily stood behind him, one hand on his shoulder.

It seemed a patently stupid question to Lily, since she had been wearing her wedding dress when the photograph was taken. "Yes. And he'll be back here soon."

"Alone, probably," Baker said, turning to look at Lily. "Won't be any trouble to kill him."

Lily felt the color drain from her face. "Why would you want to do that?"

"He probably wouldn't let us carry off his woman without a fight." He glanced back at the photograph. "Looks like a big man."

"He is big," Lily said, "and very strong."

Baker laughed and ran his bold blue eyes over Lily's body in a brazen sweep. "I reckon he'd seem so to a little thing like you," he said. He glanced toward an inner doorway, through which the big cook stove was visible. "That the kitchen?"

Lily let her eyes tell him what she thought of the question. "Yes, it is," she said, with mock politeness. "Why do you ask?"

Baker slapped his stomach. "Got me a real hankerin' for some woman-cooked food. You get in there and fry me up some eggs."

Lily could almost feel the weight and wallop of her good iron skillet in her hands. She flexed her fingers and turned to walk into the kitchen.

There was wood in the box beside the stove, so Lily fed the fire and then took the big skillet down from its place on the wall. She hated to set it down, but she did.

Just as she was taking eggs and lard from the fancy icebox Caleb had ordered she heard a shot outside. Her heart stopped beating, but Lily allowed herself only a moment's terror. Baker, cursing, had forgotten her and rushed to the window in the back door.

After muttering a short prayer for both accuracy and forgiveness, Lily swung the skillet as hard as she could, striking him in the back of the head.

His knees buckled, and he slipped noiselessly to the floor, his eyes glazed over like Caleb's when she pleasured him.

Briskly Lily took Baker's gun, checked the chamber, and

set it aside well out of his reach, just in case he woke up too soon. She tore a dish towel into strips and tied his hands behind his back.

Then, taking up the loaded pistol, Lily at last dared to go to the window and look out. Sure enough, Caleb had arrived, but he was alone, and he was being held at gunpoint. Although he was still mounted, there was a red spot on his shoulder where the blood from a wound was seeping through his shirt.

Lily pushed up the window and took careful aim at the man who had probably shot Caleb—the fat man with the funny hat. "Drop that gun and let him pass," she said clearly, "or I'll blow you into pieces so small they'll be able to sweep you up and carry you off in that hat of yours."

Caleb grinned at that, despite his wound. When the bandit dropped his rifle into the dust Caleb dismounted, strode over to collect it, and entered the house through the back door. If the others were looking on, they were apparently afraid to move—Lily couldn't see them from where she stood.

Caleb glanced at Baker, still lying unconscious on the floor, his hands bound behind him with a cloth that had part of the word *Tuesday* embroidered on it. "What happened to him?"

"He met up with the big skillet," Lily answered, peering at Caleb's wound. "Let me have a look at that."

"It's nothing," Caleb answered, shuffling her aside. "How many are there?"

"Four, I think," Lily answered, frowning thoughtfully. "Besides this fellow and the fat man, I mean."

"What do they want?"

"Me," Lily said succinctly.

"Can't blame the poor bastards for that," Caleb remarked with a wry grin, striding to the gun cabinet and taking out a rifle. "Too bad I'm going to have to kill them."

"Caleb, you're hurt—let me take care of you."

"That'll have to wait," Caleb answered, going to the front

window to stand just to one side of it, looking out. "Get out of the middle of the room, Lily, before they take a potshot at you."

Lily ducked behind the wing-backed chair, her teeth biting into her lower lip.

The glass in the window shattered in the next instant, and Caleb fired. "Never pays to stand out in the open!" he called to his victim.

"Is he dead?" Lily's fingers were digging into the leather of Caleb's favorite chair.

"No, but his mama will probably never have grandchildren." Caleb fired again, and there was cursing from outside.

Lily ran her tongue over her lips. She was perspiring under her arms and between her breasts and shoulder blades. In those moments her many differences with Caleb didn't seem to mean much.

She closed her eyes when she saw her husband taking aim again. "Damn idiots," he muttered just before another shot exploded in the summer air. Then the air was suddenly filled with the sounds of horses' hooves beating against hard, dry dirt.

"Is the army here?" Lily said.

Caleb chuckled and set his rifle down. "No. The fellas just decided it might be a good idea to ride out." He strode outside to collect the two men he'd shot. After binding their hands behind them he threw them into the shed, along with their dazed leader, to await help from the fort.

Lily was dipping hot water from the stove reservoir when Caleb returned to the house. "You couldn't have done it without me," she said, pressing him into a chair. She was peeling off his shirt when Velvet and Hank arrived, out of breath.

Hank was carrying his hunting rifle.

"We heard shootin'!" Velvet cried.

Lily was cleaning the wound in Caleb's shoulder; it looked to her as if the bullet had gone straight through. "It just so happens that we've got three outlaws tied up in our shed," she said matter-of-factly. "Hank, if you could see your way clear to ride to the fort for a doctor, I'd appreciate it."

"I don't need a doctor," Caleb protested. But he winced and drew in a sharp breath when Lily poured some of his best whiskey onto the wound.

"Well, those men out in the shed do," Lily answered, preparing to douse the injury again, this time from the back.

When she did, Caleb let out a string of curses that reddened even Velvet's cheeks.

"I'll be back in as soon as I can," Hank said, hurrying out.

"I'd better have a look at them outlaws and see if they're bleedin' or anythin'," Velvet put in when her husband was gone.

"Just you keep in mind that they're dangerous men," Lily warned, bandaging Caleb's shoulder with strips of torn sheets. "There's hot water in the reservoir."

Velvet nodded and went out.

"You were wonderful," Caleb said, giving Lily's bottom a little pat.

"Like I said, if it weren't for me, you'd probably be dead."

Caleb laughed and pulled her down onto his lap. "Probably so. You win, Lily. You were right to believe you knew how to take care of yourself, no matter what the circumstances."

"Of course I was right," Lily said, unbuttoning her fancy shirtwaist, which was now dirty and speckled with blood.

An hour later Lily and Caleb left Fort Deveraux on board the stagecoach.

They spent the first night in Spokane, in the same hotel where they had stayed during their earlier visit, but there was a new peace between them that had never existed before. Facing trouble side by side had apparently served to spawn a deeper closeness between them.

Caleb and Lily arrived in Wyoming Territory after a four-day train ride, and Caleb, his arm in a sling because of the gunshot wound, was pale with exhaustion. Lily took a room at Bolton's only hotel, a seedy place with dusty potted palms and worn rugs in the lobby, and promised faithfully to remain there while Caleb rested. At the first snore she crept out to go in search of Caroline.

Since Mrs. Daniel Pride, the woman who had originally written to her about Caroline, had turned out to be the marshal's wife, Lily looked for her to be living in the little frame house directly behind the jail.

Her instincts proved right. The Prides resided there, and the mistress of the house was a buxom dark-haired woman with overlapping front teeth, sharp brown eyes, and heavy brows that came close to meeting in the middle.

"I'm Lily Chalmers Halliday," Lily announced when the woman stepped out onto her porch to eye her visitor suspiciously. "I wondered if Miss Caroline Chalmers ever returned to Bolton."

Mrs. Pride shook her head. "No, ma'am. I guess if you want to know all about Miss Caroline, you'd better speak with the Maitland sisters. They'll tell you the story."

Lily felt a chill move up and down her spine, but she maintained her dignity. "If you could just point the way to their house, please."

The marshal's wife directed her to a large white house at the end of the street. It had green shutters and a picket fence, and roses bloomed in an arbor, giving the place a welcoming look.

Lily opened the gate and moved purposefully up the walk. She was so tense she could barely breathe.

Reaching the front door with its snarling brass lion knocker, she made her presence known.

A tiny, timid-looking gray-haired woman answered. "Yes?"

Lily introduced herself, then explained, "I'm looking for my sister Caroline."

The small woman's eyes filled with tears, and she stepped back to admit Lily into shady environs smelling of lavender and cinnamon and wood ashes. "Oh, dear. It would have meant so much to her to see you."

Lily swallowed hard, suddenly wishing she hadn't left the hotel without Caleb. She had a feeling she was going to need his strength very soon. "Would have?" she echoed softly.

The woman dried her eyes with a fussy handkerchief trimmed in lace. "We do fear she's perished, our Caroline. Kidnapped by a scoundrel who'd been camping out in the hills. Had a drunken dog, you know."

Lily groped for a chair and sank into it. "Caroline dead? I don't believe it." In the next few minutes, she presented dozens of questions, but the old woman's answers only left her more confused than before.

"Would you like to see her picture?" the old woman asked gently.

"Oh, yes."

Moments later Lily found herself staring at a small framed photograph of a beautiful dark-haired woman with creamy, flawless skin, a straight little nose, and laughter in her eyes. "I would have known her," Lily said brokenly. "If I'd seen her, I would have known she was Caroline."

"You may keep that, if you'd like. Sister and I have many photographs of Caroline—she was our darling girl, you see."

"Perhaps she's not dead," Lily ventured, feeling new hope as she tucked the cherished photograph into her handbag. "My husband and I are on our way to Fox Chapel, Pennsylvania. I'll write everything down for you, and if—*when*—Caroline returns, you can tell her I was here."

Miss Maitland nodded, though there wasn't much hope in her gentle, crinkly face. "Very well, dear."

"What is she like?" Lily wanted to know.

"She was pretty, always laughing. She liked to sing, but she had a hot temper."

"Did she ever speak of me, or of Emma?"

"All the time. It was her dream to find you both. She

wrote a little book about the three of you—how you were sent west on that orphan train and everything. She was hoping one of you would see it and get in touch with her. It'll be published next winter."

Lily was very near tears, and she longed for Caleb. She couldn't remember a time when she'd needed his arms around her more than she did at that moment. She rose from her chair. "Thank you for everything, Miss Maitland," she said, moving uncertainly toward the door.

"That's Miss *Ethel* Maitland," the woman responded. "And my sister is Phoebe."

"Y-you raised Caroline together?" Lily asked, pausing on the porch of the tidy white house.

Ethel Maitland nodded. "We like to claim the honor, though there are those who say that Caroline raised us."

Lily smiled at that. Caroline had always been bossy; Lily could easily picture her ordering her kindly guardians about and telling them just what to think about things. "Please give her my message—and my love—when you see her again."

Miss Maitland looked doubtful, but she nodded once more. "I will," she promised.

Lily walked back to the hotel in something of a daze, and when she reached the room Caleb was sitting up. The sheets lay across his lean waist, and his chest was naked except for the white sling the doctor had put on before they left home.

"Well?" he asked, making no comment on the fact that she'd left the room without him against his express orders. "Did you find her?"

Lily burst into tears. "Everybody thinks she's dead," she sobbed. "She was kidnapped by some awful man with a dog that drinks!"

Caleb's expression was solemn as he patted the mattress beside him and said gently, "Come here and sit down."

Lily dragged the back of one hand across both eyes and sniffled. "Would you like to see her picture?"

"Sure," he answered.

She brought the photograph from her bag and held it out to her husband. "Isn't she beautiful?"

"Being your sister, she could hardly be anything else," Caleb replied, studying the lovely, animated face in the picture.

"I left word that she could reach us in Fox Chapel. Caleb, I just know she's all right, that she'll be back soon."

Caleb laid the picture aside and reached out to enfold Lily's hand in his own and squeeze it reassuringly. "Yes," he said.

Lily sighed. "Oh, Caleb, I need to be held. I need you to make love to me—to make me give everything so I don't have to think."

In answer Caleb drew her close and kissed her thoroughly. "Take off your clothes, Mrs. Halliday, and I'll be happy to comply."

It was noon, and the sounds of everyday activities were drifting up from the streets. Lily undressed and crawled into bed beside Caleb.

The train left Bolton at ten o'clock the next morning, and Lily and Caleb were aboard it. They were on their way to Fox Chapel; after Caleb had met with his brother they would travel to Chicago to see what they could learn from Kathleen Chalmers Harrington's friends and neighbors.

"Tell me why you and Joss were on opposite sides in the war," Lily urged as they rolled ever nearer to the confrontation Caleb both needed and dreaded.

Caleb sighed, taking her hand in his. "Fox Chapel is just north of the West Virginia border. There were a lot of people there who sided with the Confederacy."

Lily nodded, waiting.

"Joss joined up the same day I did." Caleb shifted uncomfortably in his seat. "I didn't see him again until the day I found him on the ground with his arm blown off."

"You turned him over to your superior officers?"

Caleb nodded. "It was that or kill him, and I couldn't do that."

"Of course not," Lily answered.

"He's been furious with me ever since."

"That doesn't make sense. You'd think he would be glad to be alive."

"It was pretty hard for him in prison, according to my sister's letters."

Lily nodded. She couldn't even begin to imagine what it must have been like to be a prisoner of war on either side. "When he sees you he'll know what a wonderful man you are, and he won't hate you anymore."

Caleb grinned and lifted Lily's hand to his lips to kiss it lightly. "I'm sure you're right," he said with gentle skepticism.

Lily felt a tingle go through her. It had been several days since she and Caleb had been able to make love, as they were sleeping in narrow berths that left no room for two people. She lowered her eyes, hoping Caleb wouldn't be able to interpret her expression.

He kissed her hand again. "I think we'll get off the train for a day or two, Mrs. Halliday. I'm feeling like a neglected husband."

Lily smiled at that. "Something must be done," she replied earnestly.

"I couldn't agree more."

The next stop was a small town in Ohio, and the Hallidays left the train there. After baths and a long, often-interrupted nap in their hotel room they bought tickets to a circus playing on the edge of town.

Lily had never seen trapeze artists or lion tamers—or lions, for that matter—and she was openmouthed at the spectacular entertainments. The clowns made her laugh until she cried, and when Caleb bought her a caramel apple she wondered that such treats weren't reserved just for angels.

By the time Lily and Caleb returned to their room that

night Lily was practically walking on air. If such wonderful things as circuses could exist, she reasoned, then Caroline must surely be alive and well somewhere. And so must Emma.

"At least I know Caroline wanted to find Emma and me," Lily said with a sigh when she and Caleb were settled side by side in their bed that night, too tired to make love.

Caleb sounded surprised. "You doubted that?"

Lily shrugged. "When a woman gets involved with a man, sometimes other things don't matter to her anymore. And Caroline is involved with a man."

"How do you know?"

"I just do. That man with the drunken dog—well, I think perhaps he didn't kidnap Caroline at all. She might have gone with him willingly."

"I hope you're right," Caleb answered, settling deep into his pillow and giving a great, noisy yawn. "Good night, Lily of the circus. I love you."

Lily bent and kissed his forehead. "And I love you," she answered.

Chapter
❧ *24* ❧

The house outside of Fox Chapel was a sprawling place built of red brick and covered with ivy. A long gravel driveway lined with venerable maple trees stretched from the main road to the base of the sloping green lawn.

Caleb had rented a horse and buggy at the livery stable in town, and he drew back on the reins just as they would have passed beneath the archway of the gate. His left arm was still in a sling from the shooting, but he'd insisted on driving anyway.

Lily waited, her hands folded in her lap. It had taken Caleb a long time to come home and face his brother, and he was in no hurry now.

"I loved him," he admitted hoarsely.

Lily nodded. She certainly understood that. Sadness touched her spirit as she wondered if she would ever see either of her sisters again.

Caleb swallowed. "I don't know why I'm doing this," he

went on, stalling. "Joss won't be interested in anything I have to say."

Lily was looking at the splendid house. As likely as not, Joss and Caleb would work out their differences—they were brothers, after all—but it might take time. She slipped her arm through Caleb's and let her head rest against his shoulder for a moment in silent reassurance.

In the distance the front door opened, and Lily could see a form standing on the long, pillared porch. The man strode down the steps after a moment's pause and started up the driveway.

Caleb brought the reins down on the horse's back with a resolute slap, and the buggy jolted forward. Lily held onto her new straw traveling hat, thinking, And nation shall rise against nation, and brother against brother. . . .

The man and the buggy met midway between the house and the road. Lily saw that Joss was as tall as Caleb, with the same golden-brown hair, though his was curly. His eyes were a deep blue, and his build was so powerful that his missing left arm didn't diminish him in any way.

He glared at Caleb. "Get off my land."

Caleb sighed and climbed awkwardly down from the buggy. Lily caught the reins, or they would have slipped to the ground.

"I'm not going anywhere," Caleb answered at his leisure. His voice was low, even, and wholly defiant.

Joss's seething mood put Lily in mind of boiling jam and the way it stung it when spilled over on a person. She watched the rise and fall of the big man's broad chest as he struggled to control his emotions. "Damn you," he whispered. "Damn you for coming back here, Caleb, and making me remember how it was before!"

Caleb said nothing.

Joss's midnight-blue eyes moved to Lily, and she saw a distinct and probably involuntary softening in his expression. "Your wife?"

"Lily," Caleb said with a nod, "this is my brother Joss."

"How do you do?" Lily said uncomfortably. The air was charged with violent emotions, and she felt like an intruder. Besides, it was hot, and she was tired and thirsty.

Joss was silent for a long time, just gazing at Lily. Finally he said, "You take this man of yours, little Mrs. Halliday, and you get him out of here before I fetch my shotgun and shoot him where he stands."

With that, he turned and walked proudly away, his broad shoulders making a barrier against the brother he hated.

Lily's mouth dropped open, but before she could call after Mr. Joss Halliday that that was a fine greeting to give his own brother after fifteen years, a pretty young woman with honey-colored hair came bounding out of the house and ran up the driveway. She held her blue sateen skirts in both hands as she approached.

"Caleb! Caleb, don't you dare leave!" she cried. Lily knew without being told that this was Abigail, the sister Caleb barely knew.

Tears poured down the girl's cheeks as she flung herself at Caleb. He caught her up with his good arm and swung her around once before planting a kiss on her forehead. "You've grown up," he said.

"Of course I have," Abbie said with good-natured impatience. "Did you think I'd still be a child?"

He set her down, and she turned her attention to Lily, smoothing her butternut hair and then her skirts. "You must be Caleb's bride," she said, and the eagerness in her face was heartening. Here was a Halliday who wanted to like Lily and was ready to accept her.

Lily nodded, relieved. "And you're Abigail."

For the moment the greeting was enough. Abigail turned her amber gaze back to her brother again. "You'll stay, won't you? You belong right here with the rest of us, and this land is as much yours as it is Joss's."

Joss was now a small figure in the distance, disappearing

around the corner of one of the outbuildings. Caleb stared after him solemnly. "I don't know why, but I expected it to be easier than this," he said, his voice low and distracted.

"Go after him," Abbie urged. "He'll listen to reason—I know he will."

But Caleb shook his head. "Let him have some time to absorb the fact that we're here."

Lily got down from the buggy, wanting to walk the rest of the way to the house and stretch her legs. She was disappointed in Joss's cold reception; just as she had fantasies about her own reunion with Emma and Caroline, she'd had expectations for Caleb's with Joss.

"Let's go inside," Abbie said, linking her arm with Lily's.

"I'll be in later," Caleb muttered, climbing back into the buggy and taking up the reins.

"Maybe we shouldn't have come here," Lily said softly when he was driving the rig away toward an enormous red barn.

Abbie's bright curls glistened in the late afternoon sunshine as she shook her head. "Everything will be all right—you'll see."

Lily hoped her sister-in-law was right, but she had her doubts. She knew she'd rather not find Emma and Caroline at all than have them rebuff her the way Joss had Caleb.

After taking the horse and buggy to the stables and turning them over to one of the hands, Caleb avoided the magnificent house where he'd grown up and walked through the orchard instead. Behind it, beyond a stone wall that dated back to Revolutionary times, were the gravestones of Hallidays who had gone before.

With painful effort he removed his suit coat and slung it over one shoulder, holding it by a finger. He stopped first at his mother's grave.

It was well tended, and there were fresh flowers lying at the base of the stone.

Caleb crouched and ran one hand over the lettering of her name and the dates that enclosed her life like brackets.

"She would have sided with the Confederacy," remarked a voice behind him. "Her people were southerners."

Caleb rose gracefully to his feet and turned to face his brother. "I don't think it matters what side she would have taken," he said evenly. "In case you haven't noticed, big brother, the war is over."

"Not for me it isn't. And not for you."

Caleb was growing weary, and his patience was wearing thin. "I don't expect you to apologize for joining up with the rebs, Joss. Don't expect me to regret fighting for the Union. I'm not going to debate you, and I'm sure as hell not going to let you goad me into a fight. I came here to make peace with you."

"You're wasting your time," Joss answered.

Caleb shook his head. "You're still as stubborn as Adam's ox, and about half as bright. If you're not willing to meet me halfway, then go away and leave me alone. I want a few minutes with Mama and Papa."

Joss glared at him for a few moments, and a muscle tensed in his bull-thick neck. "I could throw you off this place, you know," he said, raising his one arm to rest his hand on his hip.

Caleb smiled. "You'd better get started right now, then," he said evenly, "because you're going to be at it for a while."

The elder brother gestured toward the sling Caleb wore. "You've only got one good arm," he pointed out.

"I guess that makes us just about even," Caleb replied. He could see that Joss wanted to hit him—indeed, he probably wanted to tear him apart—but something stopped the big man from advancing on the younger brother he hadn't seen since the war.

He clenched his massive fist once, twice, then turned and strode away again.

"That's it, Johnny Reb," Caleb challenged. "Turn tail and run."

With a bellow Joss whirled and came at Caleb with all the restraint of a runaway freight train. His powerful fist caught Caleb squarely under the chin and sent him flying backwards into the grass, past his mother's headstone.

Blood trickled down Caleb's chin, but he grinned at his brother as he got to his feet. "I'm still here, Joss," he said. "And I'm not going anywhere until you sit down and talk with me like a sane man."

Joss's thick chest heaved with the effort of his breathing. Sweat glistened on his face, and his hand was still knotted into a fist, but his eyes were wet. "Damn you," he spat, and then he walked away.

This time Caleb didn't try to taunt him into coming back.

An hour had passed when he went back to the house, no closer to reconciliation with Joss than he had been that long-ago day in battle when Joss had lost his arm and Caleb had lost his brother.

During the coming week Joss avoided Caleb completely, refusing to remain in a room with him, let alone sit down at the same table.

Caleb got to know his sister, and Joss's wife, Susannah, and his nieces and nephews. He depended on the comfort Lily gave him with her words and with her body, and his thoughts began to turn back to Washington Territory and the house by the creek.

He was out behind the orchard again, sitting on the stone fence and gazing over the sun-warmed graves of his parents and grandparents, when he felt a strong hand strike his shoulder.

Caleb barely kept from losing his balance, and he was poised to fight when he turned to find the elusive Joss standing on the other side of the waist-high wall.

"Susannah tells me you're heading for Chicago," Joss said.

Caleb nodded, watching his brother, still daring to hope there might be some part of their relationship they could save. "That's right. We'll be here another week or so—until I can get rid of this damned sling."

Joss braced himself against the wall and leaned forward. "Do you know what it was like in that goddamn hellhole of a prison?" The words were torn from his throat.

Caleb shook his head. "I wouldn't presume to say I did."

"There were rats the size of house cats. Toward the end we ate them just to stay alive."

Caleb closed his eyes against an image that would never leave him. "I'm not sorry that I let you live," he said after a brief silence.

Joss glared at him in rage. "You'd put me through that hell all over again, wouldn't you?" he demanded. *"Damn* you, you would!"

"If it meant your life? You're damned right I would. I'd put you through it a thousand times." He paused and drew a deep, tremulous breath. "Joss, step into my boots for a minute. Go back to that day. Remember the screaming, and the cannon fire, and the sound of bullets whistling past your head. This time you're the one that's on your feet, and I'm lying on the ground with my arm gone. I ask you to shoot me—hell, I *beg* you to shoot me. What are you going to do?"

Joss's throat worked as he swallowed. He hesitated for a long time as a variety of emotions moved in his face. Then he said, "I'd shoot you."

"You're a liar," Caleb answered.

The giant, the man he'd loved and admired from the first day he'd known what it meant to have a brother, glared at him. "God damn you, Caleb—"

"You wouldn't have been able to kill me, because I'm your brother. Because you taught me to ride and shoot, because the blood in your veins is the same blood that runs in mine. You would have done exactly what I did, Joss, and somewhere inside yourself you know it."

Joss shook his head as if to fling off an image. "You listen to me," he yelled, waggling a finger in his brother's face. "I hate you. Do you hear me? I hate your miserable Yankee guts, and I plan to go right on hating you from now until they put me in a box and throw dirt on top of me!"

The sun was getting hotter by the moment. Caleb dragged his sleeve across his brow. "Fine."

"I'll buy out your share of the land."

"Go to hell," Caleb replied. "It's mine, and I'm keeping it. And I'll be back, Joss. You haven't seen the last of me."

Joss's massive shoulders moved in a sudden, tearing sob, and he lowered his head, gripping the old stones of the wall.

Caleb stepped closer, daring to lay his good hand on Joss's shoulder. "I'd have gone to prison in your place if they would have let me," he said, and the words were wholly true. He'd envisioned it a thousand times over the years, felt Joss's pain and rage. In some ways he'd been as much a captive as his brother had.

Joss shook Caleb's hand away. He wouldn't come around easily, Caleb knew that, but the worst of his anger was spent. He wept for a time, and Caleb waited, absorbing the sound like blows to the midsection.

Presently Joss recovered himself, dried his eyes with his sleeve, and said, "Your Lily is a pretty little thing, but she's as fractious as my Susannah."

Caleb grinned. "It's going to take two hands and all my wits to keep her in line," he confessed.

Unwillingly, rawly, Joss chuckled. "Come on in, then, and we'll talk." And he led the way toward the house.

Caleb vaulted over the fence and fell into step with his brother. Neither of them spoke as they approached the place that had once been home to both of them.

Joss's littlest child, a girl with her father's curly hair, came bounding down the path toward them. "Papa, is Uncle Caleb really a damn Yankee?" she chirped.

Joss didn't so much as glance in Caleb's direction. "Yes, Ellen," he said gently. "He's the damnedest Yankee I ever saw."

Caleb smiled. "You wouldn't have Susannah and all these

beautiful kids if I'd done what you told me to do that day," he pointed out. "You'd be nothing but a pile of bones moldering in the brush somewhere."

Joss glowered at him. "I guess that's so," he conceded. "But don't get the idea things are settled between us, little brother, because they aren't. I'm still going to beat the living tar out of you the day your arm comes out of that sling."

This was the old Joss, the Joss whom Caleb remembered and loved. "Don't be too confident, big brother," he replied. "Just in case you haven't noticed, I'm all grown up."

Lily and Caleb had been at Fox Chapel for two weeks when Lily awakened one hot night in early August to find her husband standing at the window, looking out.

"What is it?" she asked.

He turned slowly to face her, his features in shadow. "It isn't the same."

Lily pulled back the sheet that covered her and patted the mattress. "Come back to bed, Caleb, and tell me what you're talking about."

Reluctantly Caleb came to sit on the edge of the bed, his back to Lily. "This is Joss's place," he sighed, running one hand through his hair in a distracted gesture. "*He* built it into what it is now, not me."

Lily began to massage the knotted muscles in his shoulders, carefully avoiding his rapidly healing wound. "You were born here, Caleb. This land—or half of it, at least—is your birthright."

"I want to go back, to build something with my own hands, something that's yours and mine. Our homestead seems like the best place to start."

Lily was so happy that she rose up on her knees and flung her arms around Caleb's neck from behind. "I do love you, Major Halliday!"

He laughed. "Damn it, woman, you're choking me."

Playfully Lily bit the back of his neck. "I don't care!"

Caleb whirled on her, flinging her down onto the mattress.

"Don't you?" he teased, and he began to tickle her ribs through her lightweight nightgown, causing her to writhe and shout with laughter.

"Stop!" she gasped finally, and Caleb relented, though only to bend his head and take a nip at the peak of one of her breasts, which was pressing taut against her nightgown.

Lily moaned in delicious reluctance. "I swear, Caleb Halliday, you'll wear me out."

He had taken the hidden nipple full in his mouth, and it throbbed beneath its covering of thin muslin. With one hand he parted Lily's thighs.

She gave a little whimper when he found the nest of curls and invaded that moist and secret place, and her hands tugged at her nightgown. She wanted to raise it, to be bared to Caleb, but he wouldn't allow her that for the time being. He continued to suckle until the muslin clung wetly to Lily's distended nipple.

When he moved toward the other breast Lily wrenched her nightgown up so quickly that the nipple was bare when he reached it. He chuckled as he took it into his mouth.

Lily flung her arms back over her head, utterly abandoning herself to her husband's attentions. She'd long since learned that her vulnerability heightened the pleasure for both of them, and it was safe to offer herself to Caleb because she knew he would never hurt her.

She groaned lustily when his fingers slipped inside her, and her thighs began to thrash on the smooth linen sheets. She grasped the railings in the headboard of the bed in both hands and held on.

Caleb removed his fingers to roll the small nubbin of excited flesh back and forth between heaven and hell. Lily would never have guessed the two places could be so close together.

"I want you, Caleb," she choked out. "I need you. If you don't take me right now, I'm going to—I'm going to—ooooooooh—"

Caleb continued to fondle her until the firestorm in her

senses had passed, leaving her quivering, moist with pleasure and perspiration beneath his hands.

"I wanted it to happen when you were inside me," Lily fussed.

"Don't worry," Caleb answered. "It will." He kissed Lily's mouth, and then her neck, and then her breasts and her hard, rising belly. By the time he parted her for a brief but fiery little conflict with his tongue she was ready again.

Caleb stopped her writhing by grasping her hips in his strong hands. He entered her in one hard, deft stroke, forcing a long, husky cry from her throat as her back arched to receive him.

His control shattered when she reached up to toy with his nipples, and he gave a muffled shout as he parried and then lunged, causing a delightful friction deep inside Lily.

Their lovemaking became a tender battle as Caleb repeatedly sheathed and unsheathed his manhood, the pace quickening with every stroke. Finally the inevitable happened, and for several soul-wrenching moments they were bonded together, fused into one flaming entity.

When they broke apart Lily lay curled beside Caleb, naked to the darkness and the warm night air, the back of one hand pressed lightly to her mouth. "Everyone in Pennsylvania must know what you just did to me," she managed.

Caleb chuckled. "It would help if you didn't carry on like a she-wolf, Mrs. Halliday."

Lily laid her head on his bare shoulder. "You wouldn't like it if I was quiet, and you know it," she answered. "You go off like a shotgun when you hear me."

He clasped one of her plump buttocks in his hand and squeezed it gently. "Oh, you're right there, Mrs. Halliday. I do like knowing that I'm putting you through your paces."

Lily punched him in the ribs for his arrogance. "It's not as if I don't do the same thing to you," she pointed out.

Caleb rolled over and slid down to kiss her belly. He seemed to love touching it now that it was rounding with his child. "You know, as soon as you get over having this baby, I think we ought to start another one."

Lily sighed. "I have no doubt that we will."

He came back to dally at her breasts for a while in a sleepy, undemanding way, and Lily entwined her fingers gently in his hair. Soon she drifted off to sleep.

"I wish you'd stay for my wedding," Caleb's younger sister Abigail fretted. She was flanked by Sandra and Susannah, who both took her side.

Caleb touched his sister's peaches-and-cream cheek. Like her brothers, Abigail liked getting her own way. "We need to be back home before winter," he said quietly. "Besides, we have business to take care of in Chicago. Important business."

Abigail's lower lip jutted out. "I guess I'll just have to come out and visit you, then. On my honeymoon, maybe."

Caleb grinned. "You're welcome any time, Abbie. You know that."

Sandra, who was blooming with pregnancy, had long since trained her husband, Lieutenant Costner, like a lap dog. "I don't see why either of you would want to go back to that uncivilized place anyway," she stewed. "There's nobody there but a bunch of Indians and outlaws and soldiers!"

Lily wondered if her corn was still good or if it had dried up in the hot summer sun, and she couldn't wait to see Velvet and Hank and tell them all about her trip. "It's home," she said quietly, linking her arm with Caleb's.

He looked down at her and nodded, his eyes shining.

Relations between Joss and Caleb were civil, though still a little awkward. Nonetheless, Joss and Susannah insisted on throwing a grand party for Caleb and Lily before they left, and Susannah lent Lily a wonderful ball gown to wear. It was made of ecru lace, with a full, tiered skirt and a bodice that showed off her satiny bosom.

She was sitting out a dance when Caleb took her hand, pulled her into the shadowy alcove off the ballroom, and presented her with a worn velvet box.

"This belonged to my mother," he said quietly.

Holding her breath, Lily lifted the lid. Inside was a delicate silver filigree necklace accented with a snowfall of diamonds. "Oh, Caleb."

Caleb took the splendid creation from its box and moved behind Lily to put it around her neck and fix the clasp. He bent and kissed the place where the two ends of the chain met. "Someday our son will give this to his wife."

Lily turned to look up into Caleb's eyes. If she had ever doubted his love for her, those feelings were behind her for all time. No man would have given such a cherished heirloom to a woman if he didn't care about her deeply.

"It was the best thing that ever happened to me, meeting you," she said. She smiled, remembering that day in the hotel dining room in Tylerville when the soldiers had been teasing her and she'd dropped her tray. "Though I must admit I didn't think so at the time."

Caleb put his hand under her chin and gently lifted her face for a light, brief kiss. "I knew the instant I saw you," he confessed when his lips had left hers, "that I wanted to be with you forever. I just didn't have sense enough to see that you were made to be a wife, not a mistress."

Lily was full of quiet joy. All that was needed to make her happiness complete was some word of her sisters.

"While you're dancing with all these admirers of yours," Caleb went on, with a wicked light glittering in his eyes as he nodded toward the contingent of handsome young men gathered in the ballroom, "I want you to remember whose bed you sleep in."

Lily was just about to protest when he gently lowered the bodice of her lace dress, completely baring both her breasts. "Caleb!" she gasped, aware of all the people dancing and talking just on the other side of the curtains that enclosed the alcove. She covered herself with her hands, but Caleb tucked the jewelry box into his pocket and caught hold of her wrists, holding them behind her.

Her proud breasts swelled under his perusal, and the nipples went obediently taut.

"You're mine," Caleb said, as if Lily hadn't known that he owned her soul as well as her body. And then he bent and took one pulsing nipple into his mouth.

Lily bit down hard on her lower lip to hold back a moan of pleasure, for such a sound would surely have carried. Her pride, always so formidable, was gone. "Caleb," she whispered, "take me somewhere and make love to me."

He shook his head. "Not yet. I want you to be thinking of me all the rest of the evening."

Caleb had his way, for Lily's mind and body were so attuned to him that she could think of nothing and no one else. Hours later, in their bed, he satisfied her with a thoroughness that left her exhausted.

Chicago was changed from the time Lily had lived there, of course, but returning gave her a strange mixture of emotions: nostalgia, anger, sadness, joy. She paced the hotel lobby nervously as she waited for Caleb to finish arranging for their room. When that was done she was to see a doctor, even though she wasn't feeling sick.

Lily truly begrudged the time. "Couldn't you have made the appointment for after we've talked to Mama's attorney?" she demanded anxiously when Caleb came and took her arm.

He shook his head as he led her outside. "A pregnant woman needs care, Lily. I want to know that you're all right. After all, when we get back to the homestead you won't have anybody but old Doc Lindsay at the fort to look after you, and he's hardly more than a horse doctor."

Lily was exasperated, but she knew arguing with Caleb would only waste valuable time. It was like having words with a hitching post.

They took a cab to the office of the doctor recommended by the hotel manager, and Caleb ushered Lily into a towering brick building in the middle of the city. Some of the streets looked familiar to Lily, but she'd been so young when she left Chicago that she couldn't rightly remember if she'd ever seen this part of it before.

The doctor ordered Lily to take off her clothes and lie down on the examining table, and she obeyed only because he was a kindly-looking older man with a tidy white beard and gentle blue eyes. Still, her cheeks flamed, and she clutched the white linen cover he gave her as he made his examination.

"So this baby was started in April, was it?"

Lily nodded, biting her lower lip.

The physician gave her an innocuous pat on the bottom and told her to sit up. He was washing his hands under steaming hot water flowing from a tap when Lily rose from her ignoble position.

"Is everything all right?" she asked.

"I'd say it's a boy," the doctor replied, looking back at her over one shoulder in a friendly way. "You're carrying him low, you know. A girl generally rides high, under the rib cage."

"You didn't answer my question," Lily persisted.

"The baby is large," the doctor sighed, "and you're a small woman. I don't think having this child out in the middle of nowhere is a very good idea, Mrs. Halliday."

Lily closed her eyes. Once Caleb heard that, they wouldn't be going back to the homestead until after her delivery, and that was a disappointment to her. On the other hand, she wanted her baby to be born healthy and strong. "I see," she finally managed.

"Everything'll be all right," the doctor told her quietly. "So don't you worry."

Caleb's reaction was anything but a surprise to Lily. "We'll stay right here until after the baby's born," he said, and she knew by his tone and expression that there would be no point in arguing with him. They would take a house in Chicago and travel home in the spring, hopefully in time to plow and plant.

Lily put everything but the task at hand from her mind as they drove through the city streets in yet another taxi, the wheels clattering over cobbled roads.

"Do you suppose we'll find out anything about my sisters?" she asked.

Caleb took her hand and held it tightly. "Yes. We're not going to stop asking until we do."

Kathleen's attorney was out of town, but his clerk gave Lily and Caleb an address from their files.

The place was in a surprisingly affluent section of town. In fact, it was a mansion built of brownstone, and the lush gardens buzzed with bees. The grass was a deep green cushion, and a high fence of iron kept strangers at bay.

Caleb walked straight up to the gate and tried it. To Lily's vast relief, it opened, but she stood frozen to the sidewalk.

With a gentle grin Caleb reached out and clasped her hand. He tugged her along the walk and up the marble steps to the porch. The front doorway was wide enough for a wagon to drive through, and some of Lily's nervousness faded as she imagined such a sight.

No one answered their knock, so they made their way around the back of the great house to try the other door. They got no response there either.

Lily was downcast when Caleb gave her a little nudge and scolded, "We can ask the neighbors, Lily. It's not as though we're pressed for time."

No one was at home in any of the surrounding houses except for servants, and they greeted Lily's questions about her mother with tightly pressed lips and shakes of their head. It seemed likely that Kathleen's reputation had followed her to these elegant environs.

Caleb took Lily to see an opera that night, to cheer her up, and they went back to Kathleen's neighborhood the next day and the next, and the one after that. In the meantime the

Hallidays took a house of their own not far away from Kathleen's, and hardly less elegant.

Since the place was furnished right down to books on the shelves, Lily didn't have to shop for chairs and beds and chamber pots. Her life was complicated by the fact that there were servants, for she had no idea how to boss anybody but Caleb.

He laughed and said she'd better learn.

As the days passed Lily grew plumper and rounder. She taught herself to pick out tunes on the parlor piano, read virtually every book in the library, and made Caleb tell her about every moment of his day. He spent most of his time downtown, managing their investments, but when the sun went down he was the most attentive of husbands.

Lily took to visiting her mother's empty house once a week or so, in the carriage, accompanied by Loretta, the upstairs maid. There was never anyone there.

Finally December came, with its cold winds and mountains of snow. Lily was in the narrow yard beside their house, laughing and pelting Caleb with snowballs, when the first pain struck.

It doubled her over, and Caleb was at her side instantly.

Dr. Branscomb arrived within the hour. Lily's delivery, as he had predicted, was long and difficult, but just before midnight Joss Rupert Halliday came into the world, howling with fury and weighing in at a hefty nine pounds.

"There will be other babies, won't there?" Lily demanded of the doctor. Even after all the pain of delivering her son she wanted more of Caleb's children. Many more.

"No reason why not," Dr. Branscomb said quietly. After washing his hands he signed the birth certificate, put on his suit coat, and went away.

Caleb had taken his son out of the room to be bathed, and when he returned carrying the squalling bundle his face glowed with delight. "He's mad as hell, isn't he?"

Lily smiled despite her weariness. "You would be, too, if you'd just been through a birthing."

Caleb kissed her forehead and laid the baby beside her on the bed. "I love you, Mrs. Halliday," he said, "but I think maybe we'd better stop with Joss here."

Lily shook her head resolutely. "Oh, no. I want more children, and I'll have them. Doc Lindsay may be an old sawbones, but I think he could handle the task of delivering me of a few more babies like this one."

Little Joss was still howling, so Lily picked him up and put him to her breast. Even though her milk wasn't in yet, he seemed to be comforted just by suckling, and Lily smiled at that. He was just like his father.

As soon as she was well enough to leave her bed Lily started going to her mother's house again. Every day she knocked on that door and on the doors of all the surrounding establishments, and every day she got nowhere. In a few weeks it would be time to go back to Washington Territory and resume her life there. She yearned for the homestead, but at the same time she knew leaving Chicago without learning anything about Emma and Caroline would crush her.

On the third day of March, 1879, Lily's luck changed for the better. Just as she reached for the familiar brass knocker the sound of piano music swelled out through an open window that Lily hadn't noticed before, and it was a song she and her sisters had once sung together in harmony.

Her heart thundering in her throat, Lily scorned the knocker and reached for the doorknob. A moment later she was in the entryway, and the music wrapped itself around her like an embrace, welcoming her.

A pure, sweet voice was singing.

> *Three flowers bloomed in the meadow,*
> *Heads bent in sweet repose,*
> *The daisy, the lily, and the rose. . . .*

Port Orchard, Washington
April 1990

My Dear Friends,

First of all, let me say thanks to each and every one of you for the wonderful letters you've written about *My Darling Melissa* and the books that preceded it. Your kind words have encouraged and uplifted me, as well as making me laugh and cry and think, and I'm so grateful that you took the time to express your opinions.

Lily and the Major is the first book in the Orphan Train Trilogy, but let me assure you now that each story is complete in and of itself. Novels about Lily's sisters will follow from Pocket Books next year, and I hope you'll be watching for *Emma and the Outlaw* and *Caroline and the Raider*. For me, the months I spent writing each of these books were the best of times and the worst of times, and I loved every bittersweet moment! Believe me, it was hard to say good-bye to my three "girls" and send them off into the world to make a place for themselves and fall in love with their very special men. Say hello for me, won't you?

Let me know what you think. I promise I'll answer, but be patient, please, because it will probably take time. A stamped, self-addressed envelope is always appreciated.

My warmest wishes,

Linda Lael Miller
P.O. Box 2166
Bremerton, Washington 98310